W9-ASJ-440

The Carpathian Novels

Anthologies

EDGE OF DARKNESS
(with Maggie Shayne and Lori Herter)

DARKEST AT DAWN
(includes Dark Hunger *and* Dark Secret*)*

SEA STORM
(includes Magic in the Wind *and* Oceans of Fire*)*

FEVER
(includes The Awakening *and* Wild Rain*)*

FANTASY
(with Emma Holly, Sabrina Jeffries, and Elda Minger)

LOVER BEWARE
(with Fiona Brand, Katherine Sutcliffe, and Eileen Wilks)

HOT BLOODED
(with Maggie Shayne, Emma Holly, and Angela Knight)

Specials

RED ON THE RIVER
MURDER AT SUNRISE LAKE

LEOPARD'S HUNT

CHRISTINE FEEHAN

BERKLEY ROMANCE
New York

BERKLEY ROMANCE
Published by Berkley
An imprint of Penguin Random House LLC
penguinrandomhouse.com

ISBN: 9780593638767

First Edition: February 2024

Printed in the United States of America
1   3   5   7   9   10   8   6   4   2

For my brother, Phil. He has the heart of a leopard, the courage of a lion and the sweetness of our mother. I love you very, very much. I'm so grateful I have the privilege of being your sister.

For My Readers

Be sure to go to christinefeehan.com/members/ to sign up for my private book announcement list and download the free ebook of *Dark Desserts*. Join my community and get firsthand news, enter the book discussions, ask your questions and chat with me. Please feel free to email me at Christine@christinefeehan.com. I would love to hear from you.

Acknowledgments

Thank you to Diane Trudeau. I would never have been able to get this book written under such circumstances without you. Sheila English, for stepping in to fix all the ten thousand problems of my dying computer. Brian Feehan, for making certain he was there every day to set up the pages I needed to write in order to hit the deadline. Denise, for handling all the details of every aspect of my crazy life. And to my amazing, invaluable researcher, Karen Brownfield Houton, you are a miracle to me! Thank all of you so very much!!!

LEOPARD'S
HUNT

1

GEDEON Volkov had been a fixer for years—and he was considered the best in his field. There was a reason for that, which few understood, and it was better if they didn't. He was a shifter—an Amur leopard. Not only was he a shifter; he was also elite. As far as he knew, there were only two of them in the world—his wife, Meiling Chang, and himself. There was always the chance that a rare few more might exist, but if so, he'd never caught so much as a hint of a rumor of one.

Intellectually, he knew there had to be more. Others had to have come before them. They didn't just appear out of nowhere. Anomalies. Three families in three countries: South Korea, southeastern Russia and China near the Russian border. There had to be others.

Meiling and he had discussed it and even quietly tried to find others like themselves, but if they were out there, they were hiding just as Gedeon and Meiling were. They were faster and stronger than other shifters. Their brains worked at greater speeds. They'd been born that way, and because of it their families had been targeted and destroyed. They had watched everyone they loved be betrayed, tortured and murdered. Both lived under the threat of a death sentence should anyone discover they still lived.

Gedeon had been a loner for years, feared by those who hired him, which kept him alive. He worked mainly for the *bratva*, the Russian mob, and they could be quite brutal if one didn't get the job done. He had the reputation of *always* getting it done. When he'd met Meiling, they had joined forces, another added layer of protection. Eventually they had become more than business partners and were now married.

"Why do I have the feeling this might be more dangerous than what we've been doing?" Meiling asked, a hint of laughter in her voice.

She'd taught him fun. He'd never had that before Meiling. She'd brought so much to him, had become his world in a short time. He knew he couldn't live without her. He wouldn't want to. More importantly, his leopard, Slayer, always a killer and difficult to control, would go insane. Some leopards could drive their human male counterparts to become killers. Slayer was one of those alpha leopards. Gedeon had always known there would come a day when he would be forced to suicide to protect those around him. Then came Meiling. His Lotus Blossom. Just when he was certain he couldn't love her more, there was always more.

Still, Meiling might have laughter in her voice, but there was also a bit of sobriety there. A warning. Her radar had gone off, the same as his, which didn't make sense. Drake Donovan would never have asked them to consider this job if he didn't think it was legitimate. His company was solid. Renowned. Known and respected the world over. That was the only reason Gedeon had even considered working for him.

Gedeon and Meiling had talked for a long while about getting out of the business he'd been in now that they were married and she was pregnant. He was a man of action, and he'd gone his own way for far too long. It wasn't as if he were ever going to take orders from anyone else. He needed not only the mental activity but also the physicality that he'd had for years of being a fixer.

He'd had to realistically face who he was many times in his life, and he'd learned not to shy away from the truth of who and what he was. Fixing problems within the *bratva* wasn't always about negotiating or trading favors. Often, it was about having to kill, and Gedeon was excellent at that particular skill.

He had Meiling now and his number one priority was keeping her and his children safe. He wanted her to have friends. He wanted his children to have them. Being a fixer wasn't exactly conducive to those goals.

Drake Donovan, the man who owned the Donovan International Security Company, had approached him with the offer of a job. One of his clients had specifically asked Donovan to try to recruit Gedeon for the head of his security. The client was not only *bratva* but also a leopard shifter, as were many of his men. He'd recently taken over a territory about which little was known. He was attempting to free it of all human trafficking. In doing so, he had incurred the wrath of locals who had been profiting from the business for years.

The locals weren't his only problem. Many of the men under him weren't happy he wasn't continuing that part of the business. Those his predecessor had been doing business with really weren't happy. Basically, it was a nightmare they would be helping the man with. Ordinarily, it was exactly the thing Gedeon would have jumped on.

"I've got the same feeling," Gedeon told Meiling. "What's more, Slayer's warning me to be very careful." Again, that made little sense.

He knew Gorya Amurov—at least he knew *of* him. He'd met him a couple of times, which wasn't the same as knowing him. He'd been around the Amurov family, all members of the *bratva* and lethal as hell. Gorya seemed the most easygoing of all the cousins. He seemed relaxed in the tensest of situations and played the role of the peacemaker, although now that Gedeon thought about it, Gorya faded into the background quite easily—much in the way Meiling did. He was soft-spoken, but his cousins always seemed to listen to him.

"You know, Lotus, now that I really think about it, the information we have on the Amurov family here in the States was pieced together and difficult to get. Not so much the ones in Russia. That was easy enough. But there isn't much on Gorya at all. He isn't in the news. There's no speculation on him. No one talks about him. It's almost as if he doesn't exist."

Meiling nodded her agreement. "That bothered me. His cousins run territories and are considered very brutal if crossed. There have been assassination attempts on Fyodor and his wife, Evangeline. Mitya was horribly wounded throwing himself in front of his cousin and Evangeline. There are hits taken out on all of them, but there never seems to be anything written up on Gorya. Not here, and not even in Russia."

Gedeon took his time processing that information. Meiling was good at research. His man, Rene Guidry, was equally good. Between the two of them, they should have found all kinds of data on Gorya, yet nothing of significance had turned up. Drake's people had done research as well, and he was renowned for his ability to ferret out secrets on shifters. He was close to the Amurovs, knew them quite well, but when it came to Gorya, he had very little to contribute other than that he was a good man.

"We know the Amurov family comes from the absolute worst lairs in the Primorye region of Russia," Meiling said. "Four brothers—Patva, Lazar, Rolan and Filipp Amurov—were *pakhans* in the *bratva* and ruled those lairs. Each held his own territory and ruled it with an iron fist. They demanded loyalty to the *bratva*, and by that, I mean not to their own families. They demanded that once the men serving under them were given sons, they were to show their loyalty to the *bratva* by murdering their wives. Their leopards were never allowed a true mate. They deliberately turned not only their leopards into killers but also the other males in their lair."

Gedeon knew all about the cruelty those kinds of *pakhans* were capable of. His family had been murdered by one. He didn't want to think of the suffering his mother had undergone at the hands of the leader of the lair he'd belonged to. He shut down that memory and turned his attention to the problem at hand. Those four men, the *pakhans* of those territories in Russia, were the fathers of the Amurov cousins residing in the United States.

Gedeon liked and respected Fyodor, Mitya, Sevastyan and Timur Amurov. They were tough, lethal men, but he'd found them to be fair, and they'd always kept their word. They'd been raised in brutal conditions. That had been easy enough to discover. He also knew that Fyodor had saved his brother and cousins by destroying the entire lair. The cousins were tight and loyal to one another.

What of Gorya Amurov? He was always with them.

"You've been around the Amurovs far more than I have," Meiling said. "Are you certain Gorya is really related to them?"

Gedeon brought up every encounter he'd had with the man. Gorya didn't have the obvious bulk his cousins had. He was leaner, but there was no mistaking the muscles rippling beneath his skin. He moved with the fluid stealth of a leopard. Gedeon just hadn't paid enough attention to him, not with his cousins around. They were lethal, dangerous men, every single one. Gorya, in comparison, had seemed gentle and considerate. He thought before he spoke. He soothed explosive situations and then seemed to fade into the background.

Could Meiling have the answer? Was Gorya not really an Amurov? Gedeon frowned as he stood in the shadows outside the building where they would be meeting with Gorya Amurov. They had come very early, as they always did. It was how they stayed alive. They trusted no one.

Drake Donovan had chosen the location. It wasn't in territory where Gorya was *pakhan*. That was a little-known town on the edge of the swamp between New Orleans and San Antonio, hidden from the eyes of law enforcement. There was a straight shot to the Gulf of Mexico by boat.

At Gorya's request, Drake had chosen a neutral location to meet. Gorya hadn't wanted any of his men to know he was meeting with Gedeon and Meiling. When Drake had first come to Gedeon with the proposal of working for Gorya, the job of head of his security had been for Gedeon alone. Gorya hadn't wanted Meiling. Gedeon made it clear he didn't work without his partner. Gorya took his time thinking it over before he offered a meeting.

"He has the scent of an Amurov. The eyes of one. We're missing something, Lotus, there's no doubt about it."

"Maybe the danger's to Gorya and not to us," Meiling ventured. "Just taking over this territory was a huge risk. He's made a lot of enemies."

Gedeon studied the buildings surrounding the rectangular building they were to meet Gorya in. Mostly garages and mechanic buildings, with one warehouse close. "He doesn't seem to have any bodyguards or snipers lying in wait for us."

"I'm going up on the roof," Meiling said. "If there's a way in, I'll take it."

He didn't tell her to be careful. She would have been insulted if he did. He didn't remind her that she was pregnant either. Obviously, she was aware that she was. His eyes met hers just to let her know she was his world. That was the reminder.

She nodded, and then she was going up the side of the building, a small shadow blending in with the darker side of the concrete wall.

Gedeon was grateful they were able to speak mind to mind. The leopards helped with that. He could always stay in touch with her, know exactly where she was or if she was in trouble and needed him—or the other way around.

Gedeon moved around the building slowly, checking the streets, the cars, the pattern of traffic, rooftops, every doorway and window facing the warehouse. He could find no threat to them or to the man they had come to interview.

Donovan had chosen a good location. It was off the beaten path, yet not so far out that it appeared abandoned. On either side of the small warehouse were two shops, still open. One was a garage that custom-painted cars, and the other repaired tires. Across the street was a welding shop. It was closed.

I can only detect one man inside, Gedeon. If that's Gorya Amurov, he's alone. He came without bodyguards. Does that seem right?

Nothing about this meeting was right. Gedeon was half inclined to call it off, but he knew part of that decision would be because he was becoming overprotective of Meiling. He would have gone in immediately had he been alone.

I'm going in, Meiling. Drake was adamant that Amurov needs help. He specifically asked for me. He had no idea we were considering getting out of our business, yet he reached out to Drake and asked for a meeting to be set up.

Wanting to exclude me, Meiling reminded him.

He noted that this time she didn't sound hurt. She sounded thoughtful.

Gorya's cousins weren't like their fathers. They didn't think of women as lesser beings. If anything, they treated their wives the way he did Meiling—as if they wouldn't be able to survive without them. Gedeon was sure their leopards were mated as well. That made the women doubly important to their men.

Gorya was the only cousin without a woman of his own. How difficult would that be for him? For his leopard? Now he'd been thrown into a situation demanding him to make snap decisions and contend with violence at every turn. The *pakhan* of the *bratva*, when challenged, had to respond with speed and ferocity. His men had to respect him. Their leopards had to fear his leopard. Was Gorya Amurov capable of commanding the same kind of deference and fear as his cousins?

I don't think it's about you being a woman, Meiling, he mused. Icy fingers of dread crept down his spine at his next thought, the one he couldn't push away.

What is it?

He sighed. There was no getting around Meiling. *He's leopard, Lotus. Leopards are capable of slipping into a building unseen and unheard. We do it all the time. Suppose, just for a moment, that Gorya researched us the way we researched him. Only he was even more thorough.*

I don't like where you're going with this.

It's possible he knows you're pregnant.

No one knows I'm pregnant. We haven't even told Rene.

The more he considered the idea, the more Gedeon feared he could be on the right track. *That doesn't mean he didn't figure it out. You were in heat. Leopard sex is wild. The odds of you getting pregnant were very high. Even if he's just guessing, he's got a fifty-fifty shot at being correct.* He didn't think Gorya was making a guess.

He thought the man had found a way to confirm his suspicion, and he didn't want Meiling in the line of fire.

Gedeon was more intrigued than ever. He often got strong hunches, and so far, those premonitions had always been right.

He knows we're here, Gedeon. I don't know what we did to tip him off, but he's aware we're here.

Meiling was extremely sensitive to changes in energy. He had no idea how she would know that Gorya had been alerted to their presence, but he believed her.

We have to make up our minds if we're going to talk with him. The element of surprise is gone. I don't believe he has an ambush set up. On the other hand, we're walking into something Slayer doesn't like. Gedeon was honest with Meiling. His leopard was still warning him they could be in trouble. *What is Whisper telling you?*

Gedeon and his male were fierce, brutal fighters and generally riled other males the moment he came into close proximity with them. Meiling and her female calmed other leopards. Ordinarily, Whisper had no problem around any leopard.

She's uneasy for Slayer.

The hair on the back of his neck stood up. It was unprecedented for Whisper to be in the least concerned for Slayer. He was an elite leopard, one of the few in the world. Slayer was faster than any other leopard they had ever encountered. He was a brutal, experienced fighter. He killed in seconds, all business. Whisper was well aware of Slayer's fighting abilities.

That puts an entirely different perspective on things, doesn't it? Stay or go?

Meiling emerged from the shadows to stand next to him. She looked up at him and then at the building.

She was quiet a moment, thinking the problem over as was her way. Meiling didn't make snap decisions. "I think we have no choice now, Gedeon. We need to find out who

Gorya Amurov is and what his interest in us is. There is no doubt he arranged for us to be here, and he wants to speak to us alone."

Gedeon agreed with her. "Then we do this the way we always have, Lotus. We treat him as a hostile enemy. His leopard will dismiss yours and rage over mine. Slip inside and set up to take him out. I'll keep his attention focused on me. Hopefully this interview will be legitimate, and we won't have to go after every one of his cousins. He has the kind of family that if you kill one of them, they don't stop coming after you until you're dead."

"If we kill him, Gedeon, we'll have to go after the others immediately and then disappear."

That was Meiling. Practical. With him. She didn't like their lifestyle, especially if it involved killing, but she would stand with him.

"Self-preservation, baby. Let's hope Drake Donovan is a good judge of character."

There was no sense in putting off the meeting once they decided to go. Gedeon entered the room first, careful when he pushed the door open that the heavy frame partially blocked the opening. As he did, his large body filling the entrance, Meiling slipped inside behind him, moving along the wall. The moment Gedeon opened the door, Slayer reacted, snarling and clawing, despite Meiling and Whisper, his mate, being close.

Across the room, Gorya sat behind a desk, rolling a bullet between his fingers, a gun in front of him. He glanced at Meiling, and then his gaze fixed on Gedeon. Gorya's leopard had to have reacted to the aggression in Gedeon's leopard, yet the man didn't so much as blink. That was a huge red flag to Gedeon.

Gedeon stopped close to the door, keeping Slayer under control when the leopard fought him for supremacy, clearly feeling a threat to Gedeon and Meiling.

"Gorya," Gedeon opened the conversation. "You came without any backup. Do you think that wise?"

"The things I have to say to you require complete privacy. I did my research. You will keep what is said confidential whether you take the job or not."

Gorya was soft-spoken. His voice mesmerizing. Gedeon had to resist glancing at Meiling to see her reaction. The quality in that voice edged on compelling. A gift.

Gorya turned his attention once again to Meiling. "We haven't met officially, Meiling. I'm Gorya Amurov. I hope I didn't offend you when I first asked Drake to speak with your husband about working for me. I knew the two of you were partners. It wasn't that I didn't know how competent you are; I do my research very thoroughly."

Gedeon found that low voice so compelling it was impossible not to focus on it. Instinctively, he knew that leopards could inch closer without listeners being aware. That voice, although low, was powerful, embedding the need to hear every word. It was an amazing weapon.

"Knowing that we work together and that you were risking offending me, why would you have Drake only approach my husband?" Meiling asked.

Gedeon wanted to smile. Those long lashes of hers fanned her cheeks, making her look so innocent and demure, not at all calculating and brilliant as he knew her to be. She wasn't getting trapped in Gorya's voice.

"You are very, very good at what you do, Meiling. You won't hesitate to kill if necessary, but unlike Gedeon, it weighs on you. I didn't want to put you in that position."

He spun the bullet over and over between his fingers when he turned his gaze back to Gedeon. "I saw you in San Antonio at Evangeline's bakery the night Elijah Lospostos came with his men to speak with you. One of his trainees put a gun to Meiling's head as she was going out the door. I happened to be watching you. Everyone else was talking together, but I had my eyes on you. I saw you signal her to leave."

He glanced again at Meiling, the faintest of smiles on his face. The charm showed through, but Gedeon noted there was no smile in his eyes.

"She disappears easily into the shadows. No one saw her until she had to go through the doorway. I kept watching you and I saw you move. The speed and your ability to leap over the men in that room were incredible. Later, my cousins discussed it, but because it didn't seem possible, they eventually dismissed the idea that you really were able to leap that far and fast. They convinced themselves that you were closer than you had been."

Gedeon remained silent. Waiting. Giving nothing away. Gorya hadn't dismissed what he saw, that much was clear. The bullet between his fingers continued to spin. Gedeon was certain the man hadn't blinked once.

"I need someone fast. I need someone who won't hesitate to kill. And I need his leopard to be experienced and ferocious in a fight. He must be able to shift fast and kill faster."

Gedeon kept his gaze steady on Gorya's. "Drake told me many of the problems with this particular territory."

Gorya shook his head slowly. "I haven't explained myself. I do need you for help there as well, but your main purpose will be to kill me when the time comes—and it will come."

That was the last thing Gedeon expected him to say. Those eyes didn't move from his, assessing how he took the request.

"Perhaps you could sit down and we can discuss this," Gorya invited.

He is very sincere, Meiling said. *He means exactly what he says. Whisper also cannot detect deceit. He is being very honest. He wants a commitment from you.*

Slayer agrees with you and Whisper.

"Gorya, why would you ask this of me?"

"Because I believe you are the only man who has a chance of killing me."

Again, Gedeon heard only the truth.

"When the time comes, I hope I won't be so far gone that I couldn't spare you." Gorya held up the bullet. "I've found the idea of killing my leopard nearly impossible. Every time I've tried, I've been unable to go through with it. I thought that by taking on this territory it would help relieve some of the pressure on us, but it made it so much worse."

He shook his head and once again raised his eyes to meet Gedeon's. "To clean up a territory like the one I have taken over requires brutality. Ruthlessness. Becoming the kind of psychopath I was raised with. You know what that kind of violence breeds."

He's one of us, Meiling, Gedeon told her, certain it was true. *I don't know how he can be when his cousins aren't, but he is. He knows what we are because he is, and he recognized us.*

If that's true, he's stayed hidden in plain sight, even from his cousins. I don't think they have a clue what he is. Why would he hide his true self?

Stay where you are.

Gedeon wasn't risking Meiling. He took the lead as he normally did when they were on a dangerous job. Crossing the room, he pulled out a chair and sat opposite Gorya, leaving Meiling a clear shot to the man if there was need. Gorya did nothing to protect himself from Meiling, although he had to know she was in a perfect position to kill him.

"You do realize if I killed you, your cousins would hunt me to the ends of the earth," Gedeon said.

Gorya shook his head. "I would make certain they were aware I hired you specifically for that purpose."

"Gorya, seriously, think about what kind of men your

cousins are. Do you think that would deter them? You're
family. You don't talk about emotions in your family, but
they have them for you. Their women have them for you."

"It is necessary, and you know why. They will know
why as well. They made a choice years ago, long before I
did, to live by a code. I wasn't certain I wanted to live
without the violence of the *bratva*. I fit. Once I was old
enough to hold my own against the *pakhan's* men, I could
slide into the shadows and do what I wanted. I was in my
teens when I became faster and stronger than all of them.
I could outthink them. Outsmart them. My leopard hated
them as much as or more than I did."

Gedeon understood that and the need for revenge. It
burned bright and fierce. Deep and cold. Smoldered and
never went away.

"Patience," Gedeon said.

"Exactly," Gorya said. "It became a game of wits. I am
a deceiver. My leopard is called *Moshennik*, which is why
I call him Rogue. We learned to bide our time. One by one
we took out the worst of them. Unfortunately, the two of
us thrived on violence. We reveled in it. My first memories
were of blood and death, and I don't recall much else. The
only good thing I can say for myself is, I could never stand
seeing what was done to women and children. That was a
trigger for me. Again, unfortunately, I've become a monster, and I can't seem to hold that side of me back when
that happens."

Gedeon noted Gorya didn't sound remorseful, only
matter-of-fact. He'd accepted himself for who and what he
was, just as Gedeon had.

"This territory I've taken over was run like the ones
that I came from in Russia. The women and children are
sometimes abused, but often the women are complicit in
the crimes. I've retaliated in kind when there is abuse. It
hasn't been pretty, but I'm cleaning things up fast. On the
other hand, it's brought out every negative trait Rogue and

I have. The rush for us has fed the continual need for more. We're deteriorating very fast."

There was stark honesty in that mesmerizing voice. Gedeon understood exactly what Gorya was telling him. He'd been there. Before Meiling, he'd grown more violent, barring his doors and windows with steel to keep Slayer from escaping. He'd taken refuge in rough, emotionless sex to try to relieve the ever-building need for violence. Like Gorya, he knew the only answer for him was to end his life before he killed an innocent. He'd been lucky to find a miracle—Meiling.

"Your cousins were each able to find their leopard's true mate. Why do you believe you won't find Rogue's?" Meiling asked.

Gorya twisted the bullet back and forth until it spun between his fingers, not touching his skin but remaining in the air, a hairsbreadth away from his thumb and finger. He didn't appear to notice while he contemplated his answer.

"My cousins are brutal, violent men out of necessity," he finally said. "They were raised in an environment that didn't allow for anything else, so to survive they were forced to learn those ways. They didn't like what they had to become, but they became good at being those men. That wasn't the case with me."

Abruptly, Gorya pinched the bullet between his fingers and carefully set it on the desk beside the gun. "The story of how my parents died isn't true. My father didn't murder my mother. She was acquired in the way most of the women were in that lair. She was bought with the idea that once she provided sons, she would be murdered by her husband to show loyalty to the *bratva*. As my father had no problem killing his first wife with the help of his two sons, he expected to do just that with his second. Not only did he expect that he would kill her, his sons also expected it, as did his brothers."

Gedeon couldn't detect any emotion at all on Gorya's handsome features or in his unusual eyes. Amur leopards typically had amber or even blue eyes, but Gorya's eyes, although shaped like a cat's and just as focused and piercing, maybe even more so, were slate gray. The strange and rare color made reading him more difficult than ever. His eyes could appear as pure frost or reflect back as a mirror. Gedeon would bet his last dollar that the undercoat on Gorya's leopard was gray to match those eyes, making him nearly impossible to spot when he wanted to disappear.

"No one expected that she was his leopard's true mate, or that he would fall in love with her."

"Do you have any idea where she came from?" Meiling asked.

Gorya shook his head. "No one cared. She was considered expendable. My brothers, Dima and Grisha, hated her and hated me when I was born. I knew they wanted me dead. They would sneak into the room where I was sleeping and pick up a pillow to smother me. Rogue always tore his way through the pillow, even when he was a cub. They couldn't let their leopards loose on him because it would have woken my father or mother. She always seemed alert. She watched them closely once she found the pillows ripped."

How terrible to know from the time you're born that your own brothers want to murder you, Meiling whispered into Gedeon's mind. *He was just an infant. So was his leopard.*

Gorya had had the awareness of a much older child from the time he was an infant, and he hadn't forgotten. Gedeon knew what that was like, although his earliest memories were happy ones. He'd been given that same gift.

"My father, Filipp, fell in love with my mother. That was enough to brand him a traitor with his brothers. She was his leopard's true mate. Patva conspired with Dima and Grisha to murder them both. Dima and Grisha broke Filipp's spine so he was helpless, and then, while Patva watched, they beat my mother to death in front of Filipp. I have no idea why Patva decided to keep me alive. Dima and Grisha were very angry, but Patva took me home and gave me to his wife to raise along with Fyodor and Timur."

"This might answer the question of how you are so different from your cousins in that you have tremendous gifts," Gedeon pointed out, "but it doesn't answer why you think you won't be able to find your leopard's true mate or yours."

"Patva was the cruelest of all the brothers. He reveled in brutality. He allowed the leopards in his lair to be whipped into killing frenzies. They hunted humans and fed on them. Each atrocity he committed was worse than the one before. His power grew, and so did his reputation."

Gedeon heard loathing in Gorya's voice for the first time, but he suspected the loathing wasn't for Patva; it was for himself.

"When I was a child, Patva beat me, had his men beat me. They subjected me to as much cruelty as possible without killing me. I learned to stay quiet and bide my time. Rogue obeyed me. We needed to learn from them. From all the leopards. We were sponges, soaking up the knowledge they had, the experience. After a while I barely felt the beatings, although I made certain to put on the appropriate show and then fade into the background as quickly as possible."

Once again, Gorya's eyes met Gedeon's without flinching from the truth. "I reveled in learning. I wanted to be more of a monster than my uncle. I began to pit myself against him. In small ways at first. I would steal away his small treasures and plant them among his trusted captain's things. I took great delight in the torture of his captain and his family. The woman was already dead and only his sons remained, men who enjoyed hunting humans and raping and murdering others. I always watched as Patva took his wrath out on his own loyal men, believing what his eyes saw when I had orchestrated the crime instead of listening to men who had served him for years. You have no idea the joy that brought me at such a young age, and it only increased as my acts of revenge became more complex."

Again, Gedeon understood. How could he not? There was joy in defeating an enemy, especially when that enemy thought you had no power.

"I didn't want Patva to die. I wanted him to live forever. It seemed too merciful for him to just die. I could torment him, strip him of everything that mattered to him little by little, and he would never know it was me. I knew I could best him. It was like a game of chess, and I found it exhilarating. I outthought him at every turn."

"Weren't there people in the lair suffering?" Meiling asked.

Gorya turned his frosty gray eyes on her. Gedeon knew what she was seeing. Emptiness. No soul. If his leopard looked back at her, that leopard had no real life in it either.

"I considered the entire lair corrupt, so therefore I was at war with everyone. If they suffered, that was good. It gave me opportunities to hone my skills. Patva took me with him on raids, and I practiced deceiving him into thinking I was squeamish and reluctant. His punishments were severe, but it was worth it to me. I learned to be an even better actor. He'd force his other men to take me with them, and that would allow me to wreak havoc without his knowledge."

Gorya turned back to Gedeon. "Rogue and I hunted his best fighters, first stalking them for weeks just to hone our skills, entering their homes over and over, standing over them at night, but their leopards were never alerted unless we wanted them to know we were there."

The hair on the back of Gedeon's neck stood up. Slayer raked at him in alarm.

That's what he did to us, Meiling, stalked us. He came into our home and Slayer didn't alert. Neither did Whisper. He knew you were pregnant because he heard us talking.

Gedeon found it very disturbing that Gorya and his leopard had the skills to enter their home when Meiling and he were both elite. Was he fast enough to kill Gorya? Was Slayer? He'd never questioned himself or his leopard, but he'd be an arrogant ass if he didn't consider the possibility that Gorya might be faster, stronger and even more ruthless.

All his life Gedeon had known he was superior to other shifters. He'd been careful not to take it for granted, but he'd known. He hid his gifts from others. Now he sat across from a man who was relaxed while knowing Meiling was in position to shoot him. Gedeon sat across from him within striking distance. Gorya hadn't so much as flinched.

"To answer your question, Meiling, over the years, I developed the need to feed the brutality inside me. Whether it comes from the skills I got from my mother or the DNA I got from my father or the combination of both, it's very strong in me. Far more so than my brothers. The beatings Rogue and I were subjected to so early and the way we had to survive by secretly plotting to kill only fed that side of me—of us. I can be very sadistic, and I don't feel remorse. I know my cousins often thought of themselves as psychopaths, but they are not. They are good men. I am not."

"If that's the truth, how did you end up here in the States with your cousins?" Meiling asked.

There was a quality to Meiling's voice that had always brought Gedeon peace. For the first time, he hoped it brought Gorya and his leopard peace as well. He remembered the days of believing that he was a psychopath and there was no hope for survival. It was possible it was too late for Gorya, but clearly the man was determined to find a way to keep those around him safe by hiring Gedeon to kill him after he cleaned up the territory he'd been given. That didn't strike Gedeon as a man who was completely unredeemable.

For the first time, Gorya hesitated. He wore his black hair slicked back, so it was impossible for Gedeon to tell how long it was on top, but it was thick, as all shifters' hair was. The sides of his hair were kept shaved. He wore a short, trimmed beard and moustache. He looked young, with few lines in his face until you looked very close, then you could see the faint signs of burden and exhaustion from the life he'd led taking their toll.

Gorya pushed his fingers through his hair and shook his head. He gave Gedeon that faint smile that was as cold as ice and as fake as a three-dollar bill. "I told myself I would answer your questions honestly. There's always that one moment in life when you must make a choice. My choice, until then, had been to keep Patva alive and torment him by slowly stripping him of everything he had. He was bringing in women and young girls and selling them or giving them to his trusted men before selling them. He had one of his enforcers take me along with him to inspect a house where they were keeping some of the women."

There was no expression on Gorya's face, but he picked up the bullet again and looked at it for a long moment. "I sometimes wonder, if I had just killed him, would I have spared that child the things done to her? But then I would never have been sent to that house of horrors." He looked up again and met Gedeon's gaze.

Gedeon could barely look at him. For some unknown reason, he had the feeling Gorya knew about his past, about his mother in just such a house. About Gedeon in just such a house. No one other than Meiling knew about Gedeon's past, so that would be impossible, but those frosty gray eyes seemed to see inside him, into the secrets of his dark past.

"The men openly raped and beat the women and children right there in front of one another as if they weren't human beings. They laughed and egged each other on. One little girl wasn't more than five or six. She had all this white-blond hair and blue-gray eyes. I could see she had a leopard, although I knew the men were too smug to see. She'd already been raped numerous times. There was no doubt she was gearing up to force them to beat her into submission again. I think she was going to make them kill her."

Gorya shook his head as if back in that house of horrors. "I don't think I'll ever get the sight of those women and children or the sounds or smells out of my mind for as long as I live. I think I went a little berserk. I know Rogue did. One minute we were looking at that little child, and the next I was shifting and tearing them all apart."

He sank back into his seat and regarded Gedeon, once again relaxed, accepting who he was. The change was slight, but Gedeon read it easily.

"Patva had sent a five-man team. There were two guards in the house. I had to kill all seven of them. Then I had to destroy the cameras. There couldn't be any evidence that I had been the one to kill them and in such a violent way. I made it appear as if we'd been raided by outsiders so they could get the women and sell them themselves. I had less than an hour to get the women and children onto a freighter I knew was leaving the harbor. I had to make out the proper paperwork and sign Patva's name to it, which I was very good at doing. It was the best I could do for them. I knew where there was money, and I gave what I could to them. Then I had to find a way to make it look like I'd been ripped apart and left for dead so Patva would believe I'd been attacked as well."

"How was it that you didn't kill Patva yourself when he attacked you and Timur? Even though you were so young, you must have been capable of killing him," Gedeon said.

"When he first came in, he acted very nice to Ogfia, Timur's mother. She always tried to go into another room to get away from him, even if he beat one of us. Timur never seemed to mind. He made excuses for her. When she started to leave, Patva leapt on her and began to beat her savagely. Timur immediately went to assist her, but instead of aiding him, Ogfia again tried to lock herself in another room."

There wasn't the slightest hint of disgust or loathing on Gorya's face or in his voice, but Gedeon felt disgust heavy in the air. Gorya might not be able to tolerate seeing women or children raped, tortured or misused, but he didn't have a high opinion of them.

"Patva turned on me with a knife hidden in his hand. Using a weapon was unusual, and I didn't see or expect it. He stabbed me three times as he rushed past me to get to Ogfia. Rogue spun us away from him fast, so the blade missed my heart, but I went down. He shouted at Timur and me that we were cowards and traitors. Those loyal to the *bratva* didn't give their loyalty to women."

Gorya touched his chest near his heart. "That taught me the lesson to always expect the unexpected. I was young and arrogant in those days. After Patva beat Ogfia to death, he turned his attention to Timur and me. I might have been able to take him, I don't honestly know. I'd lost a lot of blood and was weak, but fortunately, Fyodor came in. He saved us, and I just fell back on what I did best. I became the deceiver even with those I loved most."

What do you think, Meiling?

I've never met a man so lost, Gedeon.

Or so dangerous. The point is, what do we do?
I don't think we have a choice. We take the job.

Gedeon studied the man across from him. Gorya was brilliant. He'd known that the moment he laid the facts out they would take the job. He sighed. "You have yourself a couple heading your security. Your men aren't going to like us very much."

Gorya sent him that flat, cold smile. "They don't like me much either."

2

MAYA Averina paced the length of the very long basement, cursing under her breath with every step. The heat was stifling. There were only slits for windows to allow light in, and those ran along the ceiling, far too narrow for even her small body to escape through.

She meticulously inspected every inch of the prison she'd been trapped in. There was no way out that she could find—yet. That didn't mean there wasn't one. She hadn't given up. She knew cameras had been set up in that long rectangular basement somewhere. She'd spotted a very tiny one near the doorway, but there had to be one or two more.

The moment she'd realized what was happening, she should have fought her way out of the building. She just hadn't known how many were involved. She'd believed she would be able to find a way to escape the basement.

She still believed there had to be a way; she just hadn't found it yet.

"Not my finest plan, Wraith," she said aloud. "I got us into a mess this time. And when we get out, I'm going to *kill* Theo." She meant it too.

Theo Pappas had helped her escape a bad situation a few years earlier, and she had never forgotten his kindness. When they had run into each other months ago, he was the one needing help. She had a sense about people, and red flags had gone off. He seemed a completely different person. She smelled addiction on him. Not just drugs but other, darker things she had encountered in her past. She hadn't sensed conspiracy until it was too late, most likely because she hadn't spent any time with him.

She and Wraith were in a good place. She had a good freelance job, although she mainly worked for three different companies, researching whatever they needed. She was thorough and fast and didn't mind going places no one else could go if she wasn't asked how she got her information. She worked from home, avoiding people, which suited her.

She appeared to be an introvert to the outside world. She didn't interact with anyone other than exchanging emails with her clients. She kept to herself, moving often, always staying on the edge of a city, where there was plenty of room to run her leopard.

Maya took time to hunt down certain criminals. That kept her skills sharp, both on the computer searching for their whereabouts and then physically stalking them. It was important for her and Wraith to always have an edge. They couldn't ever get complacent because they were living a life away from shifters. Unfortunately, her last investigation had brought her to the coast of Texas and then the swamps of Louisiana.

She had known her quarry, Albert Krylov, was working as a courier for one of the *bratva* families in Russia. She was looking for his connections in the United States. She found it a little shocking to find not just one territory held by Russians but several. She thought they would have been Italian or American, maybe both. How the Russians had gotten such a foothold in Louisiana and Texas was beyond her. She had been very careful to avoid any contact with them, even though she was tracking Krylov and he had gone to each of those territories.

She had run into Theo in the Café du Monde in New Orleans. There was no way to abruptly leave or pretend she didn't know him. He had spotted her while she waited in line and came right over to her. She couldn't make a scene, not with Krylov at a table several feet away. She didn't want to draw attention to herself. She blended into the crowd unobtrusively, making certain she was in the shadows as much as possible and blurring her appearance so no one would be able to describe her accurately if asked later. But Theo had noticed her, because the moment he'd arrived at the Café du Monde and gotten into line he'd approached her.

He immediately told her he was in trouble and needed help. Could he call her later? He was being followed and couldn't stay. The meeting was so brief she hadn't had time to assess the situation. Instead of giving him her number, she'd taken his number and agreed to call him as soon as she could.

Thankfully, Krylov had moved out of New Orleans, a city that seemed to be crawling with shifters. She'd followed him to the Atchafalaya Swamp, the largest in the United States. With a million acres to choose from, she thought herself safe enough, but to her dismay, Krylov was visiting yet another Russian territory. This one looked as if it had been around for a while and was well established with the locals. It was run by shifters.

The *bratva*. She had thought herself safe from them in the United States. She'd stayed under the radar, far from anything that remotely resembled shifters. It hadn't occurred to her there would be leopards in the swamps of Louisiana, and yet not only were they there, but there was also an entire established town of them. Worse, they were Russian.

The *pakhan* and leader of the lair had been killed recently, and a new one had taken over. He'd been challenged just twice. From rumors she'd heard, he hadn't spared the challengers' lives, as was normal. His leopard had killed theirs in seconds. There had been no more challenges to his leadership.

This new leader wasn't just *bratva*. He was from the Primorye region of Russia, where the Amur leopards were going extinct and the shifters were the most cruel and brutal of all. Those were the ones reputed to kill the mothers of their children to prove loyalty to the *bratva*. They demanded the same from all who served under them.

Although the swamp was the best possible place for her to keep up her training, she decided to get out while she could. She wanted to rid the world of Krylov. She already had leads on three others she wanted to track thanks to his travels. She needed an opportunity to kill him and either dispose of the body in the swamp or make certain someone else would take the blame.

She called Theo, intending to tell him she was no longer in New Orleans and wouldn't be able to meet with him. Unfortunately, he was in the Atchafalaya Swamp as well. He was desperate for a meeting. He kept telling her he was really in trouble and reminded her that when she'd needed help, he had come through for her.

Maya felt unsettled. Edgy. Moody. Very unlike her. She made decisions with logic. She was decisive. She would never have agreed to meet with Theo if she'd been herself, but she was all over the place. Her body burned on and off as if she had a fever. She never got sick, and yet she felt as though she were coming down with some terrible flu.

"I should never have agreed to meet with him," she muttered aloud as she paced the length of the basement. Fortunately, the area was very long and gave her enough space to relieve some of her pent-up energy.

We were burning up with fever, Wraith excused.

As always, Wraith excused anything Maya felt she'd done wrong. That was sweet and made Maya feel loved, but it didn't help her learn from the mistakes she made. Mistakes could get them killed. They couldn't afford mistakes.

Theo insisted on meeting her in this building, a sprawling one-story monstrosity of new modern design. The building was located in a town in the swamp just on the coast. Even Maya knew most residences and businesses were built high on stilts to avoid the flooding, especially those close to the water. They certainly didn't have basements. This basement was below water level, so one little leak and it would flood easily.

The building was too new, and that was her first red flag. Theo sweated; his gaze, instead of shifting to the windows and doors, continually swept along the upper trim of wood as they walked down the hall. She could understand his nerves when he'd said he was in trouble, but he looked as if he were sweeping for cameras. Why choose a building and risk being caught on camera rather than meeting out in the swamp?

"Don't give me drama, Theo. I don't have much time." She'd been curt. Her gut told her to get out of there. The farther they moved away from the main entrance, the more her alarms were going off.

Wraith had gone quiet, very watchful. She made it plain she didn't like or trust Theo. At the same time, it was difficult to think straight, to push down the unfamiliar feelings of burning inside, of needing to rub her skin along every surface and then rake her fingernails like claws down Theo's face each time he got too close. Those feelings would rise abruptly and, just as fast, leave her.

"I took a job at one of the businesses in town." Theo's gaze met hers and then slid away. Another red flag. She should have taken him out right then and left, but he was already talking, and she was listening. "There was so much cash coming in. I'm good with numbers. Really good. I realized each of the businesses, under one premise or another, paid a certain amount to the one I worked under. Small bits of cash were disappearing, and I traced the flow back to three men. They were siphoning money steadily from three different sources and had been for a while."

He hesitated and then corrected himself. "I couldn't find the exact identities of the men, just where each of them was working and stealing from."

The long hallway ended abruptly at an open doorway. To stay a distance from Theo, Maya found herself standing in the doorway. A cool draft came from inside the darkened interior. There was no scent of anyone waiting inside to ambush her, and she welcomed the cool air on her overheated body. She tried to make sense of what he was saying over the strange roaring in her ears and the intense fire building in her body that came and went in waves.

"I swear I was going to report the money disappearing, but before I could, one of the men visited me late in the evening. He stayed in the shadows. Even with my superior vision, I couldn't make him out. My leopard couldn't smell him."

That alarmed Maya. Theo seemed to be telling the truth. *Wraith?*

He is telling the truth. His leopard confirms his story.

His leopard is weak, Maya, very weak. Sick. He is not taking care of him. I suspect that is the reason he could not scent the other male.

"He made me an offer. He told me how corrupt the leader of the local lair was and that they were siphoning the money to help human trafficking victims of this lair."

She heard that lie as plain as day, and her head snapped up. She glared at him. "You know better than to lie to me, Theo."

"Everything was going fine." He ignored her warning. "Then the leader of the territory died—was murdered—and a new *pakhan* took over. He demanded an accounting from every one of his men and their businesses. I knew he would discover the missing money. When I reached out to the others, they were gone. I knew they'd set me up to take the fall."

"Of course they did. You're an outsider. Not Russian. What did you think was going to happen? Do you have the money to give back? Can you even name the other men?"

She was burning up. Her skin itched. Her skull hurt. She could barely look at him. Her throat felt tight and swollen. She backed another couple of steps away. Wraith felt just as hot and out of sorts as she was.

Neither wanted to deal with Theo. He'd taken the money for his own personal gain, most likely for drugs. Whatever he'd been using it for had made his leopard sick.

Theo shook his head. "I don't have my share let alone their shares. But I have an idea of how we can get it."

Maya wished it were that simple. "You don't seem to understand what you did, Theo. You stole from the *bratva*. That's a death sentence. Not just a death sentence. Even if you return the money, they will torture and kill you as an example to everyone else. No one steals from them and gets away with it. If you have a family, they will kill your entire family."

Theo shook his head, a sly look stealing over his face. "Not this time. I have you."

"What does that mean?"

Without thinking, she had taken another step back, which put her solidly into the other room. Theo reached out and slammed the door closed. She heard a bolt slide into place. For a moment she stared at Theo through the thick glass window in the door as he pointed to a grille on the left side.

"I'm holding an online auction to make the money back." His voice sounded just a little tinny. "It occurred to me the minute I saw you in New Orleans and realized you still weren't with anyone. You haven't been claimed. We can say your leopard is in her first life cycle. We could repeat this scam over and over and make so much money. The bidding for you is so high already it's unbelievable."

The moment she heard the words "first life cycle" and "haven't been claimed," alarm bells went off. She was scorching hot. Burning up. Her skin felt too tight. She couldn't think clearly. She was moody. Edgy. What did that add up to? She was leopard. A female shifter.

Maya and Wraith were unusual in their world because they'd known each other since Maya was an infant. Females were rarely aware of their leopard until they entered what was known as the Han Vol Dan. The leopard and the human came together in the same cycle, ovulating together. There were many times it never happened, and the leopard didn't rise or emerge. Wraith had made herself known to Maya almost immediately, and they'd relied on each other.

"We're going into heat," Maya whispered to Wraith. "That's what's happening." A part of her wanted to laugh. "It's rather ironic that Theo is betraying us, believing he's scamming the buyers by selling us to the highest bidder because he thinks we aren't in heat."

He is like all the others. A betrayer.

"I should never have put you in this position," Maya apologized to her leopard. She wiped the sweat from her face, took her laptop from the small backpack and opened it. She had her own hot spot. "Let's see if we can find the money Theo and his friends stole. I don't believe for one minute his altruistic stealing-to-help-human-trafficking-victims story."

Even if Theo or his friends tried to hack into her computer, it would be impossible. She had built in too many firewalls for them to work through, all false and all with viruses in them. By the time they realized what was happening, it would be too late.

Theo was on his laptop, looking smug. She could have told him his insane plan wasn't going to work. He had no idea who he had stolen from or what those consequences were going to be. He couldn't possibly conceive of what kind of hell was coming his way.

Maya took her time, researching the territory first. Little was known about it. It had been kept secret for many years. Hidden away, the lair and town had grown quite wealthy, being in the perfect location to run arms, drugs and humans by land, sea and even air without anyone suspecting. The *pakhan* had died two months earlier and Gorya Amurov had replaced him.

"Amurov," Maya whispered aloud. She pressed her hand over her heart. "That's bad, Wraith. The worst. They torture and kill for the slightest infraction. They would take any money Theo managed to recoup, then torture and kill him just to show others what happens if they're crossed."

Saves us the trouble of killing him, Wraith said. *Did you find the money?*

"He gambled his share away. He has a drug dealer. Quite a bit was spent there. It's no wonder his leopard is ill. He deserves to die."

If the bratva *doesn't get him, we will,* Wraith assured her complacently. *We always do.*

The symptoms of the heat had subsided enough to allow Maya to breathe evenly and think rationally.

"Believe me, Wraith, an Amurov isn't going to let it go that Theo stole so much money," she reiterated.

Then they will kill him for us. Did you take the money from the others and put it somewhere it can't be found by them or these leopards that are disgusting?

She felt Wraith curl her lip. She held the male leopards in contempt just as Maya did. "I found the money. It was funneled into three offshore accounts. And yes, I removed it from those accounts. The names on the accounts are fake; at least I can't find anyone with those names in a quick search."

Maya closed her laptop, carefully wrapped it and put it away in her bag. Everything had to be waterproof. She began to pace the length of the room, inspecting every inch of it again. Clearly this was used to bring prisoners for interrogation. There was a small bathroom and shower, which meant there was running water to drink. Mostly, there were instruments for torture. Instead of intimidating her, she saw them as weapons.

There was a long oven; clearly bodies were burned there after the interrogators were finished with them. The entire basement had been designed like some medieval dungeon. She looked up at the slivers of windows again. Beads of sweat began to trickle down her body, and she wiped at the ones on her face with her forearm. Once again, the burning had started. This time she ached everywhere.

"Wraith, we're in so much trouble. We're giving off enough pheromones to call to every male shifter for miles. If we can't get ourselves under control, we'll never be able to hide our presence if we do break out of here. Clearly, this is a true heat." As far as Maya was concerned, it was pure hell, and it was just starting. They couldn't be anywhere in the vicinity. They would have to get out of the area as fast as possible.

I will settle again. I am very tired.

Maya didn't know if that was bad or good. If Wraith went to sleep, their bodies would settle and there would be no way for a male shifter to know they were in heat. On the other hand, she might need Wraith to escape.

"Go to sleep if you need to. I'll wake you if things get dicey."

Wraith had faith in her. She'd never let them down so far. Maya was afraid there was always a first time, and she hadn't been paying attention the way she should have been. After splashing cold water on her face, she made her way to the door and peered out the window at Theo. He was still on his laptop, looking triumphant.

"Bids still coming in?" she questioned through the grille.

Theo looked up, his eyes gleaming with satisfaction. "You wouldn't believe the amount of money men are willing to pay for you. There's a shortage of female shifters, so you're at a premium. The two of us could make so much money. Even if we just ask for half up front and then take off, we could make a killing."

"You don't think word would get out and they'd send someone after us?" she asked, putting just a single note of interest in her voice.

She appeared to be looking through the window at him, but she was studying the door. It was heavy steel. Thick. The bolt on the outside had slid easily into place and was about at the height of her cheekbones.

Maya was small and slight despite being a shifter, causing her appearance to be very deceptive. She thought perhaps being starved as a child during the time she and Wraith were growing had caused her to be smaller than normal—or maybe that was just her genetic makeup. Her size did give her an advantage in quite a few ways. She gave the appearance of being fragile and delicate when, in truth, she had the muscles of a shifter running through her diminutive frame.

Maya's size allowed her to slip into spaces few others could go, particularly larger male leopards. Over the years, she and Wraith had honed their fighting skills, something very unexpected in female leopards. Both were good at acting out whatever role was necessary to get done what was needed. There was no hesitation on either's part.

"I knew if you thought about it, you'd come to your senses," Theo said, taking a step closer to the door. "It's a real moneymaker, Maya. We can't stay here. Sooner or later, that bastard who took over the lair will come looking for me. He killed the men challenging him for leadership. That isn't done."

Her heart dropped. It was common for several members of a lair to challenge for the role of leader when a *pakhan* died. Most of the time, because every leopard was needed, the fights were bloody, but once the losing leopard submitted, the victorious leopard allowed the loser to swear allegiance and that was the end of it. The Amurovs were brutal killers. They took no prisoners. They were known for their swift retaliation and cruel ways of dealing with anyone they thought was against them.

"Are you certain they've checked the books? It's a big territory. There are so many businesses, and he's just taken over. I had one of my hacker friends do a quick search, Theo. It's possible you aren't on his radar yet." She didn't believe that for a minute. The Amurov shifters seemed to smell betrayal.

Theo's gaze had gone back to his laptop, greed etched deep into the heavy lines of his face. Now that she was free of the scorching fury of Wraith's heat, she could easily see the signs of depravity on Theo's features. His nose was red and bulbous. His eyes appeared bloodshot. His jowls had gone saggy. Once, he'd been a charming, handsome man.

We'll have to be ready for Theo to open the door. He has some kind of plan. Maya spoke telepathically to her leopard in images, her face turned away from the window. She didn't want to look at Theo any more than she had to now that she'd made up her mind to kill him. *If someone is with him, we'll have to kill both and make our escape.*

Wraith gave a sniff of disdain. *You will kill anyone coming through the door when they open it. If you do not, I will.*

Wraith was very certain they would prevail—and she had reason to be so confident. The two had tracked and hunted criminals for several years, and they had never failed to bring down their prey. That didn't mean there wouldn't be a first time they would fail. Already, Maya knew they were in trouble. One mistake and it could prove to be fatal. She didn't worry her leopard with her concerns.

"We're in Amurov territory. This part of the swamp is theirs. Their leopards will hunt us if they suspect we're in heat. They may anyway. They traffic women. We'll have to cover our scent and get out fast."

That would mean leaving her computer behind. She had learned to plan for events such as this one—dire emergencies. She had money and clothes stashed in various places if she could get to them, but she despised leaving her laptop. She'd set a fail-safe on it. The moment someone tried to access it, the hard drive would be destroyed. There would be no trail leading back to her. In any case, she would move from the state she'd been living in. She was good at hiding. She'd been doing it for some time. If necessary, she would go to Europe. That might mean a new identity, but she was good at paperwork, and she had enough money to start over somewhere else.

She swore again under her breath. This was her own stupidity. The moment she'd recognized Theo, she should have disappeared. Not acknowledged him. Not spoken. Not engaged. What had gotten into her to risk Wraith that way?

It is our first heat, and we didn't know what to expect. You were disoriented.

Of course Wraith would excuse her. She always did. Maya believed she should have been prepared. She'd considered that eventually it would happen, but nothing could have possibly shown her what it would be like to feel the way she did when Wraith burned with need. Not just Wraith. Now she knew. Hormones raged out of control.

If she was going to get them out of this situation, she would have to do so fast. What she did know of the Han Vol Dan was that the female would rise in little stops and starts. Hopefully Wraith would settle and give Maya time to get them out of the extensive and very dangerous lair and away from all *bratva* territories.

Maya turned her attention back to Theo. "Theo," she called out to him in a soft voice to bring his attention back to her. He had to think it was his idea to open the door. "Do you believe they already know about the money that's gone?"

This time Maya inserted a small tremble in her voice. She wanted to create a sense of urgency in him to leave immediately. She appeared small and lost, not difficult when she often wore clothes just a little too big. Her weapons were concealed up her sleeves, between her shoulder blades, down in her boots, around her waist, along her thighs. It was funny to her that no one ever thought to check her for weapons. She didn't appear to be a threat to anyone, and they took her at face value. Aside from her brain, her looks were one of her greatest weapons.

Theo looked up from his laptop and then scowled.

"Amurov is a real bastard, Maya. All he cares about is money. The first thing he did was demand an accounting from everyone. Every single business had to turn over the books to his people. He brought in new people to oversee everything. He knows. I'm sure of it."

Deliberately Maya looked past him, down the hall, as if fearful of him being stalked. She brought one hand up to her throat. "Those men you said brought this idea to you, they were tempting you, Theo. They'd already been stealing from the organization, and they needed someone they could blame if there was an accounting. They deliberately lured you into their scheme by lying to you and then hooking you into gambling. You know that, right?"

His eyes met hers. "How did you know? About the gambling?"

"My friend does research. That's her job. I asked her to try to find out who those men were who got you into this mess. I figured if we could find them, you would have names to tell this new leader, but they covered themselves. They hid the money under new identities. Given enough time, I'm sure she can track them, but not under these circumstances." She dangled the bait, willing him to open the door.

Theo glanced behind him and then at the laptop. "You have no idea the amount of money these shifters are willing to pay for an unmated female."

"What happens when they find out I'm not available?"

"They won't. We can ask for half up front, arrange to meet them somewhere and then get out of the area." Theo sounded not only eager but confident. "If we move constantly, we could run this con several times before we have to shut it down. We could make a fortune."

"What if I really do go into heat? It could happen, Theo. I don't want to be with a stranger."

Theo looked her over. "My leopard would claim yours. He's never had a mate."

Wraith would never accept his leopard. The male leopard was weak and sick from all the alcohol and drugs Theo had abused their bodies with. Wraith was in top fighting form. She would never stand for a mate who was less than she was.

"Do you feel as if your leopard is close to rising?"

She had no idea if Theo could hear lies. She could. She didn't dare speak aloud. She lowered her lashes, looking at the floor as if ashamed. Many females never had their leopards emerge. They were often treated as less than desirable by others. There were less and less shifters as fewer males could find mates.

Maya knew the Amur leopards were close to extinction, but that was because the Amurovs had cruelly and deliberately prevented their leopards from finding their true mates. They often murdered female cubs and always killed the mothers of their children once they gave birth to sons, just to prove their loyalty to the *bratva*. They were destroying their own species. They knew it, and yet they still continued with their sadistic practices. In her mind, that made them culpable.

"It would be better if she didn't rise," Theo assured her.

Even with his assurance, Maya heard the little superior sneer in his voice. Like most shifters, he looked down on any female whose leopard hadn't emerged. Little did he know that Wraith could run rings around his leopard. She might not have had a heat cycle with Maya before, but they had managed to work together in every other way.

Maya twisted her fingers together to show nervousness. Why didn't he get a move on? He had to realize they were running out of time. She felt a sense of urgency and wanted to insist he open the door. He was the kind of man who thought every idea was his, but the reason the three Russians had chosen him was because Theo was weak and easily open to suggestion.

Moistening her lips, Maya stepped closer to the door, shaking her arm slightly so a small blade slid into her hand. Her fingers closed around the hilt and she kept the flat blade concealed against her wrist as she willed Theo to take another step toward the door and slide the bolt free.

Her heart jumped. Clenched hard. She swore it skipped a beat. Wraith stilled. Both froze. Theo simply peered down at the screen of his laptop as if mesmerized by the various numbers there.

"The bidding is going strong for you," he announced.

Theo didn't sense the men coming up behind him. Five of them. Even if they were entirely silent, which Maya was certain they were, and their energy was nonexistent, surely he had to feel the presence of danger. His leopard had to be that aware. She was locked behind a thick door, and the threat of impending violence hit her so hard she took several steps back into the darker shadows.

As the men came closer, she could tell that the three bringing up the rear were bodyguards. They were definitely from one of the lairs in the Primorye region of Russia. They were Amur shifters, fit, muscles moving subtly beneath their clothing. It was the two men striding toward Theo that set her heart pounding. She'd never seen two men who appeared more like predators.

At first she thought the bulkier of the two was the man to fear the most. His eyes were glacier cold, and she knew he took in everything around him. The other man was definitely an Amurov, but he was . . . more. She couldn't keep her gaze from him. He didn't have obvious muscles, but they ran beneath his skin. He looked almost nice—charming—but she knew that was deceptive. She couldn't have said how she knew, but she did.

Icy fingers of fear crept down her spine. She would have moved even farther back into the shadows, but movement drew notice, and she didn't dare draw either of those

two men's attention to herself. They were the scariest men
she'd ever encountered, and she'd met a few very dangerous men.

She was careful to observe them from under her lashes,
not stare directly. Several times, despite their attention being centered on Theo, both men looked toward the door of
the basement as if they were aware they were under obser-
vation.

"Theo Pappas." The man she was certain was an Amurov spoke. His voice was deceptively low. Mild. No hint of
a threat.

Theo half turned to face them, his skin going ashen as
he saw the number of men facing him. One of the bodyguards reached out and took his laptop from him, glanced
at the screen and then handed it to Amurov.

"My name is Gorya Amurov." He studied the contents
of the screen and then turned toward the door of the basement. "You appear to be auctioning off a young female
leopard in heat. The fact that the door is bolted would indicate she might not be on board with your idea."

Again, Maya couldn't detect a hint of reprimand. She
also couldn't tell whether he thought the idea was a good
one or not. Considering the Amurov lairs dealt in human
trafficking, she was sure he would applaud Theo's scheme.

"The money's for you," Theo said hastily. "I owe you
money, and this was a way to pay you back. You can see
how much is coming in, and I only just started the auction.
Although," he added, "if you want her yourself, we could
work something out."

The bodyguards exchanged incredulous looks. Maya
allowed herself a breath. Theo was oblivious to the fact
that he was in way over his head.

"We can work something out," Gorya Amurov repeated slowly in that same low voice.

His head turned slowly, and this time his eyes pierced

the darkness to look right at her. Seeing her. He didn't look in the least bit easygoing or charming. Fear crept down her spine. Ice surrounded her heart. She gripped the hilt of her knife and stroked one finger along the small blade. She was looking at death.

3

GORYA suddenly struck Theo without even looking at him. He was so fast his hand was a blur. So strong Theo's head snapped back, the skin on his cheekbone exploding and blood erupting even as he was knocked off his feet. All the while, Gorya continued to stare straight at Maya, never blinking. The laptop didn't so much as shake in his other hand.

She couldn't help taking the cautionary step back, farther into the shadows. Her mouth went dry.

"Did you really think you could get away with stealing from me?" Gorya asked in that same low tone, as if that brutal strike had never happened. "You knew the consequences, and yet you took the money and spent it on drugs, alcohol and gambling. Now you're willing to sell a female shifter to pay for your sins. You disgust me."

Theo dug his heels into the floor. "I'm giving you the way to make money *free*," he sputtered as he tried to push backward, away from Gorya. "I could have kept it to my-self. I didn't try to hide her from you." There was a sob in his voice.

Gorya gestured toward him in disgust. "Rodion, get him out of here. We need the names of his accomplices. He didn't think of this scheme alone. Quite frankly, he doesn't have the brains or the balls to have thought of this by himself."

The entire time, Gorya hadn't taken his gaze from that window leading straight to the basement rooms. He shouldn't have been able to see Maya in the shadows, but she knew he did.

"Take the laptop with you. Have Tonio see what he can get off it. If there's a passcode, I'm certain Pappas will cooperate if you need it."

He spoke so casually, but Maya knew what was meant by cooperation. Someone would get the information from Theo by torture. It wasn't that she was opposed to Theo dying. She'd planned to kill him herself. As far as she was concerned, he deserved to die for a number of reasons. She killed as cleanly as possible, not that she thought her-self better than anyone else.

Her heart pounded as the leader of the lair waited for the bodyguard to drag Theo down the hall and out of sight before he moved close to the door.

"Are you injured?"

She shook her head, reluctant to speak to him aloud. In any case, it would be good to know if she was right. Could he see into the darker recesses of the basement?

"I'm going to open the door and allow you to come out."

No way was she going out there with four shifter males in a narrow hallway. She wouldn't have fighting room. There would be no room to maneuver. She would have no choice but to speak to him.

"No one will harm you. And no one is going to sell you to the highest bidder."

She shook her head again, keeping her gaze locked with his. He never changed expression.

"You have my word."

Those eyes were flat and dead. Ice. Colder than ice. Frosted over and piercing the veil of darkness. At the same time, they burned over her. Through her. She swore if she'd been in the fires of hell, he would have found her there. If she'd been hiding in the densest glacier, he would have seen her.

"Forgive me, but you're an Amurov. You don't have the best reputations." She was crazy to rile him, but what did she have to lose? She was already a captive. "If you mean what you say, unlock the door and leave. When I feel safe, I'll leave the building and get out of your territory."

Something changed. She didn't know exactly what it was, but she knew the moment she spoke she was in trouble. Real trouble, and she couldn't take it back. The lines in his face deepened. His eyes went from that gray frost to an eerie color even more penetrating. She could see his leopard looking straight at her, a steely bluish gray coming through that piercing stare. The blue wasn't vivid—if anything, it was still as frosty as the gray was—but she could see the difference, and she knew the leopard was aware of her.

Maya shuddered and stroked her finger along the short blade of the knife in her hand. They would be coming for her. She had promised herself she would never be taken again. She wouldn't allow Wraith to be savagely beaten, and she would never again submit to rape and other vile, depraved acts men subjected trafficked women to.

Gorya Amurov was coming for her. He wasn't going to leave quietly and let her go into the swamp and disappear. His promises of not selling her and no harm coming to her were bullshit. She couldn't trust him.

She pressed a hand to her churning stomach and fought down the rising bile. She detested male shifters. She detested their leopards. More than anything, she detested the Amurovs. She was willing to die, and she would take Wraith with her before she would let them take her. That was a solemn vow.

Maya moved farther back into the deeper recesses of the basement. If he was coming for her, he was going to have to come all the way into the room. She might have a chance to kill him. If she could face them one at a time, the man instead of his leopard, they would think she was small and weak. That was always the man's downfall.

She heard the bolt slide and her heart accelerated. She took a deep breath and forced it under control. The door opened slowly, and light spilled into the room.

"Gedeon, this is the time to earn your money," Gorya said. "Matvei, Kyanite, you are to stay out there no matter what happens. I hired Gedeon for more than to head up my security detail. His main duty is to ensure that my leopard doesn't kill an innocent."

The two bodyguards exchanged an uneasy look. One moved forward, but Gorya held up his hand.

"I've given him an order I expect him to carry out. I've already texted my cousins and let them know I've instructed Gedeon to kill Rogue if he attacks this woman, and Gedeon is not to be blamed or harmed. I expect you to protect Gedeon from them should they come. That is a direct order."

His gaze met Gedeon's. Gedeon's nod was nearly imperceptible, but Maya caught it. Immediately she wished she could see through the little window. She knew there were windows along that hallway. Her best guess was that someone was outside those windows with a high-powered rifle. If one or both bodyguards made a move against Gedeon, they weren't going to live through it.

But what did that mean for her? Maya heard truth in Gorya's voice, but he wasn't making sense. He believed his leopard might try to kill her. No, he believed his leopard *would* try to kill her. He fully expected Gedeon to have to shoot him. Why would he chance it? If Gedeon shot the leopard, it could kill Gorya. Unless Gedeon was such a good shot he was able to incapacitate the animal without killing both. She doubted anyone could do that with an experienced leopard attacking. She was certain Gorya's leopard was extremely fast.

Gorya closed the door on the two bodyguards, and the basement was once more dimly lit. He turned toward her as he toed off his shoes. "My name is Gorya Amurov, in case you didn't hear it. My leopard reacted very strongly to your voice. Pappas had your name as Maya."

She shook her head. "Keep your leopard away from me. I don't want anything to do with you or your leopard."

"I'm sorry, Maya, but he's very insistent." As he walked toward her on bare feet, he slid the buttons free on his shirt.

She swallowed fear and moved closer to the wall to protect her back, although she gave herself room to move. She couldn't control the way her heart accelerated. That embarrassed her. If she was going down fighting, she didn't want him to think her a coward. The hell with him and his leopard.

Gorya came at her in a slow, steady, silent stalk, the way a leopard would. No freeze-frame, but alarming all the same, maybe more so because he didn't take his eyes from hers.

She shook her head and moved into a fighting stance, feet shoulder-width apart, hands up to block any move he made. The blade was concealed, but she could strike with it from any direction. She'd already picked her targets.

"He isn't going to get to her." Maya made it a firm statement.

Gorya nodded. "I understand you feel you must protect her. I feel I should protect you. Gedeon will see to it that no harm will come to you or your leopard."

"I don't know or trust you or Gedeon. Back off." It was more of a plea than a command.

Gorya was relentless. He just kept coming, and the closer he got to her, the more invincible he seemed. She did her best not to let tension show, not to grip the hilt of the blade too hard and give herself away. He got into her personal space, his eyes staring right into hers.

Like frost. She could see the leopard looking at her through those gray eyes, giving them that bluish cast that by turns burned and froze her.

Gorya didn't break the stare when he reached her. "Gedeon." He caught her arms and pulled her close. "*Bog*, your scent." He took a deep breath, inhaling her into his lungs.

She tried not to breathe him in. As it was, it took every ounce of determination to rotate her wrist and step into him, to thrust the blade at his chest. At his heart.

No, Wraith protested. *I recognize his leopard.*

She should have driven it deep, but he very gently caught the blade, wrapping his fist around it and twisting it out of her hand. Blood dripped from his palm as he tossed the knife aside and turned her around, pressing her front against the wall.

That's impossible. We've never met them before. His leopard is a killer.

"What are you doing?" She pushed her forehead against the wall, closing her eyes, trying to figure out what she should do. Wraith had never gone against her decisions before. Not once.

She couldn't move. Her hands were trapped, and Gorya's body weight held her in place. He seemed driven by his leopard and as uncertain of the outcome as she was. Maya couldn't stop shaking even though Gorya tried to soothe her by rubbing her arms gently.

"Gedeon," Gorya repeated. "Rogue is insistent. For the

first time, I'm uncertain if I can hold him back. Come closer. Be ready."

"He could kill her," Maya found herself pleading. "Not like this. Don't let him kill her like this."

"Gedeon is fast," Gorya assured her.

"No one is that fast." The truth was, the leopard would kill Maya, but Wraith would be too close and feel the pain. Maya didn't want that for her.

If Gorya was allowing his leopard to claim Wraith, and the monster's intention was really to kill her, Maya might not be able to stop Wraith from rising. On the other hand, if Wraith believed the male leopard was determined to kill Maya, she might shift. These men—and the leopard—wouldn't expect that. Females didn't shift until the emergence, which happened during the first heat cycle. They had worked at it. Practiced out of dire need. Maya had been a child and Wraith had come to her aid.

He will not kill either of us. I would never allow it.

Maya could barely stand the scent of Gorya surrounding her. He was too potent. Too male. She tried holding her breath as he pushed her shirt up, exposing her spine. She froze. He would see the scars. A road map of them. Tiny white lines like a giant spiderweb spreading across her entire back. From the dimples at her bottom to her shoulder blades. No one else had seen them—not in years.

Damn him to hell. She knew he was staring at them. She felt his gaze, burning hot, right through her skin. She refused to squirm. She nearly jumped out of her skin when the pad of his finger brushed along the network of scars, following each of those thin lines. It was the lightest of touches, but she felt every brushstroke as if it sank through skin and muscle straight to the bone, branding her.

Maya shuddered. She couldn't help it. "Please, don't let him do this." She wasn't a woman to plead, especially with a member of the *bratva*. She knew better. She knew they didn't have hearts, but she couldn't stop herself. "I can't be claimed. Those scars you see, Amurovs did those." She whispered it to him, hoping Gedeon couldn't hear her make a fool of herself. He was leopard, which meant his hearing was acute and most likely he could. That only added to her humiliation.

Gorya pressed his lips against her skin, right in the center of the spiderweb of scars. "You haven't seen my scars. They're fairly horrendous. Amurovs made them as well."

She dared to take another breath. She had no choice. He smelled wild. Feral. Dangerous. His leopard was close. Listening to every word. She didn't care if he heard her beg. If Gedeon did. Gorya had to listen to her.

"I don't know how to be a partner to anyone. I don't like men. I would be of no use to you. I'm broken and there's no fixing me. I might wake up one morning and stick a knife in your heart just because you're an Amurov."

"After cleaning up this hellhole, I had planned to eat a bullet. Maybe it would be a mercy."

Gorya's voice rang with honesty. As much as she didn't want to believe a single thing he said, it was impossible not to hear the truth. She tried to turn her head to look at him over her shoulder. She needed to see his face again, but he had one hand on the nape of her neck, holding her shirt off her back and shoulders.

She grew hot as hormones flooded her body. A fist of desire knotted in her belly, and fire began to smolder between her legs.

"I can't let you do this." She tried to warn him. She couldn't live with this choice. If his leopard claimed Wraith and her female allowed it, it was permanent. Every Amurov she knew of had murdered his partner. Their reputations with women were legendary. "Don't you think I know what men like you do after you get what you want from a woman?"

"Feel him. Feel his joy. His triumph."

Again, his lips whispered over the nape of her neck, sending fiery darts through her bloodstream.

"I call him Rogue. His life has been hell—worse than hell—from the time he was born until a few minutes ago. We were both close to insanity. He knew I intended to end our lives after we took care of the problems here. We both feared we would cross the line and hurt an innocent. We were getting to the end of our control. But then, *she* came. Do you think after waiting all this time and finally finding her, Rogue would ever allow anything or anyone to harm her? Me included? That means you're under his protection. He's spent his entire life looking for her."

His voice didn't change from that soft rasp of a whisper. From that honest desperation she couldn't ignore. Tears burned behind her eyes. She couldn't prevent what was happening. She did feel his male leopard. The animal was very close. Listening. Trying to be patient. Wraith was there. Eager to accept him. Eager to betray her. That was what it felt like to her. A betrayal.

"You said he spent his life looking for his mate. Not you. You weren't looking, were you?" She already knew his answer. Gorya hadn't once said or acted as if he wanted her. This was all about his leopard. Wraith and Rogue would force their human counterparts to live together whether they wanted each other or not.

He shook his head slightly and she felt the brush of his beard against her shoulder. "Just as the Amurovs scarred you, they damaged me beyond all saving. I'm not going to be of any use to a woman. There's something terribly wrong with me. Maybe I was born this way. I just know I had to make the choice to follow my cousins' code, but it's been a struggle."

Maya was shocked at Gorya's confession. It was entirely possible he was the greatest actor of all time. She had the feeling he had the ability to deceive, but she was extremely good at detecting lies. Wraith would have known—usually. Right now, she was so smitten with Rogue, Maya doubted if Wraith was even paying attention to what was happening between the humans.

The ominous way Gorya portrayed himself sent her heart thundering all over again. She'd like to say he was scaring her, but she was just plain scared. She couldn't be his partner, yet she couldn't stop what was happening.

She felt the slide of fur against her bare back. She closed her eyes and pressed her forehead harder against the wall. Her breath caught in her lungs and just held there. Deep inside her head, where she thought no one could hear, she screamed and screamed the way she had when she was a child and there was no other outlet to express the fear and trauma of horrific events.

The leopard was heavy, all roped muscle, long and lithe, and that was just his upper body. He rubbed along her spine up to the nape of her neck. His fur felt thick and soft rather than rough and coarse. A blast of hot air startled her as the large cat nuzzled her shoulder. His teeth sank in a holding bite as he flooded her body with male hormones, calling enticingly to the female to come to him.

Maya willed Wraith not to move, but the female leopard rose eagerly, rushing to the surface, matching the male with her own tempting, very feminine pheromones as she touched her nose to his, accepting his claim on her. She subsided, retreating to rest.

Triumphant, Rogue licked at the punctures on Maya's shoulder, numbing and cleansing the wounds before Gorya shifted back to his human form. Gedeon came closer, handing him antibiotic cream and bandages.

"I guess that answered your question about your leopard, Gorya."

Gorya didn't reply. Maya didn't turn around to face either man. She still struggled to breathe. She'd never felt more alone in her life. She wanted to crumple to the floor and hide from the world. Wraith. Her only companion. Her one ally. Her friend.

I am with you.

Maya refused to acknowledge her, afraid anything she said might be too hurtful. They were two separate entities, yet they had to coexist. She wrapped her arms around her waist, hugging herself as Gorya lowered her shirt over her back. Slipping down to the floor without looking at him, she drew up her knees and made herself as small as possible. She was still in the shadows. It was too late to undo what Wraith had done. She had to decide what to do before Gorya decreed that she go with him.

The one path she did have open to her was to live the majority of her life as a leopard rather than as a human. She could avoid Gorya, and he could avoid her. If he followed the rest of the Amurovs, he had a strong sex drive. She was having no part of that. She could take herself out of that equation. If he wanted to use other women for that purpose, he had her blessing. She would disappear and let Wraith have their form.

"You can't stay here indefinitely," Gorya informed her in that same mild voice. He held out his hand to her. "Come with me. No one is going to harm you, Maya."

She lifted her lashes and studied his face. How could he look so deceptively young and easygoing? If one didn't look at his eyes, they might not see the danger lurking just below that facade.

She gave him a faint, practiced smile. Two could play at the civilized game. She'd perfected that art a long time ago. "How can you be so sure? Essentially, you said you don't trust yourself."

It wasn't easy to allow him to touch her, but she put her hand in his and allowed him to pull her to her feet. The moment she was standing, on the pretense of finding her backpack, she turned away from him, forcing him to release her.

I am with you, Wraith repeated, insistent.

Maya shoved down her sorrow and the overwhelming fear she felt at having to go with Amurov to his home. Wraith had placed her in this position knowing what had happened to her. She'd protected Wraith, and yet her leopard had chosen an Amurov leopard as a mate. It was the worst kind of betrayal.

Maya picked up her backpack and slung it on so Gorya wouldn't be tempted to touch her as they walked out of the room. He hadn't searched her for weapons. Neither had Gedeon. That surprised her. Gorya might be arrogant enough to think he could stop her from getting to him, but Gedeon was his bodyguard and he seemed deadly. Extremely competent. It was a little shocking that he didn't at least ask her if she was armed. She would have widened her eyes in innocent shock and given a little nonverbal shake of her head.

Gedeon stepped back to allow Gorya and Maya to go through the heavy door first. Matvei and Kyanite waited just outside, and both looked her over as she stepped into the hallway.

"Maya, this is Kyanite Boston and Matvei Jarvis. I've known them most of my life," Gorya said. "We're new to this lair. For now, we're careful who we trust. Kyanite, Matvei, Rodion, Gedeon and his wife, Meiling, are the only ones I want you to rely on. Stick with one of them if you leave the residence. Don't go anywhere alone. It isn't safe yet."

Maya flashed them a small smile designed to make her appear fragile, sweet and demure. "Nice to know. Thank you." She looked out the window toward the swamp, and a visible shudder went through her body.

Both bodyguards crowded closer protectively. Gorya glided between them easily. "I think she's safe enough when she's with me." There was an edge to his low tone, as if his famous control might be slipping.

Maya risked a quick look up at his face from under her lashes. He wore that same charming, easygoing, deceptive mask, but his eyes were pure silvery frost, edged now with slate blue. She saw the killer in him quite plainly. His fingers settled around her upper arm like a shackle, and he anchored her to his side.

"They can't see you for what you are, Maya, but I do. Whatever you're thinking of doing, stop. We'll sort things out between us when we get home." There was no inflection in his voice, but she knew it was a command.

She tilted her head back to look more fully at him. He saw her, did he? Well, she saw him too. He might deceive everyone else around him, but not her. He might pretend he had a nice side to him, a sweet, charming side, but she knew better. She saw right into him. He could go right ahead and look at what his family had made of her. It wasn't a pretty sight.

On the outside, Maya looked like the girl next door. When she was around others, she often dressed in feminine clothing that made her appear younger and delicate. She smiled readily and agreed with everyone. Most of the time, she simply avoided being around anyone. She was nothing at all like she appeared. If anyone took her at face value, they did so at their own peril.

She stayed very quiet and remained as far from Gorya as possible in the close confines of the car on the ride back to his estate. Twice Wraith reached out to her, but Maya didn't respond. Both times, Gorya turned that frosty bluish gaze on her as if his leopard was aware she was at odds with her female.

Maya curled her fingers into a fist and pressed it tightly against the knot developing in her stomach. Wraith had completely abandoned her. That had never been a remote possibility. Something heavy settled in her chest, crushing her heart. A vise gripped her lungs and squeezed until every last bit of air was gone and she couldn't breathe.

For one terrible moment the door creaked open, and the feeling of brutal hands tearing at her body, hurting her, excruciating pain ripping her open, and the sound of male laughter filled her mind as a thin wire tore into her back. She fought back the need to vomit. Fortunately, the car stopped moving and the door beside her opened, spilling air into the interior where there had been only Amurov to breathe in.

Maya stumbled out, nearly going to her knees. It was Gedeon who caught her before she went down. She didn't look at him as she managed to get her legs to work. She hadn't allowed those memories to surface in years. She'd built herself into a strong, confident woman, capable of hunting the men who had beaten, raped and trafficked a child.

She did have times when she could barely get out of bed. She knew she was incapable of relationships. For the most part, she was a puddle of issues. Bad ones. There was nothing left of a human being other than what she'd developed herself into: A deceiver. A liar. A killing machine. She could track anyone. She doubted anyone could hide from her once she set out to find them. She was determined to find every single man who had raped her. Who had killed her family and friends. Not one would escape her. Only then could she rest.

"He's a good man," Gedeon said softly. "Give him a chance. He needs saving the way his leopard does. The way I did. Meiling was my miracle."

Everything in her froze. Saving? Gorya Amurov needed saving? Gorya came up on the other side of her as she contemplated the absolute irony of Gedeon's statement. She wanted to burst into hysterical laughter. At least she wasn't going to vomit all over Gorya's immaculate shoes as he came up beside her. She was no one's miracle. If that was what he expected, he was in for a very sad letdown. She couldn't save herself, let alone Gorya.

The one thing Gedeon had done for her was allow her to pull her fragmented mind back together. She flashed him her first half-real smile. "You aren't very good at telling lies, Gedeon. Gorya is about as good a man as I am a good woman."

Gorya slid his hand down her arm and took firm possession of her hand. "I don't think we need to consider each other in terms of bad or good, do you?"

The moment his large hand surrounded hers, tiny embers flickered and smoldered through her veins. There was no way to stop it, so she didn't try. She had to accept the fact that physically, because of Wraith's heat, she was very susceptible to Gorya.

"I suppose that would be for the best," she agreed as they went up the walkway toward the front of the sprawling house.

"How many weapons do you have on you?" Gedeon asked.

She glanced up at Gedeon. It was far easier to look at him than Gorya. "I wondered if you or the others were ever going to do your job. If you're supposed to be keeping Amurov alive, I'm not certain you're up to the task."

Matvei and Kyanite gave an affronted huff. Kyanite answered the accusation. "Had we searched you, Gorya would have cut off our heads. Did you notice he got a little protective when we got too close?"

"Is that what you call it? Nevertheless, as his security, whether he likes it or not, your job is to keep him alive. That means you search everyone he encounters who might be a potential threat to him."

"You're his mate," Matvei pointed out.

"Wraith is Rogue's mate," Gorya corrected, unexpectedly backing her up. "I haven't convinced Maya yet that she's mine. Right now, she's thinking about slitting my throat."

She gave her laugh, the one she'd perfected over time

and everyone believed—everyone, it seemed, but Gorya. He tightened his hold on her and brought her hand to his chest. Her heart clenched. She forced herself to look at the house, not at him. She couldn't think too much, just go along with everything until she had time to herself to figure things out logically.

"You didn't answer me about the weapons, Maya," Gedeon said.

"Do you believe I'd tell you the truth?"

She stared up at the two-story house, which was surrounded by an abundance of trees with curved branches, each reaching to the next, and taller trees that held climbing vines weeping gorgeous flowers. The landscaping was wild, but with native plants clearly maintained and encouraged to grow. If the road hadn't led to the house, it would have been impossible to spot with the wealth of trees and plants around it. She found the place breathtaking, a leopard's paradise.

"There's no reason to lie, especially in light of what Kyanite told you. Gorya would object to any of us searching you."

She looked at Gedeon with a cool, assessing stare. "That wouldn't stop you."

"No, but it would be a process."

She heard the humor in his voice. He genuinely liked Gorya. Instinctively, she knew this man didn't call very many others friend. "You would have shot his leopard if he had attacked me, wouldn't you?"

"That was the plan."

She had to grudgingly respect him. She also had to consider that Gorya was telling her the truth—that he had gone against his family. That he really was there to clean up the lair and that he'd planned to kill his leopard and himself before they both went insane and harmed an innocent. If she believed that, she would have to go a step further and believe Gorya when he said his body and mind had been scarred and damaged by the Amurovs just as hers had been.

She could believe that the Amurovs would turn on their own—even sons. If Gorya had dared to oppose his father, uncles or cousins in any way, they were cruel enough to hold him up as an example, as they did other members of the lair. They would most likely make his punishments even worse. She didn't want to think about that. If she did, her own childhood would surface, and she wouldn't be able to cope.

"I honestly don't know how many weapons I have on me at this precise moment. I do hope you retrieved the one Gorya took from me. I don't ever leave them behind." She did her best to sound demure.

"I don't suppose you'd hand your weapons over."

"No."

She glanced up at Gorya as he reached past her to open the front door. She could have sworn he had a half smile on his face.

Gedeon sighed. "Why did I know you wouldn't make this easy on me? Will you at least promise me you won't kill him?"

"How can I do that? You know he's going to provoke me on purpose."

"I didn't say you couldn't stab him. Just don't kill him. Do you have any idea the problems you'd be making for me if you actually killed him? He has cousins. Lots of them. For some reason they like him. If that isn't enough, my wife likes him too. I'd never hear the end of it if I let him get killed on my watch."

"If you don't tell him you'll just stab me somewhere nonlethal, he'll talk us to death," Gorya said. "We're going in, Gedeon. Alone. No bodyguards. We have a lot to work out."

Gedeon stepped back. It registered with Maya that Kyanite and Matvei looked uneasy. They didn't know what to make of her. She hadn't stayed in character as the sweet girl next door the way she normally would have portrayed herself. She'd been too shaken. Just the name Amurov had been a trigger.

She tried another smile. "I'll do my best, Gedeon."

Gorya indicated for her to step through the doorway. Wraith had committed them to this path. She had no real choice. She squared her shoulders and stepped inside. Gorya crowded close enough behind her that she could feel his heat and smell his feral scent surrounding her. She moved all the way into the enormous room, hoping for some respite from her own pounding heart as he closed the door on freedom.

4

GORYA hadn't expected to feel anything at all for the exotic creature standing just a few feet from him. She looked pale and delicate—extremely fragile, as if the least little disagreement would have her dissolving into a flood of tears. She had steel running through her, yet at the same time she was fragile. She just didn't accept that she was.

"Our leopards certainly didn't hesitate, did they?" He had to find a way to reach her. Maya was closed off to any possibility of a relationship between the two of them. In all honesty, he had been as well.

He didn't have a soft side. There wasn't anything good left in him; maybe there never had been. If there had, he couldn't remember it. Still, there were his cousins and their wives. He was fiercely loyal and protective of them. He didn't just feel mild affection for them. He loved them. He knew he did. Twice, when he'd heard of a threat to Evangeline, Fyodor's wife, he had quietly gone on the hunt and killed whoever had threatened her. No one had ever known. He wasn't a man who needed or wanted accolades. He didn't want to be noticed. He got the job done.

Maya wasn't joking about weapons. He knew she was armed, and he was aware that if she felt threatened, she wouldn't hesitate to use force to get free.

"No, Wraith knew exactly what she wanted." Maya looked around the large room, anywhere but at him.

"We can figure this out between us."

Her gaze suddenly collided with his, and his chest felt like a vise. There was no logical reason for the physical reaction at that look she gave him. She had no intention of entering into a relationship with him. None. He brought his palm to his heart and pressed hard to ease the unexpected ache. He didn't want a relationship either.

Gorya knew he had nothing to give her. He was too damaged. Too brutal. Too violent. Too far beyond redemption. There had been a feeling of relief in making the decision to end the fight for sanity. He knew Rogue was a killing machine and he was eventually going to lose control of him. He was already losing control of himself. The more violence he used in cleaning up the territory—which was necessary—the worse he was becoming. Yet looking at Maya, something in him responded to her, which made no sense at all.

"Let's start with a tour of the house. You'll need to know your way around. It looks big, and there are escape routes, but once you know the rooms and who belongs and who doesn't, you'll be comfortable here." He kept his voice strictly neutral. Pleasant, not giving away the fact that he was as conflicted as she was. Maybe more so.

The scent of her drove him half out of his mind. He considered that it might be pheromones, but he feared it was just Maya without Wraith's influence. Wraith had subsided, as often happened during a heat. He knew because, for the first time, Rogue was at peace. He couldn't say the same for himself. He hadn't liked his bodyguards—not even Gedeon—in close proximity to Maya. None of his reactions made sense, and he was a logical man.

He didn't wait for her answer. Better to be a tour guide and show her through the house than try to figure out the impossible. He didn't like to dwell on emotions. That wasn't part of his life. Emotions led to bad things—like revenge. Like the rush he felt in the hunt or with brutality and violence. He couldn't afford to give in to that vile side of who he was, especially now that he had to protect Maya from himself. Damn his leopard for claiming Wraith. By doing so, the cat had complicated his life beyond measure.

"Obviously, this is the entryway. Italian marble. The curving stairway leads to the second story. The entire house is about eight thousand square feet." He indicated opposite the stairway, where a table and six chairs sat on a thick rug in front of a bank of curved floor-to-ceiling windows covered by heavy drapes. "Open floor plan for the most part. If the leopards are prowling around, it makes it easier for them."

He led the way past the table to the enormous kitchen. "Chef's dream right here. The cabinetry is custom." He liked the kitchen. It was the one room that had a homey feel to it, although it was extremely large. He liked the arrangement and the white with gray and black accents. The industrial stove, ovens and refrigerator were silver or black. The center aisle was very large and had comfortable black barstools with rounded backs.

Maya turned around twice, taking in the room. Looking up at the overhead lighting. "This is really nice. There's something comforting about this kitchen. You didn't design it, did you?"

How could she possibly guess that? "I had it remodeled before I moved in," he admitted. He had told himself he'd be as truthful as possible with her. "I needed a sanctuary for Rogue and me. Somewhere we might feel a little peace. I found this place for sale and saw the potential."

"The entryway and staircase are your designs as well?"

He nodded. "I didn't choose the Italian marble. Most of the materials were chosen by some very experienced craftsmen I consulted."

"Do you cook?"

"I like to eat, but I'm no cook. Gedeon has been instructing me on the grill outside. He thinks I should be proficient on that at least."

She gave him a small smile. He thought it might be genuine, because it lit her eyes to a fantastic shade of blue for the briefest of moments, just enough time for him to want to see that color again. "That Gedeon is bossy."

Gorya nodded. "I gave him far too much power over me when I hired him. Fortunately, Meiling makes up for him."

Maya turned away from him, but not fast enough, and not before he caught a look on her face that told him she might not be enamored with Meiling. That didn't make sense because she hadn't met her. It even appeared as if she'd rolled her eyes.

"Do you cook?"

"Out of necessity, but I don't love it. I like to grow things. Gardens. Vegetables. Herbs. Beautiful flowers. Mostly vegetables and herbs. At first I wasn't very successful, but I started paying attention to soil and heat and water and what needed what. It's not just tossing the seeds in the ground like I thought it would be. I liked researching how to grow the different vegetables. I also thought if I survived long enough and could settle somewhere, I would learn to keep bees."

Gorya didn't like the way she'd put that. Why the hell wouldn't she survive? What did she mean by that? He considered whether it would be a good idea to ask her, but he didn't want her to shut down. At least she was talking to him without looking as if she were on the verge of flight—or trying to kill him. Or loathing him.

"Have you gardened in a greenhouse?"

"Not yet. I thought about it. I tried barrels in a couple of the places I lived. When it was cold, I put plastic around them. The plants survived, but they weren't the healthiest. I've done a lot of research on various types of green-houses." Her voice trailed off as she followed him into the informal dining room that looked out to the back of the property.

The floor-to-ceiling windows and thick sliding glass doors gave a good view of a saltwater pool and spa and a fire pit sitting on a raised portion of the large patio.

"Do you like water?"

She nodded without taking her gaze from the pool. "How do you keep the wildlife away? The alligators? The birds and snakes? It seems to me it would be a full-time job."

"The entire backyard is surrounded by a high fence and netting."

"You do a good job of keeping it invisible."

"That wasn't my design, although I'd like to take the credit. Drake Donovan has lived in various places—rainforests, swamps, you name it—and he has experience living in harmony with all kinds of wildlife. I suppose shifters are considered wildlife."

She turned her head to look at him. Once more, there was that hint of deeper blue in her eyes, indicating her sense of humor had kicked in.

"You do give off a feral vibe."

Was she teasing him? Was she even capable of that? He raised an eyebrow. "I'm considered the easygoing, charm-ing cousin."

"Ever the deceiver. How could they possibly live with you all those years and not catch on?" There was real cu-riosity in her voice.

Gorya liked that she was interested, but confessions would only reinforce her bad opinion of him. Unfortunately, she needed to see the truth of him if she was going to live with him, and for whatever reason, he'd made up his mind that she was. Gorya wasn't a man to lose a battle, let alone the war. Rogue deserved whatever contentment and peace he could get in the time he had left, and whatever it cost Gorya—or Maya—he was going to see that Rogue got it.

He continued walking to the large den. There were comfortable chairs and a large floor-to-ceiling cabinet housing books and a television. A gas fireplace was built into the wall on one side, and two windows faced the patio.

"My cousins look and feel like dangerous men. In their way, they are. Fyodor destroyed the entire lair, killed his father, in order to save Timur and me." Gorya tapped his fingers against his thigh. "They don't believe they're good men, but I know differently. Timur loved his mother. I never understood why. I really didn't. I was brought to her when my mother was murdered, and Ogfia raised me along with Timur and Fyodor. She never once showed an ounce of affection for either of them, let alone me."

He left the den and continued through the wide, sprawling house toward the playroom, where there were several activities from billiards to bowling. Throughout the house were high perches for his leopard as well as many shadowed alcoves, with large plants concealing the entrances, where Rogue could rest while concealed.

"There's a shooting range in the building beside the garage. The garage is temperature controlled and houses five cars. Over it is a full apartment complete with its own kitchen. There are four guesthouses on the property as well as a gym where we do combat training. There is also an area for the leopards to train, with ladders and small tunnels and various obstacles to keep their skills sharp.

We have a range in the swamp for them to engage in fighting skills as well as hunt live food."

"Did you think Fyodor's mother deserved to be murdered?" There was no judgment in Maya's voice, but how could she not be judging him when he judged himself?

He hadn't thrown her off topic by his revelations on all the interesting perks of the property. He should have known. In any case, he was determined to give her the truth of who he was. If they were going to have a relationship, she should know what she was getting into.

"She never once tried to stop Patva from beating Timur or Fyodor or turning the three of us over to his men for beatings. He was a sadistic bastard, but she would hide and allow him to torture the three of us. Being gang raped or beaten with whips or chains wasn't out of the question. That didn't rally her to defend any of us, not even Timur."

He didn't sound bitter, because he wasn't. He was indifferent. Maya had ceased following him, forcing him to stop as well. He indicated the hall. "The house has eight bathrooms. This is one of the guest bathrooms. There's only one guest bedroom on this floor. There's an office, and the rest of the floor is taken up with the primary suite."

He opened the door to the bedroom to show her the spacious room. It was beautiful and had its own bathroom. The bedroom was enormous and could easily have been a second primary suite. The floor was wood, the bed large and comfortable looking, and a sitting area by the windows invited reading or visiting. A small desk with a lamp was against one wall, but otherwise the room was kept open and spacious. The closet was a walk-in and could have been a small nursery.

The bathroom was large as well, with a deep jacuzzi tub and a two-person shower. Gorya wanted to get Maya out of there as quickly as possible. She seemed to take a great deal of interest in it as she wandered around the room, looking anywhere but at him. Truthfully, it had occurred to him that she could sleep there until Wraith got further along in her heat, but his odd reaction to the close proximity of his bodyguards to Maya had him changing his mind.

She followed him down the hall, silence stretching between them. He didn't turn around to look at her face. She was a deceiver, the same as he was. She wasn't going to give anything away unless she wanted to. That little smile she'd teased him with had been as practiced as the easygoing charm he was so famous for. It was a little scary how alike they were. On the other hand, he was grateful. She might be the only woman in the world who could live with him.

He'd disclosed information about himself he had never told anyone. Inadvertently, he had also told her things about other family members he was certain they hadn't told anyone. He'd been casual about it, but she'd heard him. Maya was a woman who didn't miss much.

"I didn't think she deserved Patva's way of killing her, but was I terribly upset about her death? In all honesty? No. I wish I could say I was. I know I *should* feel emotion for her death, but it would be a lie if I said I did. I wasn't certain what she did with her time other than hide away and ignore her children."

Maya remained silent, and Gorya stopped at the entrance to the primary bedroom, turning to look at her face. The door was reinforced with steel between the thick slabs of wood. The suite was practically designed as an enormous safe room. Gorya rested a hip against the door and crossed his arms over his chest.

"Patva, like all the men in the lair, expected us to join him in beating the mothers to death to prove loyalty to the *bratva*. I wasn't loyal to them or to Patva. I don't beat women, and I knew Timur wasn't about to hurt his mother. He tried to stop his father. I couldn't allow Patva to kill Timur."

He rolled his shoulders in a slight shrug. "I was smaller than Fyodor and Timur, so no one ever considered me a threat. Rogue didn't have the obvious bulk that their leopards did. He was sleek and long but deadly fast. I trained him away from everyone, including Timur and Fyodor."

Her blue-gray eyes didn't move from his face. "Why?"

Gorya allowed his gaze to drift over her delicate features. She was beautiful. Maybe a little too beautiful. She would catch the attention of other men if they looked too closely. How had she gotten away from the shifters who should have been watching for an unattached female?

"I recognized very early that I was different. That Rogue was. Not just my appearance but the way I thought. The way I moved. My speed. The more I trained, the more apart I was from them. I didn't want my cousins to see me as different. And I was worried that the way I craved violence—the things that went through my head when I planned to take down Patva and his men—made me just like them."

He had brought his gaze back to her eyes, watching carefully, missing nothing. He interrogated prisoners all the time. He read others easily. Everyone had little subtle tells that gave them away, but not Maya. She continued to observe him with the same expression on her face. He couldn't detect judgment. He couldn't detect anything at all.

She had the longest eyelashes and a perfect bow of a mouth. The longer he looked at her face and took in each detail, the more he found himself fixated on it.

"Keep going."

Maya's voice penetrated his dazed distraction and he realized for the first time the sound had a mesmerizing quality to it. Captivating. Even compelling. She could catch a man off guard if he wasn't careful. She had far more weapons at her disposal than guns and knives, maybe much more lethal ones. He was fascinated with her more than ever, and that was dangerous.

"I had already begun hunting Patva's men. I started first by disrupting his arms deals. He supplied arms all over the world. He'd negotiate deals, take large down payments and then ship the guns after the deals were finalized. I would ruin the guns or dump them. I shifted blame to whoever was in charge, someone he'd always trusted and their crew. When I first started, I was a kid, maybe eight or nine. He never considered me a threat. No one ever did."

She nodded her head in approval. "Nice. Essentially, you let Patva punish his men. You didn't have to risk your leopard or yourself at that point by going up against grown men. You just used your brains." A little frown flitted across her face. "But you did have to sabotage the weapons. That was a big risk."

"Patva didn't just punish his men." It was important to Gorya that Maya understand the extent of what was going on in his childhood lair. "He tortured them. He wanted to break them. He destroyed their families in front of them, not that any of them had families to speak of. Most had murdered their wives already at his command. If they had daughters, they sold them or killed them—again, at Patva's command. Their sons were just as bad or worse than they were. They would take delight in raping and torturing. They let their leopards hunt humans. Again, even as a child, I didn't feel the emotions I should have when Patva blamed them and they weren't responsible. I was elated."

Again, he waited for condemnation. Again, she surprised him. She nodded. "Those were some of the men Patva gave you and your cousins to when he decided you needed to be punished."

She was astute. He rubbed his jaw to cover the sudden urge to step into her space and pull her to him. He didn't like touching others—and he didn't kiss women. That was too intimate. There couldn't be intimacy between him and anyone else. Just the thought of it made his skin crawl and his leopard rage—until Maya.

He nodded his head slowly. "I marked every one of them. I never said a word to my cousins. I made certain Rogue would never talk about our plans or our training to the other leopards. I allowed Patva's punishments, the beatings and rapes, anything he threw at me, without ever fighting back. I let him think me a coward. Fyodor and Timur protected me as best they could. I wasn't defiant when they were around because I didn't want to put them in the position of having to defend me. Timur often got in trouble coming to my defense. I had to be careful never to show my speed to him or to Patva's men."

"That must have been a pretty narrow tightrope you walked every day."

There was respect in her voice, but with her, he couldn't tell if it was genuine or not. He wasn't going to consult Rogue. He had to be able to read her on his own if they were going to live together. They had to be real together, and she had to be on the same page with him. He stepped back, away from the door, worried that once he opened it, she would slip back into fight-or-flight mode.

"It was good preparation for my life. I was able to train mentally and physically nearly every second of the day and night."

"But your family doesn't really know who you are."

He turned away from her on the pretense of opening the door. "That did bother me more than I expected, but I got used to it. I didn't want to lose them. There was a time when I was so certain I was like Patva: brutal, vicious, without any ability to feel. I didn't want Patva to die. I wanted him to suffer. I had a plan and was determined to carry it out. I wanted him to suffer every day of his life. To lose everything. To never trust anyone. The idea was too good to give up, no matter what."

He stepped aside so she could see the beautiful suite—and it was extraordinary. He had designed the room as a refuge for both Rogue and him to find peace. Once the door was closed and locked, it was the one place they could fully relax. He had made a pact with his leopard, and Rogue had given his word that he wouldn't escape while Gorya was relaxing. This place was their last stand, and they were making it together.

Maya didn't look around; she continued to stare at Gorya with her bluish-green eyes. They didn't have that flat color in them at all as she inspected every inch of his face.

"You didn't have to tell me the truth. You're good at deceiving everyone around you. If Rogue refused to tell Wraith the truth, she might not be able to discern whether you were lying to me. But you are telling me the truth. Why?"

"How can you tell?"

"I just know."

"You don't want to be in a relationship. It will be extremely difficult for you. If you choose to do this, really try with me, I'm going to give you the real me, not some bullshit person I make up for everyone else. You deserve to know who I am if we're going to do this."

Her brows drew together, and she rubbed at them. "I'm not sure exactly what 'going to do *this*' entails."

Before he could answer, she turned her attention to the room, her eyes widening with shock as she spun in a slow circle, taking everything in. "This is bigger than most people's houses, Gorya. This is your *bedroom*?"

"It's more than a bedroom."

Gorya couldn't take his eyes off her. She was very small, but for him, she was the only thing in the room. Every movement was graceful and fluid. The floor plan was wide open from one end to the other. Rather than approaching down the middle to the far side, where the room curved into the floor-to-ceiling bank of windows, she instinctively moved along the wall, where tall plants with wide lacy leaves created a haven for his leopard.

Maya didn't stir a single leaf as she slipped through the

jungle of trees and shrubs. She didn't need to be in the form of a leopard to move like one. She was absolutely silent. He had acute hearing. At times her image faded in and out, as if even in human form, she blended in with the foliage or the background around her.

What did he know about her and where she came from? He was beginning to be a little suspicious about her origins. How could she be in a territory filled with shifters with not one of them suspecting she was leopard? Not just that, but they hadn't detected her presence. She had to have passed through quite a few shifters to get to the building where Theo Pappas had imprisoned her in the interrogation room.

Maya stared out one of the tall windows, her fingers bunching the thick drapes as she looked at the massive outdoor plants. The branches on the outside trees beckoned him in both forms—man and leopard. Gorya always found the various shades of green cool and inviting. Truthfully, the trees were one more escape route out of many. He hadn't yet told her about them, but he would.

Strangely, when he had created this room for an escape from others, where he could isolate, relax and be his authentic self, where Rogue could, he found he was more at peace than he'd ever been. He had no idea what to do with Maya, but the longer he was in her company, the more he wanted to be around her. Was that the pull of a leopard's heat? Of the mating ritual? He wasn't feeling Rogue's influence at all. This was all about him, which made him uneasy.

"Yes, this was our last refuge. I wanted Rogue to have a nice place to end our days."

"Why did you decide to take on this territory if you dislike these shifters so much? You don't trust them." Maya turned around to face him.

"Have you heard of Drake Donovan? I mentioned him

earlier, but you didn't react. I notice you don't give much away."

She nodded. "I'm a freelance researcher. I mainly work for three companies here in the United States and a few in Europe, although I do take on a few other clients occasionally. Not many, because the big three here keep me busy. Donovan International Security Company is one of my biggest clients. A few years back I had to go for an interview. I made it clear I don't meet in person, so it was going to be a one-time thing, or I wouldn't work for his company. He agreed. That was the only time I saw him."

"Did he know you were leopard?"

"This is Wraith's first heat."

"Donovan, or maybe it's his leopard, is very discerning."

"He had no clue and neither did his leopard. He was interested in how I did my research. I told him if that mattered, I wasn't the best person for him. If it didn't, and he wanted a thorough but fast report, I was the right fit. He gave me someone he needed information on and a deadline to turn it in. Very simple work for a test. I had it to him in no time. Then he gave me the real work and it was much more intriguing. I knew immediately we were the right fit. I like what I do."

He could tell by her voice that she did. It was just a small note, but enthusiasm registered. "Donovan is a friend of my cousins. He came up with a harebrained scheme when many of the local crime lords suddenly began doing business with the *bratva*. They had developed pipelines and were shuffling women and children from various ports to Russia, Europe and points in the US. Donovan wanted those territories shut down. The problem is the same as it has been for a hundred years. If you cut off the head of the snake, it grows back two, even more vicious than the first."

Maya nodded in agreement. "I see the problem."

"Donovan's idea was to take out the head of a territory dealing in human trafficking. Replace it with one of ours. They would have to be believable and run the territory the way the *bratva* would run it. Since that's what we know best, our family is well suited to the work. Donovan knew that, so he came to us and asked if we'd consider it. Fyodor was already working for Arnotto, and when Arnotto died, he took over his territory, albeit reluctantly."

"That's how the *bratva* came to be in San Antonio, mixing with the Italian mob," Maya said.

Gorya nodded. "My cousin Mitya was forced into taking over another territory. He really wasn't happy about it. We agreed to help Donovan because we didn't think there was a chance of finding our leopards' true mates. Fyodor found his. Mitya fell hard. Timur. Even Sevastyan, and that was a miracle."

"But you didn't think you and Rogue had a chance."

He shook his head. "Not really, no. Like I said, I'm not like them. This territory was kept secret for a long time. It was well established and used as the main hub for distribution of arms and drugs. Suddenly, trafficking became the big moneymaker. They already had the routes set up, with buyers everywhere. Trafficking became huge for them. Rivel, the *pakhan*, hired the locals, giving them more money than they could ever make fishing. He spread money to his men, although when I had the books checked from each of his businesses, there was quite a lot of theft taking place. Braum Malcom, the man he relied on, was cheating him left and right."

"That doesn't tell me why you decided to take over this particular territory. You had to know when you did, especially if you were going to shut off the biggest moneymaker, you were going to be painting a huge target on your back. The locals would want you dead. Every shifter taking that money inside the lair would want you dead. Those cheating the books would definitely want you dead.

We aren't even talking about any of them aspiring to be the leader of the lair. And then every single person doing business with Rivel you shut out. Most likely, they'll put out contracts on you."

"I considered that. In fact, Donovan made that very clear. He didn't offer me the job at first. He wanted one of my tougher cousins. Timur would never leave Fyodor. Sevastyan wasn't about to leave Mitya. Neither ever aspired to be *vor*. They're security and they like it that way. I told Donovan I'd do it. Rogue and I needed action. We were getting too close to insanity. I thought the mental and physical action would be good for us." He sighed and rubbed at his beard. "I was wrong."

"How so?"

"I didn't realize that using violence would bring that need out in both Rogue and me. I began to crave it all over again." He didn't hesitate to tell her the truth. "I had tried to suppress that part of me over the years, but it's part of who I am, and it isn't ever going away. Like I told you, either I was born that way, or Patva and his friends made me into a sadist."

Again, her blue-green eyes studied him. "I doubt you're a true sadist, Gorya. If you were, you wouldn't have been able to keep from harming others or humiliating them."

"No? Just kill them."

"Perhaps they needed killing."

Gorya pressed his palm to his chest when his heart reacted with that strange, unfamiliar pressure, as if it were being squeezed in a vise. Was this how Fyodor felt when he had gone to Evangeline's bakery for all those months? Feeling she might be his only chance at salvation? And Sevastyan? Had he known all along that Flambe would find a way to redeem him? The man Gorya knew who was closest to sharing his sins was Gedeon. He believed Meiling was his miracle. He understood Gorya and Rogue because he had been on the verge of ending his existence before his leopard, Slayer, could kill an innocent. That time had been approaching very fast.

"I think it's possible you're my own personal miracle." He murmured the thought aloud, not truly believing in redemption for someone like him, but if there was a way, she might be the path.

Her expression changed to absolute rejection. She drew back. Tears even shimmered in her eyes. She shook her head several times and then burst out laughing. The sound was low, but very close to hysteria.

"Is that what you think? Your own personal miracle? Like saintly Meiling? That's what Gedeon said. Is that what everyone thinks? Expects?"

She was in such distress it felt as if he had tortured her. The emotions came off her in such strong waves that it was all he could do not to go to her and pull her into his arms. In his entire life, Gorya had never had such a reaction. He'd seen women in tears. He'd seen them in life-or-death situations. He'd seen them lose loved ones, but not once had he been affected the way he was by Maya's reaction to his statement. He couldn't even believe it.

Her breathing was ragged, as if her lungs burned for air and she couldn't find it in the spacious room despite all the plants.

"I can't even save myself, Gorya." Maya sounded hoarse, her vocal cords shredded, as if she'd screamed and screamed where no one could hear her. The shadows in her eyes increased. "What you see isn't real. There isn't one single thing real about me."

"Maya—" He broke off. What was there to say? She couldn't hear him. She was so upset she looked broken. Absolutely broken.

"The Amurov family raided our homes and killed my father and brothers. They took my mother, sister and me when I was barely two." A visible shudder went through her body. She wrapped her arms around her middle and rocked herself gently in a self-soothing manner. Her eyes had gone almost completely gray-blue as she turned inward, recalling the terrible nightmare of her childhood.

Gorya remained silent, needing to hear the trauma his family had caused this woman—the one he was certain was destined to be his partner—and her leopard, Rogue's mate. He found it difficult not to go to her. He *needed* to go to her. Still, he held himself rigid, inwardly cursing his uncles, wondering who had ripped her life apart. If any lived, he would hunt them down, destroy their lives and then kill them for her.

"The *pakhan* seemed to hate my mother more than anyone. He wanted something from her, but she wouldn't give it to him, no matter what he did. He gave my sister to his men. They did horrible things to her in front of my mother—and me. I can still hear her screams. Sometimes I wake up hearing her screaming. He tortured my mother. He let his men torture her. One man was so angry with my sister for fighting back when he tried to rape her, and the men laughed at him when she managed to kick him in the balls. She was only four. He beat her badly and began cutting her legs with a knife. He dragged her out of the house, with a bunch of other men egging him on. We never saw her again. The *pakhan* grabbed another little girl and skinned her alive in front of my mother, telling her he was looking for her leopard. I was next if my mother didn't give him what he wanted."

She choked on her silent sobs. "I was two, almost three. I remember him looking at me after she died. She was on the floor in a pool of blood, her eyes glassy, and I knew when he looked at me he meant what he said. My mother hadn't made a sound. Not one single sound." She choked again and jammed her fist into her mouth as if that would stop the tears from falling down her face or the silent screams she refused to allow anyone to hear.

He heard. Gorya heard. Not through Rogue. Just as he

had been aware of Maya when he'd entered the hallway, just as his entire being seemed to be tuned to her, he could hear the screams of anguish, and it tore at him as nothing else could. He despised where he had come from. If he could have torn that part of him out of his body and mind, he would have.

"He told my mother that he would train me himself to please his guests. He would let his men use me. If she didn't give him what he wanted, eventually I would. Right there, with that little girl lying dead on the floor, he attacked me. He was deliberately brutal, and he hurt me. His men laughed. I didn't make a sound. Inside, I screamed, but outside, I didn't make a sound. That only made him angrier."

Gorya could well imagine. In the *pakhan's* mind, he'd been defeated by a child. He would retaliate in ugly, vindictive ways.

"I was raped constantly by his men and by him after that. Then one day he became so angry with my mother that he whipped me with a thin wire on my back until I was so bloody no one could hold on to me. He killed her the way he killed that little girl. I was taken to a house where there were several women and girls. He would sell them to outsiders as brides or allow his men and guests to use them. That was more hell for me."

She bit her lip and lifted her gaze to his. Once again, he could see she was deep in the past. "A couple of days after my fifth birthday, several men came in and they gang raped me. Then the door opened and more came in. They were some of the worst, the *pakhan's* guards. They really liked to hurt me and the other women. I just felt like I couldn't take any more. I was going to fight them and force them to kill me."

Gorya's heart dropped. His breath left his lungs in a long rush, leaving him frozen, staring at her in shock. He shared images in her mind—all too familiar images. That moment she was sharing with him was the exact moment that had changed his life. Evidently, it had changed hers as well. He'd temporarily lost all sanity. Rogue had as well.

Gorya was in his teens and the men he'd arrived with were used to bullying him, beating him and treating him as if he were one of the sex slaves instead of one of the ruling members of the Amurov family. They paid no attention to him as they began to join in on the fun the guards were already having.

Gorya's gaze had been instantly riveted to the child with the platinum-blond hair. She was so tiny, her body smeared with blood. The men surrounding her appeared monstrous. Evil. Gorya forgot all about hiding who and what he was. He didn't think to hide his superior gifts or what the cost to him would be. The men in that room weren't human beings. They were depraved demonic beasts and had to be destroyed.

He used a curved blade, one that he had concealed in his sleeve, slashing throats and arteries as he moved through the enormous room with blurring speed, killing every man in his way. He saw a pattern in his mind and had already marked each target for maximum efficiency with the least amount of effort or risk to him. Most were dead before anyone knew their friends were falling.

Rogue and Gorya shifted back and forth—one moment the leopard ripping throats out, the next the knife slicing through insides of thighs and driving into the backs of skulls as he pulled the men off the child. He found the room eerily silent as he kicked the dead bodies away from her, adrenaline rushing through his veins.

The other women in the room said nothing. Although one just looked at Gorya and shook her head. It was Rogue who warned him. He spun around to find that the little girl had picked up a knife and was about to cut her own wrists.

Gorya caught her arm and took the weapon from her. "You don't let them win. You've been strong this long. Let me tell you how to live. I know you're strong enough. I'll tell you, and Rogue will tell your leopard. He says you have one."

Gorya drove his fist into the wall. He'd done this to her. To Maya. He had been the one to poison her entire life. He'd stopped her from suiciding as a child and in his arrogance had shown her a way to live—for revenge. He'd given her a brief but thorough lesson on how to deceive the outside world. On how to hunt and kill those who wronged you and the ones you loved. How to survive in a nightmare.

He'd been the one to cause those silent screams. He'd been the one to put that look of terror and horror on her face at the thought of anyone—especially him—expecting her to have a relationship. She believed she couldn't save herself or her leopard. He'd done that.

The pressure in his chest intensified. His vision blurred. His gut knotted and churned and bile rose. He spun around, facing away from her, fists knotted against his thighs. There was nothing he could say to her. He had no defense. None. He wasn't about to force her to stay.

Rogue had to have known. Wraith had to have known. The two leopards hadn't cared how difficult it would be for their human companions. They had staked their claim, believing Gorya and Maya would have to live with the consequences. That meant Maya would have to go through the mating heat with Gorya. No way in hell was he doing that to her.

He cursed his leopard. *Clearly, you don't know me as well as you thought you did. I would slay the two of us before I would hurt her like that. You should have known I would.*

5

HE saved us. Wraith had repeated that to her.

At the time, Maya hadn't had a clue what her leopard meant. As far as Maya knew, she'd never seen Gorya in her life. She certainly didn't remember meeting him. Although, now that she really thought about it, she had been aware of him the moment he'd walked into the building.

Her pulse pounded and she automatically slowed it down. Gorya was beyond upset and she sensed that was out of character for him. Because he was so distraught, she immediately calmed. He knew she was that child. Somehow, she'd shared the images of her childhood with him and he'd recognized those memories.

"You saved me. You got us all out of there and onto a ship that was scheduled to leave within the hour. You gave Nadia money for all of us. No one else would have tried to get us to safety. They said there was no way to hide those bodies. There had to be repercussions. The women talked about it, what he would do to you. No one thought you would live through it."

He cleared his throat. "I'm sorry, Maya. I thought I was doing the right thing for you. I had no business imprinting on you the way I did. I didn't realize what I was doing, but that isn't an excuse."

"Imprinting? I don't understand."

Gorya wasn't facing her, so Maya allowed herself the luxury of twisting her fingers together in agitation. She was slowly regaining complete control. She had a strange need to comfort him, an emotion she'd never felt in her life.

"It's when two people are bonded. My leopard bonded with yours. Essentially, he claimed her. You have a mark on your shoulder. You were hurt, and when he bit down in a holding bite, you barely noticed because you were so traumatized. He flooded your body with his hormones to call to your leopard and she answered. He needed to know she would keep you alive for me. He knew she was his mate. I don't know how he knew, but he did. I held you, and I must have known on some level. I didn't want you to die. That was more important than me living. More important than Patva finding out my secrets. I spoke directly into your mind rather than aloud to you, just as Rogue spoke to Wraith. That's imprinting. You did everything I told you to do. I fucked up your life, Maya. That's what I did. I didn't save you."

He sounded tired. Utterly tired. If she knew how, she would have wrapped her arms around his waist and held him, but she didn't know how to even step closer to him without panic setting in.

"Wraith and I wanted to survive, Gorya. You gave that to us. I panicked for a minute when I thought you might have certain expectations from me, but that doesn't mean I don't enjoy various aspects of my life."

Did she? She considered the truth of that statement.

She was the ultimate liar. A perfect deceiver. She lied so much she didn't know if she even told the truth to herself.

"I don't have expectations of anyone, Maya." Gorya's voice had gone back to that low, compelling timbre that he used all the time, indicating he was completely under control again.

Maya felt Wraith's instant alarm as she woke. *He means to suicide. He will destroy himself and Rogue to protect you.*

Maya didn't need her leopard to tell her Gorya's intention. She'd already guessed; she just hadn't been certain of his motivation. Part of her feared that he regarded her as so damaged he thought it useless to even try with her. She herself thought that. She was broken beyond repair. But there were the leopards to consider. And there was Gorya. He wasn't nearly as bad a man as he thought himself.

Mostly, if she was admitting the truth to herself, every cell in her body and mind rejected the idea of losing him. That was how conflicted and confused she was. It wasn't logical and made no sense, but she couldn't bear the idea of any harm coming to him.

Rogue will stop him, she assured Wraith.

Rogue is very strong, but Gorya is stronger. My mate cannot prevent him from doing what he intends. You are the only one who can.

Now suddenly I'm important to you. You didn't consult me when you accepted Rogue's claim on you. It didn't matter to you in the least how I felt. And it didn't matter to Rogue how Gorya felt.

That isn't true. You were too afraid. I accepted his claim, and that gave you time to accept Gorya. If I hadn't, you would have run. You would have been unhappy. This way you have a chance to be happy. Rogue and Gorya have a chance to continue to live.

"I'll have Gedeon escort you away from here as soon as you've rested. He'll make certain you're completely clear of all shifter territory. I never should have allowed Rogue to put you in this position."

Maya sighed. She knew she wasn't capable of a relationship with Gorya. What could she possibly give him? She was damaged goods. How could she fight for him if she wasn't prepared to live with him? She struggled to think of a way out for them both. She knew there wasn't one. Either she accepted the situation and his claim on her or she took the out he was giving her and walked away, leaving him to do whatever he felt he had to do.

Gorya still faced the window, refusing to look at her. He might have regained control, but that only added to the determination in every line of his body. From the back, he looked relaxed, once more the man who appeared to command everyone around him when he chose. She found it interesting that he could appear so easygoing and charming, and yet the moment he entered a room, those around him knew he was in charge and listened to every word he said.

"Maybe before we make permanent decisions, we should just slow everything down."

Maya couldn't think what else to say to him. She needed time. Sliding the pack from her back, she placed it on the bench at the end of the bed.

"It's best if you just go now, Maya. I'll text Gedeon and have him come get you. Grab a bottle of water. Use the bathroom. If you're hungry, Gedeon and Meiling can feed you before you take off. He'll let me know when you're safely away."

She noticed his fingers had curled tighter into fists. The fists were pressed against his thighs. His hands were back to displaying tension.

"Are you saying you've finally come to your senses and realized from my panic attack that I'm too much trouble and you don't want to be with me after all?" She forced a note of self-deprecating humor into her voice.

"Don't be ridiculous, Maya. I'm doing my best to save you. It isn't easy letting you go. I have no idea how to have a relationship. None at all. But I can't imagine living in this world without you. I'm doing my best for you. You have to get out of here now."

There was sincerity in his tone. Her stomach rolled, and heat rushed through her veins unexpectedly. He didn't want her to leave any more than she wanted to go. He was in the same dilemma as she was. Neither one of them knew what they were doing or how to fix what was broken in them.

"I think we should slow things down, Gorya, and not make decisions so fast. We're both a little tired and hungry. I'm not quite ready to say we can't make this work."

"Really? You're prepared to be my partner in every way? Sleep in my bed?"

There was a harsh rasp to his normally charming voice. A note of desire. Maya winced, grateful he wasn't looking at her. She swallowed the first six things she considered saying, choosing her reply carefully.

"I have no idea if I'm even able to be a partner in every way. Honestly, I very much doubt it. The idea of it terrifies me, but I'm willing to consider ways to do this. We haven't explored any possibilities. If you really want to give up this easily, go ahead and text Gedeon to come for me. I won't believe for a moment that it's because you're trying to save me. You have a leopard. No one wants to deprive their leopard of its mate if they find the right one."

She poured a wealth of challenge into her voice, daring him to deny the truth of her statement. She had no idea what she was doing. What if she couldn't stay with him? What if she had another panic attack in front of him? She didn't want to appear weak to him.

Maya spun around and stalked toward the primary bathroom. She needed to find some breathing room. She didn't spend a lot of time with other people, and she needed space—especially from Gorya. She never expected to be the one fighting for something she didn't even believe possible.

Fingers settled around her wrist. Gently. Firmly. A shackle, yet barely felt. She swung around, prepared to fight, her heart wild, adrenaline rushing through her system. She recognized his scent. His touch. Yet she was still wary. No one put hands on her, yet she hadn't pulled a knife and stuck it into his chest. That was something. That was progress.

Her eyes met his, her heart skipped a beat and her stomach did that funny flip. She didn't know how to interpret his look. It was soft. No one had ever looked at her like that before, and she wasn't certain how to respond. There was a melting sensation she didn't want to admit to. Instinctively, she tried to pull away, but it was a halfhearted attempt and they both knew it.

"Maya." His thumb stroked over the inside of her wrist, sending a thousand fiery embers sparkling through her veins. "You don't want this. Once we commit, you know there isn't going to be a way to turn back."

She knew he was right. She knew, but she couldn't let him go. She detested that he could feel her trembling. It made her look weak when she wasn't a weak woman.

Maya lifted her chin at him. "At least we need to give ourselves time to sit down together and discuss the possibilities."

He *had* to stop brushing her bare skin with the pad of his thumb. An electrical current flowed from Gorya to her and back again in a continuous loop. She felt sparks over her skin, in her bloodstream and even in her mind. She told herself to pull away from him but found she couldn't.

"You don't find my touch entirely repulsive?"

She wanted to lie, but he was a man who could read women. He could see he was affecting her breathing. She was fairly certain he would affect any woman's breathing.

"Not entirely, no." She interjected a teasing note into her voice in an effort to show him she wasn't as affected by him as he might think.

The color of his eyes deepened to a frosty, silvery blue. It was quite a beautiful color and she didn't want to get lost there, so she looked at his knuckles instead.

"You might want to leave the walls alone. It's nice in here. Holes in the wall won't improve the look." She used her strength to twist her wrist, subtly reminding him to release her. "I'm going to sit in one of those really comfortable-looking chairs by the windows and put my feet up. We can continue the conversation there if I don't fall asleep."

"Where were you staying? I can have someone get the rest of your things."

"I wasn't staying anywhere around here."

The chair seemed to embrace her as she sat down and leaned into the curved back. The seat was positioned perfectly to look out the bank of windows toward the trees and brightly colored flowers just outside. She liked that the thick brush gave the primary bedroom even more privacy. She hadn't realized how tired she was until she sank into the comfort of the chair.

"Since we've decided to establish that we're going to do our best to work things out," Gorya said, moving to the other side of the glass coffee table to sink into the opposite chair, "the first rule we should agree on is to tell the truth to each other. No one else ever has to know us, but we need to be honest with each other about everything, no matter how bad it gets."

Maya's long lashes swept down, a ploy she often used to give herself time to think. She had been certain Gorya had been honest with her all along. She'd been deceptive, trying to figure out a way to make a run for it, afraid there was no way to resolve the situation. She still didn't have a clue how they could—but she couldn't bear the thought of Gorya destroying himself or his leopard.

"I can try, Gorya." She lifted her lashes and met his penetrating gaze. Her stomach dropped. He saw too much.

"That isn't going to cut it, Maya, and you know it. We both need to commit, all the way. It has to be the two of us. Not our leopards, not anyone else. The two of us. We're both damaged. Broken. Any way you want to put it. We're dangerous to others and to each other. The only way we have a chance is if we both say we're going to do this thing. We have iron wills. We make a vow to dedicate our lives and loyalties to each other. Tell the truth no matter how bad it gets. Depend on each other. Have each other's backs. It won't be easy. It will be a learning process, but we're both highly intelligent, skilled, and if we make up our minds, I know we can succeed."

"I wish I could be as decisive as you are." That much was the truth.

He gave her a little self-deprecating smile. "All the years of having to make decisions quickly, I suppose."

She bit down on her lower lip, regarding him soberly. For this one moment, she would have to be brutally honest with them both. "I want to do this, Gorya. I believe we might make good partners in some respects, but I have no doubt that you would expect a physical relationship, and I'm not capable of that. I'm just not." She was a little ashamed to admit that to him, especially in light of what he'd revealed of his past to her.

His gaze grew even more focused. More intense. "Maya. You don't have any idea of what we're capable of together. You're on step one hundred. We need to start on step one."

"But that's a huge step, and it will matter. I've tried to figure out ways around it. Sleeping in a different room or even a different building. You having other women when you need to." The thought of it made her feel murderous, but she forced herself to put the idea out there.

"You know that isn't going to work. Aside from the fact

that I don't want another woman, Rogue wouldn't tolerate
it. Let's concentrate on getting to know each other before
we worry about the minor things."

She was getting close to another panic attack. How
could he just dismiss what was the biggest obstacle in their
relationship as if it were nothing?

"Gorya, you can't just discount this. What would be the
point of us working out ninety-nine steps and then getting
to this and finding out we can't overcome something so
important?"

How could he not see that was the real deal-breaker?
Even if they were the best at working side by side, it
wouldn't matter. They would eventually despise each
other. She would never be able to take him sleeping with
other women. She really thought she could sleep in the
guest room, and when he had other women—discreetly of
course—she would simply look the other way. What
would it matter? She would welcome him turning his attention elsewhere, right? The moment the thought entered
her mind, reality hit her.

Maya was already bonded with Gorya. That bond was
strong and growing stronger with every moment in his
company. There was no way she could tolerate him with
other women. And in a lair, everyone would know that he
was disrespecting her. She pressed her fingers to her temples to counter the pounding.

Gorya slipped smoothly from his chair. No effort. No
noise. One moment he was across from her with the glass
coffee table between them. The next he glided across the
short distance and was looming over her. Maya immediately went into fight mode. Every cell in her body reacted
to his closeness and the way he was looking at her with
such intensity.

"What are you doing?" She held up her hand, palm out,
a flimsy defense when adrenaline rushed through her

veins, and it took everything she had not to draw up both legs and do a double kick to drive him away from her.

Not even blinking as he stared straight into her eyes, he slowly knelt. Her heart nearly exploded when his hands dropped to her knees and he pulled her legs apart, allowing him to move between her thighs. Heat pounded through her veins and pulsed in her sex. Heat that had nothing to do with Wraith and everything to do with her as a woman. She had no idea what to do with that—or with him.

"What are you doing, Gorya? This isn't a good idea."

"It's the only idea. Where's your knife?"

"My knife?" She echoed his words faintly. She felt faint. She wished she could faint. Fainting might just save them both. She wasn't making a good showing here.

"Yeah, baby, your knife. I know you have several on you. Pull one out and hold it in your hand."

"That would be dangerous. When I get nervous—and you're making me a little crazy—I tend to strike out like a cobra and run for it." He wanted honesty; she was giving it to him. She wasn't about to apologize for learning how to survive.

"Your knife, Maya. You'll feel in control when you have that blade ready." His gaze never left hers.

She shook her head but pulled one of the blades from the sheath on her belt. The moment her fingers wrapped around the familiar handle she should have felt stable, but instead she feared for Gorya. She wanted to shove the knife back into the scabbard. She lowered the blade to her thigh, just inches from his hand.

"Tell me what you're going to do."

"We're conducting an experiment to see if you can stand me being this close to you."

His voice was that same low, matter-of-fact, mesmerizing tone that brushed over her skin like velvet. This close to him, she could see that his eyelashes were long and dark, like the soft bristles of his mustache and trimmed beard. His jaw was strong. From a distance he might look young—because technically he was—but this close she could see lines carved into his face that aged him.

The knots in her stomach unraveled a little, but the heat didn't lessen in the least. "I had no idea you were so dramatic. I think we both know I don't mind you being close to me, Gorya." It was all she could do to keep her hands from trembling—and not because she feared he might hurt her.

The look in his eyes intensified. His fingers stroked along her inner thighs and then, when she gasped and involuntarily jerked her legs, his palms settled around the tops of her thighs.

"The question is, how close? We will be sleeping in the same bed." This time the fingers of his hand brushed along the top of her right hand around her fist and stroked her tense muscles where she clutched her knife. "I know you have the harebrained idea you'll be taking the guest bedroom, but that isn't going to work for either of us. Mainly me. I want you right next to me." His voice dropped another octave. "Close."

Her stomach dropped right out of her body. Her lungs quit working. Every instinct told her to raise the knife, but her brain had stopped functioning. She could only stare at him in shock. He didn't move back; he just continued to stroke her thigh as if he didn't notice she was frozen—or that blue flames were flickering like magic inside her. She wasn't certain she liked the sensations he was creating in her, but a part of her was glad she couldn't move so the feelings had no chance to end before she could decide.

"I think, going forward, Maya, you'll see being close to me isn't so bad. I like that you don't want others close to you. I've never liked them near me or touching me. It feels different with you. Does my touch feel different?"

His fingers moved to her face. Gentle. Barely there. A stroke along her cheek. Tucking hair behind her ear. Tracing her ear before bringing the pad of his thumb to her lower lip. She swore her heart skipped a beat.

"You have to remember to breathe."

"I've forgotten how," she managed to blurt out.

His lips curved into a slow smile that took time to find its way to his eyes. When the light finally hit the frosty gray, it turned his eyes that bluish color that made her melt inside. "We're just getting started, my little hellcat. This is step one in a long list of steps."

She shook her head, not taking her gaze from his smile. She would have tolerated a lot to see him smile. "I think step one is as far as we should go. I might pass out from lack of oxygen." She tried to interject humor into her voice, but she didn't think she'd pulled it off.

Was this what it felt like to want a man? She hadn't thought it was possible for her to feel desire. She tried to touch Wraith. Was she rising again? Feeling her heat? No, Wraith was sleeping soundly. Maya couldn't blame her leopard for the edgy, unfamiliar, turbulent sensations Gorya was producing in her with just a few brushes of his fingers on her skin, his voice and the dark passion in his eyes.

"I'm quite capable of giving you mouth-to-mouth."

This time his smile was so seductive it bordered on sin. Her heart ceased beating and then began to pound. He shouldn't be so appealing to her, not when she knew what he was. Not when he couldn't deceive or hide from her. She knew that beneath that easygoing facade was a deadly killer, and that only excited her more. He matched her in every way. She could never live with anyone she couldn't show herself to.

What was she thinking? Living with him? She looked at his hands. He didn't have them covered with gloves. He wasn't trying to hide the fact that he was Amurov, shifter or *bratva* from her. The tattoo that started just below his knuckles took all four fingers to create the Amur leopard. Most, when they saw it, thought it represented the *bratva*, specifically the Amurovs' territories. They were feared throughout the world. Few realized that the tattoo was an identity for the family, and they were the ones to be feared.

"I'm quite capable of biting."

His white teeth flashed at her. Pressure coiled hot and tight in her stomach. Was she actually flirting with him? Encouraging him? She couldn't want this to go any further. His fingers were still moving over her face. Just little strokes on her skin. Tracing her cheekbones. Stopping for a moment while she caught her breath. Brushing over her lips just for a tiny second so that she felt sparks. Anticipation.

Need swamped her. Of what? Him. Gorya. It was a slow seduction. He hadn't really done anything other than kneel in front of her looking like temptation itself. Whispering outrageous things that made her want to laugh—or tease him back. She had no idea what to do with him or what he was leading them into, but she found herself relaxing more and more. Very slowly the feeling of being safe with him crept over her despite the unfamiliar sexual tension he produced.

"I believe I'd like your bites," he murmured.

"You're outrageous."

He shifted closer. Gorya was so close already, she wasn't certain how he did it, but now she felt the press of his body against hers. Heat came off him in waves, penetrating her skin until she felt him like a brand on her bones.

"Are you ready for step two?"

She shook her head and raised both hands, forgetting about the knife as she tried to put her palms on his shoulders to push him back. At the last minute, she wrapped her fist tightly around the hilt. "No step two. Step one was scary enough. I think we need a break. A cool shower or something."

His eyebrow shot up. "You want to shower with me? That's step ninety. You're getting *way* ahead of yourself. I'm not ready for that yet."

She laughed; she couldn't help it. "Gorya, do your cousins know you're a menace?"

"They think I'm cute and cuddly and need looking after."

The laughter faded as she studied Gorya's face, feature by feature. Maya thought maybe someone did need to look after him. She didn't think anyone ever had, because he'd never let anyone see him. Just as she'd never let anyone see her. It made one too vulnerable. His life had been just as horrific and unhappy as hers had been.

Maybe he was her only chance at a real life. She had always thought she would have to end her life eventually when it all got to be too much. There was the possibility she would be killed if she was a little too slow on the hunt. She'd never envisioned herself with anyone, but then she hadn't known someone like Gorya existed.

"This is our one chance, Maya." There was an ache in his voice. "Take the risk with me. Let's try it. If we fail, so be it, but at least we can say we gave it a shot."

He echoed what she'd been thinking. Her gaze drifted over him again. To her, he had a beauty unequaled by any other man she'd come across. There was strength in him others might not see. A will of absolute steel. He would be implacable in his resolve. If he made up his mind that they would make it, he would pour everything he was into ensuring they did.

Maya knew herself very well. She might deceive others and even herself occasionally, but when it came to what she was like inside, she knew if she gave her word to Gorya, she would honor it. She was just like him. She had that same will, and she wouldn't give up unless he became abusive—and then she'd kill him, if she could.

Without thinking, she shoved the knife back into the sheath at her waist, a gesture of capitulation when she still wasn't certain she could manage to do everything needed.

"Gorya." The answering ache was in her voice. "You know I want to say yes. I am different with you. I don't seem to mind your touch so much. I am attracted, but that doesn't necessarily mean I'll be able to have sex with you. The thought of a man touching me fills me with revulsion." She had to be truthful.

"The thought of a man touching you fills me with more than revulsion." His large hands framed her face, piercing eyes looking straight into hers with the intense, focused stare of a leopard, only there was no leopard—there was only Gorya. "Just the thought fills me with murderous rage."

Her lashes swept down as her heart jumped. At the same time, her sex clenched. She didn't want to be that person—the one who was a little thrilled that he might get violent if some man came on to her physically. Still, no one had ever wanted her with that fierce possessiveness or the protective streak she sensed in Gorya. She'd never had that, and in just the short time she'd spent with him, he'd set up a craving for it in her.

"Sex is far down the line when it comes to our steps, Maya. We have time before Wraith is fully in her heat. I have control. You'll learn that I can keep you safe even during the times she rises. Those times will be short, and I can handle them for us until you're ready."

Trust. He was asking a lot, but at the same time, he was giving her his trust. His life hadn't been any better than hers. She stroked a finger over the tattoo, tracing the Amur leopard.

"I deliberately took off my gloves," he said. "I can't

wear them all the time, and if we do this, you will have to get used to seeing the tattoo. I know it must be a trigger for you and very offensive. Later, I can have it lasered off."

She continued to brush her finger over his, tracing the powerful muscles of the leopard tattoo on his hand. "None of the men who attacked me when I was a child had this tattoo. Patva kept his gloves on. I saw the tattoo when you held me after you had killed everyone. You'd taken your gloves off to shift. You lifted me onto your lap, and I remember staring down at your hands and seeing the leopard. For the first time, with your arms around me, I felt safe, even when I hurt everywhere and there was blood from one end of the room to the other."

He cleared his throat. "I didn't realize that."

Maya nodded. "It's true. I shut the door on those memories to stay sane, but I always remembered the tattoo. For some reason, that had become a symbol of safety to me. I had considered getting a similar tattoo until I looked it up on the internet and realized it was considered by many to represent the *bratva*. I certainly didn't want to put anything on my body that would mark me as theirs. I already had enough reminders."

"Many people think the tattoo is *bratva*," Gorya said, "but it's a family tattoo, and no one else has it but those of us born of Amurov blood." He tipped up her face, his gaze moving over hers as if to assure himself she was telling him the truth. "It's nice to hear that for once, our family ink symbolizes something good, especially for you."

She could see, beyond his casual words and tone, that it really did mean something to him that she found his tattoo comforting.

"There isn't a guarantee I can do this, Gorya," she reminded him. She wanted honesty between them. Maybe in learning to be honest with him, she'd find out who she was meant to be. Someone better.

"Did I ask for a guarantee, Maya? You persist in thinking you're the only damaged one in this relationship. I might implode, and you'll have to be another Gedeon."

She laughed. She couldn't help it. "I think Gedeon would have to worry about me because I'll have your back. He's going to be creeping around, scared I'll be stalking him. I'll have to be on alert for his wife somewhere on top of a building with me in her sights. Your cousins would show up. It would be a hot mess, so best to just stay sane, Gorya."

The frost in his eyes softened to a pale blue. "Before my knees give out and Rogue tells me I've ruined him for fighting, we have to get to step two."

"Step two?" Maya should have panicked, but she was too intrigued now. She was past being totally panicked around him. She wanted the relationship and was willing to work for it. Once she recognized she wasn't the only one struggling, it was easier for her.

Gorya was back to using his hand like a seductive weapon, his palm stealing around to the nape of her neck, where his fingers settled in her thick hair. It was impossible not to be aware of the way he gathered the mass into his fist, and she slowly tilted her head up toward his.

"Kissing. I'm going to kiss you."

Thunder roared in her ears, nearly drowning out his soft murmur. She was sure she hadn't heard him correctly. "Kiss me?" she echoed faintly. She should have expected it.

"Yeah, baby, I'm going to kiss you. If I don't, you're going to start thinking about it and you're going to panic again."

He was right, but she might panic now. "I don't know how to kiss."

"That's fine. We'll learn together. We'll just practice until we get it right."

His head had come closer to hers. Much closer. She could see the fine lines etched into his skin. Those lines

represented the trauma he'd suffered as a child. Just seeing
those creases settled her. She identified with him. She
wasn't threatened by him. She was needed by him.

His lips curved as if he knew what she was thinking.
His warm breath reached the left corner of her mouth. Her
entire body went taut in anticipation. Every nerve ending
came alive. Little goose bumps rose on her skin. His lips
brushed hers lightly—a delicate touch, but she felt it like
a brand. Her stomach fluttered. A thousand butterflies
lifted in flight.

Kissing was so intimate. She should close her eyes, but
she was mesmerized by the way his eyes continued to
change color, darkening with desire to a deeper blue, the
silver ring around the blue thicker. This time she could
read the stark passion mixed with growing affection for
her. Growing need. Not just the need of a lover. There was
that, but it was so much more. Like her, he wanted a much
deeper relationship. He wanted something real with her.

Her hands came up of their own volition. She wasn't
going to be passive and put this all on him. He didn't kiss
women. Like her, he found kissing others much too familiar. If they were in this together, she was participating
fully. She was terrified that she wouldn't be able to be
sexually intimate with him. She was the one afraid her
past experiences would prohibit her from having a normal
relationship. He was being gentle. Taking care to introduce her to their world of shared intimacy and vulnerabil-
ity slowly and carefully.

His lips merely feathered along hers. Teased and
coaxed. Always gentle. Little flashes of flickering flames
seemed to touch her and were gone, leaving her wanting
more. He didn't try to rush into kissing her. He took his
time, savoring the taste of her. The feel of her. Outlining
the curves of her lips with his tongue. Memorizing her.
She caught the images in his mind. All the while, he never

closed his eyes, staring into hers as if he could see right into her soul.

Maya had never been so aware of another human being. He was everywhere. Surrounding her with his strength. His heart. Letting her into his mind. Pouring into hers slowly. Carefully. It wasn't an invasion or a takeover. It was a joining. A promise. He deliberately shared himself with her. Opened himself up to her. Made himself vulnerable.

Maya did the same, staring into his eyes. Giving herself to him the same way. A vow to him that he would be her only. She would give him everything she was. There was no expectation of perfection. Both accepted the other for the broken, damaged person they were. They were going into the relationship with their eyes wide open.

He slanted his head, and his mouth settled on hers. Her lashes fluttered down as he rubbed his lips over hers and then traced the seam with his tongue. The floor tilted and rocked. She gripped his shoulders, needing an anchor so she wouldn't go spinning off into space.

6

GORYA couldn't believe he was kissing a woman. *Kissing*. The world seemed to be going up in flames all around him. The floor beneath his knees tilted and rolled. It had been her eyes, staring into his, grounding him. Her long lashes had come down and he was thrown immediately into a turbulent vortex, a combination of terror and exhilaration.

He hadn't known true terror since he was a child watching his mother and father being murdered. He'd faced death so many times during his childhood and teen years, he'd become immune to fear. When one didn't care if they lived or died, fear became ineffectual, completely powerless. He was always in control. He'd learned to accept torture and never break character. Never give away his superior skills. Everything had changed for him in one single decision. One woman.

Her scent. Her touch. And now this. Her taste. He hadn't

expected to want to keep her. To want to be with her. It took every ounce of discipline he had not to tremble when he knelt before her, between her thighs. He hadn't realized he had anything gentle or tender in him. He'd thought there was only violence left in him—the brutal side that had become dominant. It had grown to the point he hadn't wanted to be around his cousins because it was getting harder for him to want to hide his differences.

Almost from the moment he'd entered the building where Theo Pappas had trapped Maya, he'd felt different. He just hadn't known why. He'd only ever felt that insane protective instinct once—when he'd been in his teens and he'd seen those grown men raping a child. He'd never thought more clearly, and yet he hadn't been thinking logically when he'd killed every single one of Patva's enforcers. The reaction had been instinctive. Necessary. When he'd breathed in Maya's scent, that same protective drive had begun to form in him and grew in strength the closer he got to her.

He hadn't believed anything in the world could terrify him. He'd lived through torture and loss and seen depravity at its worst. He was ready to let go. He wanted to leave before he completely succumbed to the brutality that lived inside him. He didn't want his leopard to betray their code any more than he wanted to do it. Just when he had formed their plan to exit the world, Maya and Wraith had entered their world. Rogue reacted instantly, claiming Wraith.

Gorya told himself he had no choice; he had to claim the woman and give Rogue his chance at happiness. He felt the joy in his leopard. His cat deserved happiness after the truly miserable life he'd led. But the truth was, Gorya wanted Maya for himself—he just didn't know what to do with her. He had no idea if he could be decent to her—and she deserved decent.

He had talked her into trying with him, and now he was pushing for more. What was more? An actual relationship where they stripped each other bare. He would have to be real for her. Show her who he was. He didn't know if he wanted her to see the truth of what he was. Hell. He didn't know if *he* wanted to see what he was. He only knew that if they didn't stand before each other in their true skin, a relationship would never work between them.

He was tired of deceiving his cousins—the only family he had. He doubted they would accept him for who he was. He couldn't accept himself. Could Maya? If she couldn't, he would strip himself bare, lay himself wide open, only to be rejected by the one person he had ever wanted for himself. That would shatter him. He knew it would. He'd never allowed himself to be vulnerable with another human being, but in such a short time Maya had crawled into his mind and somehow managed to fill all those empty places he hadn't even realized he had. Losing her would make life unbearable.

He had no idea how to kiss her. He was a man. Not young anymore. She would expect him to lead. To make the experience good for her. He wanted it to be good. To be amazing. Perfect. He didn't want to make one mistake with her, but he knew nothing; kissing her had changed everything.

He wasn't certain if it had made things better or worse. He didn't know what the hell he was doing, but then, neither did she. That didn't seem to matter; the world around them tumbled away. He might not be any good at intimacy or kissing, but it didn't seem to matter when he was with Maya. It was heaven and hell. He never wanted to stop. Fortunately, she wasn't trying to hide her reaction from him. She didn't want to stop either.

Gorya felt her tremble. Melt into him. Despite the clothes separating them, it felt as if they shared the same skin. He had learned intimacy wasn't necessarily sex. It started in one's mind, and she had firmly entrenched herself in his. She was wrapped in him now, and he was never going to get her out. He found he didn't want to—and that was what was so damn chilling.

He lifted his head and looked down at her. She was beautiful beyond his imagining. Her lashes fluttered. Lifted. He found himself looking into blue. Her cheeks had flushed a shade of rose. Her lips were swollen, thoroughly kissed. A slow smile brought light to her eyes.

"I think step two is a major success."

"I think step two scares the hell out of me." He was honest.

Her smile widened. "It scares me too."

"I don't think for the same reason."

Her eyebrow went up. Delicate. Blond. He couldn't help himself. He traced the line of it above her eye.

"I was a monster long before I met you, Maya. I had this strange idea that my mate was supposed to tame the beast. Now I'm concerned that if another man gets near you, I'll tear him apart."

The sound of her laughter was soft and musical, the notes sliding through him, sending an emotion he was unfamiliar with. Happiness? Could this be happiness? Was she showing him what that was? Fun? Sharing laughter? She didn't know it, but she was a miracle after all.

He stood up slowly and backed away from her, needing a little respite. He hadn't been this close to anyone for as long as he could remember.

"You laugh, woman, but it could happen. I'm not all that nice."

"Neither am I. I think we might be suited after all." She leaned down and removed her shoes. "I'm going to order clothes. I just have one change of clothes, and out here in this humidity, that's not going to last very long."

"That's a good idea." He was grateful the subject had turned to the practical for a few minutes. They needed a break. Touching her had been a success. So had kissing.

She hadn't stabbed him with a knife; he counted that a real success.

"Who's the best man here in the lair with a computer?"

That put him on alert. She had asked casually and she wasn't looking at him. Instead, she removed her socks and stuffed them into her shoes. He remained silent. Waiting. She looked around for her backpack and then finally met his gaze. He continued to wait.

Maya sighed. "I only had a few minutes to see what Theo was up to. There was no way he had come up with his scheme to steal money from you all by himself. He just isn't that bright. He told me he found that money was being taken from several sources, and before he could tell you, he'd been approached and asked if he wanted to go in with them. That's not exactly what he told me, but something close. He was lying. He wanted the money for gambling and drugs."

Gorya nodded and remained silent. She hadn't gotten to the part she was withholding from him. The important part.

She drummed her fingers on her thigh. "I knew he wasn't the mastermind, so when I was stuck in the torture room, I decided I would try to find out who was actually doing the stealing. They'd been at it for some time, long before Theo came on the scene. He doesn't belong here. He isn't Russian. He came along about a year ago and was hired. That stealing has been systematically taking place for at least two years and by three different men. Clearly, they're in on it together. But I don't think the three of them are the masterminds. I think someone else is orchestrating the thefts."

"You got all that in the short time you investigated?"

She nodded, her fingers drumming faster. "Yes. I traced the money on three accounts, but the names didn't come back to anyone here. They were false identities. I took the money from the accounts, so they are going to be royally pissed." She flashed him a grin. "That's my specialty. Give me enough time and I can find those three for you."

"I've had a couple of computer experts working on it for three weeks and they haven't found out anything."

She shrugged. "I hunt this way."

She sounded so casual, as if the criminals she chased couldn't possibly turn the tables on her. He knew better. Gedeon and Meiling had explained how easy it was for anyone with good skills to trace someone if they become aware they are being stalked through a computer. He had nearly zero skills in hunting with a computer. Maya sounded very confident.

"Babe, I've been told someone with excellent skills can turn the tables on you unexpectedly."

Her smile was a little smug. "So true. I'm not easy to catch, Gorya. In fact, it's never happened, but I don't take chances. I started hunting for the men who originally raped me and killed my family. Then I branched out to find the ones who killed the women I traveled with when we came here."

Gorya sat down and leaned toward her. "The women you traveled with were killed? When you were a little girl? Just getting off the freighter?" The monster in him roared. Why hadn't he expected that the women would run into trouble? The freighter had been captained by an Amurov crew. He cursed under his breath. "Were there men waiting to take you to houses to sell you?"

Why hadn't it occurred to him that the women would be passed on to a land crew? He'd been so focused on getting back to the house where the dead bodies of Patva's crew were so he could create a believable scene of raiders coming in and taking the women, saving his own hide. Damn him to hell. In his arrogance he had wanted to best Patva once again. He had wanted to save his own skin.

He leapt up and paced across the room, stopping near the wall, adrenaline rushing through him like wildfire.

"Don't." The command was soft. "I won't tell you another thing about my life if you keep taking responsibility for something you had no control over. You weren't there. There was nothing you could have done. You saved us. Got us out of that place. What happened after that wasn't your fault or your failing. No one blamed you, least of all me."

Gorya realized she meant it. Maya had a will of steel. She wasn't going to bend. If he wanted to hear about her life, he had to use discipline to get through this, because he needed to know everything that had happened to her in the years since he'd seen her. He was used to giving orders. Commanding her to tell him what he wanted to know wasn't going to work.

Forcing control, he made his way to the small bar and dragged a cold bottle of water from the refrigerator. "Would you like one?"

She nodded. "Yes, please."

He didn't like the soothing quality to her voice. He didn't need soothing. He needed to go to the workout room and beat the shit out of someone. He needed to run for miles in the swamp as both a man and a leopard. He didn't need her to soothe him when he'd let all those women down.

"Gorya, you do remember you were a teenager when you killed all those men, right? I don't even know how many there were, but there were quite a few of them. You weren't prepared and you only had about an hour to get us out of there. Then you had to go back and face the leader of the *bratva*. The women were sure he would kill you."

"I remember putting you on a freighter and forgetting all about you. I thought you were safe because I wanted to believe you were. Had I given it any thought at all, I would have known better. Please tell me what happened to you."

She studied him for a few minutes, and he kept his features a mask. He didn't like that he was deceiving her, but he had the feeling she was aware he was doing so. When she remained silent, he sighed and shoved his hand through his hair.

"I can't help being upset, Maya. I promised you and myself I would be real with you. Would you want me to be deceptive? I'm under control. I'm not going to hit the wall or go torture a prisoner."

She lifted an eyebrow. "You would do that?"

"I'd consider it."

"Well, don't. This is all in the past. If we're going to talk about it, keep it in the past. It has to stay there, that's how I cope. If you make it about now, I can't deal very well. That's me being honest with you. We both have crazy shit to deal with in our past, Gorya. I keep that door closed pretty tight. Maybe you don't. I'm not the 'talk to strangers and get it all out' kind of girl. You're the only person who's ever going to hear about my life, if you really want to know, and only because you're mine. I think you're kind of nuts to want to know details, but so be it. I might want to ask you questions about your life. That makes us both a little insane, but we knew that going into this. So behave yourself."

He liked quite a bit of what she'd said. Mostly that he was hers and he was the only one who would ever get her past. No one ever told him what to do, not since he'd gotten free of Patva. His cousins had given him security orders, but that didn't count. He'd gotten up in the middle of the night and destroyed threats to them without their knowledge. He didn't mind the pretense of following orders, especially if it saved their lives.

"Are you going to spend the rest of your life telling me what to do?"

She broke out laughing. The musical notes filled the space between them, lighting it with merriment. How could he feel like smiling when just a few minutes earlier he wanted to smash something—or someone?

"Most likely. Someone needs to. Everyone seems a little afraid of you."

"I think you're a little afraid of me."

"Not for the same reasons the rest of the world is." She flashed him another smile that got him right in the pit of his stomach.

You see? She is your mate. She belongs to us. She is needed.

Now Rogue was suddenly going to add his two cents. *I don't think you need to sound so self-righteous. You put her in a terrible position, and I haven't forgiven you.*

Without her, we would both be lost. They would be lost. Look at her. She is everything you could possibly want. I feel the difference in you.

Gorya swore at his leopard. *Don't act like you didn't claim her leopard for yourself, you smug bastard. You didn't think about how afraid Maya was going to be when she had to face me. She was terrified.*

If Rogue dared to point out that Gorya echoed that same terror, he might cut the cat right out of his body and burn the two of them—man and leopard—in a hideous ceremony. Gorya shared the images with the animal. Rogue didn't seem in the least disturbed, but he didn't pursue the conversation. If anything, he sent an image of the curl of his tongue, almost as if he had a sense of humor about the entire subject.

Keep it up. I might never let you out to see your mate.

Rogue didn't deign to answer what he knew was an empty threat. He gave a little sniff and subsided, pleased with himself.

"My leopard needs to be shot. Not killed, just shot. I don't suppose you would do the honors for me."

She laughed again, just like he knew she would. The sound made him smile. He wanted to record the sound on his phone and play it whenever he was alone. That probably made him some kind of first-class fool, but he didn't care. He didn't dare tell her she was a fuckin' miracle, because that was definitely a trigger for her, but she was. And whether she liked to think it or not, she might just save him. He had to figure out what he could give her of equal value in return.

"I thought you hired Gedeon for that particular job."

That teasing note in her voice sparked little stirrings of arousal in his groin. He savored the natural stimulation. The feeling wasn't dark and terrible or overwhelming; instead it felt intimate and emotional.

"Turns out the man has a strict code he refuses to violate for any reason."

"And Meiling?"

He heaved an exaggerated sigh. "She has scruples. Lots of them. That woman has a conscience and insists on giving Gedeon one. It's ridiculous. She could have been his greatest asset. She's a crack shot with that rifle of hers, and I'm telling you, if anyone dares to mess with her man, she'd take them out in a heartbeat, but he isn't going to have much fun when it comes to putting a bullet in my leopard's ass."

"I can't imagine why not. Especially since shooting Rogue in the butt means winging you as well. That's a double bonus right there." Maya's eyes sparkled.

Gorya thought he might be able to sit there forever with her, teasing back and forth. It was an entirely new experience for him and one he found he enjoyed. Watching her was half the fun. He'd never had fun. He hadn't really known what it was. He'd built the house in order to relax and to allow Rogue the same peace once they were inside, away from others, but that wasn't the same.

"Are you saying you wouldn't have a problem shooting me in the ass?"

"Not at all. You or that despicable leopard of yours,"

she assured him. "Knife, gun, doesn't matter. Either one of you gets out of line and needs a little reminder, I'm your girl. I have no scruples at all. I have all kinds of flaws."

"I'm not sure that particular character trait is a flaw."

Her musical laughter spilled over again, filling his heart with joy. Joy was another emotion he hadn't known. For just a brief moment, light shone into that place inside him where it was always cold and dark, illuminating something ugly, sending it scurrying away from the brightness.

"That's a good thing, Gorya, if you're really planning on living with me. I feel very comfortable when I'm carrying weapons and extremely naked without them."

Deliberately, he ran his gaze over her, leering a bit and wiggling his eyebrows, trying to look like a lech. "Naked?"

The throwing knife shaved a thread from his sleeve as the blade sank into the curved back of the chair. He laughed. The sound startled him. He couldn't remember actually laughing before. Even Rogue sat up and took notice.

"We're going to need new walls and furniture if the two of us keep this up," he pointed out. She'd been fast—so fast he hadn't seen her draw the knife. The throw had been a blur. She was damn accurate.

"I like these chairs too," she said. "I'll try to restrain myself, but don't do the eyebrow thing. It's just nasty."

But she was laughing. Really laughing. He liked that he'd made her really laugh. Her eyes had gone a deeper blue and seemed to sparkle like gems. That beautiful bow of a mouth gleamed, lips parted, her white teeth showing as she threw her head back. She even pressed a hand to her stomach as if all the laughter hurt her. He suspected genuine laughter was as rare for her as it was for him. It felt good to give her that. A gift for them both.

"I'm going to practice in the mirror every morning," he threatened. "I'm impressed with your throwing skills. I should be equally as good at provoking you."

"I have no doubt you won't need to practice. I think you're going to be so obnoxious naturally that you won't have to. And that leopard of yours is going to be worse."

Gorya nodded in agreement. "He isn't cute and cuddly." *Do you hear that? She's got your number, you old rogue. She isn't going to be deceived the way her leopard has been. She doesn't think you're adorable.*

Wraith knows I'm a capable fighter. She appreciates that in me.

She knows you prance around with your ridiculous swagger, bragging about what a fighter you are.

It isn't bragging if it's true, Rogue pointed out.

"Are you arguing with your cat again?" Maya teased. "Because it sounds like it to me."

Gorya went still. Rogue did as well. "You can hear us?"

Maya's smile vanished instantly. She gave a little shake of her head. In that instant she was transformed. Her blond hair flew and then settled around her chin, giving her a pixie appearance. She looked innocent, her eyes wide and once more that blue-gray that gave away nothing.

"Of course not. It was just a way of speaking."

Gorya couldn't detect deceit in her voice, but he knew she was lying. The disappointment was overwhelming. "Maya." He kept his tone low. Made certain there was no judgment, no reprimand. This was a learning process. They were both going to make mistakes. "We're in this together. We promised to tell the truth to each other."

Maya didn't look away from him, but faint color stole up her cheeks. "It isn't easy when I'm used to protecting myself."

"I know, baby. I'm right there with you in that same boat. I'm fairly certain you're going to be reminding me often." She'd taken his prompting well. Leopards were secretive creatures. Shifters were even more so.

"It isn't as if I hear the talk between a shifter and his leopard. I see images the leopard is projecting to the shifter. I connect mainly to the leopard. That's one of the ways I track the man I'm hunting. Once I lock onto his leopard, he can't escape me. His leopard never gives me away. I can go right into his house and stand over him."

"I can enter a shifter's home without detection by his leopard or him. Fortunately, we have the same gifts."

"Technically, once I'm there, it isn't that the leopard ignores me; it's because he's unaware of me," Maya explained. "I blend. Like an apparition. A wraith." She flashed him a small smile.

"I'm capable of the same thing," Gorya said. He found that strange. What were the odds that both of them would be able to go into the house of a shifter undetected? Had they exchanged a chemical of some kind when he had rescued her all those years ago that allowed her to do the kinds of things he had done? Or was it the other way around? There was no doubt in his mind that she had gifts few leopards had. Gedeon and Meiling had them. He did. He'd never met any others. Some came close, but there were no others with those telling traits that he knew of.

"These men you hunt, these are the ones that you were turned over to when you first arrived from Russia?" he asked, grateful to return to the subject. He'd been trying to find a way to naturally turn the conversation back ever since he'd blown it, but hadn't known how.

"Some of them."

"Tell me what happened, Maya. Please. I won't go berserker on you."

She looked at him warily. He could tell Wraith was close by the rings of green surrounding the blue of her eyes, but she only nodded and continued her story. "When the freighter got to the harbor, someone told us we were in Houston and we had to get off very fast before anyone saw us. We were taken to a large container and had to stay there for a long time. I had to use the bathroom. It was awful and smelled like onions. I dislike onions to this day."

"You were locked in a storage container?" He forced himself to repeat her words in a calm, neutral tone. "Who did they send to meet you?"

"There was a man by the name of Blum. He said in order to work we needed papers, and they had to be paid for and were expensive. He would get them for everyone, and a place to stay and work, but it wouldn't come cheap. I didn't like him. He was really mean. He snorted like a pig all the time and his eyes were close together and beady. The women hid the money you gave us, but his men found it and took it."

Gorya sighed. That was the oldest scam in the book. They kept the women working like slaves, owing them money, withholding their rightful earnings on the pretense that they never paid their debt.

"We lived in a small house together and eventually could go to the market and shop. It wasn't too bad at first until some of the women wanted more of the money they earned. Blum beat them. His men beat them. The women would hide me from them when they came to have sex with them. We were there about two years when Blum brought two other men to the house."

Something in her voice warned him he wasn't going to like what she was about to tell him.

"The men said they wanted women to work at a very exclusive party for them. Blum laughed. It was a nasty laugh. I knew it was not a good thing. They acted as if the women would make extra money and maybe even be able to leave, but I knew they would never come back. I tried to tell the women, but they wouldn't listen to me. They wanted out from under Blum."

Gorya studied her face. "You were about seven."

She nodded. "I looked much younger and was able to merge with the shadows. Wraith and I practiced her coming out every chance we got. We didn't allow anyone to see her, even the other women. I saw too many of them trading favors with men to trust anyone. But I remembered names. I made certain I listened to conversations and gathered as much information as possible. If anyone touched me, I never forgot his name and I promised myself I would track him down someday. If they hurt any of my friends, I did the same. If they made the women disappear—and I always knew the truth, even when they lied and said the women were allowed to leave—I put them into my memory banks."

Maya's tone hadn't changed and neither had her expression, but deep inside, he felt her resolve. Her determination was every bit as strong as his. Her killer instincts had been developed at a young age. She didn't forget those who had shaped her into a vengeful, relentless hunter.

"I learned so much very fast in those early days. I studied my enemies, following them through the streets. At first, with the cars driving so fast and the maze of freeways and alleys and neighborhoods, it was daunting, but I have an excellent memory, and after the first couple of times, I could follow them to their bosses' offices and businesses and then to their homes. It wasn't that difficult to familiarize myself with their residences and the surrounding landscape as well as their guards and their schedules."

She'd had the natural instincts of a hunter even at such a young age. She'd taken her time, developing her skills, not striking too fast and giving herself away.

"There was one woman, Polina, who always looked after me."

There was an ache in Maya's heart that tore at Gorya. Her features were composed and her tone serene, but he felt her sorrow. Polina meant a great deal to Maya.

"She made sure I had clothes and food. She protected me as best she could from the men coming in and from Blum." A small note of humor crept into her voice. "She insisted on tutoring me with books she'd get from stores.

Sometimes I'd steal books so she wouldn't spend what little money Blum would give her as her share of the wages she'd earned. She never asked me how I got them, but she suspected."

"She sounds wonderful." He'd had his cousins growing up. At least she'd had Polina.

"She was. The others were very nice too, but she went out of her way to treat me like family. She knew I could slip out under the guards' noses and kept urging me to leave, but I didn't want to leave her. And it seemed like I was acquiring knowledge at a faster rate."

She fell silent again, and with her silence came the heavy pressure of sorrow weighing down her heart. Again, sorrow didn't show on her face.

"Keep going, Maya," he encouraged gently. "What happened to Polina?"

Maya's hand dropped to her thigh, and her fingers slid up and down over her muscle in a small self-soothing motion. "The men came looking for women to take to their party. By this time, everyone knew that whoever went wasn't coming back, and it wasn't because they were set free. Polina would pretend to be sick. She would make herself vomit, and Blum's men wouldn't choose her to go with the two men who came for them. One was Carl Bortsov, the other Davyd Chugunov; both had insisted they wanted Polina on more than one occasion. I think everyone knew she wasn't really ill."

Gorya followed the graceful movement of her hand as it came up to stroke her throat. He could almost feel the lump there.

"When she wouldn't go with them, Blum's men dragged me out of the shadows, tore my clothes off, beat me with a wire hanger and raped me in front of her. They told her they would keep it up until she went with Bortsov and Chugunov of her own free will. Bortsov and Chugunov thought it was great sport and joined in."

Gorya's gut tightened into hard knots. Fists formed. He locked down the demon in him, roaring to be released. This was about Maya and how extraordinary she was. How she built herself up from a child ripped apart by monsters and made herself into pure steel.

"Polina said she would go with them. I never cried. I made certain I didn't, but she said she would go anyway. Then she told me to stick to the path. I knew what she meant. She wanted me to get out of there. Blum and his men had their eyes on me. I had turned thirteen. I might look very young, but age didn't matter to them. We knew we'd never see each other again."

She raised her eyes to meet his. For one moment, her eyes glittered with tears. "I knew what it had been like for you when your leopard burst free and you killed all those men. I struggled to keep from doing the same thing. I wanted to. It took everything in me not to let go. I didn't care if I died, as long as I could kill them and keep them from taking Polina. She was the one who prevented me from shifting. She kept shaking her head and murmuring that she loved me, and it mattered to her that I lived—that I had to live."

She was breaking his heart. Two tears dripped down her face, but she appeared unaware of it, while that was all he could see. His heart ached—a new sensation for him that was rapidly becoming too familiar. He felt he'd known her a lifetime, and yet he'd barely spent more than a few hours with her. Why did it seem as if she belonged with him?

"I left right after they took her. I followed them to the party house and watched. I shouldn't have. I knew better. There wasn't anything I could do to save her from the things that went on there, but I wanted to never forget. I wanted to be there with her. She wouldn't have wanted me there, but I needed to be for myself. And I saw the man who orchestrated the parties."

Again, her eyes met his. "Some nights, when I fall asleep, I see those men. Their faces are burned into my brain. There were so many. Young, old. So depraved. They conducted meetings, and the women were expected to serve them meals and drinks and anything else they desired. They were treated as if they were toys, not humans. As the evening wore on, the men became worse than any animal."

Gorya knew what she was talking about. He'd seen it. Alcohol and drugs flowed freely. Deliberately. Deals were struck. Men became richer. The women were nothing to them. They were going to be dead at the end of the night as the depravity grew. The woman who had been the closest thing to a mother for her had been subjected to that kind of evil, and his Maya had witnessed it all. No wonder she had turned to a life of vengeance.

He stood up and held out his hand to her, needing the connection even more than she did. "Let's go outside. I need to breathe fresh air."

7

THE sun sank into the swamp, bathing the trees in shades of purple and dark blue with splashes of deep lavender. The lighter colors poured through cypress trees with the fading light, while the darker shades of purple crept like silent raiders through the veils of hanging moss dripping from branches that hung over the water's edge. The sinking sun turned the duckweed carpet covering the water into a strange silvery blue.

Gorya inhaled the night. He always found he could breathe easier outside. The air was heavy with many scents, the humidity trapping the fragrances of flowers, shrubs and trees as well as rotting vegetation. The swamp was a world of its own, and it was one place he felt free to be himself.

He glanced down at Maya. She looked around her at the water as the wind gently played with little ripples on the surface.

She tipped her head up toward his. "This is a beautiful piece of land."

"I agree. I tell myself I come here to stay sharp and run every night or let Rogue run to train, but in reality, I feel free when I'm out here."

Groves of tupelo and cypress graced the water's edge along the inlets and banks. Several great blue herons walked on sticklike legs, dipping their long beaks in the water, fishing, before spreading their wings and rising toward the large, bulky nests high in the trees. Bats were out in abundance, wheeling in formation, dipping and darting at the multitude of insects hovering over the water.

Several raccoon families made their way through the heavy brush and fallen trees to the water's edge. A fox barked at them from where he stood on an old log, warning them away from his den. They paid him no mind but continued toward the bank. The flutter of wings overhead told Gorya an owl had joined them, watching the animals congregate along the banks. It was very still, in hunting mode.

The swamp came alive at night. The sounds were louder than ever. The steady drone of insects. Rustling mice scurrying in the vegetation to gather up the last of the seeds to take to their nests before they retired. Lizards using little stop-and-start motions as they foraged for food. His hair acted like a guidance system, allowing him to read air currents, supplying him with information about his surroundings in the way his leopard's whiskers did.

This night was theirs, and he was going to make the most of it. Enjoy every moment he could with her. He looked down at her again. *His.* His other half. Made for him. He knew he was made for her. That truth came to him. He might have been so damaged that it was impossible to fulfill the destiny he'd been born to, but looking at her, he knew it was the truth.

The light from the small sliver of moon shining through

drifting clouds caught her just right, spotlighting her. He saw her with vivid clarity. His breath caught. His lungs burned. His heart seemed to stutter. The various colors in the thick blond hair falling around her face—so light it could have been called a true platinum. Woven in were strands of gold and silver. Her eyes were large for her oval face, adding to the innocent look. The color was blue-gray, with flecks of green. Her lashes were thick and pale, like her hair and eyebrows. Where most leopards were dense and curvy, she was very slight, adding to her waiflike appearance. Despite that deceptive build, he knew she was all woman.

Color crept into her cheeks, turning her pale skin a deep rose. "Why are you looking at me like that?"

He wasn't going to lie to her. It was possible all he had to give her was truth. He cupped the side of her face with his palm and slid his thumb over her lips. "I have no idea how I realized so quickly that I was born to be your man, the one to care for you, but I know I was before my brothers and uncles fucked me up. Now I honestly don't know if I'm capable of doing what I was put on this planet to do."

He felt sorrow for her—for himself. He stepped back, all too aware that the bond they'd formed when she was a child had strengthened and she could feel his every emotion. He was used to commanding every situation. He didn't like feeling less than a man.

A slow smile curved her lips. "Silly. You're more a man than any other I've ever met, because you admit your emotions to me. I feel as though I was born to be with you, and yet I have no idea if I can give you the things you need either. I want to. More than anything, Gorya, I want to be that woman for you. Your partner in every way, but like you, I'm not the person I was born to be."

There was pain in her voice. Pain in her eyes. He *felt* that emotion coming off her in waves. "Maybe we were both meant to be exactly who we are now so we can be together," he murmured. He smoothed back her hair. "I can't imagine being with anyone else."

"Let's hope you're right, Gorya. If you're not, at least we have this time together."

He liked that it mattered to her that they were together because it meant everything to him. "You ready for a run, Maya?"

"I'm looking forward to it," she answered immediately, and stretched her arms over her head. "You have the advantage because you know the area."

"We aren't racing. This is a very hazardous section of the swamp. There are some places where the surface appears stable but it's thin and you could fall through."

She lifted an eyebrow. "I've got good instincts. And if I get into trouble, I'm sure you'll rescue me." She batted her eyelashes.

"Follow me and don't get cocky." He gave her his best scary face, but it didn't seem to faze her.

She gave a little sniff of disdain. Her answering grin said she was teasing him.

Gorya turned and began to jog along a narrow path that led into the interior of the swamp. Long veils of moss hung in silvery drapes from branches, fluttering in the breeze. Ropes of woody vines spilled from the highest canopies to swing gently. Various varieties of flowers wound around tree trunks, climbing toward the sky and infusing the air with fragrances, adding to the smells of the swamp.

He ran along a thin track of land, leapt over a fallen log, avoided a termite mound that was nearly as tall as Maya and maneuvered through tangled brush that held sharp thorns. There wasn't a sound behind him. He didn't look over his shoulder to see if she was there. He felt her and knew she instinctively stepped in his footprints.

She kept up even when he quickened his pace. If a

fallen log was higher than her head and he leapt over it, she cleared it without breaking stride. She had amazing springing capability. He was pleased to discover she had nerves of steel. Swerving close to the embankment where a bull alligator guarded his territory didn't deter her in the least. She didn't hesitate or try to swerve from the course. She always found foliage to cover her presence from above and around her. She had the advantage in that she was small enough to disappear into the vegetation.

He indicated they were going up into the trees as they approached the river, and she immediately leapt into the higher branches of a cypress tree and ran along the curving limb that stretched toward the next one. He chose a larger cypress growing beside the one she was in, racing her, using longer strides; the arboreal highway was one he knew intimately. The tree branches extended across a narrow spot in the river, and he ran lightly. Even with his weight, he didn't disturb the leaves.

Maya was in the tree across from his, but he would never have known. She could have been a ghost, the wraith she called her leopard. There was no sound, no movement; he knew she was there, yet he couldn't spot her. He had no doubt he wouldn't have been able to see her leopard either. She was just behind him as he leapt from one tree to the next, clearing the large gap between branches to the opposite shore.

She laughed softly, the sound of joy filling the space between them. Gorya found his entire mind and body reacting to the sound. He hadn't known happiness until Maya.

Do you see now? Rogue's smug images mixed with the new emotions. *Wraith and I made the decision for the two of you because you wouldn't have chosen the right path.*

Gorya had to admit the leopard was right. Maya would never have accepted him, and he wouldn't have pushed for a relationship, not even for Rogue. He considered himself too far gone. *The verdict isn't in on whether or not this will work.*

The leopard curled his lip. *Shifters must overthink everything. I do not understand why. You belong together. Wraith is my mate. Maya is yours. There is no doubt. It is meant to be, therefore it is. Why make it complicated with all the—* The leopard broke off, searching for an image that conveyed what he was thinking. *Drama.*

You think my concerns don't have merit? If Gorya could have strangled the cat, he would have.

Rogue gave the idea consideration. *Maya is very afraid. You believe things about yourself that are not all true. Both can be overcome.*

Not during a leopard's heat. Gorya knew he was right about that. A leopard's heat was intense, out of control. Hormones raged and, in most cases, ruled. Maya would never be able to accept him during such a time. She'd be terrified of him.

But you will have a plan in place. Rogue had absolute faith in him. *Whatever you decide to do, I will follow the plan and help you carry it out.*

If Gorya could be shocked by anything Rogue said or did, this was the time. It had never occurred to him that the animal would have such faith in him that even during the most important time for all four, shifters and animals, he would put his trust in Gorya and believe the shifter would guide them through a very dangerous path.

It would be a very difficult one for us both. His mind was already racing with possibilities.

We are used to difficult situations. Rogue sounded placid, almost bored.

Gorya turned back toward the house. He didn't want Maya too exhausted. She needed to eat something before she went to bed. He had to plan out carefully what to do when her leopard showed herself each time. The sexual needs between the shifters would grow more intense, much more brutal, until the leopard finally emerged. He would have to find a way for them to cope with those out-of-control hormones.

Once they crossed the river again and were back on land, he motioned for Maya to take the lead, needing to assure himself that she could find her way back to the house through the maze of swamp. He should have known she would have no problem at all. She ran a faster pace on the way back than he had set and never once hit a spot where the ground was too thin to support his weight. She knew when they were coming up on wildlife and instinctively avoided disturbing any creatures that would give their position away.

"I'm impressed," he praised as he held the door open for her.

He had to admit she looked good, her body gleaming with a light sheen of sweat. She shot him a quick grin.

"That was fun, but I'm hitting the shower. Then soaking in the bathtub. Give me an hour before dinner. We are going to eat, right?"

He nodded. "We'll eat." If they didn't eat, all he was going to be thinking about was her in the shower or bathtub, and that wasn't safe.

He watched her disappear into the primary bath and he gathered up a few clean clothes and headed for the largest guest bathroom, texting Gedeon as he went down the hall. It had been impossible not to smell the barbecue when they'd come up on the side courtyard. If Gedeon was at the grill, chances were, he'd put on enough for the two of them.

After being assured there was plenty of food for Maya and himself, Gorya checked on Theo Pappas to see if he had known more than he admitted. Matvei confirmed the man was aware there was someone else behind the three men he knew were stealing money, but he didn't know who any of them were. Matvei was certain he had gotten everything out of the man they could possibly get.

Gorya trusted Matvei to know when the prisoner was done. He gave the order to terminate the man. If he was of no more use, there was no sense in keeping him alive. He had already proven himself to be a drug addict, a thief and a man willing to sell a female leopard who had come to do him a favor. He needed to be put out of his misery.

After showering, he went back to the bedroom just as Maya came out of the primary bathroom, leaving a trail smelling oddly enough of fresh snow and a flower Gorya identified as Tashkent, a marigold he remembered from when he'd traveled to Uzbekistan. The fragrance had managed to sweeten the hot summer night air. He had never forgotten that scent. No other marigold had smelled the same no matter where he went. He was a leopard shifter with an acute sense of smell, and even though she seemed to be able to mask her smell from leopards when she wanted, she didn't bother hiding it from him, and he found himself elated. In the short time they'd been together, they were finding a balance. A rhythm. And they were doing so quickly.

"Would you mind if I used that little room for an office? The one you showed me that is just sitting there with nothing in it?"

He barely heard her. She was wearing nothing but the shirt he'd given her earlier. He knew she didn't really have much in the way of clothing. They'd discussed it once already. She'd told him she was going to order clothes, but knowing she wore nothing under that shirt was instantly distracting.

"The room?" he echoed, trying to remember the location of the room. There were a lot of rooms in the house. Which room was she talking about?

"I need an office for my work. It's best if no one knows about it. If all your men here think others are doing your computer research for you, it's best if everyone continues to believe that."

She pulled her laptop from the backpack and set it on the end table beside the bed. He noticed the way her fingers moved over the lid in a small stroke of what could have been affection. The laptop had a waterproof case, and the backpack was waterproof.

"In case you're wondering, I did ask Gedeon to bring us dinner."

"I'm hungry," she admitted. "I was considering heading to the kitchen and looking for whatever you had in there to make a salad."

"Fortunately, Gedeon is grilling tonight. He's got everything covered for us."

"Handy man to have around."

"I think so." Gorya indicated her laptop. "How did you learn your computer skills? Computers aren't my strong suit. I can use one if I have to, but I prefer to have someone else who really knows what they're doing do all the heavy work."

Her lashes fluttered—those long lashes that made her look so incredibly young. He was beginning to know the subtle telling signs she gave when she was uncomfortable answering his questions. He found it interesting that she didn't want to tell him how she'd learned to use a computer.

Maya traced the logo on the lid of the laptop. "I happened to stumble upon three men attacking a woman. Well, teenager. She was seventeen. Initially, I think they were stealing her car. She had a very cool Porsche 911 Carrera. I didn't know anything about cars at the time, but even I could see it was awesome and worth stealing. I didn't, by the way, steal cars, because I didn't know how to drive back then. I would have let them take the car had they stopped there, but once they saw the driver, they decided they wanted more."

Gorya's gut knotted. He kept his expressionless mask. There was a good reason she didn't want to tell him about her introduction to the computer. He noticed immediately she didn't give the woman's name. She was still in touch with her. The woman knew her. She *knew Maya's name.* That was unacceptable. He had no doubt in his mind that Maya was hunted.

He was already suspicious that she was like his mother, like Gédeon and Meiling. If Maya had rare gifts—and he already knew she did—and the remaining members of the Amurov family left alive in Russia found out she lived, they would hunt her. So would any of those who had banded together to wipe out families with superior gifts. Patva seemed to have realized her mother had rare gifts and wanted a child from her. Somehow her mother had managed to prevent conception. He had turned his eyes toward the child. Others might do the same. This woman would always be a threat to Maya as long as she was alive. He didn't dare let on to Maya what he was thinking.

"Keep going," he encouraged, careful his voice sounded like he was interested but not in the least threatening. "You must have stopped them."

She leapt up to pace across the room to the fireplace, her feet not making even a whisper of sound. "She fought them, and the more she fought, the angrier they got. I despise that, as if women don't have a right to say no. Or to protect our bodies. In any case, after what was done to Polina, that's a trigger for me—multiple men raping women and angry that they dare fight back. By that time, Wraith and I had practiced, with her fully or partially emerging at will. We could fight together smoothly, and we did. We killed all three of them. Two of them had guns and one had a knife. I believe they would have killed her. As it was, they did stab her, and one shot me before I could finish them off."

Again, Gorya noticed she didn't put a name to the

woman. He filed away that the girl was seventeen at the time. She had to come from a very wealthy family in Houston in order to be driving a Porsche. The car she named was a top-of-the-line sports car. Maya might not know much about cars, but he did. Only a very wealthy family would give their daughter an expensive and, in his opinion, dangerous car.

"Shot you?" he echoed.

She nodded. "I didn't want any of my blood at the scene. I knew she would have to call the cops, and I ripped my shirt and bound my arm. It wasn't too bad, but it hurt like hell. I needed to make certain her wound wasn't so bad that she'd bleed out before the ambulance got there. I tried not to let her see my face, but that was impossible. The stab wound was bad. I kept talking to her to keep her alert. I told her no one could know about me, that I lived on the streets. She hadn't seen Wraith, so she had no idea my leopard had helped. In the end, she agreed not to identify me. She said she would say she was unconscious most of the time, which she was. She had a bump on her head. She gave me her address and told me there were security cameras everywhere on her estate, but if I could get past them or call her ahead of time so she could distract the guards, she would see to my wound."

"You trusted her?"

She looked up at him through the crescent of thick pale lashes. "I don't trust anyone, Gorya. At least, I'm struggling to trust you."

He heard the honesty in her voice. He detested the fact that this woman meant something to her. Maya knew the woman was a threat to her safety and was willing to take the chance in order to keep her in her life. He wasn't. That was the bottom line. He wasn't. In just a short time, Maya had become the world to him. Without her, there wasn't a way for Rogue or him to exist. There was no joy. No hope. She was the miracle whether or not she believed in miracles or that she was capable of someday saving him. She at least gave him these moments—something he'd never had. No one could threaten her and live.

He gave her his gentlest smile when he didn't know gentle. "I'm doing the same. Clearly you developed a relationship with her. Are you going to continue to refer to her as 'she' and 'her'?" Deliberately, it was a challenge. Was she going to make up her mind to trust him?

"She's the only person I consider family."

There was no mistaking the underlying warning in her voice.

He had promised honesty. What was honest? "You know my family. I told you the cousins that matter to me." He had. Timur, he thought of more as a sibling than a cousin. Fyodor. Mitya and Sevastyan. They were his family, and he was intensely protective of them.

He couldn't kill her family. He couldn't. And the woman was innocent. He didn't murder innocents. What the hell was he going to do?

She nodded. "That's true, but it isn't as if I couldn't have found that information easily. They're notorious crime lords. Well, not Timur or Sevastyan, but Fyodor and Mitya." She didn't take her gaze from his.

He didn't look away or blink. He was used to deception. It wasn't that he wanted to deceive her. He didn't want to harm the one woman she considered family. He'd made it a policy never to kill an innocent. It wouldn't be an easy decision.

Rogue stirred. *To keep them safe we would have no choice.*

There is always a choice. Gorya was uneasy. Killing had become too easy for both leopard and man. It was a way of life, a solution when anyone got in the way. Granted, everyone they ran across was depraved and out to kill them or someone they loved, or they were someone they had hunted down from their past, but it had become far too easy for them to dispose of human beings. *This woman is innocent. She is someone Maya cares for.*

She is a threat. She knows Maya, and if this woman's identity is discovered, she will be tortured until she reveals Maya's real name and location. She cannot live. We can be merciful when we dispose of her.

Gorya liked that even less. *We do not murder innocent women, especially if Maya considers them family.* He'd just been considering the exact same thing, and yet when Rogue sent him the images, he knew it was wrong. Very, very wrong. Maya would never forgive him any more than he would forgive her if she killed Timur.

"You're arguing with your leopard again." Maya made it a statement.

Gorya sighed. "Yes. He can be adamant with his opinion at times. Over the years we have had many discussions. I've had no one else to talk things out with, so it has become a bad habit to let him voice his concerns at the worst possible times, like when we're in the middle of an important talk."

Her eyes narrowed, focused sharply on his, all too intelligent. He cursed his cat. *She's going to question me.*

That won't matter. Tell her what she wants to hear.

Gorya cursed the cat again. That was his inclination. Lying. Deceiving. That was who he was. What he did.

"Are you going to tell me what you were arguing about, or do you want me to take a stab at guessing?"

Her tone was mild. She was giving him every opportunity to come clean. To tell the truth. He had no doubt he could convince her with a lie. He was adept at it, but once he told a lie to her, he would tell another and then another. Their relationship would be built on lies. There would be no real foundation, and those lies would always be between them.

"Rogue believes it's safest for me to kill your friend. He's afraid eventually the *bratva* will find her and torture her. That in doing so, they'll be able to locate you. His concern is for your safety."

Her expression didn't change. She didn't blink. She looked more leopard than she ever had, yet he knew Wraith wasn't close.

"Naturally my first thought was to protect you, but I've never killed an innocent that I know of. That would be murder and make me as low as Patva. Aside from that, you consider this woman family. If that's the case, there should be a way to protect her. I may not have figured out how, but you must have. You're intelligent and you've lived in the situation a long time. I didn't have a chance to voice that to Rogue, but I will. I have faith in you. I don't in this woman, but I do in you. If I'm being strictly honest, if it became evident to me that she was a threat to you and I couldn't protect her, I would kill her."

He wasn't going to lie to her no matter how tempted he was. He was ruthless. He didn't pull his gaze from hers. He wanted her to know he meant it. She had to see the real person she was dealing with. Know who he was. He wanted to show her. She had to know if she could live with him. He had to know.

It took what seemed a lifetime, but eventually her eyes brightened to silvery blue. A hint of laughter crept in. "It seems we think alike. I've thought of quite a few ways to take out your bodyguard Gedeon before he can kill you when you order him to shoot you. I have to always know where his wife is. That makes it difficult because she's very good at concealing herself."

"You plan on killing Gedeon?"

She shrugged. "Only if you insist on your idiotic suicidal plan. It isn't that I want to. He seems like he's willing to protect you, but he's all business, and I have no doubt that he'd shoot you in a heartbeat if you ordered it."

"That's the reason I hired him."

"There you go. It's my job to have your back. I have a

few concerns for your safety just like you have for mine. If Wraith wasn't so lazy right now, we'd be having arguments as well."

"That's the reason you've been so reluctant to see anything good in Meiling. You don't want to chance liking her because you're afraid you might have to kill her."

Maya nodded. "I can't be friends with either of them."

"I should have known. I thought because Wraith was in heat you were reacting to a female being around." He felt the smile before it flashed briefly on his face. "You wanted me to think that. All this time when I've been showing you the house and you were going to the windows, you weren't looking at the view so much as studying where Meiling would position herself to cover Gedeon in any situation, weren't you?"

Gorya couldn't keep the admiration out of his voice. She really was good. Excellent, in fact. As for an asset, he couldn't ask for a better one. No one would ever have an idea that his mate was as deadly as she was. She looked sweet and innocent, just about as nonlethal as one could get. More, she really could disappear into the shadows. And she could soothe a leopard into ignoring her presence.

"Naturally."

"I don't want you to think that my leopard did anything I didn't do. My first thought, really, was that I would have to hunt down your friend. He would have come to the same conclusion I did."

You still are not certain, Rogue interjected.

Shut the hell up.

"It's nice that Rogue is looking out for me, but Lexie doesn't know my real name. She doesn't even know where I'm originally from."

He didn't mind playing devil's advocate even as he filed the woman's name away to make certain he could find her. "Yet she is presumably good on a computer if you learned your skills from her."

"Not just good, Gorya, she's elite. The best. Incredible. And so are her friends. She taught me everything I know. It was just luck that I had a knack for computers and caught on fast."

"How are you safe, then? She has to be able to find you. That means if she's discovered, you're at risk."

She rolled her eyes at him. "I didn't give her my real name. The minute I hit the streets I became someone else. I knew they'd look for me. I told you I listened to every conversation. I heard about all the freighters coming in. Also, there were refugees, families coming in from other countries, paying to get papers to be able to work in the States. It was a pretty brisk business to enslave them to work for years to pay off the papers. I had heard of a family, parents and a daughter about my age, who came from Ukraine. The father refused to hand over their money, and when they threatened to put his wife and daughter into the whorehouse to pay off his debts, he shot his wife, his daughter and himself. His daughter ran, she was bleeding profusely, but she jumped into the water and was washed away. They didn't recover her body. Some said she lived, that they saw her on the streets. Her name was Teona Kyva. I became Teona Kyva."

She'd been no more than twelve or thirteen when she'd left the house after Polina had been taken, and yet she'd had a cover in place. Gorya admired her even more.

"I suppose Lexie helped you get identification because you had none."

"She did. I stuck to the story of what happened to Teona. It's easier to tell the truth as much as possible. If she investigated it, she would find there was a man from Ukraine who shot his wife and himself. He had also shot his daughter, but she disappeared. Her body has never been found. I was very up-front that no one could know I was alive or else those who brought us here would demand I pay my parents' debts and I would never be free."

"Very clever. You knew she would investigate."

Maya nodded. "She had to know if I lied. She was letting me into her parents' home. Into her sacred circle. She didn't tell her parents. Her friends were anonymous for the most part, especially at first. They participated remotely, some from other parts of the country. She let me stay in her house. It was an enormous risk she took. I couldn't believe my luck. She taught me so much. Everything from my computer skills to driving cars. She treated me like a sister even though I wasn't at all very trusting in the beginning."

Gorya could tell she was a little ashamed that Lexie didn't know her real name. She really cared about the woman.

"Not giving her your real name was as much for her protection as it was for yours," he reminded her gently.

"I know, but it still feels wrong. She's all I've got."

"You have me."

And me. Rogue spoke directly to Maya. *And Wraith.*

Maya looked startled. "I do, don't I?"

"You do." Gorya was decisive. "We'll find a way to make this work."

"You always sound so sure that we can do it, but I know you're not that certain, Gorya."

"I wasn't," he admitted. "But Rogue said something to me that made sense." He flashed a fleeting smile at her. "He does that on rare occasions—make sense. I don't like admitting it where he can overhear me, because he's a smug bastard, but in this case, I have to give him credit."

Those long pale lashes fluttered, drawing his attention. He really loved her lashes. Her lips curved, giving him the idea that kissing her before they went to bed might be a good habit to start.

"What could your leopard have said to you that made sense?"

"He said we belonged together, and he trusted me to

work out any problems because I always did. Shifters always overthink things."

She burst out laughing. "That simple?"

"He knows it isn't quite that simple, but he said whatever it took, he would help."

Her eyes went silvery blue. "I think I'm going to like your leopard."

He hoped so. If he had his way, they'd be together a lifetime.

8

THE food was delicious. Gorya knew it would be. Gedeon was amazing at grilling anything, from vegetables to steak. Gorya and Maya sat in the comfortable lounge chairs under the stars, eating with Gedeon, Meiling, Matvei, Rodion and Kyanite. The fire pit wasn't necessary as the night was cool but not really cold. Still, it added ambience.

Maya looked calm and relaxed, not in the least uneasy surrounded by men she knew were not only leopard but *bratva* and had been raised in the Amurov lairs. Gorya knew differently. She hadn't shut him out of her mind, and he felt her discomfort.

I can make an excuse to take our dinner inside. He made the offer sincerely. He didn't like that she was in the least uncomfortable. There was no need for it. *You've been through enough today.*

Her eyes met his, the moon catching her just right, so

that her blue eyes shone like gleaming jewels. His gut reacted with a strange roll.

I've never had anyone looking out for me before. It feels odd.

Odd good or bad? he prompted.

Her smile washed through his mind. Intimate. Only for him. It was such a new concept for both to have someone else to think about. To worry about. To care for. He liked that he was continuously uppermost in her mind. He couldn't get her out of his.

Good, I think. I could get used to it. She glanced at the circle of people in the chairs around the fire pit. *These men are the ones looking after you. I need to get used to them. Get to know them. Eventually, I'll feel more at ease with them. It's important for me to know for myself that they would never betray you.*

He was in her mind, so he knew she was hoping what she said was true, but she didn't think it would come to pass. She didn't believe she'd ever be truly comfortable around men, especially a large group of them, humans or shifters.

It's us. They would never betray us. If you're certain you don't want to go inside.

I am. And the food is good. You were right about Gedeon and his ability on the barbecue.

Gorya inclined his head and forked another bite of steak and mushrooms into his mouth. Gedeon was a master on the grill.

She's pregnant. Maya narrowed her gaze at Gorya. *Meiling, she's pregnant. There's no way you didn't know.*

Gorya kept his features an expressionless mask but laughed when he spoke intimately to her. *Of course I knew. I thought it best to allow you to find out for yourself.*

"Gorya," Rodion announced. "The Amurov helicopter landed a few minutes ago. You're about to have company."

Gorya sighed. "I should have known. How many?"

"Timur and Ashe," Matvei said. "They brought Kiriil Sokolov and Arman Morozov with them."

I was raised with Timur, and Ashe is his wife. Kiriil and Arman are shifters from the Amurov lair. They left when we did.

Do you trust them?

I trust Timur. The others I trust as much as I trust anyone I've known for a long time. They've never betrayed us.

That tells me very little.

That tells you, Maya, that I'm very careful.

Gedeon heaved an exaggerated sigh. "Gorya, you did send the text to your family telling them you gave me the order to shoot you. Most likely, Timur is here to murder me."

Meiling put her feet up. "Sorry, honey, but I'm just too tired to save you tonight. If he comes in guns blazing, you're on your own."

Maya brushed the back of her hand across her mouth, but Gorya could see the laughter in her eyes. She liked Meiling despite her intention to stay distant from her.

"Don't look at us," Rodion said. "I'd miss the food, but I'm not tangling with Timur when he's in one of his black moods. Gedeon, if he thinks you're going to kill his favorite cousin, no doubt he's got a target painted right in the center of your forehead."

"Thanks," Gedeon said. "You're making me feel better every second."

Kyanite waved his fork around. "You were the one crazy enough to take the job. The three of us would have said no. Timur, Fyodor, Sevastyan and Mitya? They're all insanely protective when it comes to family. You should know that, Gedeon. You've been around them enough."

"I did tell him," Meiling said. "I think he was a little too eager to shoot Gorya and didn't think it through."

"In all fairness, Rogue rubbed Slayer the wrong way deliberately," Gorya said. "We thought that might help Gedeon make up his mind."

Meiling laughed. "That was just mean, Gorya. You know he likes you."

"Not anymore," Gedeon declared solemnly. "I'm back to being a loner."

"You never stopped," Matvei pointed out. "You're antisocial, Gedeon."

Kiriil Sokolov opened the heavy gate leading to the center courtyard, glanced around and stepped back to allow Timur Amurov to go through. Timur was a big man, with wide shoulders and scars on his face. He perpetually wore an expressionless mask on his stone-cold features and a threat in his dead ice-cold eyes. His trench coat swirled around his boot-covered ankles, the inner lining covered in dozens of loops to hold the weapons he carried with him.

His gaze took in everyone and then settled on his cousin. There was no smile as he strode right up to him. Gorya rose to greet him. "Timur. What a surprise. You didn't let me know you were coming to visit."

Timur gripped his shoulders. "Did you think I wasn't going to come when you sent a text that said Gedeon had orders to shoot you and I wasn't to retaliate? I'm not losing you, Gorya. If something is wrong, you reach out. We'll deal together. If you need to come home, then do it. We'll all pull out of this thing we have with Donovan. We all made that promise to one another."

They had. When had Gorya forgotten that his cousins had sworn an oath to one another—to him—that they would be family? That their women would be family. Sons and daughters. All would be put first and guarded carefully. Gorya had never believed himself worthy of that oath. He watched over his cousins, guarded them, but didn't expect that same loyalty in return.

Gorya. Maya filled him with a soft feeling of something that bordered far too close to what might be growing love. *You are not less than he is. How could you think such a thing? For me, you will always be so much more.*

Whatever emotion it was Maya filled his mind with, he felt far more intensely for her, and it was growing every minute in her company. The sincerity in her quiet statement caught at him. Whether they would have a few days together or a lifetime, Gorya knew they were meant to be together. They had been destined mates. He wanted a lifetime with her.

We were right to do as we did, Rogue interjected with his smug attitude.

Between Timur's intensity and Gorya's struggle with having so many males close to Maya when he was feeling vulnerable, he might have reprimanded Rogue, but Maya's soft laughter entered his mind like rays of pure sunshine.

"I appreciate your coming, Timur," Gorya said, ignoring his cat. "Although I warn you, other than those right here in this circle, you can't trust anyone in this lair or, for that matter, the territory. Not even the locals. They made far too much money in trafficking. Shutting it down has made me very unpopular."

"I brought Arman and Kiriil with me, and if we need more, we can send for them," Timur said, indicating the men behind him. "Ashe is with me as well."

Maya stood, and Gorya took her hand, drawing her beneath his shoulder. She seemed much smaller standing that close to him. "This is Maya, my woman. Maya, my cousin Timur; his wife, Ashe; and two of the men from his security, Kiriil and Arman."

Maya smiled at them a little tentatively. She appeared the picture of innocence, the young girl next door. It would be difficult to identify her as a shifter. Timur didn't bother to hide his frown as he looked her over. He'd obviously been hoping for a warrior to aid his cousin, and looking at Maya, his hopes had been dashed.

Ashe gave her a welcoming smile. "I'm so pleased to meet you. Evangeline and Fyodor send their greetings. They were eager to come, but Timur wanted to check out how safe it was first. They have children, and we're a little protective of them."

Maya gave her a small smile. "It's nice to meet you." There was just the smallest hesitation in her voice, as if she might be intimidated by Timur, Ashe and their companions.

Gedeon and Meiling exchanged frowns. Matvei, Rodion and Kyanite appeared protective and concerned.

It was easy to view Maya through the lens she wanted others to see. She had perfected the image since she was a child. She looked and sounded vulnerable and nonthreatening. She projected the feeling of needing care, causing those around her to want to protect her. Gorya didn't see that Timur had that reaction to her, but Ashe did.

"Are you hungry?" Gedeon asked. "There's plenty."

Timur inclined his head. "Very."

"He's always hungry," Ashe said. "I'm the world's worst cook. If there's food in the vicinity, he's got to take advantage."

The men broke out in laughter at Ashe's confession as they added chairs to widen the circle around the fire pit.

Gorya explained to Maya as they sat down, "Ashe tried to help Evangeline with the bakery when Evangeline was too sick to go in one morning and nearly burned it down."

Ashe nodded solemnly when the men continued to laugh. She didn't look in the least offended. "They can laugh all they want, but don't let anyone tell you baking is easy. Evangeline is a miracle worker. She should be given a medal. I'd like to see any of you do what she does. I'm not in the least ashamed of what happened. In any case, that horrible Jeremiah was distracting me."

"Jeremiah?" Maya asked, knowing it was required of her.

"Jeremiah Wheating is our problem child," Gorya explained. "He wouldn't be if the women didn't spoil him rotten. Where is he, Timur? I half expected you to bring him along, especially since Ashe treats him like a sibling. She jumps to his defense the moment anyone dares to reprimand him for his million and one mistakes."

Ashe gave a little sniff of disdain. "I do *not*," she denied.

A chorus of "bullshits" went up from the men around the fire pit. Gedeon had taken orders and was busy at the grill, but even he turned back to lift an eyebrow as if to say Ashe might not be telling the truth.

"She does," Timur confirmed. "The kid is originally from Panama, from a big family, and I think his sisters and momma spoiled him."

There was no change in Maya's outward appearance, but Gorya felt her sudden stillness. He captured her hand, pressing her palm to his thigh.

What is it?

Not here. Wait until we're alone.

He didn't like waiting. He had patience when he needed to be patient, but she was really disturbed, and he wasn't sure why. Jeremiah? He knew the kid.

Jeremiah saved my life. I'm not the only shifter he's saved over the last couple of years.

Jeremiah had put his life on the line dozens of times for other shifters. He was eager to learn, eager to prove himself—a little too eager, which got him into trouble, but that was just his youth. What kid wasn't? He wanted action all the time. He'd nearly been killed in Panama when he was protecting a female shifter, and he'd never speak exactly the same again. Gorya didn't push Maya to tell him what was wrong, knowing it wouldn't do any good.

Ashe sent Timur a little grin. "Jeremiah is a goof. He saved Gorya's life and mine."

"You saved his," Timur corrected. He went to the grill to help Gedeon plate the food for his men and Ashe.

"See, if Jeremiah were here right now," Ashe said, "he wouldn't be able to resist commenting that Timur never has to worry about being poisoned after eating so many of my meals. He'd say he's built up a cast-iron stomach or something equally as obnoxious as that."

Timur frowned and lifted one eyebrow. "I can eat anything thanks to you, Ashe. Are you telling me this entire time you didn't ruin all those meals on purpose?"

Again, laughter erupted around them. Ashe joined in, clearly uncaring that it might be at her expense.

Even with the teasing and laughter and the disclosure that Jeremiah had saved Gorya's life, Maya didn't relax, but she softened a little toward Timur, watching him serve his wife her food.

He does seem to love her.

Gorya followed her gaze to see Timur brush a kiss on top of Ashe's head and murmur something that made her blush as he handed her the plate of food.

Ashe is his world. I have no idea what he'd do without her.

Timur went back to the grill to retrieve two more plates for Arman and Kiriil. Gorya could tell Maya was shocked that Timur waited on the two security guards rather than having them wait on him. He could have told her Timur might appear arrogant, but when it came to the men he worked with, he didn't expect them to do anything that he wasn't willing to do himself. He knew if Maya observed the behavior for herself, it would have a greater impact on her. He wanted her to like Timur, although his cousin tended to rub people the wrong way at their first meeting.

Don't worry so much, Gorya. I like that he came to check on you. You matter a lot to him. I don't have to matter to him. He sees me the way I show myself to him. He wanted someone like Ashe for you.

Gorya choked on his coffee. *I'd strangle the woman.*

Immediately, he had Timur's attention. "Everything all right?"

Gorya nodded. "Absolutely. I'm glad you're here, Timur. This is one fucked-up lair. Not only is everyone in the lair corrupt, but the locals rely on the money coming in from trafficking. I'm slowly unraveling who I can count on and who I can't, but it isn't easy."

Timur had settled in his seat and started eating, but his head went up alertly and he frowned, pausing in the act of bringing his fork to his mouth. "You've always been able to discern lies faster than any of the rest of us. How can these people possibly keep the truth from you?"

"The locals can't," Gorya said. "But those in the lair have been mixing truth with lies for so long, I think they believe what they say. Many of these men have their mates, yet the women convinced themselves, for whatever reason, that there was nothing wrong in what was being done."

Ashe scowled at him. "They knew? You're certain they knew?"

"They knew," Kyanite answered for Gorya. "It's been slow, but we've uncovered evidence that in a few cases, they helped lure women here to be sold."

Timur shook his head. "That's crazy. Women shifters aren't like that."

"They can be," Gorya said. "You should know. You just never wanted to see."

Be careful, Gorya. Don't say anything against his mother. What would be the point? Maya advised gently.

He's living a fantasy. He needs to grow up and face reality.

Why? Why shouldn't he be able to keep one nice thing for himself? Why shouldn't he be able to believe his mother loved him? Maybe she did in her own way. Let him have that.

Gorya sighed but changed tactics. Maya was right. He didn't want her to be, but she was. "Female leopards can be selfish and greedy. They're leopard, just like males, Timur. If they get used to having too much and don't want to let go of it, they're just as capable of being cunning and manipulative."

Timur switched his attention to Maya as he took Ashe's empty plate and handed her a cup of coffee. "Are you even of legal age? You look about thirteen."

Gorya bristled instantly. "What the fuck, Timur? Are you deliberately being rude to my woman?"

"She does look like a little kid. Am I the only one to think that?"

"I do look young, Gorya," Maya said unnecessarily.

"He doesn't have to sound so damn belligerent."

"Is that how I sounded?" Timur asked.

"Yes," Kyanite confirmed, smirking a little. "Maya, he always sounds like that. He can't help himself."

Maya sent Kyanite one of her sweet smiles. "It's good to know he isn't disapproving of me, since I'll be with Gorya a long time."

Ashe settled back in her chair and regarded Maya over the top of her coffee cup. Both Gorya and Rogue bristled protectively at the speculative look in her eyes.

"Since we're on the subject, as you must be aware, Timur and Gorya are very close, so naturally, the family investigated you. We couldn't find a single thing about you. Not one thing. Not even a birth certificate. You'll have to forgive me, Maya, but that sent up more than one red flag."

Maya didn't change expression, nor did she blink. It didn't matter to her that every shifter had their full attention on her. She looked as innocent and sweet as if she were sitting in a church. Gorya couldn't help but admire her.

"She doesn't owe you or anyone else an explanation," Gorya said. He kept his voice low. Ashe was the closest thing he had to a sister, but he still couldn't prevent the hint of menace from creeping into his tone. Rogue clawed at him, determined to get out to protect Maya.

Timur's head went up alertly. "What the hell, Gorya?"

"There's no need to defend me, Gorya," Maya said softly, "but thank you." She looked directly at Ashe. Her voice changed, became expressionless. "I gave Gorya what I believe is my real name, but it isn't one I've used or heard in years. He gave it to you because you're his family."

Her gaze jumped to Timur. "I suppose you feel it's perfectly fine for you to defend your woman, but for some reason your cousin shouldn't defend his. Why is that, I wonder?"

There was a short, shocked silence and then Meiling laughed. "Nice call, Maya. I was wondering the same thing. Shifters have such short tempers. I think most of the time they should just pound their chests and crow like Tarzan in the jungle. That way everyone will know they're a force to be reckoned with, and we'll take notice and bow or something."

"We don't want you to bow, Meiling," Gedeon corrected. "Just do everything we say."

Ashe rolled her eyes. "Like that will ever happen."

"Keep dreaming, honey," Meiling said.

Gorya was always impressed the way Meiling defused a situation. He'd seen her do it more than once, and it was smooth and with humor. Gedeon followed her lead and others went along. He glanced at Timur, who looked a little rueful.

"What name do you normally go by, Maya?" Ashe persisted. Her voice was much friendlier.

Gorya wanted to strangle her. *You don't have to answer*

her. Every cell in his body was on alert. Rogue was prowling, as if he were caged and waiting to be released to attack some great threat to them.

She's your family. Either we're doing this or we aren't. They have to know who I am eventually. It may as well be now. I'm not going to disclose more than my street name.

Even as she soothed him, he *felt* her uneasiness, that same ominous feeling as when their company had mentioned Jeremiah Wheating and Panama.

Maya's inner turmoil didn't show. "I assumed the identity of Teona Kyva when I was very young. I was able to perfect that identification over the years."

Meiling and Gedeon exchanged a long look. "I recognize that name," Meiling said. "You've done work for us."

Maya nodded. "I do independent research work for a few select clients in this country and some overseas. Rene Guidry has been one of my clients for years. He investigated me, and before I ever take on a client, I investigate them. The moment I heard your name, Gedeon, I knew who you were, but I don't reveal my clients to anyone. I had no idea whether Rene told you he used me for his research. I assumed that he did, but I had no way of knowing."

Gorya held up his hand before Ashe or anyone else could ask more questions. "I didn't interrogate you, Ashe, or Evangeline or any of the other women in our family. They answer to their mates. Maya answers to me and only to me. There is no need for her to disclose anything else of her past to anyone. As it is, we don't want this information going beyond those sitting here. This is my inner circle and the people I trust."

That edgy feeling was spreading through his body, his radar going off, but he had no idea why. He sent his senses reaching far into the swamp but couldn't find evidence of intruders.

"It's really that bad here, then?" Timur asked.

Gorya nodded. "The others in this lair are considered

potential enemies and we don't want them aware that Maya knows anything about computers. Also, no more researching her. She has people she protects. If you investigated her, you would put those people in danger."

Ashe looked at Timur with a little smirk. "I told you he wouldn't like it."

Gorya turned to his cousin. "You put her up to this?" He wasn't in the least surprised. Naturally Timur would have Ashe ask the questions. The knots in his belly tightened. He was growing edgier despite the way the conversation kept turning humorous. There was something out there, something he couldn't quite catch. A scent. A shadow. Or was Maya growing moodier?

Rogue? Is Wraith rising? He didn't feel her close to the surface. Maya appeared calm, although she was tense.

Timur shrugged, a roll of his wide shoulders. "I thought you'd take questions better from Ashe than me. Not that you did. Who knew you'd go caveman? You're supposed to be the easygoing Amurov."

Matvei coughed into his fist. Gedeon and Meiling exchanged a knowing smile.

"He is charming," Meiling said. "You'll have to watch him around the ladies, Maya. They fall at his feet when he walks past them."

Ashe nodded. "I can attest to that," she agreed.

Maya raised her eyebrow. "Is that so?" She nudged Gorya with her foot. "I see you've neglected to tell me a few things about yourself."

The men erupted into laughter. Gorya glared at the women. "You're supposed to be talking me up. What's wrong with you? I expect this from Timur, but not the two of you." He gave Maya his innocent mask. "Baby, I never flirt."

Ashe threw her hands over her head. "Everyone duck. Lightning is about to strike."

Maya kept her straight face, but for him, in his mind,

she stroked a small caress, barely felt. It was her first real touch of contact surrounded by the others, reaching out to reassure him she knew he was hers alone, that all the teasing was just that.

He was falling. Hard. Right off the cliff with no safety net. That made him even more dangerous than he already was, because he would do anything to keep her safe. Anything. He would sell whatever was left of his soul for her.

"I see I have my work cut out for me to keep you in line," Maya said as she got gracefully to her feet and took his empty coffee mug. "Would you like anything else?"

She moved around the outside of the circle and paused between Kiriil's and Arman's chairs as she half turned back toward Gorya. She was very still, her attention centered on the two men. For a moment, Rogue rose, clawing, raking, raging at the close proximity of the males to his female and the way she was studying the men. Gorya fought back the red sheets of jealousy he wasn't used to dealing with. The emotion was powerful and intense, and reining it in took more discipline than he expected.

"What the fuck, Gorya?" Timur muttered.

Just to show how far gone he was in that moment, he hadn't realized he was giving off waves of danger until his cousin's demand penetrated. He pulled himself out of his animalistic response and took a slow, careful look around, using every heightened sense. His security team had gone on instant alert. Gedeon had an eyebrow lifted, asking silently what was wrong.

What are you doing, Maya? Get away from those shifters, Gorya ordered. *I don't have nearly the control I thought I would, and neither does Rogue.*

Something isn't right. Don't you feel it? I thought the threat might be coming from one of them. I don't know them, but it isn't. It's farther away, coming toward us from three different directions. Reach out, Gorya. Get past the heat.

Maya stepped away from the circle, placed the mugs on the ground and paced closer to the high fence surrounding the patio.

Gorya immediately got up to join her, signaling to Gedeon as he did so.

"What is it, Maya?" Gedeon asked as he rose.

"Gorya? Gedeon? Meiling?" Maya's voice was barely a thread of sound.

Gorya felt them now. Rogue went crazy. A male leopard in his prime was approaching through the swamp. There was no mistaking his intentions. He had come to challenge for leadership—and for the female in heat. Gorya was already reaching for his shirt.

Maya's hand stayed his. "Wait, there's something else going on here. Those other two coming in aren't in leopard form, Gorya. We need to know what they're doing."

He gently removed her hand. "I cannot refuse a challenge, Maya, nor would I want to. Rogue is going insane. No one will take you from me, and I will not give up leadership." This was what he'd been feeling all along. The threat coming at him. These men had been a great distance away, but his radar had picked them up, even miles out.

"He hasn't challenged you yet," she pointed out. "He's still far out. He has no idea you're aware of him. We need to see what the other two men are doing. I believe they mean to harm you if you win."

He shrugged, uncaring. "They want to continue with what they were doing before I came into leadership and shut down their largest moneymaker. They don't like the changes. They keep coming at me, Maya, and they aren't going to stop."

She lifted her chin at him. "They don't get to have two

snipers in position when you've been challenged to fight for leadership."

He framed her face between her palms and looked into her eyes, knowing Rogue was looking as well, that she could see both. "I'm declaring that you're mine, Maya. And Wraith belongs to Rogue. If they have shooters, Meiling and Matvei will take them out." He poured confidence into his voice and mind so she would believe him. He had confidence in his security team. "Gedeon will be with me. There is no way this leopard will win."

"I'm not in the least bit concerned that he will, only that if they spot you and they're in a position to take the shot before our people are ready to take them out, I won't be too happy with you."

Gorya liked that she was already calling his security *our people*. He smiled at her. "We wouldn't want that."

She shook her head. "You know how I can get."

"How does she get?" Ashe asked curiously.

"My woman has a little bit of a temper," Gorya answered without taking his gaze from Maya's.

Meiling touched Maya's shoulder. "No one will shoot him. I give you my word. I don't miss."

Matvei didn't touch her, but he gave her a small salute. "Got your man covered."

"I appreciate you watching out for him," Maya said, breaking the eye contact with Gorya, but she reached for his hand, keeping him from shifting and rushing out into the swamp.

I'm still uneasy, Gorya. Even knowing they have this setup, there's something else.

As Meiling and Matvei slipped into the night shadows, Gorya did his best to reach beyond the chaos of the leopard's rage at another male entering his territory, daring to challenge him for his female. It was difficult to process anything else when the need to confront the other leopard was so strong.

Timur came up to stand beside his cousin. "How did your leopards feel the approach so quickly? Or scent them? I'm just now getting a faint warning, and it comes and goes. They're very far away and staying downwind as best they can."

Standing beside his cousin, another powerful male, increased the difficulty for Gorya. Disapproval of Maya came off Timur in subtle waves, but it was there. Both Rogue and he reacted despite every effort not to. Maya had to be aware of it. She was even more empathic than he was. Gedeon and even Meiling would know what Timur thought of Gorya's chosen mate. It was one thing not to care what his cousin thought of him—that he was weaker and needed looking after—but he didn't like that Timur had a poor opinion of Maya.

We are deceiving him. How is that his fault?

Maya's gentle calm flowed into him, pouring serenity into his mind over the heat-influenced male rage building against his cousin. Gorya took a deep breath and hung on to his discipline and years of developing who he was.

"You've always known I could find other leopards fast, Timur, unless they were masking their scent. These leopards aren't. Gedeon and Meiling have the same ability."

Timur glanced over at Maya. "Your woman seemed to be the one to catch them first, yet her female appears to be sleeping at the moment. None of the males are reacting to her."

Gorya inhaled Maya's unique fragrance. "She's much more sensitive to her surroundings than the rest of us."

Timur looked as if he was pleased with that news. "At least she'll be a help to you with your warning system."

The wind shifted, bringing the offending scent of the approaching male leopard. It mattered little to Rogue how far away he was. The leopard fought to emerge, to meet the challenge of the other daring to enter his exclusive territory.

Wait, Gorya whispered, stripping away his shirt altogether. *He will issue his challenge for leadership. He'll issue his challenge for Wraith. We will be on him before he is prepared.*

He crouched low, leapt over the wall, kicked off his shoes and stripped away his trousers. Shifting, he allowed Rogue the freedom to hunt, but in absolute silence.

9

ROGUE streaked through the swamp toward the intruder. The leopard had familiarized himself with the entire area and knew every shortcut, every trail, every branch that took him through the trees above their heads to make the route faster. Even Gedeon found it difficult to keep up with the leopard, and he'd run these trails hundreds of times in preparation.

Timur, Rodion and Kyanite refused to be left behind. Timur was a stranger to the local swamp. He knew his cousin's scent well and could follow it easily, but he allowed Kyanite to lead the way.

Rogue was always cognizant of the small figure slipping fast and silent through the arboreal highway above him, nearly as fast in human form as he was in leopard form. Maya was so swift in the trees, her size allowing her to move rapidly without disturbing the leaves as she raced from branch to branch. Gorya found his heart pounding in

fear for her, afraid she might make one misstep and plunge
to the swamp floor, but it never happened.

The wind shifted and the scent of the male leopard
once again filled Rogue's lungs, inflaming him further.
Rage turned red and he flung caution aside, racing to the
attack.

Slow down, Gedeon cautioned. *Meiling hasn't indicated she is in position to take out the sniper.*

Gorya barely heard him over the roar of thunder rolling
in his ears. He was wholly focused on defeating his enemy. The animal had taken over, gaining ground, digging
claws into the rotting vegetation to get traction so he could
sprint faster toward his enemy.

He was a silent apparition weaving in and out of the
trees, the gray fog concealing him. His thick coat blended
with the mist threading through the thick trunks, masking
his presence.

The sawing roar of challenge filled the swamp, startling birds and bats into flight. Insects suddenly ceased
their steady drone. An owl called a warning. Lizards and
mice scuttled for cover in the leafy vegetation on the
swamp floor.

Rogue rounded the last tree, burst through the veil of
fog and hit the intruder in his side, driving him from his
feet, sending him sprawling. Only then did he let out
his answering roar, shaking the swamp with the sound of
his lethal snarl.

The challenging leopard was large, a brute of a male, a
good two hundred pounds of dense muscle. The fur was
dark, with gold dusting beneath and darker rosettes scat-
tered throughout the thick coat. Gorya recognized the
leopard immediately. The animal was called Punisher.

The shifter was Ivan Kovalchuk, a great bear of a man.
His former job had been to oversee the women and chil-
dren sent out to other countries on freighters and planes.
It was rumored he delighted in sampling the wares before

sending them to their final destinations. He'd sworn fidelity immediately and without hesitation, although Gorya hadn't believed him for a moment. He had a ready smile that was as false as his word.

His leopard was vicious and enjoyed inflicting punishment on other leopards, especially those smaller than him and females. The former *pakhan* had used him to enforce his laws, and the others feared him. Gorya had been surprised that Ivan hadn't challenged him for leadership the moment the *pakhan* had died.

Rogue ordinarily would have been all over the leopard, killing him then and there, but he needed the fight, partly to show his female his expertise and abilities. He wanted his female to know he could always take care of her in any situation. He also *needed* to indulge in the violence. He had to pit himself against the other leopard and feel the tearing of muscle and bone under his teeth and claws. It seemed as necessary as breathing.

Do you see, Maya? There was despair in his voice, in his mind. He doubted he would ever be able to overcome the need for violence.

At once her soothing peace stole inside him, filling him with feminine amusement. *You are a shifter. A leopard. What do you expect of yourself? It is natural for you to need combat. Rogue is a fierce fighter. Accomplished. You are as well. Have at it; just don't get so complacent you make a mistake.*

Bog, but he had fallen hard for her. Just that easily she made him seem as if he were almost normal, whatever that was.

Normal is whatever we make it, she reminded him. *This is our relationship. No one else is invited.*

Punisher was on his feet, head low, snarling, showing teeth, eyes filled with malice. The leopard circled cautiously, his powerful muscles rippling beneath the loose fur. He wanted to intimidate his opponent.

Rogue watched him, not moving a muscle, his eyes that flat silvery frost that disappeared in the gray background with many rosettes. He looked slightly leaner than the dense leopard, but he was longer. He held himself very still, as if frozen, ears flat against his head. While Punisher snarled and roared, swiping at the ground to throw up dirt and leaves, Rogue remained silent and still, not posturing after the first answering challenge.

Gedeon, Rodion and Kyanite arrived with Timur and his two bodyguards, Arman and Kiriil, and Ashe. They hastily pulled on clothes from packs they carried around their necks. Maya came out of the trees to stand in the shadows on the other side of Gedeon.

Matvei and Meiling are in position, Gorya, Gedeon assured him. *Take him out anytime.*

Timur uttered a gasp, and his hands went to the jeans he'd just pulled up. "Gorya, as *pakhan*, you shouldn't have to deal with this clown. I'll fight him. He's nothing."

Gorya knew Timur was worried Punisher would be able to defeat Rogue. He'd never seen Rogue in a real battle.

"As *pakhan*," Gedeon corrected, "when a challenge is issued for leadership, Gorya has no choice but to meet it."

How many are normally sent in an assassination squad? Maya asked just as Punisher exploded into action.

But this is not an assassination squad, baby. This is just a run-of-the-mill conspiracy to kill the leader so they can take over.

Rogue rose up into the air to meet Punisher, slashing with claws at the underbelly, slicing four precise, deep wounds before he whipped his body around and disengaged.

I'm not betting your life on it.

Five.

Rogue circled the wounded leopard, who came down spilling ruby drops on the leaves and dirt. Howling and snarling, showing his teeth, Punisher's eyes deepened to an evil reddish hue as he stared at his rival. Once, he glanced into the swamp, upward toward a tree in the distance, before lifting his head and roaring another challenge. He hadn't been expecting Rogue to score lacerations deep enough to hinder movement.

Stall for a couple of minutes.

Gorya thought it ironic that Timur didn't want him to fight the leopard, in fact was willing to take his place to protect him. Maya had such faith in his abilities that she was asking him to prolong the match with Punisher for some unknown reason, and yet she'd never seen Rogue fight. It was always dangerous battling another leopard. Anything could go wrong. One slip, especially with an experienced fighter such as Punisher, and Rogue could go down just as easily as Punisher.

This time it was Rogue who attacked. He gave no warning. He rushed Punisher before the larger leopard could ready himself for the attack. Leaping on him, Rogue brought the big brute down, burying his teeth in his spine and his claws deep in his neck to control Punisher's head. He held him helpless. For the first time he allowed the other leopard to feel his enormous strength. Punisher fought, clawing and biting at him desperately, alarm showing in his eyes.

After a few minutes of struggling against Rogue's relentless grip, Punisher gave a last-ditch effort to roll. Rogue allowed it, and the two leopards somersaulted several times, flipping back and forth in a maelstrom of gray and dark fur, claws, teeth and tails. Rogue never lost his grip on the large cat. Punisher's fur was streaked with dark red.

Punisher lifted his muzzle from the dirt and howled in terror but refused submission. To claim leadership, the leopard couldn't submit. At his call, Ivan expected one of the two snipers lying in wait to put a bullet in Rogue. The sound of a rifle, followed by a second, reverberated through the swamp.

For a moment Punisher's eyes glowed with triumph. Rogue's teeth sank deeper into his spine. Snapped it. He backed off, leaving his opponent unable to rise.

Maya?

Go for it. I'll meet you back at the house.

He didn't like the way she sounded. She held herself away from him, not moving all the way into his mind. What was different about her voice?

Rogue, finish this one off fast.

Rogue didn't hesitate. He considered Punisher beneath him. The animal had not come to fight in an honorable manner. He'd brought along two snipers to assist him. To *cheat.* No self-respecting shifter would ever do such a thing when challenging for leadership. And no leopard would ever cheat in a fight for a female. She would never accept him. What would that mean for Maya? Would they try to sell her when they started up their human trafficking ring again? He knew that was the intention. Just the thought enraged him.

I would kill him, Maya said calmly.

Now she sounded more like Maya. Gorya felt he could breathe again. There was no doubt in his mind that she would have killed Ivan.

There was zero possibility that Rogue would be defeated. If Meiling and Matvei did their jobs, you were going to prevail.

Now she sounded downright smug. Rogue even preened a little with that remark. He liked that not only did Wraith believe in him, but Maya did as well. Rogue slammed his paw into the dirt, throwing leaves and dirt over Punisher's panting muzzle to show his contempt for the other cat. He clamped his jaws around him and bit down, smothering the other leopard with a bite to his neck. He was relentless, shaking Punisher viciously as the cat succumbed to the slow death.

He dropped the heavy weight of the carcass on the ground and paced away a few feet, roaring another challenge, daring any leopard to try to take his female from him, then raced back to show more contempt for the shifter by once again throwing dirt and rotting vegetation all over the carcass.

Gorya became aware of a disturbance around him. Timur swearing, in a heated argument with Gedeon and Kyanite. Then Timur was stripping and racing through the swamp back toward the house, one bodyguard rushing to keep up with him. Ashe and the other bodyguard were nowhere in sight. Gorya presumed Timur and Ashe had gotten into one of their many disagreements and he'd taken off. He allowed Rogue two more triumphant rushes at his fallen foe.

"Gorya, get Rogue moving. Your hothead cousin thinks he's going to educate Maya on what he thinks she should be doing when Rogue is fighting for her. I don't think that's going to go over so well with her," Gedeon said.

Gorya instructed Rogue to back off immediately. The leopard was still in the throes of the animal hormones. It was difficult to get him to back off and took massive persuasion. Rogue reluctantly turned away, snarling and hissing, but raced back even after Gorya started them toward home. When Gorya reprimanded him, Rogue responded with rage, reiterating that the leopard had conspired to cheat. It took patience to overcome the massive amount of male hormones running amok in the leopard.

Gorya felt the same rage and triumph and had to fight to stay focused. He was alarmed at the idea of his cousin confronting Maya without him being present. Timur was a good man but also a bulldozer when he wanted to get a point across. Maya wouldn't accept Timur's domineering ways. It could turn into a shit show in seconds.

Once he was able to regain control of Rogue, he forced him to turn toward the house. Even though shifters had an advantage, leopards were built for shorter sprints. Rogue had expended a tremendous amount of energy when racing to meet his challenger and then fighting with him, although he had ended the battle quickly. He was forced to go slower on the way home.

The moment he went through the open gates, Gorya knew he'd arrived far too late. Across the long patio Timur towered over Maya, his broad, muscular body clad only in his jeans. Standing so close to her without clothes would be a trigger for Maya, let alone doing so in a threatening, domineering Amurov way. Gorya hastily shifted, dragging on a pair of jeans from his pack.

"What the hell is wrong with you?" Timur snapped at Maya. "A female leopard always stays close to watch the match between the males fighting for her."

Maya stepped back, eliciting Timur's dictatorial nature. He caught at her arms to stop her, giving her a little shake to emphasize his point. "You *never* leave your man. You always have his back." He snapped his command through gritted teeth.

Ashe gave a little cry of alarm as she swept into the yard, shifting and trying to pull on clothes all at the same time.

Gorya sprinted toward his cousin and Maya. Gedeon and Ashe did the same. Then everyone froze in place, including Timur.

Maya didn't utter a sound, but with blurring speed she retaliated, slicing through jeans at his inner thighs, his belly, under his arms and ending with her hand at his throat. Thin lines of blood appeared on his skin directly over every major artery.

The air went electric. Ashe gasped, shaking her head.

Timur's bodyguards drew their weapons and aimed them at Maya's head. Kyanite and Rodion took aim at Timur's bodyguards. Timur was utterly still. Gorya's gaze took in the blood leaking through Maya's shirt on her left side. Her hand was rock steady as she held the small blade to Timur's neck.

"Don't you ever put your hands on me again, or I'll kill you." Her voice was low, but there was no doubt she meant every word. "I purposely didn't slash your arteries, but I could have."

Gorya ignored everyone but his woman. "Maya. Look at me. Only me." He walked toward her, making his way through the others, taking his time, reverting to absolute calm. Gedeon paced along beside him, every bit as relaxed as he was.

"I can't do this, Gorya. I thought I could, but you can see what happened. I'll get my things and leave." There was quiet despair in her voice.

"I'd just go after you, baby. You know I would. This is a little bump in the road. We expected them. We talked about them."

"I almost killed your cousin."

"But you didn't. You didn't because he's family." He stood in front of her, blocking her smaller figure from Timur's bodyguards. "I can see you have an injury. Tell me what happened."

Her expression changed. A little shudder went through her body. "I almost got you killed. It was so close. When I asked you about an assassination team, you told me it was usual to send a five-man squad. I included the leopard challenging you in that. Meiling and Matvei were taking care of two of them, and you had the leopard covered. That gave me two others to find and kill before they could shoot you."

Gorya had to resist comforting her. The tension was so thick he could cut it with a knife. She was too shaky. Fortunately, Timur was experienced enough not to move, and he wanted to understand what was going on. He had affection for Gorya. Everything he'd done had been because he loved his cousin and wanted only the best for him. He was willing to stand there with knife cuts and be humiliated in front of his men to hear the explanation. That was Timur. He might be overbearing, but in the end, he was always fair.

"It seemed to take forever before I located them, but I did. The sniper had a spotter with him, so that meant they were together. That feeling of impending danger didn't leave me the way it should have. I knew something was wrong, that I'd missed something. I heard Meiling and Matvei both take their shots. That meant Rogue had taken the other leopard down and I'd run out of time. That's when I realized that the leopard Rogue was fighting was a sacrifice."

Gorya couldn't take it anymore. Very gently he reached out and wrapped his palm around the blade of the knife, pulling it slowly from Timur's neck. "Give me the knife, Maya."

She took a deep breath and did as he asked. Her long lashes fluttered as he shackled her wrist and drew her away from Timur, tucking her beneath his shoulder.

"What happened next?"

"I had to find him fast before he could shoot you. He had to have a good line of sight on you. He wouldn't have a spotter. I made the best guess possible and then made the decision to use my speed even though I knew there were others watching." She lowered her voice and glanced at Ashe and her bodyguard, and then at Kyanite. "It was the only way to save your life."

He stroked a caress down the back of her scalp. "It was all right, Maya."

She shook her head. "They're Amurovs."

He leaned down and kissed the top of her head. "I'm Amurov," he reminded her.

"Not like they are."

"Tell me what happened."

"He was up high, and I had to leap to distract him, to prevent him from taking the shot."

Gorya's heart clenched. He had been slowly walking her toward the house, but he stopped abruptly. "Tell me you didn't leap in front of the fucking rifle."

"I came in at a side angle and kicked it hard enough that the rifle went flying out of the tree. I landed on the branch hard though, and he was on me with a knife. Wraith rolled and kept rolling, so we fell and landed on the ground below. It was a good forty feet. We hadn't shifted, not even partially, and neither had he. He dropped right in front of me, and I swept his legs out from under him. As he went down, he slashed across my ribs." She lifted her palm to show the blood spreading on her shirt.

Gorya's eyes met his cousin's over her head, and then he looked at Gedeon. *Send for the doc. The one we can trust. She'll need a shit ton of antibiotics.*

Gedeon nodded. There was only one shifter doctor Gedeon allowed any of his men to use, and it wasn't one from the present lair. They didn't trust anyone from there yet. The doctor would have to be flown in from New Orleans. It was a relatively short flight, but still, it would take time. Gorya wanted a doctor in residence, at least until he cleaned up his territory.

"We're going inside, Maya. I'll see to your wound, and you're going to rest until the doc gets here. The others will do cleanup and burn the bodies."

"You know I can't stay, Gorya." Sorrow dripped in her mind.

"We'll discuss that inside." He was very firm with her. "I want to see that laceration."

Timur paced alongside them. "Maya, I owe you an apology."

"Not now, Timur. We'll sort things out later," Gorya said. "I appreciate that you want to make things right, but I just want to make certain this wound isn't too deep and I can clean it out immediately. I think Ashe is eager to say a few things to you."

Reaching around Maya, Gorya opened the door for her, giving her no other choice but to enter, using his larger, heavier body to physically push her inside. He closed the door firmly behind them and walked her briskly down the hall to the primary suite.

"They saw me. I didn't hide who I was from them. Ashe and her bodyguard. Kyanite. All three of them saw me. There is no way I can explain what happened." She spoke in a low voice.

When he touched her mind, Gorya read guilt. Shame.

"For fuck's sake, woman, you saved my life. You can't be upset at how you had to do it. You're the superstar here. The rock star. *My* rock star. I wish I'd been there to see it and to see their faces."

He carefully peeled off her shirt, drawing it over her head. Frowning, he bent to examine the long, thin gash in her flesh. "Let's take this into the bathroom." He didn't wait for her consent but grabbed the bloody shirt and, taking her hand, led her into the primary bath.

"That's too many people knowing I'm different, Gorya."

"Wraith is Rogue's mate, Maya, and you and I belong together."

For the first time she gave him a little half smile. "You're so arrogant. You just had an assassination team come after you. You've had how many challenges for leadership already? You may have to kill ninety percent of the shifters in this lair, and yet you think because we're together no other male will decide he can claim me."

Gorya couldn't help himself. "Brace yourself, baby. I'm coming in for step two."

Her head snapped up and her eyes went wide. "Wait. What? You can't. I have swamp breath. Gator breath. The green vapor of death. After saving you from snipers, I'll kill you with poisonous breath and your obnoxious cousin will find a way to murder me after all. Most likely through one of his vile superior-male lectures."

She tried her best to backpedal away from him but came up against the long marble sink. He'd always thought that sink would come in handy. Now he was very fond of it. He captured her chin in his palm. Her eyes went from green to blue—that blue he was coming to love.

"Stay still, my little assassin. This isn't going to hurt. We've established that already. And if you're worried about noxious swamp breath, remember, I fought Punisher, the treacherous leopard, for you and then gallantly ran through the swamp to save you from my foulmouthed, overbearing cousin. I have to say I loved it when you went hellcat on my cousin. That brought on the need for step two, so consider it your fault this time."

Her mouth quirked, just as he knew it would. One eyebrow lifted. Those light-colored, innocent eyebrows that made him want to brush kisses over them too. "Foulmouthed and overbearing? Didn't you just use the F-word? And you're arrogant and bossy most of the time. *Dictatorial*, I think, is the word you might be looking for to describe yourself."

"Clearly he rubbed off on me. He's such a bad example." Gorya kept a straight face. His thumb shaped her cheekbones and traced her lips. They were trembling. She looked like a wild animal on the verge of flight, even though she had that hint of laughter in her mind.

"Are you certain step two is a good idea, Gorya?" There was anxiety in her tone.

His smile was genuine, because she made him genuine when he'd been a deceiver for most of his life. He brushed kisses over her innocent eyebrows and then along her nose. "Step two is the only idea, my little hellcat. Right now, if I don't kiss you, I won't be able to continue breathing."

"Well then, we can't have that after all I did to keep you alive. That insufferable cousin of yours nearly did me in."

Her hand came up to shape his jaw. A whisper of a touch only, but he felt it all the way to his soul. It was terrifying how much she could reach inside him and shake him like the worst earthquake, yet he was getting so used to the feeling, the terror was receding.

He turned his head to kiss her fingers as they retreated. "You have to curb your penchant for running away. If we ever need to run, we're going to do it together. That's *after* we clean this lair up. Frankly, this place stinks. Someone has to get rid of the riffraff. It may as well be us."

She sent him another small smile, and it was too much for him to resist. He bent his head and took possession of her mouth. Her lips parted under his. Turned soft. Melted. She seemed to come alive. Every cell in his body reacted and he came alive, as only Maya could make him do. Heat rushed through his veins and fed his addiction.

Maya felt soft and pliant, her body made for his. Part of him. Then she winced. He felt that just as starkly as he felt the flames rolling through him. Instantly he pulled back. He glanced down at the wound and then crouched low to really look at it. It was going to take more than a trip to his bathroom and the small medical kit he kept. He straightened, kissed her again, much more gently, and then lifted her to take her back to the bedroom.

"Kissing you is kind of like taking a trip into another world, Gorya," she whispered, one arm circling his neck. "I feel like I'm flying."

He liked that. They were just starting out. Feeling each other. Finding their way. "We're getting fairly good at step two," he acknowledged with mock seriousness. "Doc should be here soon. I'm going to undress you completely and wash this laceration." He laid her on the bed and took off her shoes, setting them neatly beneath the end table.

"I don't need a doctor. You can handle it."

He couldn't help smiling at the stubborn note in her voice. He wasn't going to argue with her, but a doctor was going to examine the very angry-looking laceration. "Tell me about your reservations over Jeremiah Wheating. You had a reaction the minute his name was mentioned," Gorya said, more to distract her from what he was doing, although he did want to know why Jeremiah's name would bother her.

The kid was a hard worker. He'd practiced shifting so much he was lightning fast now. He'd always been a good shot, almost as good as Meiling. He might be overeager for action, but that was just his youth. He could be counted on. There was no way he was anything but loyal. He'd been savagely clawed in the throat, and his voice was changed, but women seemed to find the sound of it attractive—or maybe it was his ready smile. The boy had charm.

He removed her trousers, sliding them over her hips and down her legs, careful to keep from jarring her before bending over the bed to examine the laceration closer, making certain the edges were clean. It looked nasty and deeper than he'd first thought. He was going to disinfect it and leave it for the doctor to look at. He raised his head to meet her eyes.

She sighed. "I told you I started hunting the men who raped me and then the men who raped and killed Polina. I also went after the ones who killed the others I traveled with. I started backtracking, looking for any of those who might be involved in human trafficking. It wasn't that difficult. One name would lead to another. I didn't want to just take out the bottom-feeders, I wanted to find out who was at the top."

Of course she would want that. His woman was no slacker. She would set her sights high and not take her eye off the prize. He was exactly the same way.

"This is going to hurt, baby. Take a breath and let it out."

She did as he instructed, and he didn't hesitate or prolong the anticipation, pouring the solution over the laceration to clean out the knife wound. She gasped, clamping down on his wrist, tears leaking from her eyes, but she didn't cry aloud.

"I'm sorry. I know that hurt. Knife wounds are notorious for infection."

"It's all right."

It wasn't, but there was little to be done about it. "Keep talking." He sank down onto the mattress beside her, brushing back her hair with as gentle a touch as he could manage.

"I started this loose ladder, trying to figure out who was at the top. Someone had to be directing the various shipments. They were too organized. I carefully followed each man who had anything to do with trafficking and studied those around him, keeping track of names and places and where they came from. Who they associated with. Eventually, patterns began to develop."

That was exactly what Drake Donovan had been trying to do for some time with the help of Gorya and his cousins. Jake Bannaconni, a very wealthy businessman, had been helping as well. He found it ironic that his woman was attempting to do the exact same thing he had been doing all along.

He wiped the tiny beads of sweat from her face with a cool washcloth. "How did Jeremiah figure into your ladder?"

"I was working up the ladder. My ladder became a tree with quite a few branches. I found names leading from New Orleans, Houston and San Antonio and traced them back to Borneo and then to Russia and Panama. When you said Jeremiah came from Panama, that was a major red flag."

Gorya didn't like the sound of her tree. Mitya's wife's family had been couriers, and someone had killed them for a notebook that contained damning evidence against Drake Donovan and Jake Bannaconni. Her grandfather hadn't delivered the notebook from New Orleans to Houston. He'd hidden it from everyone. He'd been murdered before he could tell anyone he had it. Her father had been murdered as well. No one knew who wrote the notebook and sent it to Houston or where it was supposed to be delivered.

"Do you have solid evidence against the men you have on this tree or only suspicion?"

"If they are suspects, they're posted in one color, and if I have investigated them thoroughly and know they are part of the trafficking ring, they are in another color. I have them color-coded by the rank they hold as well."

"Do you know absolutely who is involved from New Orleans?"

She nodded. "Yes. There are three men from New Orleans. One was a plant and two are native to New Orleans. The strange thing was, I had already tracked down and investigated them when a woman contacted me through Donovan and asked me to investigate one of them for her. I was a little shocked. I found the two locals through the plant. He was the one I had been tracking down. He had been sent from Panama to Borneo to be trained with Donovan. Donovan has no idea how many of these men he's taken on and trained for the Panama shifters."

"Like Jeremiah. That's why you were concerned he was a plant."

"How do you know he isn't?"

Gorya knew, but he didn't know how to explain to her his gut reaction to traitors. He lifted the gauze from the wound. She was still bleeding. He wanted to snarl at the doctor. Why was it taking so damn long?

"I know he isn't, baby, but I'll make certain you know it too before we're finished. I'll want to see this tree of yours. Drake is going to have to be protected. He's leader of the lair in New Orleans. If he has three traitors in his lair and doesn't know it, it's imperative we warn him immediately. But you have to be absolutely certain."

"I've got proof." Her lashes fluttered. "I'm feeling sick. So is Wraith."

"Doc is on his way, Maya. Gedeon just texted. He's about four minutes out. Try to rest."

"Don't leave me alone with him." Her eyes closed, but her fingers crushed the sheets in her fists.

"I won't."

"And I need my weapons close."

"They'll be right where you can reach them, but Rogue and I won't leave your side. I've given you my word, Maya. We're in this together. The two of us."

"I let them see me, Gorya. No one has ever seen what I'm capable of."

Her voice was a soft murmur, but there was alarm in it. She knew she was gifted, and she would be hunted if others knew about those gifts.

"I will protect you with my life." It was a vow.

10

DRAKE Donovan was young to be head of an international security company. His name alone commanded respect throughout the world of shifters and humans alike. Along with running a huge security company responsible for bringing home kidnap victims from all parts of the world, he was leader of the lair in New Orleans.

Donovan was built like a shifter, with ropes of powerful muscles, chest dense and muscular, shoulders wide. His hair was thick and blond, and his facial features were carved in strong lines. He had the fluid movements of the leopard and wore the mantle of authority easily. Drake wasn't a man to lead by throwing his weight around. He was quiet, but when he spoke, he did so in a way that had everyone listening to him—even Gorya.

They sat around the large conference table with Donovan and Jake Bannaconni, a shifter businessman with shrewd gold eyes with flecks of green that could take over quickly if he became angry. He was a billionaire and brilliant in everything he did, especially finding oil and taking apart companies and putting them back together. The two men were accompanied by Jeremiah Wheating.

Gorya greeted the newcomers. "Thanks for coming on such short notice. I realize my message must have sounded cryptic, but I couldn't take any chances. I have disturbing news and I couldn't take chances it would get out. I know this room is secure and those in it are one hundred percent loyal to Drake and his cause."

Maya sat in the shadows in the corner of the room, her smaller figure nearly disappearing, but he knew the men were acutely aware of her. They were respectful. Gorya hadn't drawn attention to her, so other than glancing her way once, the men didn't comment or look again, waiting until he introduced her. He was grateful for that sign of respect. She would always be uncomfortable around other men, although she didn't show it.

Timur had positioned himself in front of her, partially blocking the others' view of her. He wanted to point that out to her, but didn't, hoping she would see it on her own and realize his cousin was taking his screwup seriously. He regarded her as family now and was determined to make amends. It was hard not to admire Timur. The life he'd led had shaped him into a very protective, dominant alpha, but when he made mistakes, he owned them.

"My woman has been tracking criminals for quite some time, and her investigations have run into ours. She has uncovered far more than we have, including traitors in our lairs. Jeremiah, you were invited to this meeting for a specific reason, but I'm going to give you a warning, and I need you to listen carefully. While we know and trust you, she doesn't. She has had to conceal her identity her entire life. My family is one of the worst offenders, but the fact that you come from Panama condemns you as well. She will have to determine for herself that you are no threat to her. If you are asked questions, answer honestly and without your usual attempt at charm or sarcasm. If, for any reason, and that includes being disrespectful to her, I have to tell you to leave, you will no longer be included in this circle and will not be privileged to any information. Is that understood?" Gorya willed the man to understand he meant what he said.

Jeremiah nodded. "Of course."

"She saved my life three days ago, but unfortunately was wounded and is recovering from an infection. We would have waited longer, as her leopard is also coming into her first heat and is unpredictable, so it isn't the best of situations for her. Still, the situation is problematic enough that we thought it best that you be informed as soon as possible."

"We appreciate the complications," Drake said.

Are you ready, baby? You don't have to do this. I can explain it as best I can if you want to duck out. He'd made the offer several times. She was still running a fever on and off, although the antibiotics were doing their job. They were also holding Wraith's heat at bay, which was fortunate, because shifting would hurt like hell with that laceration. In fact, it could open it all over again. Leopards healed quickly, but three days was asking quite a bit.

I have to get used to working with your people sometime.

That was true. He would have to get used to sharing her. If he was being honest with himself, he didn't like the idea. He was that selfish. He wanted her all to himself. She'd slept most of the last three days, and he'd slept next to her, something he'd never done in his life before with another person. He hadn't thought he'd be able to do it, yet he'd fallen asleep, and it felt right. Much to her astonishment, Maya had slept as well.

"Drake, she has worked for your company using the name Teona Kyva. She also has done research for others connected to our project, as well as the research she was doing on her own, looking for leads she needed."

Drake turned his head for the first time to pierce the shadows where Maya sat very still. "Teona Kyva? She happens to be the best researcher of anyone we've ever hired. Not once has she let us down. What a crazy and fortunate coincidence that she turned out to be your woman, Gorya."

"And that you found her," Jake added.

Neither sounded as if they doubted her in any way. That was a relief to Gorya.

"Teona, you have no idea how many times you've helped us rescue kidnap victims. You've saved countless lives," Drake said. "That talent you have is beyond anything I've ever seen, and I've come to rely on it. I try to convey to you each time our mission is successful so you realize what you do is truly valuable."

"I've always appreciated that you let me know lives were saved," Maya answered. "That's part of the reason it was important to push this meeting forward as quickly as possible."

She emerged from the shadows, and as always, Gorya was taken with how completely innocent and young she appeared. Even knowing she was wounded and undergoing treatment for an infection, she looked pale but perfectly composed and serene. He knew what it cost her to face those seated at the conference table, but looking at her, nerves didn't show at all. She appeared completely at ease.

She smiled at Drake as she moved around the table with the fluid ease of a leopard, coming to a halt near Jeremiah's chair. She was just to the right of him, at an angle, where Gorya knew a swipe of blade could cut Jeremiah's throat. He had no idea he was in peril, but Timur did. His cousin froze, but to his credit didn't protest or make a sound.

No one else seemed to realize Gorya's woman was a threat at all. He couldn't blame them. She had perfected her role as a deceiver, the girl next door, an introvert, shy and reclusive, with a gift for tracking criminals with her computer. It would never occur to them that she took her work a step further and assassinated the criminals she hunted.

"Jeremiah, your family comes from Panama. Would you mind telling me the lair you belong to?"

Such an innocent question. Gorya heard that mild note in her tone as if it were a casual inquiry, not mattering in the least, but he felt the stillness in her. That waiting.

"My father, very early on, disliked the direction of the lair and he took our family away from the others. We were all very young. He wanted us, especially my sisters, to stay away from the other shifters. I thought that was short-sighted of him. They would need mates."

"I suppose you told him that," Gorya said with a little sigh.

"Yes," Jeremiah admitted. "More than once." He rubbed his ear, a faint smile on his face. "He cuffed me a few times, but my mom and sisters protested. He said they babied me."

"What happened to him?"

"He didn't come home one night, and my mother and I went looking for him the next morning." Jeremiah's voice was devoid of all emotion, but Gorya could feel the sorrow in him. "We tracked him through the forest and came to a spot where there had been a terrible fight. I could see where he'd attacked three men who had trapped a woman. That was like him. He stood up for others."

That explained a lot about Jeremiah. Early in his life he'd seen his father stand up for others he didn't believe could defend themselves. Gorya could see what an impression that had made on the boy, whether Jeremiah knew it or not.

"He'd killed two of them, but they had torn him to

pieces. He was dead before we got there. The woman was dead, and the third man was gone. I wanted to track him, but my mother wouldn't let me. I was only eleven. He was a shifter, and wounded. She said it would be suicide and she was probably right. We burned the bodies and buried the ashes. My mother contacted a local tribe, who packed us up, and we left that night. We relocated completely to the other side of the jungle. The tribe made certain there was no trace of us left behind."

To Gorya's relief, Maya moved away from Jeremiah, back toward the shadows, although she didn't make her retreat noticeable. She simply eased toward Gorya as if to stand behind his chair. As she approached him, he wrapped his arm around her waist.

Are you satisfied he's clean?

Yes. I could feel his sorrow. He has nothing at all to do with the shifters in Panama.

Timur was concerned you were going to cut Jeremiah's throat. Gorya couldn't keep the amusement from his mind.

I was aware. I like that he's protective of Jeremiah. And of you, she added. *I like him for that.*

Gorya tightened his arm around her, careful of the wound. *You should probably sit down.*

Sitting hurts more. When I stand, it feels better. I'm still weak, but getting stronger. This needs to be said.

"Where is your mother now? You said you have sisters?" Gorya was concerned for Jeremiah's family.

"I sent them money at first, but after what I discovered had been going on in Panama, I was uneasy with my mother and sisters being alone, so I asked my mother to relocate to Borneo. It took some persuasion, but she finally did. A few of Drake's men helped her." He flashed a grin. "I keep trying to talk her into coming here."

"I hope she does come," Maya said, surprising Gorya. "Family is a good thing. Drake, you've been very patient.

You must be wondering why Gorya asked you to drop everything to come here."

Drake nodded. "I knew he wouldn't ask me if it weren't important, and finding out that you were involved has added to the mystery."

"I'll start from the beginning so you kind of get the entire picture. I was tracking a man by the name of Albert Krylov."

Timur's head lifted immediately. He spun around in his chair to look at Gorya. "He grew up with us. His father was one of the worst and beat the shit out of him all the time. By the time he was a teen, he was nearly as bad as his father."

Maya nodded. "He made quite a name for himself with his ability to kidnap women and children and get their cooperation for the whorehouses they were sent to. Eventually, he moved up the ladder and began to branch out of Russia to teach some of the other lairs how to handle the product more efficiently. It wasn't just about the women and children; it was about the customers and how they could pull them in deeper as well. He was extremely good at his job."

Ordinarily I would have simply killed him, but I realized he would lead me to others even higher up the food chain. It was then I knew he wasn't alone. He wasn't the top dog.

Gorya rubbed her neck, easing the tension out of her. He understood the parties her friends had been taken to now. The women had been considered expendable. Albert Krylov was luring insanely wealthy customers to commit more and more depraved acts in order to ensnare them further in his world. Apparently, he was quite brilliant at his job.

I don't know how you managed to keep from killing him.

It wasn't easy, she admitted. *But I wanted to know who he answered to.*

"I was in Houston when I encountered Krylov. In Houston he spoke with several men who worked on the docks, which isn't surprising. When you bring in new women and children, you must have someone to receive them. Freighters come in. Planes. So airstrips as well. That's why this place is so perfect. It's remote and has both, and it's central. Houston is a regular hub."

"Were you able to get any of the names there?" Jake asked.

"Of course. I followed Krylov. He met with two men from the Anwar family at a café and again on the docks at around three in the morning. Enrico and Samuele Anwar. Both are shifters. I'm certain you're aware the Anwar family has held the territory in Houston for generations."

The men surrounding the table exchanged shocked looks. "Are you sure of this information, Maya? The Anwars gave up the port to the Carusos some years ago," Drake said. "Marzio Caruso and his family came from Florida to Houston and negotiated with Bartolo for the ports. They came to some sort of understanding. There was no bloodshed, and they've gotten along as allies. Everyone was shocked; they've never so much as had a fight between their crews. We suspected the Caruso family, especially with them having roots in Florida."

"Florida has connections to the Amurovs," Timur added. "We suspected the Caruso family had been dealing with Krylov's older brother, Artur, but couldn't catch them at it."

"I even went through their books," Jake said. "But I got nowhere."

"Bartolo Anwar set up the Carusos to take the fall if anyone ever finds out what is going on at the docks. They know. They're controlling the trafficking, not the Caruso family. The Anwars have been eager to have Giacenta marry one of the Caruso brothers," Maya continued. "She's been seeing the youngest, Cristo. He's the most susceptible."

"I've heard Giacenta is very sickly and her brothers and father guard her carefully," Drake said.

Maya shook her head. "Giacenta is every bit the shark her brothers and father are. She isn't sickly in the least, although she puts on a great performance. She's been after Cristo for some time, acting as if her leopard is rising."

"She can't fake a female leopard going into heat," Drake pointed out.

"She can if she has the right connections," Maya told him. "And she just happens to have them in New Orleans. I followed Krylov from Houston to New Orleans. He met with three men there. One by the name of Armande Mercier was very much in charge. He's running the operations out of New Orleans."

"Mercier?" Again, Drake reacted, turning toward Timur and then Gedeon. He swore under his breath. "Charisse, his sister, phoned and asked to see me as I was boarding the plane to come here. She said it was urgent, that she had to talk to me confidentially. I told her I was out of town but would meet her as soon as I returned. She sounded extremely upset. She told me she was going to a convent for a long retreat and would be emailing me important documents I needed to see. They would be self-explanatory."

Drake's eyes met Maya's. "Is she a client of yours?"

Maya sighed. "I don't ordinarily talk about my clients."

"Charisse came to you and asked you to investigate her brother, Armande," Drake stated. "That must have been the most difficult thing she'd ever done in her life. Her mother was a proven serial killer. She is extremely close to her brother. He handles the business end of their very lucrative worldwide perfume industry. Charisse is the master. Without her, there would be no products. She's very different, but as honest as they come. I can't imagine what this will do to her."

"You aren't as shocked as I thought you'd be," Gorya said.

"I've had my suspicions about Armande," Drake admitted. "Like Charisse, he's a genius, there's no doubt about it. He's pulled some shady things in the past but has always come up with excuses. I never quite bought them. Like his mother, he seemed to have a very twisted side to him. Because the Merciers are eccentric, everyone around them excused him."

Drake pulled his phone out. "Give me a minute. Let me access the file Charisse sent to me. I want to know what she had to say."

I'm grateful he isn't asking me to tell everyone what I said to Charisse, even though I'm essentially giving them the same information. I don't want to feel as if I'm betraying her. She's had enough betrayals, and I know what that's like.

Gorya tightened his arm around her and continued to massage the nape of her neck with strong fingers, trying to find a way to soothe her. She appeared serene and at ease, but he saw into her, and she was anything but. A part of him found the intimacy of being the only person to know the real woman both sexy and exciting.

"Charisse became suspicious when her brother began asking too many questions about a hybrid plant she had been working on that could nearly reproduce the scent of a female leopard in heat. The plant had gotten out of the greenhouse somehow. Any male leopard getting near the flowers was instantly ready to fight. She ordered the plant to be found and eradicated. When she realized the perfume she'd been trying to create simulated the scent of a female leopard in heat, she scrapped that project. Armande didn't want her to stop working on the perfume. They argued about it. He had never taken an interest in any of the perfumes before. He'd gotten very angry and had demanded to know the composition."

Drake looked around the table. "That would explain Giacenta possibly tricking Cristo into thinking her leopard is going into heat."

"Could Armande produce the perfume without Charisse's help?" Jake asked.

"No, but according to her letter to me, she was destroying the batches she had been experimenting with when he came in and tried to physically stop her. He even shoved her to the floor. Of course, he was very sorry and apologized profusely and helped her up, then proceeded to agree with her that everything should be destroyed. He even helped her get rid of it, but she knew he stole some. She has a nose like few others, and she could smell it on him. That's when she contacted me to ask who was the best investigator I knew. I didn't know why she needed one, but I gave her your contact information." He glanced at Maya.

"She really loves her brother," Meiling said. "This must have crushed her beyond everything. As I understand it, her brother was all she had left."

Drake nodded his agreement. "She relied very heavily on him. She's extremely fragile."

"Yet, when she believed he was betraying the lair, she turned him in to you and didn't let him know," Timur pointed out. "That shows strength and loyalty."

Drake again scrubbed his palm down his face. "Charisse is very complicated. I don't want to lose her. She knows Armande can't survive this." He glanced at Maya as if he needed her to take over.

Gorya's fingers tightened on her shoulder for just a moment, giving her strength. None of them knew the cost to her because she didn't show it.

"Armande is deeply embroiled in human trafficking. I think Charisse found that out herself, and that's when she called me. The hybrid plant she had developed, Lover's Leopard, had somehow escaped the greenhouse and was growing wild. She knew that someone who had access to her greenhouse had to have taken the plant. The Tregres had the plant growing on their land, and then it was found in Fenton's Marsh. Her mother had killed several people in Fenton's Marsh, but there wouldn't have been a reason to transplant the flower to that marsh. I found all of that out easily, along with the fact that the marsh was regularly used for smuggling arms and drugs. Armande was behind that operation."

Drake leaned his forehead into his hand, elbow on the table. "The Tregre brothers were the ones running the drug smuggling. That was proven."

"Armande took it a step further," Maya clarified. "At first, he continued business with the drugs, sending them out with the perfumes and soaps. He managed to establish the original connections and soon had a brisk business going all over the world. That wasn't enough for him. Along came Tonio Escabar Alba, straight from Drake's security. He's highly recommended. He was trained in Borneo by Drake and his men, worked for Jake Banna-conni on his ranch and then asked to be transferred to New Orleans to work with Drake again. Drake sent him to the Merciers when Armande requested a bodyguard."

Drake nodded. "I did that."

"He's the youngest son of Jaoa Escabar Velentez. A woman by the name of Imelda Cortez held a huge territory in Panama and conducted a reign of terror for years," Maya continued. "Her family held it before her. They were killed and the territory vacated until Jaoa Escabar Velen-tez took over with his shifters. He's quite a brilliant man and very patient. He planned carefully and didn't make the mistakes Cortez did. Unlike Cortez, he didn't try to rule those living in the forest; instead, he did his best to befriend them."

Drake looked directly at Maya. "I know quite a bit about Jaoa, but I've only heard positive things about him.

There've been a few rumors about him being friends with various factions in Russia and Florida, but all of us have these rumors surrounding us on occasion."

Maya leaned more of her weight against Gorya. She was hurting. Her body had grown a little warmer.

It's getting time to shut this meeting down. You're getting shaky.

A few more minutes. They've come a long way. Drake is taking a lot of hits right now. I feel bad for him.

Feeling bad for him doesn't mean you have to suffer. You have so much compassion in you, baby. I love that trait, since you make up for my lack of it, but not at the expense of your health. He can read the rest in a report.

"Maya, would you mind telling me who was with Mercier when he met with Krylov?" Drake asked.

"You know Tonio Escabar Alba was."

"Yes, I took him personally under my wing when he first arrived in Borneo from Panama. He didn't have a clue what he was doing. Nothing like training my own enemies." He kept his gaze fixed on Maya.

"The other man was Gaston Mouton. He's local in New Orleans, born and raised."

Drake scrubbed his hand down his face again, swearing under his breath. "So much for me being the wise leader. Gaston might be an ass, but he's never once indicated that he was in any way a traitor and would embrace human trafficking. He seems respectful of the women in the lair."

Maya's fist bunched in Gorya's shirt, down low where the others couldn't see. He felt the slight tremble. She was definitely getting tired. He was going to have to shut this meeting down. She was determined to give Drake and the others the information they needed to be safe, but she'd typed up a thorough report. As far as Gorya was concerned, they could read it.

Babe, I want you to shut this down before you fall down.

Nearly there.

"Gaston isn't alone in this, Drake. His brother, Jules, is as well. You need to be careful. So far, Armande and the others are concentrating on the trafficking and drug pipelines, but if they get wind of what you and Jake are doing, getting the Amurovs to take over territories and wipe out those criminal activities, they'll go after you both."

Drake frowned. "Are you absolutely certain, Maya? Ordinarily I would never question your information, but those two have impeccable reputations. Remy Boudreaux would vouch for them, and he rarely vouches for anyone. Remy is my brother-in-law and a homicide detective. He's very discerning." His gaze fell on Gedeon. "You've met them a time or two."

"They seemed dedicated to their work. They have a small welding shop and fix boats. They were friendly enough." Gedeon shrugged. "I wasn't put off by them."

Maya didn't defend her work. She just waited for Drake to accept her information. Like Gorya, she knew she'd delivered a great deal of very bad news all at once. It was a bitter pill to swallow. She leaned into him further without seeming to be aware of it. Gorya liked that she did it. More than ever, he felt their commitment, even in that room filled with powerful shifters.

Timur broke the silence. "Maya, I know this sounds terrible, but in all honesty, I think you should consider acting as if you've never been around a computer in your life. Aside from those of us in this room, no one else knows who you are. Gorya, if word gets out that she's capable of the kind of research she does, it won't be Drake and Jake on the top of the hit list, it's going to be Maya. Better everyone thinks the way I did when I first met her. Let them all underestimate her and keep her safe."

Instead of looking at Maya or Gorya, Timur looked around the table, and then his fierce, penetrating gaze settled on Jeremiah. "No one must ever find out where this information came from or what was said in this room. Maya is family. Gorya's woman. That means she's protected by every single one of us. Is that understood? It's a killing offense if she's betrayed."

You see why Timur is my brother as well as my cousin? He may be the proverbial bull in the china shop, but he's also an amazing man.

I will agree with you.

Gorya could feel her smile. She didn't change the expression on her face, staying sober on the outside for Drake, keeping her gaze locked with Gorya's, but inside— for him—she smiled intimately.

Jeremiah jerked his head up. "I'm part of this family, Timur. I understood the magnitude of what was being said and how dangerous it was immediately. There is no way I would allow any of this to slip out."

Timur nodded as if Jeremiah's word was enough for him. Gorya wasn't as sure about any of them in the room other than his cousin, mostly because it was Maya's life in jeopardy. He didn't give a damn about his own life. They'd come together to warn Drake and Jake to be more careful. The two were shifters, but they were kept out of the criminal spotlight. No one suspected they had anything to do with helping to place the Amurovs in fallen crime lords' territories or orchestrating the downfall of those crime lords in the first place.

"I believe you're right, Timur," Gorya acknowledged aloud. "I already told Maya it would be best if we kept her abilities known just to us. In all honesty, I would have preferred to keep her out of this and just present a written report from Teona Kyva to you. Maya felt there were too many things you might have a difficult time accepting, and she would need to be on hand to answer questions."

He looked up at her. His woman. It was impossible not to fall deeper and deeper for her. Just the fact that she was not yet fully healed but would put herself out for strangers.

For his people. He knew she did it for him. The cliff was steeper. Higher. And he was free-falling.

Gorya felt another tremble go through Maya's body. *That's it, baby. You're done. I'm taking you out of here.*

She turned fully into him, her eyes blazing frost blue directly into his. Expressive. Telling him things he'd never heard before from anyone else and didn't ever expect to. Her palms framed his face right there in front of everyone. They might have been partially in the shadows, but he knew everyone in the room was a shifter and could see her. She didn't really look directly at the others. She mostly kept her gaze fixed just above their heads or between them. With Gorya, she was always so intimate. Intense.

What is step three?

That threw him. He hadn't been expecting the question. A slow, genuine smile spread through his mind. Lit his eyes. *I have no idea. I hadn't thought that far ahead. I chose the last two. It's your turn. Any ideas?*

I've been giving it some thought. Her fingers stroked around the curve of his jaw, sending little darts of fire through his entire system. *Quite a bit of thought actually.*

What have you come up with? He couldn't believe how hard his heart was pounding.

This. Kissing you in front of your family and friends.

She sounded very decisive. Her eyes continued to look straight into his. Seeing into him.

His heart nearly stopped beating. His lungs couldn't find air. His world narrowed until there was only Maya. *Is that even a possibility?*

I have no idea, but we're about to find out.

While being careful of her wound, he slid his hands down her sides to her hips and dug his fingers possessively into the curves to pull her between his thighs. She didn't even stiffen. She fit there smoothly, as if she was already used to that spot. Close to him. Close to the heat of him.

He nearly forgot there were others in the room. Nearly forgot she was injured. The fragrance of her enveloped him. Seeped in through his pores and wrapped around his soul.

You're sure about this? He kept his tone light. Teasing. Stroking the inside of her mind intimately. She might be certain, but he wasn't. This was a bad, bad idea for so many reasons.

She traced his lower lip with the pad of her finger. *Very sure.*

Timur cleared his throat. "It's getting hot in here." There was a trace of amusement in his voice.

Gorya ignored his cousin. The sound registered from a distance, but as if he were underwater, and the words were muffled and distorted. Sweat trickled down his chest. What had gotten into her? She was so skittish in public. They were surrounded by shifters. The doors to the room were closed.

Baby, just wait. I'll kiss you when we get back to the room. He was beginning to panic. He never panicked. He was the smooth one. The charming one. Always in control. Why the hell was he on the verge of picking her up in his arms and making a run for it?

What's wrong, honey? Tell me? It's just us. No one else.

Her lips moved against his, feather light. A breath. His entire body reacted. He was so lost. What would he do without her? He hadn't known he could fall so hard so fast. It wasn't supposed to happen like that. He couldn't lose her. He *couldn't.* Maya believed she was fully committed—and she was. But she was always on the verge of flight. She was terrified she couldn't measure up. She couldn't meet his needs. He had to control the pace. He couldn't make a single mistake. This could turn into a disaster very quickly, and he wasn't about to lose her because he hadn't controlled the situation.

*I'm not taking the chance that you're not ready, Maya.
I can't lose you.* Her fingers stroking his jaws were sending little flairs of heat rolling through his body.

You aren't going to lose me. These are steps, remember. We might not be perfect each time. We might not even make it through this the first time. If it doesn't work, you can just carry me out of here, and we'll end up laughing about it. That's how we roll together, right?

In love. That sucked. He hadn't thought he would ever feel that for anyone. *I didn't know I was capable, Maya.*

The briefest of hesitations. *I didn't know either.*

Her lips skimmed his. Burned like the hottest flame. Her entire body trembled so badly he was afraid she would fall. He slid his arm around her back and locked the other behind her knees.

Already? Just like that, all panic was gone and he was once more fully in control. There was amusement in his voice. Teasing her. *You can't panic when we haven't even kissed, and it was your idea.* He swung her into his arms and stood, cradling her against his chest.

I don't care about them. It isn't the kissing. Kissing in front of them is step three. Declarations are like step fifty or something. Definitely fifty. She wrapped her arms around his neck and pulled her head back to look directly into his eyes, a silvery circle around the blue accusing him. *You took us* way *beyond step three.*

"I'm taking my woman back to our room and giving her more antibiotics. The doc wants her resting. As soon as I have her settled, I'll be back. Gedeon will get you whatever you need, and you can finish reading the report."

Gorya didn't look away from Maya as he opened the door and took her inside. "You didn't have to tell me how you felt back there. I made the declaration, but you could have waited."

She scowled at him. "I'm no coward. We promised each other we'd tell the truth. If you're going to put yourself out there, then I have to do the same. And you were all wimpy and whiny, so I had to show you how to be courageous."

"Wimpy? Whiny? If you weren't injured, I'd toss you onto the bed and show you who's wimpy."

For the first time ever, a true giggle escaped. The sound of it lit up his soul. She was changing him. She *had* changed him already. He thought of her from the moment he woke in the morning. He viewed life differently. He could look at the landscapes around him and actually see the beauty. More importantly, he recognized that he was beginning to care for those around him. She had done that. Maya.

Whether it was because Rogue no longer wanted to kill everything and everyone or because the rage in the leopard had subsided thanks to finding his mate, Gorya didn't know, but the animal no longer raked and clawed at him night and day with vicious cruelty. The cat didn't suffer anymore like he had before. He was calm and patient, waiting for his mate to rise.

Both leopards were aware of Maya's fears and her injury, and Wraith was doing her best to suppress her heat to give her partner time to heal and get used to Gorya. He admired the female leopard for her enduring strength. He found that same strength in Maya.

He carried Maya into the primary bath. "Get ready for bed, woman. You must be hurting like hell. And stop hiding that from me."

"You sound so commanding. I might swoon like all the women Ashe was telling me about if you keep it up." She fanned herself as she batted her eyelashes at him.

Her little laugh played over his skin in a sensuous melody. Unable to resist, he bent his head and took her mouth. There was nothing playful about his kiss. It might have started out gentle, but suddenly everything changed. The dominance in him welled up and took over. He poured himself into her, claiming her. Branding her. Loving her. Possessing her. Giving himself to her. He wasn't gentle in the way he knew he should be, but he couldn't hold back no matter what his brain told him. The roaring overcame all good sense, and instinct took over.

Maya's body melted into his chest, pliant, boneless. All his. She gave herself to him. Surrendered everything. He tasted love, whether she meant to give that to him or not. It wasn't just her heart being offered. Or her soul. She didn't realize what she was offering into his keeping. She was trusting him with her body. She just didn't realize the enormity of her trust yet. Their relationship was so fragile. So intimate.

He lifted his head reluctantly, slowly, rubbing his lips against hers and then kissing his way over her delicate nose and back to the corners of her mouth.

She looked up at him, her eyes wide with shock, her trembling fingers over her lips. Her breath came in ragged gasps. When she could manage, she chastised him. "Gorya. We have to stop skipping steps. That was definitely *way* beyond steps three and four. Not as far as fifty, but certainly ten or eleven. Or fifteen. You're leapfrogging."

"I refuse to take responsibility for that."

He set her feet on the floor, mostly because he was nearly as unstable as she was.

She gave him a fierce scowl, but there was that little hint of humor he really loved. It both steadied and reassured him every time.

"You seem to duck responsibility for any of these steps."

"You started it." He pulled her shirt over her head to get her moving. She had grown even paler. "I'm beginning to think Wraith is getting out of hand. I'm not sure which of you is worse."

She raised an eyebrow. "She's being good."

He couldn't help laughing. "You walked into that one,

coming to immediate defense of your leopard. That means you're the naughty one." He laid his palm across her forehead. "And don't you dare run a fever again."

Her laughter erupted, just like he knew it would. "How am I supposed to control that?"

He wanted to kiss her again. Instead, he inspected the wound. It was healing, but still looked a little nasty to him. Any wound on her was sacrilegious as far as he was concerned. The doctor had assured him the infection had subsided. If Wraith could manage to wait a couple more days, they would be okay.

Gorya studied her as she got ready for bed. She tried to cover up the fact that she was hurting, but he could see it. Not only did he watch her every move; he was also in her mind. He had Rogue and Wraith watching her as well. She didn't realize how valued she was by all of them.

She had been so careful to protect Wraith as well as Gorya and Rogue. The only one she hadn't protected was herself.

"Stop persisting in thinking I'm so nice." She laid her palm against his jaw as she leaned against the sink. Her long lashes feathered down. "If I wasn't so tired, I'd argue with you and point out that I nearly killed your cousin just for touching me."

"But you didn't. He was being an ass and he deserved it, but you didn't." Gorya once more cradled her against his chest, carrying her into the bedroom. Placing her carefully on the bed, he found he couldn't just leave her. He should go back to his guests, but instead, he curled his body protectively around hers and snapped off the lights. "Go to sleep."

"What are you doing?" She didn't open her eyes, but she smiled, her hand reaching for his.

He threaded his fingers through hers. "What I do most nights. Watching you. It's my favorite pastime."

"That's creepy. And kind of weird."

He brought their joined hands to his lips. "I *am* creepy and kind of weird. Haven't you figured that out yet?"

Her voice dropped to a mere thread of sound. So low that had he not been leopard, he wouldn't have heard. "I think you're the most beautiful, amazing man in the world. I'm the luckiest woman in the world because you're mine."

11

MAYA woke with her body on fire. Every nerve ending. Every single cell. The fierce burning between her legs was pure hell. Alarm spread through her. Instantly she was aware of Gorya's male body wrapped tightly around her. Pure muscle. She couldn't stop moving. Writhing. An erotic slide over the sheets, her body gliding sensuously against his no matter how much her brain screamed at her to stop.

"I can't stop it. I can't make it stop." She tried rolling away from him before she did something unimaginable, like lick up from his belly to his chest. She couldn't have sex. She couldn't. She couldn't lead him on. That would be the worst. She wouldn't do that to him. He was so good to her. He'd been so patient.

I'm sorry. I'm sorry. Wraith was distressed, calling out to her. *I tried as hard as I could. I can't stop it, Maya. I'm so sorry.*

It wasn't her leopard's fault. Maya detested that she made her leopard feel ashamed of what should be a wonderful, exciting time for her. Ordinarily, a female shifter didn't even know if she had a leopard until her reproductive cycle and the leopard's lined up together. If they did, the leopard would rise to the surface and eventually emerge fully. She could then be claimed by her mate.

It took extraordinary circumstances for a female leopard to ever show herself prior to that occasion. To save Maya's sanity, Wraith had revealed herself to her human counterpart and later emerged when Maya was a child. The leopard had always been there for her. She detested that she was letting her down this way.

You've done nothing wrong, Wraith. You're supposed to rise. Don't try to suppress your nature. I'm the one that's sorry.

She was. She couldn't cope with even the thought of sex, let alone feelings this violent. Her body was completely out of control. No matter how hard she tried to overcome the screaming in her head or sudden terrible vision of her childhood memories, her body continued to crave the man lying beside her.

There was no way to stop the flames coming in waves, rolling through her veins and burning low. She couldn't stop moving along the sheets. She hadn't known material could inflame her further, but the friction against her nipples felt like electricity sparking.

No matter how much she might want to have sex with Gorya, no matter how much she wanted to do the right thing for her leopard, she knew she would fail them. The screams in her head grew louder right along with the vicious images from her childhood.

"I can't. I can't. I want to. But I can't." She could barely get the words out. Her voice was no more than a thread of sound, vibrating with shame and horror and even reflecting terror.

How was she going to repay her beautiful, wonderful leopard for everything she'd done? She would kill her. She would probably kill Gorya and Rogue. All because she was a coward. A sniveling, horrid, weak, worthless woman. How could Gorya stand being close to her? He must loathe her. This strong, powerful, *beautiful* man had aligned himself with her. Put his faith in her. Trusted her with the life of his leopard.

Her body burned hotter than ever. She cried out, reaching for Gorya, calling his name, her only salvation when she was so terrified. She was condemning them all to death when they deserved so much. Deep inside, just like always, she heard herself screaming. Silent tears were locked away because it wasn't safe to let go. It would never be safe. If she broke apart, she could never be put back together. Never. She couldn't trust herself to do the right thing for any of them. Utter chaos reigned in her head and roared through her body. The darkest, ugliest, most brutal memories began to surface in spite of every attempt to suppress them.

"Maya. Be calm. We knew this was going to happen," Gorya soothed. Steady. He rose above her. Bare-chested. So perfect. All muscle. That glorious male body right there for the taking. Any other woman, any shifter, would have been beyond happy to have him as a partner. But her . . . She didn't deserve him. She didn't deserve Rogue. And she really, really didn't deserve Wraith.

He touched her with exquisite tenderness. Gathering her close despite how she stiffened and tried to pull away from him. "I've got you, baby. I'll always have you. I promised you I would. I'll see you through this."

His palm caressed the side of her face. "You keep looking inward. Don't do that, Maya. Look only at me. See me. Trust in me. Know who you're with. You're with me. You'll always be safe with me."

Maya shook her head. "You don't understand, Gorya."

Her voice wasn't her own. She couldn't look at him. Couldn't meet his eyes. She was too ashamed.

"You have your eyes closed, little love. Open your eyes and look into mine."

His hands. Oh, God. His hands. So gentle. No one had ever touched her the way he did. She tried to feel just that. His hands. Not her body. Not the fire roaring through her veins. She wanted to hear only his voice. Gorya. No one else. Not that taunting laughter. Not those memories slithering like evil snakes into her mind to taunt her and tear her apart. To make her into nothing all over again. Gorya had made her believe that she might be able to live life with him. To give Wraith everything she deserved. Now she knew it was impossible. She was so worthless. Too far gone.

She had to tell him. Make him see. She whispered the truth to him. "I can't save us. I want to. I want to be everything for you. For her. For Wraith. For Rogue. But I can't. I can't do it. I can't stop this. What's happening to her. To me. I'm tempting you, but that's all it is."

The tears hurt, but she couldn't shed them. They burned behind her eyes. They burned the way her body did, the well inside like a volcano so close to erupting she feared she would die in the inferno. The ice surrounding her soul couldn't crumble or she would disintegrate. Implode.

She felt Gorya's body sliding against hers, sending what felt like lightning strikes throughout her veins as he slowly, with great caution, sat up.

"I'm going to pick you up and put you in my lap, baby. Don't panic on me."

She was already panicking. Just the thought of him wrapping his arms around her and setting her bottom over his inflamed cock panicked her. The caring in his voice panicked her. The thought of him holding her against his bare chest sent her into a frenzy of fear. "You can't. Gorya, get out of the house. Save yourself."

The moment he left she would somehow find the courage to take her life. To free him from the claim Rogue and Wraith had bound him to. Her body shuddered repeatedly in an effort to contain the emotions that were as out of control as the rest of her.

Gorya murmured to her soothingly as his hands cradled her as if she were a child, not a sensual woman writhing erotically, enticingly, against his hot skin. He ignored her struggles and protests and held her tight against his chest, his arms protective, not in the least reacting to the way his own body was as inflamed as hers. He settled her on his lap and locked one arm around her while one large hand cupped her chin to lift it when she tried to hide.

"Look at me, my love. Open your eyes and look into mine."

His voice. That voice. So gentle. So caring. It pierced the ice, sending so many cracks spreading across the glacier, threatening her even more. "I can't."

"You can because I asked you, and you always do what I ask you," he reminded her. "You trust me, Maya. You trust only me the way I do you. We get through things together. You don't see the way out, but that's what you have me for—to lead you through the labyrinth when you can't see the path."

She clutched at his wrist. Gorya. He didn't seem to pay the least attention to the heat of her feminine body writhing continuously against his masculine one. She could feel his thick, hot cock against her buttocks, but he didn't move, not even to rub himself against her. Instead, he held her tight, comforting her. Protecting her.

Just the feel of his palm cupping her chin and then the way his knuckles skimmed her lips sent a shiver of painful awareness streaming through her. Maya forced her wet lashes to lift slowly. She didn't want to, but this was Gorya. She caught a glimpse just before he opened his hand. The leopard tattoo was there. The one from her childhood. The safety and beauty of that savage, feral leopard that spread across his fingers just below his knuckles. The sight of it shook her. The cracks in the glacier widened. Deepened. Her heart accelerated, beat far too fast. Her lungs squeezed down, driving the air from her so that she couldn't find a way to breathe properly.

Her lashes fluttered, and she lifted them all the way in total panic, her gaze meeting his. Clinging. Expecting to see loathing. Disgust. Or pure lust. What she saw was Gorya. *Her* Gorya. His stunning frost-gray eyes holding sheer love. *Love.* She knew it was love. She felt it burning through the heat of Han Vol Dan. Through the sickening memories of her past. Through her own inadequacies and self-loathing. He was there. Her rock. Her partner. He'd said to trust him. That she could count on him. That Wraith could count on him. A small part of her hadn't believed.

It felt as if her entire chest split apart. Her heart and soul shattered, broke into millions of pieces, just as she always feared they would if the ice inside her ever cracked. Tears poured down her face. Once the storm broke, she couldn't stop that either. The sound of her sobs was horrific even to her own ears. Not at all Maya. Raw. Unrestrained.

Gorya simply held her tighter, his arms and body surrounding her with a tower of strength, a fortress no one could penetrate. It didn't seem to matter that she was completely falling apart. She didn't understand how he could have fallen in love with her when she had so many flaws, but she felt the emotion surrounding her the way she did the security of his body.

After a few minutes of wild crying, some of the things he whispered into her mind began to slip past the wild emotion raging in her.

That's right, little love, share with me. All of it. We promised to be there for each other. When I need you, you stand for me. When you need me, I'll always be here. That's what we said, and we both meant it.

It wasn't so much that black-velvet voice smoothing the dark edges of pain spreading through her mind, it was the very essence of Gorya's strength filling the jagged, empty cracks her ugly past had created. He didn't flinch away from her memories, not one, but then she'd never flinched away from his. She'd accepted everything about him— everything she'd ever glimpsed in his mind.

Why would you think I could ever think less of you? You are courageous and strong. You saw my past, every bit as brutal and ugly as yours, and gave me unconditional acceptance.

His fingers moved on her scalp, a soothing, loving touch she couldn't help realizing held nothing but care. There was no doubt he felt passion for her or the terrible fire of the Han Vol Dan. It didn't seem to matter to him. He stayed in control. She had no idea how he managed when she had heard it was impossible for the female or male shifter to control their leopards' brutal sexual needs, but although Gorya was as hard as she'd ever felt him, he made no move to take advantage of her despite the way her body moved over his.

He rocked her gently, murmuring comfortingly to her, occasionally brushing kisses into the thick mass of her hair at the top of her scalp, waiting patiently for her to calm. Eventually the tearing sobs were reduced to ragged whimpers and then hiccups as she managed to slowly regain a semblance of control.

He brought a handkerchief to her face and dabbed away the worst of the catastrophe. She had no idea how long she'd been crying, but her head was pounding, and her nose was running. She took the white square of cloth from him and blew her nose, certain she was a hot mess. That didn't seem to matter to him in the least.

Gorya tipped her face up to his, kissed her wet eyes and then the tip of her nose before making his way to the corners of her mouth. "Did you really think I would ever let you go now that I've found you, Maya? I would never survive without you. Never."

"But Gorya." She tried her best to explain to him. He didn't seem to understand the problem. He kept looking at her as if she was his world. "No matter how much I love you, and I do, I can't do this. I want to, I want to. For you. For Wraith and Rogue, but I'm not ready for a physical relationship. It's too soon. I'll lose my mind."

He framed her face with his palms, his eyes holding her captive with that same look of complete love. "I know you're not ready. This isn't the way I want our first time to be. It should be *our* time together. You and me. Making love. Not a crazy leopard's heat. That's Rogue and Wraith. Their time. This is for them."

"But my body is on fire." She had to protest, to point out the obvious. She couldn't keep the despair from her voice or her mind where he could feel and hear it. It wasn't that she didn't trust him. How could she not? She did love him, but he wasn't making sense. This was a shifter's inevitable nature. Neither of them could stop it. "Your body is just as inflamed as mine. I can feel how much you need me."

"I've always had discipline and control, Maya. It has only grown stronger over the years. I realized I was born to be your partner, and that discipline was needed for this very reason. I have no doubt about it."

She could tell he wanted to assure her as his thumb slid gently over her lower lip. Gorya's voice was absolutely calm. His mind was penetrating the utter chaos of hers and helping to steady her further. She still couldn't think as clearly as she would have liked. She couldn't find solutions, and yet he seemed to feel there were answers for their very major problem.

Her eyes searched his. "You know this is Wraith's first real awakening in her heat. She'll rise with even more heat at least once or twice more before she's completely ready."

He nodded, a faint smile curving his mouth.

He wasn't getting it. She rubbed at the darker bristles along his jaw. "Each time will be worse than this one."

"I'm well aware, Maya. And prepared. I've come up with a plan."

Her eyelashes fluttered. She could so easily let herself get caught up in his illusions, but then if she did, how could she save him? Save Rogue? Or even Wraith? "I love every single thing you've said to me, Gorya. I know it's all true. You're the strongest man I know. But you can't overcome nature. No one can. It's impossible."

Again he dipped his head and brushed kisses over her mouth as if he found her irresistible. "Nothing is impossible when it's the two of us. We were born with gifts, Maya. We are lucky that way. Amazing, astounding gifts, but we weren't the only ones."

He nuzzled the top of her head. "I've had quite a lot of time to think about things while you've been recovering from this wound. We aren't alone in this relationship. It's new to us, and neither of us has any idea what we're doing, but it's ours and we have the trust we decided to give to each other. What we both left out, or at least I did, was that there are four of us here, not just two. Rogue and Wraith are of equal importance."

She leaned out away from him to look at him once more. This time, much of the despair was gone, replaced by interest. She wasn't certain where he was going with this, but he was right, she hadn't thought about including the leopards other than that they needed protection. What was Gorya considering?

"The two of them have been with us every step of our

lives, through every phase, no matter how traumatic. Every triumph. Every kill. They brought us together when we would never have come together. You would have run, and I would have let you. We were both too broken to believe we had a chance at a life with each other. Rogue and Wraith believed in us."

Maya had to agree with his assessment. She would never have accepted a man's claim on her. She would have suicided if she hadn't believed she could get away—or kill the man attempting to claim her. Wraith had been so certain Rogue and Gorya were right for them. She recognized them to be their past rescuers. Maya was very thankful for Wraith's interference, although she hadn't been at the time.

"Just as we have extraordinary gifts, so do Rogue and Wraith. They're stronger and faster than other leopards. They also have discipline and they're much more intelligent as well. We watched out for them, but all along, they've guarded us. We were never alone, not for a single moment during the times we were so viciously treated."

She couldn't argue with that. Wraith had made herself known when Maya was a little child. The leopard had been her constant companion. They'd worked together to learn how to have her emerge. It hadn't been easy, and it took a great deal of time, but eventually they had been successful.

"I always thought of myself as the strategist," she admitted. "And perhaps the guardian. We both guarded each other. She was quiet and allowed me to talk to her when I was upset."

Gorya smiled at her. "Rogue was a little more vocal. He's never liked anyone, and his solution was usually to kill them."

In spite of the dire situation, Maya found herself wanting to laugh. "That sounds like him—and maybe you. And me. We're such a combination."

"We are." Gorya brushed more kisses over her mouth. "We're lucky that Wraith has emerged before the Han Vol Dan. Few females have ever done so. That will give you relief. Both of us, in fact. Wraith and Rogue will go into the swamp and run. She'll be seductive and lead him on a terrible chase."

Maya gasped, pulling back so she could stare into his eyes. "No, there's a reason a female leopard won't emerge until she's ready to mate. She isn't ready. She'll be calling every male within miles and marking everything with her scent. She'll entice him and tempt him and tease him and then very cruelly rebuff him. She's very small, Gorya, and he's larger and stronger. He could really hurt her if he got upset with her."

"He's prepared for her behavior."

"She'll call to other males," she reminded him, feeling desperate. Her heart accelerated so fast that her chest hurt. She was afraid for Wraith.

"I've sent them away."

I would never hurt Wraith, Rogue unexpectedly assured Maya directly. *I am fully aware nature will drive her. I will watch over her and protect her until this time passes for you both.*

"I'm going to carry you to the window where the tree branch dips low, Maya. You're going to shift, allowing Wraith to emerge," Gorya decreed.

She wound her arms around his neck, pressing her body tightly against his. "If you sent all the males away, you have no security. It's too important to have guards around you, Gorya. You know you're a target. I know you're trying to protect me, but you can't forget the people in this lair want you dead."

"We can handle them if they come after us," he assured her with complete confidence. "I appreciate that you think you need to guard all of us, Maya, but for now, let the three of us watch over you."

Gorya lifted her, standing smoothly, as if the leopard's heat didn't affect him in the least. She wrapped her legs around his waist as he carried her over to the window. She rested her head against his shoulder, her heart soaring.

Wraith, are you certain you want to do this? Rogue? This won't be easy.

It was such a sacrifice. She was supposed to take care of them, not the other way around, yet the three of them, Gorya, Rogue and Wraith, had come together to protect her. No one had done such a thing in her entire life— except when Gorya and Rogue had when she was a child. Tears burned behind her eyes, but this time it was from sheer happiness. She did have a family. She did have a partner. Three partners.

I love you so much, Gorya. All of you, she amended.

Gorya reached around her to shove open the window while setting her on the windowsill. He kissed her quite thoroughly.

I love you too. Let Wraith have fun. Remember, female leopards do this all the time in the wild.

I hope you know what you're doing. It was going to be such a relief to shed her human body and allow her leopard to emerge. The fierce sexual burn was too much, even with Gorya distracting her.

Right there on the windowsill she let go of herself and allowed Wraith full ownership of their form. Wraith easily slid into her long, thick fur. She was small, with her frosty undercoat and wider-spaced rosettes. Her coat was quite beautiful. Brilliant frost-blue eyes shone out of her face. She tossed her head, swished her long tail, leapt from the branch and raced into the underbrush.

Maya felt her joy of freedom. Not just of her freedom, but of her ability to be in the wild and call to other males. To declare she was fit and strong and looking for partners to see her sensual, alluring, very playful self.

She raced over fallen logs and through shallow creeks,

heading away from the house as fast as she could to put as much distance between her and Rogue as possible. She wanted freedom while she could get it. She wanted a real chase. He should have to work to get her. She deserved that much from him.

Maya found herself smiling at Wraith's images and emotions. Hormones wreaked as much havoc in the leopard as they did in the human. Wraith had turned almost entirely into a leopard of the wild, rushing into the swamp to announce her lovely presence to as much of the world as she could with a loud, sawing call and spraying the trees with her scent to entice any male who might be in close proximity.

She splashed through shallow creeks and dashed around two termite hills and then playfully rushed up a slope, marking two more trees before rolling in a thick pile of leaves. She sent them scattering in every direction before she was up and running again along a narrow game trail.

Wraith became aware of the big male coming up slowly behind her. He was silent. Stealthy. He was worthy of her attentions. She made certain to show herself to her best advantage.

Maya found herself sharing her laughter with Gorya at the female's antics. *She's so impossible. What a terrible little hussy she is.*

She felt so different to be out of her human form and allow Wraith to take over. The relief was tremendous. She hoped it felt the same to Gorya.

She is, isn't she? There was amusement in his voice to match hers.

She loved sharing with him. She'd never really had that before. It was the little things others probably took for granted, she decided. Laughing together. Gorya consoling her, holding her when she was terrified of letting the other three down. Feeling safe with him. She'd never had the luxury of feeling safe before. Neither had Wraith. They'd depended on each other, but they lived so carefully and lied so much to everyone, she'd forgotten what telling the truth was until she'd made the pact with Gorya.

The relief on my body is tremendous, Gorya. Thank you for thinking of this. She hesitated but had to know. *I hope you're feeling that same relief.*

I am. It also helps to see how joyful Wraith is with her newfound freedom. She likes running wild.

Maya could honestly say she'd never felt Wraith's happiness the way the leopard was now experiencing the rush of independence and coquettish, kittenish behavior. She deserved to prance around like a wild, free leopard. The cat had been forced from near infancy to be a warrior, a killer, just as Maya had been. They had been shaped into warped killing machines at an early age just to survive. Maya loved feeling Wraith's joy at the new experience of just being able to have freedom to be a leopard.

Thank you, Gorya. I love this for her.

Gorya flooded her mind with such tenderness and love, she would have dissolved into tears all over again if she had her physical body. She couldn't remember being so emotional. All the hormones racing through her. She was putting it down to the unfamiliar leopard's heat—that and the completely unfamiliar feeling of care that another human shared exclusively and seemingly unconditionally with her.

I'd like to take all the credit, but Rogue and Wraith were in on the plan. Rogue and I talked it over, and then he consulted with Wraith. He didn't want her afraid of him if he had to fight off any other males vying for her attention.

Maya would have bitten down hard on her lip if she was able to while she contemplated what Gorya had told her. She turned that information over and over in her mind. It was almost as if Rogue expected to have to fight off other rivals.

I thought you sent the males away. She didn't want Rogue to fight any of the male leopards who worked security for them. Those men were Gorya's friends, or as close to friends as he had. They were men willing to risk their lives for him. In the fury of a battle for a female, Rogue could easily kill one of them.

I sent away our males, baby, he soothed. *Her call is loud. The night is carrying it far. It's possible other leopards will be drawn to her.*

Gorya didn't sound as uneasy as she thought he should be. *Gorya, if other leopards come to fight Rogue, he could be injured.* She had seen the leopard fight. Few, if any, could defeat him, but she didn't want him killing male leopards unless they were enemies.

Rogue is too fast and too skilled. Right now he's a little indignant that you would think he could be injured by another leopard.

You know as well as I do that anything can happen in a fight.

She felt Gorya's amusement. *Rogue appreciates your concern.*

Maya couldn't help but fret. He didn't seem to understand the larger implications of what could happen.

What if they are not our enemies? They could simply be males looking to acquire a female. Wraith is acting like any female leopard in heat. This is really my fault because I couldn't handle the thought of a sexual experience yet. Any death would be my fault.

Stop, Maya. We're past that. Rogue isn't going to kill a rival unless the leopard refuses to submit. Most leopards will unless there is an underlying reason, for instance, if he's a shifter and his human counterpart is refusing to allow it. If that's the case, the shifter is an enemy.

She couldn't argue with the logic. The relief was tremendous. She allowed herself to relax and just enjoy the outing through Wraith's eyes and emotions. Wraith ran and played, rolling through leaves and rubbing along tree trunks, giving her sawing call every few minutes to announce her alluring presence to the world.

She took great delight in knowing Rogue paced along behind her, admiring every step she took. He came close and brushed against her, his large body muscular and fluid. Rogue ran his muzzle along her spine, scent-marking. Claiming. He didn't make the mistake of trying to mount her. He didn't push her in one direction or another. He simply ran with her playfully, allowing her to lead, letting her see his interest and admiration.

Wraith was more coquettish than ever now that she had the exclusive attention of a male in his prime. She rubbed her body along his, playfully throwing dirt and leaves up in the air before running through another shallow creek and over two downed moss-covered trees. She sniffed in disdain at a bellowing alligator and laughed at startling a family of raccoons.

Rogue is taking the heat very well.

He is leopard. He knows how a female will act when she isn't ready for his advances. She would rebuff him if he tried to mount her. He's content to stake his claim.

Rogue not only made certain to cover Wraith in his scent, but he also raked the trees and scent-marked the territory, warning every other male leopard away. Maya was amazed at how playful the giant cat was with Wraith. She would never have guessed he had it in him. It was clear he watched over her, but when Maya allowed herself to connect with the male leopard, she found he was enjoying himself as much as Wraith was.

Just the fact that Rogue was reacting as a leopard in the wild—the same as Wraith—rather than being impatient and having difficulty with her heat lifted the last of Maya's guilt. She still felt shame that she couldn't handle Gorya's needs. And she still worried what would happen the next time Wraith began to feel the mating urges.

Gorya groaned. *You meet every single one of my needs and you always will. You're in such a hurry.*

You were suffering.

So were you. I didn't alleviate your suffering. I could have.

I would have fought you. You know I would have. It would have been horrible. I was too scared.

Baby, I could have talked you into anything.

She wasn't as certain as he was. *I don't know. I was so terrified. I still am.*

The time isn't right. We aren't there yet. You have to trust me implicitly before we make love. And when we come together, I will make love to you, not take you in a leopard's heat.

She liked that he felt that way. *I do trust you. You're the only human being I do trust.*

Not all the way, Maya, but you're getting there.

Didn't she? She felt as if she did. She wanted him. She loved kissing him. But letting him touch her so intimately? She didn't know if she could do that. The idea was both terrifying and, in the back of her mind, arousing. She wanted to be everything for Gorya. Everything to him.

Already, Wraith's heat was subsiding, allowing Maya to think much more clearly. She had instigated kissing him in public, yet he had balked at that, afraid of the repercussions—afraid they were going too fast. In the end, he had declared his feelings for her. In turn, she had told him she loved him. She'd never thought to say those words to anyone. Not ever. Certainly, she didn't think she'd ever mean them. But she did. She knew with every breath she took that she loved Gorya Amurov. And she did trust him.

She was the problem, not Gorya. She didn't trust herself. She didn't think she would be able to give him the physical things he deserved, no matter how much she wanted to share her body with him.

Stop worrying about it so much. You're building up the problem, making it insurmountable in your mind when it isn't.

Not only was there truth in what he was saying, at least the part about her building it up, but she also felt she needed to take another calming look at the situation. If Gorya and the two leopards were so certain they could overcome every obstacle, she needed to listen. She wanted to make it work. She just had to have more confidence and give things time, like Gorya said. She had to stop being so afraid. She wasn't sure how to do it, but she was willing to try. Having Gorya and a life for all of them was worth it.

12

YOU'VE got company, Gorya."

Gedeon's voice was quiet, but the low warning brought both Gorya and Maya awake instantly. He was out of bed and dressing in clothes that were easy to shed if he needed to shift. Maya was doing the exact same thing.

"He's alone," Meiling reported. "Clearly doesn't want to be seen. He's watching his back trail."

"Do you recognize him?" Gorya asked, his tone curt.

"Yes. Leo Bugrov," Gedeon answered. "Definitely more worried about his back trail than having you or me come after him. I've always liked Leo. Never thought he'd be a traitor."

"I didn't get that from him either." Gorya swept his hand down Maya's hair because he couldn't resist touching her. "He's married. Seems devoted to his wife. He has a daughter around fourteen or fifteen. He always laughs when he's with his family, but I noticed he doesn't so much when he's around quite a few of the other families in the lair. He and his wife own one of the local businesses, a clothing shop."

"Why would he be skulking around in the dead of night?"

"That's the question, isn't it?"

"He isn't approaching as a leopard," Maya pointed out. "He's coming to the front door as a man."

"But he doesn't want to be seen."

"Let me answer the door," Maya said.

"Not on your life. You stay out of sight." His voice didn't just rasp, he growled the order.

He should have known Maya would laugh. She seemed to do that a lot when he issued commands. Everyone else in the vicinity took him seriously, but not his woman. Her eyes lit up and that mouth of hers curved into sweet temptation. It was a kick right in the gut.

"Gedeon and Meiling will handle the door and security," Gorya said, attempting to cover his mistake with her. Ordering Maya to leave his security to others was never a good idea unless he could give her a good reason. "You stay out of sight and be backup, especially when we bring him into the house. If he doesn't see you or know where you are, you're my ace in the hole."

That should satisfy her. And it was the truth. Maya was fast and she could kill in seconds. So could Gorya. If Leo had come to assassinate him, he would never get near Gorya. He'd be dead. It was important to him that Maya was as protected as possible. It wasn't that he didn't think she was lethal as hell, he knew better, but she was his world. If anything happened to her, he wouldn't be able to overcome it. Neither would Rogue.

"No worries," Maya agreed as they moved together toward the front door.

Gedeon met them in the foyer. Meiling was nowhere to

be seen. It didn't surprise Gorya to see Timur moving into a position to defend his cousin. He stayed out of sight on the second floor landing overlooking the great room, where he had a clear view of most of the seating area.

Gedeon opened the door without turning on lights. "Leo, strange time of night to come calling."

Leo nodded. "I'm sorry, Gedeon. I couldn't take the chance of warning you. I need to get inside as quickly as possible. I can't be seen."

Gedeon stepped back to allow him entry and closed the heavy door after him. Leo stood just inside, not making the mistake of moving until Gedeon thoroughly searched him for weapons.

"Sit down, Leo," Gorya invited, waving his hand toward one of the comfortable chairs facing the fireplace. It also faced Timur and put him directly in Maya's path. She was in the shadows just to the right of the fireplace.

Leo dropped into the chair as if his legs could no longer hold him upright. He put his head into his hands. "This wasn't always such a bad lair, Gorya. There was a time when most of the families here were worthwhile. Now I can't say that. I don't know who to tell you to trust. Not that there aren't some who would stand by you if they could."

He lifted his head and looked directly at Gorya, his dark eyes drowning in sorrow. "It's too late for most of us, but it isn't too late for you. Get out of here. They plan to kill you. They'll kill your woman and Gedeon's woman. No one is safe. A few of us thought, when we saw you fight for leadership and you immediately gave the order to shut down the trafficking, there was a chance, but there isn't. We thought we could protect you." He shook his head.

"Leo." Gorya's voice was very low and compelling. "Something happened to bring you here tonight. I want you to tell me what that is."

"I was too outspoken from the beginning against trafficking, even back when it was first starting. My wife and I kept away from the business as much as possible. There's been a group of us. Forgive me, Gorya, but we watched what happened to your families in the lairs in Russia, and part of the reason we came to this country was to ensure we weren't a part of that. At first, we had a good territory. The gulf was close, we had access to highways and could fly small planes out, so we were able to slowly build a good business. We were under the radar and thrived. Everyone seemed happy."

This time his hand came up to rub his temples. His hand was visibly shaking. Leo appeared to be a man in his prime, around forty, solidly built. He didn't seem the least bit afraid of most things, yet clearly, he was beyond all hope. From the little Gorya knew of him, he was devoted to his family. That was about it.

"A couple of years ago, Braum Malcom's son, Derk, came home from college and brought a friend with him. A kid from Panama. He called himself Raul Escabar Alba. Seemed like a nice enough kid at first. Everyone liked him. Really intelligent. But eventually, I found I didn't like the way he treated the women. Neither did my wife. Some of the other wives noticed as well. Braum brushed off his mannerisms as his age, just a brash young college kid, same as his son. Rumors began circulating about the treatment of some of the girls he and Derk dated, but they were hushed up."

I have the feeling this is the heralding of a visit from Albert Krylov. This sounds like what I saw happen in New Orleans and Houston, Maya informed him. *Not that I ever encountered Raul Escabar Alba, but I'd heard of him.*

Gorya passed the information on to Gedeon, Timur and Ashe. "I've heard this name before," he told Leo by way of encouragement to continue when he seemed to falter or expect Gorya to become impatient with the way he was getting around to what had prompted him to be there that particular evening.

"A couple of years before you challenged for leadership, our *pakhan*, Rivel, was visited by a man introduced by Braum and Derk. He came with Raul. He was from Russia."

Albert Krylov, Maya guessed, breathing the name into Gorya's mind.

"Albert Krylov," Leo echoed aloud. "He was here for just a brief visit but arranged to return, with the intention of hosting a party for everyone the next time he came. He would arrange everything."

The women, the drugs. The cameras to record everything that went on. He's so good at leading them down the path of complete debauchery. Maya's mind was filled with disgust. *He preys on the weakest first. He strips them of their inhibitions and frees their monsters. Those men help him persuade their friends to join him until it becomes a domino effect. I saw that with Polina and the women I knew when I was a teen in Houston. Albert was so good at leading men to do despicable things even then, when he was young. He filmed it all, and then he had them. They would be willing to do more for the rush of power. Or if they balked, to keep him quiet so he wouldn't use the evidence he had against them.*

"Quite a few welcomed the parties that followed. There isn't a lot to do here and Krylov seemed to know how to entice not only the men to his parties but some of their partners as well. I didn't go, and some of the others didn't either. I think, in the end, that's what set us apart. Braum noticed and tried to get us to come several times. He wasn't happy that we didn't attend, but I'm not the party type. I'm a family man."

"You were uneasy with the way the others began acting." Gorya made it a statement.

Leo rubbed his jaw. "Yes. They were all . . ." He frowned, searching for the right word. "Different," he finally settled on. "The men weren't as respectful toward the women, even their wives, not like they used to be, and that's when Rivel introduced human trafficking into the mix. We had no say in the matter. We had to accept it, just as we did everything else. Rivel knew we weren't happy about it. He showered us with money, but it left us feeling dirty. There was no getting out. We understood that. We talked about how we might find a way of taking our daughter and leaving without making it seem as if we were trying to leave. An illness, maybe, but we knew it wouldn't work. We'd been too vocal in our protests. Braum was watching us closely, paying attention to everything we said and did, even if Rivel wasn't."

He isn't getting to the point. What prompted him to come here tonight? Gorya asked Maya. *He doesn't want to say.*

Maya hesitated. She knew exactly why Leo wasn't telling Gorya what he'd come there to say to him. She knew because she'd held back for so long, unable to reveal details not only to Gorya but to herself.

Tell me, baby. His voice gentled. Was compelling. Surrounded her with warmth.

It's too traumatic. Whatever it is, once he states it aloud, it becomes too real. She knew. She had finally shared with Gorya the images of her past, something she'd refused to do with anyone. *I couldn't even reexamine my memories for so many years. That made them far too real.* The brutal memories had come spilling out despite her determination to never open that door again.

I'm honored that you had the courage to share with me, Maya. The things we share will always only be between us. No one else ever.

Knowing he meant it increased the intimacy between them so much.

"I wasn't the only one happy when you arrived and banned trafficking. We thought you were the answer we'd waited for. We should have known Braum and the others wouldn't stand for their new way of life to disappear," Leo continued. "Braum may have sworn allegiance to you, but he and the others are plotting to kill you. They have help from the outside, bringing in assassination teams if they can't get it done, although their plans are solid." He raked his thick hair with both hands and once again raised sorrowful eyes to Gorya. "I don't see how he can fail."

When Gorya would have prompted him for the information, Maya cautioned him against speaking. *You have to allow him to say it his way. I know it's difficult to wait, Gorya, but he's putting the courage together to tell you whatever it is.*

She couldn't keep sympathy for the man out of her mind. She knew she was supposed to keep her distance emotionally from him, just in case she was the one who would have to kill him, but she found it impossible. He was putting off waves of such intense sorrow mixed with guilt and anger.

Gorya remained quiet but reached out once more to Maya, pouring warmth and love into her mind. *Whatever it is, baby, we'll do our best to help him. He feels hopeless because he doesn't know his new* pakhan. *I've led with fear because I've had to, not because that's necessarily what I believe is right.*

How could she not love him? The determination to give aid to this man was already in his mind. She hadn't asked him; as the leader of the territory, it was natural, no matter the danger to himself. He didn't know what the problem was, but he was certain he would be able to find a solution—just as he had worked to get ahead of the problems the two of them had in their physical relationship.

You persist in looking at me with stars in your eyes. You deserve to be looked at through stars.

Baby, someday you're going to be so disappointed.

I see the real you, the one no one else will ever see. You even hide from yourself. Rogue and Wraith see the man I see.

"My daughter, Alicia, was spending the night with her best friend, Mindy. Her parents are George and Vera Morozov. George works closely with Braum. I should have known better than to allow Alicia to have such a close friendship with Mindy, but they grew up together. They were always together. Vera treated her like a second daughter. It never occurred to either one of us—my wife, Yelena, or me—that Vera would betray her. Alicia is barely fifteen."

Leo pressed his fingers to the corners of his eyes as if he was keeping himself from weeping. "We received a visit from Braum and George tonight. They told us they'd taken Alicia and were holding her in one of the cells, waiting to be shipped out if I didn't cooperate. Then they took Yelena. They informed me Yelena would be shipped out in the opposite direction. They insisted I challenge you for leadership tomorrow. They have a team waiting to assassinate you whether I win or lose. There is no way my leopard can defeat yours. They know this. I know this. It is a setup to kill the both of us and take my daughter and wife and traffic them. Vera was in on it all the way. She helped them."

"You're absolutely certain Vera helped them?" Gorya asked, his tone lower than ever, but even more compelling.

Leo nodded. "They knocked me out, but when I woke up, I attempted to track them in the hope of getting my wife and daughter back. I couldn't find either of them. I do know where most of the holding cells are, and I checked them. They weren't in any of them. They use some kind of scent blocker so even the leopards can't find traces of them."

He sounded so hopeless that Maya's heart went out to him. *Wraith and I can find the women,* she assured Gorya.

I was certain you would be able to. I think Braum and Albert Krylov have forgotten what it's like to go up against an Amurov.

Maya wasn't certain she liked the underlying note of what she could only identify as eagerness.

Did you suspect Braum was the person behind the others siphoning the money?

Yes, but only because of his position with both you and the former pakhan. *He's in the best position to know everyone's business. Gorya, I need you to get this man's address for me now.*

Maya. Gorya's tone was cautionary. *We'll get the women. We can't tip off the others until we're ready to deal with all of them.*

I'm not waiting to get to the daughter. She's been gone too long. I know what happens and it isn't pretty. I can handle it quietly.

Not alone.

Alone is quiet. You have to have faith in both Wraith and me. I trust you to take care of your end of things. I've been hunting these people a long time. Albert Krylov spent quite a lot of time in Houston giving those parties, and eventually he convinced the men we were with to use the women in sick, depraved ways. When I was able to, I tracked him and found he went from lair to lair doing the same thing. At first I planned to kill him, but then I realized he was acting as an emissary for someone else. That's when I decided to follow the trail back to the head of the entire organization. Leo's daughter isn't safe. She's been in their hands too long. Right this minute something bad is happening to her.

She said it with conviction because she was certain of it. The longer she looked at the misery on Leo's face, the more convinced she was. An ominous feeling had been spreading through her since Leo had shown up. She willed Gorya to understand that this was something she had to do. More, she *was* going to find the girl whether he gave his blessing or not.

She felt Gorya's sigh, yet his expression gave nothing away. *You'd better keep me informed every minute. And don't do anything rash. If you need reinforcements, I'll get to you.*

Maya didn't wait.

The trail wasn't so difficult to follow once she knew each of the scents. She visited Leo's home first and familiarized herself with both Yelena's and Alicia's scents. Then she went to the residence of George and Vera Morozov. She didn't make the mistake of hurrying, because her warning system was shrieking at her. She knew part of her fear for Alicia was from that door in her mind cracking open and the terrible trauma of her childhood spilling out. She knew what these men did to women when they had them helpless in their possession. She couldn't allow that to cause her to make mistakes. That wouldn't help anyone.

Maya pushed the past from her mind and concentrated on the female leopard. Surprisingly, it was always the females who were the hardest to take over. Most were strong and independent—if they were healthy. The moment she connected with Vera's leopard she could tell the animal was groggy, disoriented, repressed even. She was barely able to detect Maya's presence.

Maya flowed into her mind very slowly, careful not to alert the leopard's mate or her human partner. This was the most important moment, when everything could go wrong. The female leopard couldn't fight her presence or become agitated in any way, warning the others there might be an intruder in their home. She matched the rhythm of breathing and brain waves perfectly until she was sure she had the right path and then she simply took the leopard from her human counterpart and mate. She did so carefully and subtly, but the animal retreated far back, leaving Maya completely in charge.

Next she examined the animal's memories. They were very ugly in regard to her human counterpart's actions against young Alicia, Mindy's friend. The leopard had always liked Alicia. The accusations Vera had leveled against her were lies. No matter what the leopard said, Vera ignored her and insisted to Mindy that the young girl had attempted to seduce her husband. She slapped her repeatedly and called her names. In the background, two young men smirked and leered as Vera ripped at Alicia's clothes and thrust her toward them. She demanded that if Alicia wanted to be a whore, they teach her a lesson she'd never forget.

Mindy had been frozen in the corner, her hand covering her eyes as the two men jerked the sobbing girl to them, laughing and assuring Vera it would be taken care of. Alicia begged to be taken home to her family. Vera slapped her again and told her she was never going home, that there was no home to go to. Her stuck-up parents should have been friends with the right people.

Maya recognized the two young men. One was Raul Escabar Alba from Panama, and the other was his college friend, Derk Malcom, son of Braum. It didn't surprise her in the least that they were the ones Alicia had been turned over to. She was certain Albert was staying in the Malcom home or at least in their guesthouse. She instructed the leopard to sleep peacefully.

The male leopard was a little more difficult, only because he was confused and angry with his human counterpart. Like the female leopard, he showed signs of drugs in his system, but the drugs were slightly different. Where the drugs in the female had caused her to be more compliant and submissive, whatever the human male was taking and passed on to his leopard ramped up his sexual needs, removed all natural constraints, bringing out the worst traits shifter or leopard could have. That left the leopard in a continual state of arousal and confusion, as his human counterpart had ceased being faithful to his wife and was using many women who had been brought in, women the leopard found itself despising and wanting to take part in the violence against. He longed for his own mate, yet at the same time hated her for her subservience. She no longer felt the same to him, adding to his confusion.

Maya was doubly cautious as she entered the male leopard's mind. She didn't want to trigger violence when he was confused and on edge. She took longer to merge with him, but once she did, she was able to examine his memories. Even confused, the parties hosted at Braum's home and put on by Albert Krylov were more than perverted. Each party had seemed to take those attending further down a depraved path of drugs and deviant behavior. Apparently Braum, with Albert, was holding a meeting much later that evening with his trusted members to put the finishing touches on their plan to get rid of their present *pakhan*. They would also reestablish the transports they had from the gulf on freighters, the light planes going out from their small airport and the trucks that would haul cross-country to the eastern states. She got the time of the meeting from the male leopard and sent him to sleep as well.

It was easy to move through the house knowing the leopards wouldn't alert the humans to her presence. Wraith would let her know if either of the humans woke, but she doubted they would. They were feeling safe and smug. She quickly found her way to Mindy's room, where Alicia's scent was everywhere. Fear permeated the rooms and hallway. Fear and the sexual excitement and what Maya had come to think of as the depraved scent of men who enjoyed hurting women.

She inhaled to take all three scents deep into her lungs. *Can you find them, Wraith, even if they use a blocker?*

Yes. The men stink and she is terrified. They will never be able to hide from us. There was a purring satisfaction in Wraith's tone, in her images. She was no longer the sex kitten. That leopard had disappeared, and in her wake, the predator had come alive. Like Maya, Wraith was more than eager to hunt and kill the men who had taken the young girl.

Maya reached for Mindy's leopard next, seeking to find whether the teen had one. She did. The leopard was there, not even close to emergence, but disturbed by the events of the day. Mindy had protested, yelling at her parents that Alicia had been with her the entire time and couldn't possibly have done the things her mother had accused her of. Her mother had slapped her viciously and then proclaimed she knew Mindy had coveted her father. She'd seen her trying to get his attention.

Mindy was horrified at the accusations, clinging to Alicia, trying to prevent the two men from taking her while warding off her mother with one hand. Vera's rage increased while her husband looked on with a smirk, and the two men offered to take Mindy with them to teach her manners.

In the end, Alicia was dragged away, Mindy was thrown into a corner of the room and her mother was wrapped in her father's arms while he cooed to her how proud he was and assured her he would take care of her and said she could go with him to the next party and participate with him. No one comforted Mindy or even looked at their daughter crumpled on the floor, not understanding how her family had gone from happy to torn apart. She was isolated, terrified, and knew it was only a matter of time before she would suffer the same fate as Alicia had.

It was all Maya could do to leave the girl there. She desperately wanted to comfort her, tell her things would be all right, although she knew this child's family would never be put back together. Her parents were too far gone. It seemed as if the drugs given to them had created damage to their brains, almost as if they'd been hit head-on in a car crash.

Resolutely, she left the house and began to follow the trail through the back streets of the small town leading toward the outskirts and the swamp. She was nothing more than a small shadow within the darkness, making no sound, giving off no scent. Maya and Wraith had perfected the art after years of practice. They'd started trying to "disappear" when Maya was a child, merging into the shadows of rooms and buildings, desperate to escape notice of the men coming to rape and torture.

Abruptly, the scent lessened considerably, nearly disappeared altogether. This was where Alicia and the two men had been sprayed with scent blocker. She was familiar with the use of it. It was odd that it had never hindered her ability to scent-track when it did for other leopards. Despite the blocker, she could still detect that trail. It was faint, but it was there.

Heat images in the form of splotches of color rose and she followed the path unerringly, jogging, not sprinting. She knew better than to waste energy. She would need it. There were two men to deal with, and no matter how depraved they were, they were young and strong and leopard. She was a huntress and fully in control. Fully determined to find and kill her prey.

The trail twisted around the edge of the swamp, looped into it for a few yards and came out near the building Theo Pappas had taken her prisoner in. She should have known. It was the perfect place to keep a prisoner. They would be able to do whatever they wanted to young Alicia and no one would hear her screams. If they brought her mother to the same torture room, they could easily dispose of her body if they killed her outright, or they could make her see and listen to her daughter's agony. Maya wouldn't be surprised if Braum's son, Derk, and Raul were that cruel.

The basement appeared to have only the one entrance,

which might present a problem if the two men had anyone else with them or if they were watching security cameras. The doors locked from the outside. In this case, she knew the two men wouldn't have locked themselves in. Maya had seen this scenario dozens of times. She was certain they would be secure in the knowledge that they had the upper hand with their fifteen-year-old prisoner and wouldn't bother to monitor the cameras.

Even though she had that alarming urgency driving her, she took the time to secure the building. She didn't want anyone unexpected spotting her and coming up behind her. When she found the controls for the cameras, it was easy enough to disrupt the feed throughout the building.

Maya approached the door to the basement with caution. As she expected, it was unlocked. She didn't hesitate to open it just enough to allow her slender form to slip inside. Immediately she glided into the shadows and froze, letting the sounds and scents feed her the information she needed.

Two men, Raul Escabar Alba and Derk Malcom, nearly swamped the long rows of rooms with the musty odor of their arousal and the adrenaline flooding their bodies. Alicia gave off waves of terror. Maya smelled another woman, detected a heartbeat, but she was unmoving, perhaps unconscious.

Raul seemed to be instructing Derk in how to view Alicia. "It doesn't matter that you grew up with the bitch, Derk." Raul reached down and casually caught Alicia by her hair, jerking her to her knees. Ignoring her sobbing, he caught her jaws between his fingers and pinched ruthlessly, forcing her mouth open. "See that? That's all you need. That's all she is to you. She's nothing but that hole right there. She's got two more for you to take your pleasure in. You want this job—training the bitches, keeping them in line and selling them to the highest bidder—you

have to control them. To do that, they gotta respect you.
They gotta know you mean everything you say. They obey
your slightest wish. They got no rights, Derk. You *own*
them. You want to cut them into little pieces just because
it amuses you, that's your prerogative. Why? Because
you're the fuckin' man and she's nothin' but a doll for you
to play with."

How often had Maya heard that speech? Nearly word
for word. It had been said far back in the Amurov lair
when she was a child and Gorya's uncle had come in with
his men and their sons, training them how to treat women
and little girls or boys. Hatred rose for just a moment.
Rage. Deep inside, Wraith snarled. Maya breathed away
the emotion. Emotion had no place here. That way could
lead to mistakes. She had to stay distant, completely removed from what was happening, so she could kill these
two men and free this young girl.

You aren't much older than she is. Gorya's voice was
soft in her ear. Calm. Steady. Sure of her. He had been
there to save her when she was a child in this same position. Rogue had been there to save Wraith.

She took her time, reaching for Raul's leopard first. It
was agitated, sensing a threat, but Maya's verve was so
low and Raul was in such a state of arousal and flooded
with aggression and testosterone, the leopard couldn't sort
through the waves of powerful energy swamping it. She
simply rode those waves into the leopard's mind, absorbed
the animal's memories, became part of him until he was
surrounded by her, accepting and at peace. She took him
over with care, separating him from Raul, and the shifter
didn't notice. He was too high on his own power.

She viewed Raul with fresh eyes. He had been taught
this lesson by Albert Krylov. Albert was a little older than
Gorya, perhaps by one or two years. He was one of the
boys brought by the *pakhan* and his men to prey on the
women and learn how to properly "use" them. His father

had died by Fyodor's hand in the bloodbath that followed
Patva's attack on his son and nephew, but somehow Albert
and Artur had escaped his wrath.

She didn't know the full story of how Fyodor had, for
all intents and purposes, wiped out the Amurov lair before
he'd left, but he had killed his father and every one of the
high-ranking members of Patva's organization. She knew
the Amurov name had been legendary long before that
night. It was even more so after. There were few *bratva*
who dared to take on the Amurovs. That was one of the
reasons she found the way the lair was opposing Gorya's
leadership so odd.

His leopard had not only defeated every challenger but
also ruthlessly killed them—in a matter of minutes. Less.
They continued to challenge his authority using men who
had no chance, backed by teams of assassins. *Do they
think your cousins won't retaliate because you aren't a
sibling? You're still an Amurov. Their cousin.*

Maya tried to puzzle out the reasoning of their oppo-
nents as she inched closer to the two men with the weeping girl sandwiched between them. She had to block out
the sight of the teenager stripped naked, bruises and
swelling marring her body. She couldn't let the girl's pleas
to Derk influence her. Maya had to stay focused on the
ultimate goal—killing the two male shifters, both in their
prime, both capable of killing or capturing her if she made
one mistake.

You won't make a mistake, Gorya said, his voice low
and intense, whispering into her mind like a caress. *You
and Wraith have done this too many times and you're like
a machine together.*

*Why would Braum Malcom think he could defeat you,
Gorya? Even if he did, your cousins would come. He
would be annihilated. He must know that.*

She reached for Derk's leopard next, confident Raul's
wouldn't sound the alarm even if he caught sight of her.

She had instructed him to accept her, and he had done so. Derk's leopard wasn't as aggressive as Raul's had been but was just as agitated as Raul's, with the levels of arousal and excitement the shifter experienced listening to his friend's instructions. The man paid no attention to his leopard. Unlike Raul, Derk had drugs in his system that further confused the leopard and affected its senses. She took this one over with much more ease than she had Raul's leopard.

Once Maya was certain she had both leopards under her control, she glided closer to her target. Of the two men, Raul was the more dangerous, the more experienced. She would have to kill him first. He was totally concentrating on instructing Derk, acting the big man. Showing off. Enjoying himself. Drunk on his own power. Power over the girl. Over the man he was instructing. He was so high on his supremacy—forcing Alicia's mouth open, telling Derk to pull her hips to him so they could use her together—he never saw the small figure emerging from the shadows to his left. He never saw the blade that slammed deep into his jugular or the one that severed his spinal cord.

Derk's eyes widened in a kind of horror as blood sprayed around them in a geyser and Raul seemed to slowly crumple like a rag doll. Before he could react, a blade sank deep into his chest directly over his heart. Another followed, then a third and fourth. Each blade hit a vital spot, and blood erupted as if he were a fountain.

Maya hooked Alicia under her arms and dragged her free of the two falling bodies and spraying blood. "It's over, honey. You're free. Your father went to the *pakhan* and he's taking your enemies down. You're free. Let's get your mother." She sent up a silent prayer that Yelena was alive. This girl needed her mother and a trauma counselor more than she needed to shower the blood from her body.

Alicia started to turn her head, but Maya stopped her. "Don't look."

"I need to see. I need to know they're dead and can't ever come after me again," Alicia whispered hoarsely.

Maya understood completely, because wasn't she the one still trying to track down and kill every man who had brutally assaulted her as a child? She let Alicia look her fill and then they went to the corner where her mother lay on the floor. She had been assaulted, but she was alive. Maya was calling that a win.

13

BRAUM Malcom looked around the large conference table at the thirty men he considered trustworthy serving under him. He'd spent a lifetime working up to this moment, and satisfaction always warred with the need to do more. To do better. To seek revenge. To do penance for his sins. He had no desire to be *pakhan*. The money man and the adviser/enforcer were the true powers. He was always both. Behind the scenes, directing the lair, running the territory. Running the *pakhan*. If the leader forgot who was really in charge, he simply had him killed and put another in power.

He always faced his weaknesses. He made himself look every day at how he'd failed, what he'd been responsible for. He vowed he'd make up for those weaknesses. Truth was, it was impossible. She was dead. His beloved Celine. She'd been his world. He'd loved her too much. Given her everything she'd wanted. Been too lenient with her. If he'd just been a man and taken charge as he should have, she'd still be alive today. With him. Raising their son. Giving him her brightness and beauty.

He'd failed her by giving in to her. She'd been too kind. Too compassionate. He'd seen the other women, known they were jealous. Petty. They pretended to be her friend, but they weren't. They came on to him constantly, were upset that he hadn't chosen them and wouldn't succumb to their attentions. So they had targeted her.

He despised women. *Despised* them. Greedy, grasping, jealous bitches. Not all, he conceded. He'd watched Gedeon's woman, Meiling, carefully. She was worthwhile. Devoted to her man. A woman worth having, but then Gedeon was a man who clearly took charge—as he should have done. Braum owned his mistake. Had he taken charge of Celine, put his foot down, dictated to her for her safety, she would still be alive.

He'd made promises to her. Stood over her burning body and made solemn vows to her. He meant every last one of his assurances to her, and he'd carry them out until the day he died. If he could come back from hell, he'd continue. Their son would never make the same mistakes he had. He'd be strong, and when he found the right woman, he would devote himself to her, but he would be able to tell her a firm no when she needed it.

His gaze settled on each of the men. Most of them were weak. Followers. They were needed, and they'd fight for their way of life, but they weren't leaders. He needed a leader. It was too bad Gorya Amurov didn't believe in trafficking. That had surprised him. Shocked him even. The Amurovs had been one of the wealthiest families in their homeland and they'd made a good portion of that money from trafficking.

They weren't weak men, allowing their women to run them. They lived for the *bratva*. Were loyal to the brotherhood. They knew better than to put anything before their brotherhood. These thirty men—plus Derk, along with his private security, another five members—were the men in the lair he could count on no matter who was *pakhan*.

Any man in the lair who was not seated at the table was not as committed. Their women influenced them. They'd grown soft. They went along with the order of things, but they had never fully agreed to the one real profit-making deal the lair had started. Their businesses flourished, and he was generous, giving them shares, but those with mates found the idea distasteful. Any who remained alive after this cleansing would be obligated to participate in Albert's parties. Inside he smirked. So would their wives.

His information on Gorya hadn't been as good as it should have been. He'd been told he was the weakest of the Amurovs. He hadn't just been given reports by his best investigators, he'd been told by Albert Krylov. The man had grown up with him. Known him. They'd all said Gorya's cousins protected him. Fought his battles. It was whispered he might not even be an Amurov. He looked different.

Gorya Amurov had turned out to be a pain in the ass. A real one. His leopard was reputed to be extremely fast. Braum hadn't seen the bastard in action. He always made certain he had an alibi just in case. Every eyewitness said the leopard killed within a minute, quite viciously. When every challenge had failed, Braum had brought in assassination teams, and somehow, those teams had been slaughtered. Gedeon and his woman, no doubt. The fucking bodyguards. Or just bad luck.

He had a foolproof plan now to rid himself of Gorya Amurov, and at the same time, he was going to either bind the traitors in his community or have them killed as well. Leo Bugrov would be the first to go, and every one of the others would know exactly what had happened to his wife and daughter. The rest of them would know what would happen to their precious families if they crossed him. As it was, he would be taking their businesses and most of their money. Let them see what it was like to cross him.

Albert Krylov was seated to his right at the table, something never done, bringing an outsider in. Braum wished he could make Albert *pakhan*. Or adviser. The man was honed as sharp as a razor blade, but he still missed things, making him malleable. Braum sat back in his chair, once more looking around at the prospects who were talking in low tones to one another. With Albert, it made thirty-one sitting with him. A good solid number.

None of them, including Krylov, realized he had chosen his son's college because Raul Escabar Alba was attending that school. He had instructed Derk to cultivate a friendship with the boy, a slow one, not making it seem as if that relationship was his idea. Raul had taken the bait when Derk had talked about his home in the Atchafalaya Swamp.

Krylov did his research. He had a private connection no one knew about that he sometimes used to gather information. That researcher had found a mysterious family located in Panama, one he was certain was the power behind the trafficking. He wanted in. Raul Escabar Alba was his way in. It just had to be their idea. Negotiations were always important.

He pushed down feelings of smugness and pride. He might be a brilliant man now, but he hadn't been when he was young. There was always more to learn. Always more to do.

Without warning, not even from his leopard, the doors to the conference room swung open—and there were three of them; two were double doors—and Gorya and *his* security waltzed right in as if they owned the place. Braum cursed under his breath. His own security should have notified him, but there wasn't the slightest warning. He didn't allow his shock to show on his face as he assessed the situation.

The security team included Gorya's cousin Timur. He hadn't personally met Timur Amurov, but the man's reputation preceded him. He was a big man who didn't try to hide the killer in him. Wide shoulders. Thick, roped muscles rippling down his back, arms and chest if he moved at all. His face bore scars, and the lines were carved deep all the way to his strong jaw.

He shifted his gaze to Gorya. He could see why so many underestimated Gorya Amurov if they saw him next to his cousin. He was built differently. Leaner, although if one looked, muscle ran densely beneath his skin. He was extremely handsome, where Timur had scars on his face and looked rough as hell. Gorya seemed charming and very young by comparison, although they were reputed to be close in age. Timur looked the part of a mobster while Gorya did not.

Braum looked beyond all that charm. Gorya was Amurov. There was no doubt in his mind. He was ruthless and cunning, and judging from the reports of his leopard's ability, he was lightning fast. Everyone else might underestimate him, but Braum wasn't going to make that mistake.

"Gorya, welcome," he greeted, making as if to rise from his chair.

Gorya waved him to his seat. "A meeting without your *pakhan*, Braum?"

"I like to clarify things before I bring them to you. It's much better to have all the books in order and know details so you don't have to be bothered with them," Braum replied smoothly. It was a lie and yet not quite one.

"Four o'clock in the morning seems a little early and smacks of something altogether different." Gorya looked around the table. "Not all the heads of the businesses are here. Why is that, I wonder?"

Braum noted that Gorya's security force had spread out around the table behind the chairs, covering the room. It bothered him that none of his security had entered. He had to assume they were incapacitated—or dead. His leopard hadn't responded to him when twice he had reached for him. There were dozens of shadows in the room, and he was certain Gorya had more of his security force hidden within them. How the man was blocking him from speaking to his leopard, he couldn't imagine, but he needed the animal to confirm it.

"I already know where they stand, Gorya, and can give you that information." That much was the truth. If the present *pakhan* was capable of reading lies, he couldn't be caught in that lie. Hopefully Gorya would be confused and believe all he was saying. He willed those at the table to stay silent and let him handle everything.

"I see you have company. Albert Krylov. It has been years."

Krylov nodded but made no move to greet Gorya properly, clearly determined to get the upper hand. "It has. I hear you recently found your mate." There was a slight edge of contempt in his voice. "Dare I say congratulations?"

Braum winced at the disrespect. That wasn't the way to handle Gorya Amurov. He wouldn't have been shocked if Timur stepped forward and backhanded the man.

Gorya lifted an eyebrow. "You needn't bother, not when you don't mean it. What you might do is tell Braum and the others the story of what happened so many years ago when Patva sent one of his trusted teams to his whorehouse. You weren't there, but you heard the story. I was there, the only survivor."

Krylov lifted an eyebrow. "You mean when you were forever after branded the coward? Why would you want me to relate such a story of their *pakhan*? The shame of just that story would be too much for them to want to follow you, but the aftermath and what you became would be too much for them to endure if they knew."

Krylov was clearly taunting Gorya deliberately, as if he could blackmail the man into silence—into leaving.

Gorya didn't look in the least upset. In fact, his expression didn't change at all. "I think Braum will understand why it's important to hear that particular story. He'll find it very entertaining and pertinent. So please, tell all of it, every detail."

"If you insist," Krylov said.

He proceeded to explain in detail how the men had gone to the whorehouse to use the women.

"And children," Gorya added quietly. "Don't leave out the part of grown men using children for sex."

Braum flicked his gaze to Gorya's hard features. There was no change in expression. No change in that soft tone whatsoever, but a chill went down his spine. For the first time, instead of the thrill he got from facing a brilliant opponent, he had the impression of a dangerous predator looming over him. Not just dangerous. Far more than that.

Children. Was that Gorya's trigger? Was that why he was here at four o'clock in the morning? Braum desperately wanted to text his son and ask where he was. A dark premonition crept in. They'd taken Leo's daughter. Did Gorya consider fifteen to be a child?

Albert Krylov didn't seem to notice that Gorya was a predator. He had a fixed idea of who the man was and refused to entertain any other version.

Even as Krylov told the story, Braum kept his gaze fixed on Gorya's features, studying him carefully. He was aware of the others in the room, the security spread out, but they had faded into the background. Gorya was the one who mattered. He was lethal, at the top of the food chain. Braum had carefully avoided Gedeon, knowing his reputation and sensing the man would see more than Braum could afford for him to see. Gorya had hidden the predator under a charming facade, easily bought. His reputation had been the weak link in the Amurov family, one he had clearly cultivated over the years.

Krylov's tone turned almost gleeful as he described the massacre found by Patva and his men in the whorehouse. The dead soldiers. The dead guards. No women or children. No tracks other than a few leading inland away from the harbor. Only Gorya had survived with a few injuries, his body hidden among the dead.

Patva had beaten him thoroughly in front of the others and branded him a coward. They determined a rival *pakhan* had declared war by stealing the whores they had contracted to sell. Gorya never so much as blinked when Krylov, his voice filled with disgust and contempt, told those at the table how Gorya was punished with torture and rape since the whores were gone and the men would need a body to use until the next shipment came in.

There was silence following the story. No one so much as scraped a chair or moved. Braum's heart nearly ceased beating. Krylov wasn't nearly as intelligent as Braum had thought. Another terrible mistake on his part. *I'm sorry, Celine.*

"How long did it take you to kill them all, Gorya?" Braum forced his gaze to meet those flat, dead eyes. Pure frost. Ghost eyes.

"It was a standard team of his men, plus the guards. Once I started killing, they all had to go down. I had seconds, so less than a minute or so." Gorya made it sound casual. Easy.

Krylov bristled. "That's impossible. He was a kid. A scrawny teenager. A coward. I lived there, *knew* him. A grown man couldn't have done that alone. Those killed were trained soldiers."

Braum ignored him. The man was dead already and didn't know it. No one would allow such a story to be told if he planned on letting those hearing it live. Gorya had spent far too much time fabricating his reputation as charming and easygoing.

"Then you had to get rid of the women and manufacture enough evidence to make it believable that another *pakhan* had raided."

Gorya shrugged calmly. "Freighter in the harbor was leaving. I'd perfected Patva's signature by that time and wrote out orders. I'd already stolen money and was able to give them that for a new start. It was a matter of creating enough of a trail and then inflicting wounds on myself so I looked like I'd taken a beating."

"Nobody would have taken the kinds of things done to him without fighting back," Krylov snapped. "I don't care what he says. He just lay down and took it. Why would anyone do that? If he could get those women out, why didn't he go with them?"

Braum wondered if the man could be any less intelligent. He kept pouring triumph into his voice as if that could make him right. No one else moved. No one else spoke. Braum knew it was because they were beginning to sense—or already had—that they were in the presence of a much larger predator. No one wanted to draw his attention.

"Braum knows why, don't you, Braum?" Gorya said in that same soft voice.

Another chill went down Braum's spine. "If you hate enough and you want to learn to be a monster, to learn everything from them you can, and then exact your revenge, plan it out step by step, you will do anything, take anything to get there."

There was silence again and then Krylov burst out, "He would have just killed Patva." This time he didn't sound so certain.

Braum shook his head. "No, he would want him to live. To suffer. To take everything from him. Killing him would be too easy. I would guess things were already beginning to go wrong. Shipments interrupted or missing. Money stolen. Patva becoming paranoid against his own trusted men. Total chaos."

He didn't take his gaze from Gorya. No change in expression registered. None. Those frosted ghost eyes stared right back at him.

"That's true," Krylov conceded. "Patva nearly went insane with the continual losses."

"I consider myself a fair *pakhan*. You might not be used to my ways, but I state the truth and I'm always clear about the rules and consequences. I gave an order," Gorya stated. "No more trafficking. I don't think anyone sitting at this table could possibly have misunderstood that order. Every single person in this room swore allegiance to me. You were given the opportunity to leave. You didn't have to swear on your life and the lives of your families, but you did. I stated very plainly the consequences of trafficking."

Braum could hear accelerated heartbeats throughout the room. His heart raced as well, not for himself but for his son. Someone in the room, four chairs down and across the table, was stupid enough to try to pull a gun. Something stirred in the shadows and moved with blurring speed right past the security team. At the same time blood erupted from the man's jugular, the sound of a gun firing echoed through the room, and his left eye was gone. He slumped forward, his weapon slipping from nerveless fingers. The hilt of a knife protruded from the base of his skull. That blur retreated into the shadows as if it had never been.

No one made a sound. Bile rose in Braum's throat. He forced himself to stay seated and not reach for his phone. Derk. This was bad. A huge mistake. He'd underestimated his opponent based on information given to him by others rather than sizing up the new *pakhan* for himself.

"Tonight Leo Bugrov's daughter, Alicia, was taken by force from the home of George and Vera Morozov."

For the first time, Gorya broke eye contact and looked directly at George Morozov. "Both Vera and Morozov aided Raul Escabar Alba and Derk Malcom in taking this child. Escabar Alba and Malcom were caught outright beating and raping the girl. There is no question that George and Vera provided help in taking her. Shifter and leopard memories were examined. Leo's wife was also taken forcefully by several men in this room. She was beaten severely and raped by Escabar Alba and Malcom."

The security team had moved up behind the men in complete silence, put guns to the backs of their heads and nearly simultaneously pulled the triggers. George and the others named slumped forward. Just like that, the *pakhan* had slaughtered eight men in the room.

"Vera has been executed as well," Gorya said. "The sentence is absolute."

Once more the pitiless, frosted eyes of Gorya Amurov met Braum's. Braum had held out a small splinter of hope that his son might still be alive until Gorya had used the word *child* when he referred to Alicia. He knew immediately that Derk was dead. There had been instant retaliation.

He moistened his lips and drew in a deep breath. "Raul is the son of a very important man in Panama, Gorya. His death may bring retribution down on your family. Perhaps I could try to act as an intermediary." He made the offer woodenly, but he wanted confirmation that Derk and Raul were dead.

"That won't be necessary. I know who Jaoa Escabar Velentez is and exactly what he does. I may be a new *pakhan* here, but for years I've kept up with business through my family. He'll be informed of his son's death and the reasons why."

The piercing through his heart was worse than any knife could have been. Braum looked around the room at the remaining men. They had no idea what was in store for them. He did. They were all condemned to death. Every man at that table.

"I challenge you for leadership." He issued the confrontation listlessly. His leopard wasn't in the least responsive. It didn't seem to want to fight for him.

"I challenge for leadership," Krylov echoed. He seemed suddenly aware of the death sentence hanging over them. "As long as you fight me and don't have your brother fight your battles for you."

"Do you mean you would like me to fight fair?" For the first time there seemed to be a trace of amusement in Gorya's tone, although if so, there was none in his eyes. "You don't think I should have Timur fight my battles for me or an assassination team waiting in the swamp to shoot you if I fail to get the job done?"

Braum instantly had a bad taste in his mouth. He felt that lash of contempt from the *pakhan*. They all did. There was no honor in the challenges sent to Gorya. They'd wanted him dead and had set him up to be killed after the first three official challenges.

"Yes," Krylov demanded, choosing not to see the irony.

Three others quickly followed suit. The three were unmated men, strong, with fierce leopards. Braum knew they stood little chance against Gorya, but he could tell they thought they did. Vinn and Edik were brothers. It didn't surprise him that they would challenge for leadership. They had been entrenched in trafficking, guarding and training the girls who were delivered into holding and passing them through to the various destinations.

Karol was a little more surprising. He worked at the harbor and oversaw the loading and offloading of the arms, girls and drugs. He was methodical at his job, which made him excellent at supervising his crews. He wasn't a drinker and rarely did things to excess. Braum had kept an eye on him for grooming as a future *pakhan*. He had the makings.

It was possible to turn this thing around. It would only take one challenger to win the battle. Gorya's security team couldn't interfere. His cousin couldn't either. Once a new *pakhan* was leader of the lair, Gorya's people could be ordered to leave—or imprisoned. There was no doubt in his mind that if they were killed or imprisoned, his lair would be at war with every Amurov territory surrounding him. He didn't have the manpower to fight them.

The question was, how could they win? He needed a strategy. If they cheated, the challenger would be killed instantly by Timur or Gorya's security. This had to be a fair fight, but somehow, he knew he had to stack the odds in his men's favor. Once more, Braum studied Gorya. That charming mask was so deceiving.

"I want you five to make absolutely certain that you want to make the challenge to face Rogue. He has no mercy in him. He's a vicious killer. He despises traffickers. In particular, he despises men with children who would, without thought, take other men's children from them and sell them to the highest bidder. His justice won't be a clean, quick execution. Once you decide this is the way you want to go, there is no backing out."

Braum knew the warning was for him. *He* had given the orders to take Leo's daughter from the man. Although his name wasn't anywhere to be seen, he had been the one to accept women and children coming in on boats and planes and in trucks and then shipping them out to the other territories.

Albert Krylov gave a little sniff of contempt. "I don't think scaring us with your big bad leopard is going to stop anyone from challenging you."

For the first time, a hint of satisfaction crept into the cold, ghostly eyes and Braum found himself shivering. It wasn't a good idea to bait the predator, but Krylov couldn't seem to keep his mouth shut. Perhaps he had a childhood grudge against the Amurov family. Whatever the reason, he continued to taunt Gorya.

"I presume your new mate will be there to witness the challenges, unless she's hiding for fear you won't win. She'll be the first one we train to send to the homeland. My brother and his men will welcome her properly."

This time it wasn't Gorya reacting. It was his security team and Timur. A wave of outright laughter swept through the rank. It was low, but it was sincere.

"Do you think I said something funny?" Krylov bristled. He was used to others deferring to him.

"Who do you think killed both Raul and Derk on her own with no backup?" Timur all but growled it. "Who do you think destroyed your assassination teams when Gedeon and his security teams were surrounding Gorya during what was supposed to be a fair challenge for leadership? You really are a dumb fuck, Krylov."

Braum hadn't thought that through either. He hadn't given a thought to Gorya's new mate. Was she that blur that had come out of the shadows and disappeared again? He knew female leopards could fight, but he hadn't heard they could take down two grown leopards in their prime. Not alone. Did he believe Timur? His voice rang with truth. More, the entire security crew had laughed when Krylov had made his ridiculous boast. Yeah, he believed him.

Braum figured Gorya's leopard would want to teach Krylov a lesson. They would urge him to challenge first. Let his leopard tire Gorya out. The longer the *pakhan* spent tormenting his prey, the more time there would be to inflict even minor damage on him and perhaps wear down his stamina. With stupid comments like Krylov had just made, no doubt Gorya and his leopard wouldn't be able to resist teaching him manners before slaying him.

"I'd rather go out fighting," Braum said.

Vinn, Edik and Karol added their agreements to Braum's.

Gorya gave the slightest of nods, nearly imperceptible. On silent feet, his security crew stepped up behind the remaining men seated at the oblong table. The shadows moved. Men slumped forward. That shadow plunged knives into two men simultaneously. Braum saw the results, but not the person behind the chair. Shots rang out and four men fell with the others. In the end, all were dead, leaving only the five challengers alive.

"Gentlemen, you will stand one by one and be searched for weapons," Gedeon said. "Once you are free of them, your leopard will be returned to you, and you'll be escorted to the place we've chosen for the match. The last assassination team was located and destroyed. To be on the safe side, we've chosen our own arena, so if we missed any further treachery on your part, they will have to find us."

Braum couldn't imagine Gedeon and this crew missing anything. They seemed to be very thorough.

"What do you mean return our leopards to us?" Braum inquired, trying to sound as casual as possible, not alarmed in the least. How was it they had the power to overtake one leopard, let alone every leopard in the room? He'd never heard of such a thing. He hadn't known it was possible.

Krylov and the others took their shaken gazes from the dead men surrounding them and stared at Gedeon with shock. Braum realized it was the first time any of them had reached for their leopards. What was wrong with them? How had they not known? No one had been warned. Shifters were always told by their leopards if danger was close. When had they all grown so excessively reliant on the security force when they had their meetings?

No one answered him, but then, he hadn't really expected an answer. One by one they stood up. Gedeon was very thorough, taking his time to ensure no weapon could possibly slip by. Braum was very aware that no packs were given to them so they could dress in their clothes on the off chance that one of them would defeat Gorya. They would have the clothes they took off at the site where the battle was going to take place, but often in their haste to get them off, trousers and shirts could be shredded.

Before it was Braum's turn to be escorted from the room, a small, slender woman emerged from the shadows. She was tiny like a little pixie. Her hair was blond and her eyes big, a slate blue with long, sweeping lashes. He'd never seen a woman look so young and innocent as this one did. He wasn't even certain at first that she was a woman until she glided gracefully across the floor to come up behind several of the dead men. Removing the blades from their bodies, she wiped them clean and shoved them out of sight. She did it so fast that at first, he wasn't certain what he'd witnessed.

The woman turned her head and looked at Gorya. She looked like the sweet girl next door, totally incapable of killing anyone. For one moment, when she looked up at Gorya and took his outstretched hand, she smiled up at her mate, and her smile was absolutely beautiful. Right there, surrounded by death, she didn't seem in the least fazed. Gorya pulled her close, uncaring that anyone saw the way he acted possessive of her, tucking her under his shoulder as he escorted her out to a waiting SUV.

Braum suffered the indignity of cuffs when he was placed in another vehicle along with guards. He still didn't have his leopard back. None of the others rode in the same car with him. Gorya—or Gedeon—was too intelligent to allow them to talk together to conspire.

Braum found it both undignified and rather humiliating that the new *pakhan* thought so little of him. He had betrayed the one man he could have admired. Not that they would have ever seen eye to eye on their moral codes. He doubted if Gorya would have understood why he believed in trafficking even if he agreed to drop the underage, which his contracts with the other territories would never agree to. There were always regrets. He had to stay focused on the task at hand—defeating Gorya's leopard.

They were taken to a section of the swamp Braum wasn't familiar with. There was a clearing, so he should have known the area; he'd been living there for years. As he stepped from the SUV and the cuffs were removed, he took a good look around him. Gorya's security force was much larger than he remembered. There were several unfamiliar faces. Most looked very seasoned. Fighters, every single one. The ones with expressions held contempt on their faces. That added to his shame, and it seemed to goad Vinn and Edik into needing to shift as soon as they could. Both men began to strip, toeing their shoes off and ripping shirts over their heads.

Braum stepped back, indicating that either man could make the challenge first. As he did so, he felt the awakening of his leopard, Jago. The animal woke abruptly, shook itself and brushed up against him in reassurance. Braum wanted desperately to know what had happened, but all his concentration had to be on studying Gorya's leopard's ability.

Gorya shrugged out of his shirt. There were bullet scars, whip marks, and burns covering his chest and back. Muscles played smoothly beneath his skin. His shoes were off and he bent his head to brush a kiss on top of his mate's head before he slid his jeans from his hips. As he did, Vinn's leopard, a roped, golden-furred creature called Kingston, rushed the *pakhan*.

A single leap took Kingston across the distance separating Vinn and Gorya. Gorya hadn't yet removed his trousers, yet by the time the golden leopard landed, claws extended, snarling teeth exposed, yellow eyes wild with malice, Gorya was gone, his clothes on the ground. A long, dense leopard with thick, shaggy, scarred fur and fierce burning eyes met Kingston in the air, sweeping past him, wicked claws shredding his underbelly, gutting him before whirling in midair and sinking claws onto the golden leopard's back. They landed heavily, Rogue's entire weight on top of Kingston, breaking the leopard's back. Kingston lay gasping in pain, blood and intestines leaking from his belly.

Braum couldn't believe how fast it was over. Rogue had defeated the challenger in seconds. *Seconds.* If he'd blinked, he would have missed it. As it was, he hadn't seen Gorya shift. He'd been too fast.

Edik's leopard, Prince, didn't wait for Rogue to lift his head or get off Kingston. He charged, intending to hit the *pakhan* in the side and drive him away from his brother. At the same time, he would break ribs and hopefully incapacitate Rogue. At the last possible second, Rogue, as if he had eyes in the back of his head and springs on his paws, launched himself into the air so that Prince rushed past him.

Rogue seemed to fold himself in half, a tornado of fur and claws and teeth raking both sides of Edik's leopard so that long furrows of fur flew into the air, fur that should have protected the animal's muscles. Instead, pieces of flesh hung open, as if the other leopard had carved him up on either side with sharp knives. Rogue landed easily right beside Prince, rearing up as the other leopard did, so fast he was a blur of movement, raking the underbelly and genitals viciously so that only torn flesh hung as he leapt away. Rogue returned with a powerful bite to his hind leg, snapping the bone on the left side and then crushing the bone on the right so that Prince could only lie in a pool of blood, staring at his opponent with hate-filled eyes.

Krylov cursed under his breath. Braum could only admire the efficiency, skill and speed of the leopard. He didn't seem to have a weakness. Jago studied him as well, and his leopard seemed just as reluctant to face the challenge as Braum was. Neither spoke or offered the other advice. They had watched both battles closely, hoping to find anything that might give them a glimmer of hope in their coming fight with Rogue. He had defeated both challengers in seconds.

Karol was a thoughtful, methodical man, and his leopard, Duke, was much like him. He didn't rush his attack. He didn't try to catch Rogue off guard while he was distracted fighting another leopard. He waited and then circled around cautiously, eyeing his opponent.

Braum waited to see what Rogue would do with this new approach. Gorya's security had formed a loose circle around them, locking them within the arena so there was no hope of escaping into the swamp. They would have to fight to the death. In any case, Gorya's leopard was utterly fascinating. Braum had never seen an animal so fast, vicious or accurate.

As Duke circled, he continued growling a warning, the sound growing in strength as he became more and more aggressive. His head was low, eyes on his prey, teeth bared. Rogue was still, seemingly frozen in place, and then he began to pace about six feet from Duke so they were side by side, matching him step for step. For some reason, with the way Rogue moved, he seemed mesmerizing, like a ghost, almost disappearing in the tall grass.

Braum found his heart accelerating. He wanted to call out to Karol to be cautious. Gorya moved with blurring speed. His woman did. That leopard was a demon. They couldn't be deceived by or hypnotized by Rogue's disappearing act. The cat was silent. No challenging rumbles. That wasn't natural.

Krylov's leopard, Master, was a big Amur leopard. He paced close to Gorya's security team, his malevolent gaze fixed on the two challengers. He watched them carefully, as if he were trying to absorb Rogue's every fighting technique.

Duke suddenly turned and leapt sideways at Rogue, striking out at him. As Rogue twisted with blinding speed to meet Duke in the air, Krylov directed his leopard straight at Gorya's mate, charging at full speed, crossing the six-foot distance in one bound.

Braum's breath caught in his throat at such treachery—at such balls. Only, the little blond was no longer there. Just a hairsbreadth from the large male cat was a creature, half woman, half leopard. Back claws dug into the dirt to give her purchase and strength as she drove a knife into Master, ripping mercilessly across his entire left side, allowing his momentum to drive the blade deep. The wound ran all the way along his side, down low, close to his belly—close to his genitals.

The woman continued to shift, flinging the knife unerringly straight toward Gedeon, who caught it. Rogue had already abandoned his attack on Duke and slammed into Master, driving him off his feet. Knowing he was dead if he didn't get up, Master rolled desperately, trying to avoid the vicious claws raking his body and the teeth clamping down mercilessly on his right hip.

The two male leopards rolled over and over, kicking up dirt, leaves and rotting vegetation. The snarling and roaring had to be heard for miles as they fought on the ground. Rogue was enraged. Furious. He was in a murderous frenzy. He shot to his feet and began to circle Master. Methodically, he rushed in, delivering vicious blow after vicious blow, striking with precision, tearing deep lacerations in his enemy without mercy. Each time he jumped away, he delivered a contemptuous plume of dirt and leaves into his rival's face with a sweep of his giant paw.

Duke grimaced and scowled his displeasure at Master,

tail lashing as he stalked back and forth, his roaring adding to the din that was rising to the canopy of the trees surrounding the meadow. Gorya's security didn't take their eyes—or weapons—from him, but the leopard made no move to aid the challenger who had tried to take advantage of Rogue's distraction to attack his mate. Braum admired Karol's sense of honor even as he knew the shifter's leopard didn't have a prayer of defeating Rogue.

Krylov's leopard tried again and again to rise, but his attempts were decidedly feebler. Finally, he lay on his heaving side, his fur matted with blood, the dirt and leaves soaked in blood, and Rogue backed off to look around him. His muzzle was streaked red. His malicious demon gaze became riveted on Duke, and a chill went down Braum's spine.

There was no time to shout a warning. Duke hadn't even begun his charge when Rogue took him down and delivered a suffocating killing bite to his neck. Rogue held the heavy body, shaking it once or twice before dropping it to the ground, casting Braum a malevolent look and then returning to swipe with vicious, punishing claws at the other three downed leopards.

Braum slowly eased his shoes off and removed his shirt. There was no mistaking that look from the ferocious leopard. He despised the three incapacitated leopards he hadn't killed. Their deaths wouldn't be quick the way Master's had been. The way Rogue had looked at him, there was no doubt in Braum's mind his death would be ugly as well.

Rogue ran up to the little female leopard nearly hidden by the grasses of the swamp. Head and shoulders emerging for a brief moment.

Gorya put both hands on either side of the female leopard's muzzle. "Do me a favor, wild one, go home. Rogue and I prefer you to wait there for us."

They stared into each other's eyes, and the intimacy of that look broke something in Braum. She nuzzled Gorya's throat and turned, disappearing into the swamp. At once, two of the security guards followed. Rogue turned back toward Braum. There was nothing left of that soft man. Nothing. He was all vicious killing machine. All vengeance and fury. All rage. And he was coming for Braum.

14

GORYA lay on his back, staring up at the ceiling fan as he contemplated his life and wondered what the fuck he was going to do now. A lifetime of discipline seemed to be heading right out the window. Watching his woman nearly get shredded by that weasel Krylov had taken ten years off his life, but *Bog*, how easily she had switched from her innocence to her warrior. It was a thing of beauty.

He had come home to her drenched in the blood of how many men? So many. He should feel remorse. He knew he should. There were stains on his soul. The foul coppery taste of blood would remain in his mouth for days to come. Rogue may have torn those bodies apart, but he had participated. Directed. Strategized. Been an integral part of the process. Rogue didn't ever kill without his permission or cooperation.

What had Maya done? Had she condemned him for being a monster? He hadn't just come back coated in blood. He had ordered the deaths of the others involved in the trafficking ring—and that included the corrupt wives. He'd expected her to look at him with fear and loathing. He wouldn't have blamed her. He often looked at himself that way. There were times when he looked in the mirror and saw a dead man looking back. A ghost.

But Maya? His sweet, adorable Maya? She'd been up waiting for him. Her eyes clear and guileless. Gentle with compassion—for him. She didn't speak; she simply held out her hand to him and led him into the primary bathroom. He was so damn tired he could barely stand up. The day had started long before dawn and gone on until far into the night before he was satisfied they'd rounded up all of Braum's men and cleared out the traitors.

He had to rebuild the lair quickly with the few people he had left. They needed homes for the young children left without parents and hoped they could shape them into productive members of the lair. Fortunately, Meiling was able to read other leopards the way Maya could, and she'd found good families willing to take them in and provide loving homes. He would sort out more in the coming weeks and appoint others to help him, but all he had wanted to do was go home. At the same time, he had dreaded facing Maya.

How could she accept him after seeing the true monster in him? After seeing Rogue at his worst? They were vicious and cruel. Both of them. They had no problem with not only killing but also torturing. He had wanted to prolong Braum's and Krylov's deaths. After they had forced hundreds to suffer, they didn't deserve to die quietly. How did that serve justice? But then, that made him every bit a monster, just as they were.

He went to her exhausted. Barely able to stand. Barely able to look her in the eyes, and yet she simply took his hand and led him to the primary bath without a word. This time it was her thumb rubbing along the back of his hand in a small caress. Feather-light, but he felt it like a small earthquake moving through his entire body.

Without hesitation, she stepped right into the shower with him. Reaching up, she tugged his shirt from his body. He had to help because he was so much taller than she was, but when she got it free, she retained possession of it, crumpled it into her hand and tossed it out of the shower onto the floor.

He had walked into the bedroom barefoot, unwilling to bring grime from the swamp into their home, so she simply dropped her hands to the closure of his trousers. They were specially made, no zipper, no buttons, just a thick Velcro fastener to quickly rip free to shed when he was forced to shift on the run. She peeled it away, her lashes veiling her eyes as she freed his cock and balls and swept the trousers down from his narrow hips. He stepped out of them, one hand on her shoulder as if he had to steady himself.

"Turn on the shower, honey," she instructed. "I'm going to wash you."

He did as she said, careful to keep his body between hers and the water until he was certain the temperature wouldn't hurt her. He liked it hot. And he wanted steam. "There isn't any way to get me clean. I won't be sleeping for a long, long time."

She removed the robe from her shoulders, tossing it after his shirt, her blue eyes shimmering through the clouds of steam. He didn't want her to look at him. Inside him. Into his mind. She saw too much with those eyes of hers. "You're already clean, Gorya. See yourself through my eyes, not yours. You'll have no problem going to sleep tonight. I was proud of you and proud of Rogue. Thank you for sticking up for Alicia, Yelena and Leo and all the others Braum would have forced into his way of life."

She picked up the gel body wash and sponge and began soaping his body. Nothing in his life had prepared him for

Maya and the way she cared for him that night. She took her time, her hands gentle as they moved over his entire body. She didn't seem shy or inhibited or in the least bit worried he might attack her. She seemed—trusting. She'd given her trust to the monster.

He turned his face up to the spray of water and let it fall on him, mingling with the unfamiliar burn in his eyes as he pulled her to him and clung, holding on to her as if she were his lifeline. His savior. And she was. She'd said she couldn't be. But she was. How could he not want her—need her—with every cell in his body? How could he not love her?

Hell. He hadn't known he was capable of loving anyone. Not real love. Not the deep, soul-crushing, gut-wrenching, all-encompassing emotion that overwhelmed him when he looked at her. Or thought about her. Or just woke up, heart pounding because, with that first breath he took, he had to breathe her in to know his world was going to be right.

There she was, curled right against him the way she did, hardly taking up any space, yet she filled his universe. He could breathe. He could live. Rogue could live. So what the hell was he doing lying on his back, staring up at the ceiling fan, wanting more. Needing more. Instead of getting on his knees and thanking every god there was that she was his, his mind was filled with every erotic, lustful, dirty thought he could possibly have.

Love and lust were so twisted together he didn't know where one started and the other ended. They had no covers over them. The night was too damn hot. Muggy. Sultry. Perfumed. *Her* perfume. Her natural fragrance drove him insane. Sometimes he dreamt of her right before he woke, of burying his tongue in her and having her come apart for him. Moaning his name. Fingers digging deep in his shoulders. In his skin. He fucking ached for her.

He couldn't just lie there next to her. He didn't trust

himself. Sighing, he started to sit up. Her hand slid along
his bare thigh, and he froze. That whisper of a touch was
like a brand burning her name into his skin. His cock, already as hard as a rock, became a thick shaft of pure tita-
nium.

"Baby." His voice came out more of a growl. A deep
rasp. A warning.

"You're burning up. You went to sleep relaxed, and
now every muscle in your body is as tight as a drum. What
is it?"

They had made a vow to be honest with each other. He
turned his head to look at her. Her large eyes stared
straight into his. No fear. Where had her fear gone? She'd
had a complete breakdown when Wraith had gone into a
fever pitch of heat, and yet now she looked at him with
speculation, desire. All woman. Temptation. Not good
when he was in such a state.

Gorya took her hand—the hand that was so small in
comparison to his. Very slowly he brought it to his swollen
cock and wrapped her fingers around the hot, pulsing
shaft. He waited for her retreat. Her fear of him. She'd
completely fallen apart a few nights earlier, yet she didn't
flinch now.

Her fingers tightened, long lashes sweeping up and
then down to look at the sight of him with their joined fists
surrounding his girth. "You feel like a combination of silk
and steel."

His heart clenched in his chest. She didn't try to pull
away. Instead, she seemed fascinated. More than fascinated. She even shifted slightly closer to him as if getting
a better look. She had never avoided looking at his body
and he'd never hidden himself from her, but she'd never
looked at his cock, not with that particular look in her
eyes. Was it real? Desire? Had her fingers tightened and
pumped along with his of their own volition?

"I want you." He barely recognized his voice. The rasp

had deepened. It didn't matter how low he spoke; she heard him. She couldn't fail to hear the ache. She still didn't freeze or pull away.

"How is this any different from any other night? Every night when you're curled around me, I can feel how hard you are." Her lashes lifted, and once more her gaze met his. Steady. A slight flush began to spread over her entire body.

He found her not only sexy but endearing. Adorable. She couldn't help blushing, a full-body blush, and he loved that about her. Hell. He loved everything about her, but it only increased his need for her, and that was extremely dangerous when he was riding the very edge of his control. He didn't want her hand to go away, but he didn't dare stay where he was.

"I want you with every fucking breath I take, Maya, but add to that the buildup from Rogue's battles. It's all come together in a perfect storm. I just don't trust myself tonight. I think it's best if I go spend time working off my energy away from you."

The pad of her thumb slipped out from under his fist and caressed the long vein running along his shaft as together they gave another slide up and then down. He stifled a groan. He was playing with fire, but it felt so good, he couldn't make himself get up and leave her. Her legs moved restlessly beside him.

"You always seem so ready. So ready. Are you always like that? When you're around other women do you get hard like this?"

She bent her head toward his cock as if examining him—or as if she might take a taste. He felt the warmth of her breath bathing his cock's head, and his heart shuddered in his chest. She tilted her head back to look up at him, her eyes wide again.

"Not other women. Just you. I can't walk into the same room with you without getting hard. If I breathe you in, I get hard. Most nights I don't want to fall asleep because I just want to stare at you, afraid you'll disappear on me. I don't want to miss a single one of your expressions. Just looking at you while you sleep makes me hard. It's only you, Maya. But tonight . . . tonight is different."

Her small teeth tugged at her full lower lip while she contemplated what he'd said, but she didn't pull her gaze from his. He could see she struggled to find the right words to tell him whatever it was she wanted to say. Eventually the tip of her tongue moistened her lips, making him want to groan. His cock jerked, making her fingers react, tightening her fist around him almost possessively.

"The thing is, Gorya, if I'm being honest with you, I think about you day and night. I have very erotic dreams about you and things I'd like us to do together." Her lashes swept down and then back up, and the flush on her skin deepened from a pink to a blushing red.

Gorya found that her voice alone was an aphrodisiac, her hesitant, innocent admission uttered so low, as if he were a priest and she was making a confession of a great sin.

"I want you, but I have no clue what I'm doing or how to go about making it happen without panicking. I was counting on you to take the lead in that department."

Her voice trembled just a little, letting him know that trepidation was there, but her gaze was steady, telling him she meant every word. She looked at him as if he might be the devil tempting her to commit sin, but she was willing to follow him down the path. Hell, she'd just confessed that she was willing.

"Baby . . ." The last thing he wanted to do was talk her out of anything, but if it was too soon for them to make any progression, he didn't want to set them back.

The pad of her thumb moved again as their combined fists did another slow squeeze up and down his shaft, and sheer pleasure burst through him.

"When you kiss me, I can't think straight. When you touch me, my body belongs to you. I just don't quite know how to control my fears, but I want you so much. I want us to find a way to be together the way we're supposed to be."

Gorya looked down at the woman the universe had somehow gifted him. She lay beside him, looking up at him with the trust he'd asked her to give him. The world had given her a shit deal from the day she was born. His family had most likely been part of the raid murdering her family. They'd certainly been responsible for the torture and rape, the trauma and nightmares. But there she was. His. His gift.

Just like that, she took away every selfish inclination he had. She melted him with her resilience and strength. Her loyalty. And that sexy combination of innocence and siren.

Gorya gave her a mock-stern look. "We have rules. Steps. An order we agreed to follow."

A little frown flitted across her full lower lip—the one he was tempted to bite. "We already skipped a few of the steps. What's a few more?"

"You really don't like rules, do you? Or authority figures."

"No. And I don't acknowledge *anyone* as my authority figure."

That was a challenge if he ever heard one. Amusement sliced through him. Genuine amusement. She'd given him that when he'd never had such a thing. She meant him. He was not going to be an authority figure to her. He didn't want to be. He wanted to be her partner. Her lover. The one man in the world she trusted with the real Maya. But he had to earn that privilege.

"So you think we should skip a few more steps."

She nodded. "I think it would be a good thing, Gorya. We have the *entire* rest of the night, and you could maybe think of ways to make me not so afraid of . . . um . . ."

He raised an eyebrow. "Me touching you? You touching me? You're touching me now. How does it feel to touch me? Do you like it? You washed my entire body earlier. Did you like that?"

Maya once again used her thumb, this time to trace the rim of his cock's head, sending shivers of heat and flames racing through his veins and down his spine. It was a lesson to him how much she did trust him and how innocent she could be about pleasing a man even though she'd had sex countless times.

Rape wasn't making love. Fucking wasn't beautiful intimacy, not unless done with one's partner in an intimate, loving way. Maya didn't realize that every touch of her hand, no matter how feather-light, inflamed him even more. She had no idea that a man in love with his partner wanted to spend hours exploring her body, learning how to bring her the most pleasure possible. That just the slightest touch from her could set his body off the way no lap dancer ever could. He knew because this was all new to him as well.

"Maya," he encouraged. "We should talk about this. The more you're able to communicate with me what you need or want, the easier it will be for me to give you those things. And I want to. I want to take us there."

One finger traced little patterns on his thigh, betraying her nervousness. He covered her hand with his to give her courage. She'd been so brave and trusting so far. They were making huge strides far faster than he'd ever dared to hope. His woman.

Her eyes met his again. "I loved feeling like I could touch you without being afraid when we were in the shower. Sleeping next to you is one of my favorite things because I can feel your body wrapped around mine. I don't want to be afraid of you. Afraid of what happens or how I'll react when we come together."

"Are you afraid I will hurt you?"

A little frown drew her eyebrows together, and he rubbed at the tiny lines to erase them.

At once the tension eased from her soft features. "I told you I loved you and I meant it. I tell you I trust you and I mean that too. I love when you kiss me. I want to be able to kiss and touch you freely. I'm not afraid of you; I'm afraid of the door in my mind that creaks open and ruins what we have when something—and I don't know what that something might be—triggers it. That's what scares me the most. Me ruining everything for all of us." Her voice dropped so low that even with his acute hearing he could barely discern her words. "Me losing you."

Gorya's heart fluttered in his chest. He unwrapped his fingers from around hers, releasing her hand, albeit reluctantly. His cock felt bereft, but he shifted his weight so he lay on his side, his body partially covering hers without putting weight on her. He knew that was important—not to hold her down. She couldn't feel like a captive. She had to feel as if he was protecting her, not caging her in.

"You're never going to lose me, Maya. *Never*. I'd find my way back from hell to get to you." He meant that too. "You're always going to have triggers. I'm going to have triggers. You saw them yesterday. You saw them in both Rogue and me. That monster is never going away, baby."

Her gaze softened even more. Rings of silver circled the blue of her eyes as she looked up at him with so much love he had to press a hand over his heart.

"There isn't one part of you I don't love, Gorya." There was sincerity in her voice. In her mind. Her lips curved into that slow, mischievous smile that sent his heart into overdrive. "Although sometimes I want to smack you in the head with a wet towel."

He leaned down and nipped at her full bottom lip, unable to resist, while one palm slid over her right thigh, urging her to part her legs for him. "A *wet* towel?"

Maya's eyes darkened with desire at his touch, but she followed the silent command he'd given her. "It really stings when you snap a towel and the tail hits bare skin. If it's wet, the sting is even worse. When I was living at my friend Lexie's house in Houston, she showed me how to snap towels."

"What else did she show you?" He kept his voice low and mesmerizing. Slightly teasing, distracting her from feeling fear at what was happening between them.

"Pillow fights. I didn't know how to play. She taught me how to have fun. It was a foreign concept to me."

Gorya bent his head again, nipping her earlobe with his teeth—a tiny sting that made her gasp, her eyes widening with shock. He flicked his tongue out and licked away the sting until she took a shaky breath.

"I love how you're so soft everywhere, baby," he murmured, nuzzling her neck. He blazed a trail of fire from her ear to her throat with small kisses and nips. He had a primitive desire to leave his mark everywhere on her. A claiming. He wanted her to look in the mirror the next morning and know she was his. She was loved.

"Do we want to jump all the way to step seventy or stay in the sixties?" he asked, his voice muffled against her skin. He licked at her chin. Bit down. Kissed his way up to her mouth and then simply brushed his lips over hers.

He didn't give her the satisfying kisses she sought; he had other things in mind. She gave him a frustrated sigh and her brows drew together, but she didn't protest because once again his palm had slid around to the inside of her thigh. He began to slide his hand up and down her leg in a long caress, bringing the nerve endings to life.

The tip of Maya's tongue made her lips glisten. She began to pant, her breathing ragged enough to lift her small breasts up and down, drawing his heated gaze. Her nipples had peaked, coming to attention. Good signs her body was coming to life for him.

"Since we're jumping steps, seventy sounds like a good start."

If it was possible, his cock hardened even more against her hip at her answer. That was his woman. Very courageous. He permitted a wicked smile to escape. "I should have known my woman would be the naughty one. Spread your legs wider for me."

She complied immediately. With just the very pads of his fingers he found her clit, a little hidden treasure he had wanted to touch almost from the first time he'd realized the depth he felt for her. A tremor ran through her body as he tenderly stroked caresses over it. He used a light touch, never rubbing or flicking, just keeping up that gentle motion as he watched for her reaction.

Her hips shifted and she spread her legs a little wider to accommodate his large hand. He felt the first signs of wet arousal as her body began to slicken, readying itself for him. There was no sign of alarm in her eyes, only a kind of dazed shock and wonder.

"I want to know all the things I can do to you that make you feel good," he admitted, bending to pull her taut nipple into the heat of his mouth.

Maya might be small, but she was soft and pliant, a perfect mouthful. So very sensitive. She shivered when he sucked at her nipple, and stroked and teased with his tongue and teeth. She arched her back, both hands coming up to catch at his head. He wasn't certain if she intended to pull him toward her or push him away.

A little moan escaped from her throat, and she dug her heels into the mattress so that she pushed against his stroking fingers as if seeking more pressure. He didn't give it to her. He kept stroking those same gentle caresses over her clit, occasionally circling, and then using the wide pad of his thumb to add to the sensations he created for her.

Gorya. His name exploded in his mind a bit brokenly. The sound was sexy. Exactly what he wanted to hear.

Now that her mind was open to his, he felt the heat shimmering through her veins, arousal whispering through her. Her body had gone from pink to a flushed red. She was unable to hold still. Her gaze clung to his in a kind of dazed wonder. Her focus was entirely on her body and what she was feeling. Flames licked at her, smoldered in her veins, threatening an impending inferno. The pressure built and built toward an explosive detonation. One small hand gripped his wrist as if she might try to stop him.

There would be no stopping, not unless he could see or feel that she was becoming terrified. She needed to see what loving a partner was—giving pleasure to them generously. He wasn't expecting anything back. Hell, at this point, it didn't matter to him if she ever touched him. More than anything, he felt as if his entire future was centered on this one moment. He needed success.

He continued petting her clit, a relentless caress that kept her focus centered on her body. His entire focus was on her and her reactions. Her heightened color and breathing. He breathed in her whimpers. The sounds were music to him. She began to writhe against the sheets, slipping and sliding in a kind of mindless pleasure. The friction of her soft body rubbing against his hard cock sent shocking waves of heat down his spine, but he kept his attention centered on her.

He leaned closer to her again, his breath in her ear connecting them in the same way his fingers connected them as he caressed her in her most intimate place. "My little treasure." He meant Maya, the woman, as well as her clit. "No other man will ever have the pleasure of seeing you like this. You only give yourself to me."

Her lashes fluttered as if they were too heavy to lift, but he wanted her to see him. See who gave her bliss. Ecstasy.

He would do that for her every time. No other. He brushed kisses over her small shell of an ear. "You're so wet for me. That's all you, Maya. That's not Wraith. That's Maya needing Gorya."

You're taking your sweet time about it.

Impatience was in her mind, and he had to work to prevent himself from smiling. *My woman is always in a hurry. It's best not to hurry these things.*

Another whimper escaped. Her head tossed back and forth on the pillow, her pale hair shimmering in the light spilling through the window. He was in her mind, so he could feel the building of her impending orgasm. So close yet still hovering just beyond her grasp. She didn't even know exactly what she was reaching for—only that she needed it more than her next breath.

I don't know what to do, Gorya.

That was what he'd been waiting for all along, that whispered admission. Maya needed to ask him. To trust him. She wanted to follow their silly step one and step two because it made her feel safe. *He* made her feel safe. She let him touch her intimately because she trusted that he would guide her body to absolute euphoria, and he had every intention of doing so.

When I tell you, baby, you're going to let go. Give me all control. Sex isn't about control. It's beautiful and messy and should be absolute bliss. Trust me to keep you safe.

She closed her eyes, and he immediately lifted his fingers away from between her legs, although he continued to stroke his hand along the inside of her thigh. The moment he stopped, she gave a little keening cry and her long lashes lifted instantly.

"Eyes on me, Maya. Keep your eyes on me."

Once more he settled the pad of his thumb over her clit, caressing tenderly. This time he very gently slid a finger along her wet entrance. Her eyes widened and the hand on his wrist tightened, but she didn't attempt to stop him. Her hips lifted slightly off the sheets as she moaned his name. He curled one finger into that hot, tight, oh-so-wet slit. He didn't see how his cock would ever fit in there, but it wanted to try. Against her hip, his shaft jerked hard, pulsing and raging to be in that tight, hot channel.

Gorya ruthlessly shut down all thoughts going in that direction to concentrate on bringing his woman an explosive orgasm. He wanted her first to be spectacular. Rockets going off. Start off slow and keep building and building in waves. He wouldn't be finished—this was just the start—but it was step seventy, not seventy-one.

Her gaze clung to his as the heat coiled into a massive fist. He used his fingers and thumb with merciless intent, driving her up until she peaked. Her mouth formed a round O, eyes going wide, gaze clinging to his for an anchor as her body found release for the first time. The orgasm washed over her in waves, flowing through her, shooting her toward the stars, but she was bound to Gorya, safe with him.

She gave a soft little cry—no screams, but he hadn't expected her to scream. That wouldn't be like Maya. Her breathy whimpers and pleas, the intimacy of her demands in his mind, were sexy and just for him. He licked his fingers, looking down into her dazed eyes as she stared up at him with a shocked look on her face.

"I think step seventy is going to be one of your favorites." He couldn't keep the satisfaction out of his voice. Her body was totally relaxed. Every muscle loose, as if she were boneless on the sheets. He placed one hand on her belly. Splayed his fingers wide, covering her entire tummy. "I want to proceed to step seventy-one."

"You might have to give me a minute. My brain is mush. I don't think I can move, Gorya."

He tugged at the little blond curls at the junction between her legs. They were white-gold. "You don't have to do anything but lie there relaxed. This is all for me. I need to taste you. I've needed to since the first time I caught your scent there in that basement when Rogue claimed Wraith. Some nights it's all I can think about."

He bent his head and touched his tongue to her skin, running it over the curve of her breast. "That fragrance is elusive, all yours. It isn't soap or shampoo. It's you. I chase after it at night. When I kiss you, I can taste it in my mouth, but it isn't enough."

Maya raised an eyebrow, looking intrigued, but she didn't protest when he took her hands and placed them over her head.

"Try to keep them right there for me."

"Since I'm feeling as limp as a dishrag, I don't think that's going to be a problem, Gorya." She gave him a tentative smile as she left her arms stretched above her head.

His heart accelerated, going wild with excitement. So close. They were so close. His cock was in a frenzy of need. He knelt up on the bed, a hand to each of her ankles. "Widen your legs for me, baby. As wide as you can and still be comfortable."

For the first time unease crept into her eyes. He smoothed his palm up and down her slender leg. "We can stop if you'd like." He knew he looked enormous looming over her much smaller body as she lay on the bed. "I'm not going to lie over the top of you. I want to be between your legs." He should have explained that to her. He'd been so eager to get his tongue inside her, he hadn't thought to go slowly enough not to scare her.

"I don't want to stop. Will this really give you pleasure, Gorya?"

Her voice trembled, and beneath his palm he felt a shiver go through her. He bent to press a kiss to her belly button. "You have no idea how much. This is one of my biggest fantasies. Devouring you." He lifted his head to deliberately leer at her. "The big bad wolf."

She laughed, just as he knew she would, her body relaxing again. "Well, who am I to say no, then?" She widened her legs, giving him more room than he'd anticipated. His shoulders would definitely fit. He could wedge himself between those slender thighs and feast.

"That's my girl." He didn't wait. Couldn't. He kissed his way over her belly to those golden curls as he stretched out between her legs, one hand going under her bottom and the other dropping casually to her tummy to hold her in place.

He lifted her bottom slightly. "Put your legs over my shoulders and keep your knees open."

She did so, legs quivering, her eyes on him, watching his every move intently. Gorya turned his head and ran his tongue from her knee to the heat emanating from her slick entrance. He felt the answering clench of the small muscles through her abdomen. Her orgasm had brought her nerve endings alive. She was focused on her body's reaction to his smallest attention.

Very gently he nipped his way down the inside of her thigh to behind her knee, where he massaged and then continued down her calf and back up. Her nipples had grown hard, two taut peaks. The muscles beneath the hand he held on her belly clenched and unclenched. He did another slow lick up her thigh, and right before his tongue reached her slit, he flicked her clit with the flat, wet heat.

Maya keened, nearly exploding out of the bed. Above her head, her hands curled into fists, with the sheets bunched inside. She writhed, or tried to, but he held her easily. He repeated the exact same pattern on her other leg, taking his time, an unhurried, leisurely exploration driving them both a little insane.

Gorya.

What is it, baby? I'm just getting started. This is for me. I gave you yours, this is mine.

I didn't know it would feel like this.

He pressed a kiss to her greedy little clit, thankful she was sensitive and responsive to him. *We're only getting started.*

I could pass out.

If you pass out from pleasure, I'll be okay with that.

Gorya lowered his head to the feast; he felt as if he'd been waiting a lifetime for it.

15

MAYA wasn't certain she would survive. Gorya looked like a hungry predator about to devour his prey. She should have been terrified with the way he was holding her, looking at her, so focused on her, but the reality was that the intensity made her feel wanted and loved.

He not only told her she was beautiful, he also made her feel that way. He made her feel sexy. Feminine. Special. She'd never had what he gave her. The way he looked at her now—with his eyes so intent on her, so centered, as if nothing else mattered in his universe but her—was thrilling.

She wouldn't have moved if the ceiling was coming down on top of her. His face was carved with deep lines of lust. That should have terrified her. But she saw the love shining so starkly and unashamedly in his fierce hooded eyes. He did lust after her and she wanted him to. She wanted that look on his face, his eyes looking over her so possessively, as if she were his last meal and he was starving.

He lowered his head to her. She felt the heat of his breath against her slick entrance. Heard his deep inhale and knew he was taking her scent deep. Every internal muscle in her sheath clenched in anticipation. There was a gush of welcoming liquid. She'd always been dry. No matter what, she hadn't responded to anything she'd tried, such as toys or her own fingers, to coax a climax. She'd always assumed her childhood trauma had made her frigid. That assessment was entirely incorrect.

Watching him, his focused expression, seeing his need, was as much a turn-on to her as the things he was doing to her body. She braced herself for an assault. She got gentleness. That same gentle lick over her clit that his fingers had done. The petting motion. Only this was heat and moisture. A lick of flame. She felt that whisper of a touch like a twisting flood of arousal spiraling through her veins.

Gorya. She whispered his name into his mind like a prayer. With love. With adoration. He had given her so many gifts. So many firsts. She hadn't known her body could feel this way, that she was capable of soaring so high. He was the miracle saving them, not her. Never her. He could think whatever he wanted, but she knew the truth. Gorya was her truth.

His tongue circled her clit almost lazily. Flattened. Swept up and back in a long, slow lick, savoring what he was doing. Then he was licking at her entrance, using that same gentle lapping as if he were tasting a delicacy. Savoring it. Committing it to memory. Each sweep of his tongue was a hot brand burned into her flesh. He drove the air from her lungs until she felt raw with need, and he hadn't even gotten started.

He'd said this was for him, but she didn't believe him. Not the way he treated her so gently. It felt like worship.

His strong features were stamped with pure sensuality. Moisture glistened on his short beard and mustache. The feel of both against her sensitive feminine parts added to the fire beginning to spread through her body.

He looked like sin incarnate. The very devil. His gray eyes had gone nearly pure steel blue and were filled with such raw desire she found she couldn't breathe. It didn't seem to matter how terrifying he looked, how enormously strong, or how much he said this was all for him; his touch said otherwise.

Tears burned behind her eyes, dripped down the walls of her mind. A deep craving took hold of her. She wanted to be just as giving and as generous to him as he was to her. Her body felt soft and feminine. Beautiful. Burning from the inside out. Needy. More needy than even the last time he'd built her up so slowly. This was different and so much more.

Golden sparks went off like fireworks behind her eyes, warring with the tears. *I can't breathe without you, Gorya. I'll never be the same.*

I haven't been able to breathe without you since the moment I laid eyes on you. We belong together. The pair of us. Broken. Damaged. We work together. No matter what happens, we fit.

His tongue danced in her, and a storm of fireworks burst through her body, raining through her mind like colored stars. She didn't know how to control that overwhelming need building and building inside her. Thunder roared in her ears. Forked lightning struck from her core to every sensitive nerve with each stab and lap of his tongue.

Gorya. Too much.

Feel how much I love you, baby. This is love. This is me loving you. Replacing those memories with our memories. Every stroke of my tongue is my way of telling you I worship the ground you walk on.

Her mind seemed to go into shock as the glittering

pleasure rushed through her like a storm. Her hips bucked of their own volition, the heels of her feet digging into his back. Flames burned her from the inside out. Every nerve ending was alive, raw and aware of him. It felt as if a million electrical impulses sparked over her skin. Tension gathered into a tight, coiled knot. Her breasts ached and her nipples burned, as if he'd lit matches to the tips.

The throbbing ache between her legs became a roaring fire. An inferno burning out of control. A wildfire running away with her. She needed . . . Was desperate.

You have to stop before I go insane. She was sure she would go insane if he stopped.

I waited a lifetime for this. It came out a growl. Possessive. *I told you I needed this.*

That rasping growl in her mind, along with his admission, only added to the leaping flames, making them burn higher. Hotter. Making that coil in her core tighten to the point that she thought her mind was unraveling.

I won't survive. I'm really not going to.

Then neither one of us will. His mouth and tongue and teeth were relentless. Merciless. But he was gentle. So gentle. Tender. She couldn't say there wasn't care and love mixed with lust and desire. She just couldn't tell where one started and the other left off. The implosion building in her was big, and she knew if she allowed it to detonate, there would never be a Maya without Gorya. They would never be separate.

Baby. We're already woven together. The same heart. The same soul. The same skin. They broke us to pieces, and when we put our pieces together, we became one. You. Wraith. Me. Rogue.

She had to believe in something for survival. In someone. She hadn't been enough to save Wraith and herself. She could never have saved Gorya on her own. Her childhood had damaged her beyond repair—until Gorya.

He was taking her apart and putting her back together.

Giving her life, but seriously, this fire was too hot. Both might burn in the inferno. Her gaze was riveted to him—to that beloved face. Despite being gentle, his mouth was more aggressive, more determined to collect from her every drop of what he considered his. His tongue plunged into her again and again, drawing out hot liquid and finding secret sensitive places to stimulate until she was bucking in his hand, only the palm on her belly keeping her in place. His mouth suckled and bright, hot pleasure radiated through her like rockets to every part of her body.

Hold on, baby, just a little longer. I need this.

She had to find a way to give him whatever it was he needed, but it was impossible to think clearly, not when the earth tilted and spun. She couldn't see anything but those sensual lines carved deep into his face. Sin incarnate. He wanted complete surrender from her. She knew that was what he was asking. If she gave him that she would be giving up that last little guarded piece of herself. She wanted to give him everything.

Panic warred with her need to please him. To unite them once and for all. To taste nirvana. To allow herself to shatter and trust him to pick up the pieces just as he'd done before. She wanted to give him that, wanted him to know he was hers and she would do anything, stand by him always.

She bunched the sheets in her fists, holding as tight as she could, trying desperately to breathe while he continued to devour her like a man on a mission. Leisurely. Savoring her. Taking her further than she thought it possible for anyone to go. The tension coiled, winding tighter and tighter until the fierce need was growing so out of control, she grew afraid.

Gorya. Fear edged her mind. Touched his. She reached for him, her body shuddering and writhing beneath his hands and mouth. Desperate for something only he could give her.

Gorya raised his head to look at her, his eyes nearly silver with love and darker blue with desire, his beard gleaming in the light spilling from the moon. Her heart stuttered.

Then come for me, baby. Soar free.

He bent his head to her again and she felt his tongue flick and dance. For one moment her back arched and her bottom nearly came out of his hand, and then the flames rolled through her, waves of them, streaks of colors bursting behind her eyes and a million fireworks exploding.

The orgasm went on forever, aftershocks rocking her while heat rolled in her veins, and she was vaguely aware of Gorya's beard on the insides of her thighs, the friction adding to the waves of sensation rocking through her. His hands were gentle, his voice soothing, raspy, loving, but even though he was in her mind, she wasn't completely aware of what he was saying to her.

Maya drifted in a sea of pleasure. An ocean of brightly colored stars. There was only pleasure—and Gorya. He was right there with her. She felt him. Mind to mind. If anyone had told her real love existed and she would find a soul mate, she would have laughed at them. She didn't consider herself romantic or poetic, but she knew she'd been born to be with Gorya. Destined for him.

Take a breath, baby.

She felt the pads of his fingers tracing a path along her cheekbones. Down to the corners of her mouth.

I don't believe breathing is all that important.

Masculine amusement filled her mind. There was satisfaction in making Gorya laugh. He so rarely did. She would have basked in that accomplishment, but she couldn't move, and her brain was too fried to think. Even the mechanics of breathing was too much for her to figure out.

Still. Gorya took her hand and brought her fingertips to his mouth, biting down hard enough to sting. That penetrated her blissful euphoria. *Take a breath for me anyway. And while you're at it, stop crying.*

Am I crying? Was she? *I didn't used to cry. Not ever. I think you've turned me into a sobby crybaby.*

I'll take the blame if you breathe.

He pressed her palm over his bare chest where she could feel his heart beating. He inhaled. She followed his lead automatically. She was beginning to come to life again, the bright colors receding and the magic electrical sparks fading to leave her wanting more.

You can't offer to take the blame on conditions if you are *to blame,* she pointed out.

His soft laughter filled her mind, and his lips followed the trail of a tear down her face. *You're coming around from your sex-induced high.* The purring male satisfaction in his voice was almost too much to take. He was definitely feeling smug.

Maya had flung one arm over her eyes as she lay there trying to find a way to catch her breath. She turned her head and peeked out from under her arm to look at the man who gave her so much and never seemed to ask for anything in return. She wanted him. Wanted to give him everything. There was no putting her mouth on him yet. She didn't have that kind of courage. She would have to work up to that. But she wanted to be part of him. Skin to skin. His body in hers. She felt empty without him. And he needed. No matter what he said, he needed.

She was slick and wanting right at that moment. Still trusting and unafraid. There was trepidation, but if she took the initiative, didn't put it on him, gave him a gift instead of him being the one doing the giving, she might figure out a way to make love to him.

Gathering her courage, Maya sat up and rolled onto his large frame, sprawling over him, straddling his hips, careful to align her body perfectly so the heat of her feminine core was just inches below his thick shaft. He rose like a tower against her belly, between her legs, so hot he felt like a furnace. Excitement coursed through her along with a sense of power.

Gorya lifted his head, his eyes meeting hers in shock. Both hands caught at her shoulders as if he might launch her into the air. His fingers tightened into iron bands, but he didn't move, his body frozen.

"What are you doing?"

She raised a hand and traced the lines in his face with a fingertip. "I love your face. I love looking at you. Staring into your eyes. I see love there and it always astonishes me. Takes me by surprise. I keep thinking it won't be there, but you never fail me."

Maya bent forward to feather whisper-soft kisses from the corner of his eye to the corner of his mouth. She rubbed her lips back and forth over his, savoring the feel of his soft bristle before she sat up again.

"I've been thinking."

Gorya regarded her warily as he gently pushed a strand of hair behind her ear. "It's always dangerous when you use that tone and get that wicked look on your face."

"Don't worry. I'll take good care of you," she promised, doing her best to look sober and innocent. Deliberately she wriggled her body, letting her slick heat slide along his lower belly right next to his cock's head.

She felt the tremor run through his body, and his hands slipped to her hips. Once again, his fingers dug into her flesh.

"Baby, seriously, this isn't a good idea." Little beads of sweat broke out on his forehead.

"Hear me out, Gorya." Deliberately she looked down at his cock, swollen and desperate. Pearly cream dotted the broad head, and she couldn't resist wrapping her fist around the shaft as he'd taught her earlier and smearing those drops with the pad of her thumb.

Gorya shuddered beneath her, his legs moving as restlessly as hers had. "I'm listening, baby, but you'd better talk fast or start working on giving me a hand job."

"I wasn't thinking hand job. I thought we could skip all the way to step one hundred."

Gorya froze again, his gaze fixed on her face. She felt she could drown in his eyes. Be lost there. She wanted to drown in him.

"Baby." The sound was a cross between a groan and a sexy rasp.

"No, I mean. I want you right now. This way. I don't know what I'm doing, so you'll have to help me, but I want you inside me. Filling me up, part of me. Skin to skin. The way we're meant to be. I want to make love to you. I'm asking you to help me do that."

"Damn it, Maya, you know I can't refuse you. I don't even want to, but you have to be sure. Be certain. You can't do this for me. I can wait."

His voice sounded hoarse. Broken. Sexy. He might think he could wait—and he probably could because he loved her that much and he would sacrifice anything for her—but she wasn't willing to let him do it. And she wanted him. *Craved* him.

She tightened her fist around his cock, thumb moving in swirls through those drops. "I want this for me. For both of us. Right now. I know this is the right time." Her hips gave a little undulation, spreading fire along his lower thighs. "I need you in me. I just have to be the one controlling how at first."

Kiss me, baby. I need you to kiss me.

That was unexpected. She had geared herself up for climbing onto his cock, but that wasn't Gorya, no matter how much he might want her there. He needed to connect them first. And their connection was the intimacy of their minds and his blazing kisses. His arms swept around her. Tight. Firm. That wall of protection he gave her where she always felt so safe.

Very gently Gorya pulled her body to him. She slid deliciously over his straining cock. Sprawled over his chest, her legs on either side of his ribs until he cupped the back of her head and simply brought his mouth to hers. The earth stood still. Time stopped. Her heart clenched hard in her chest and her sex fluttered. This man.

His lips brushed over hers gently. Once. Twice. Barely there. A whisper of a touch, no more, but it was a brand. His brand. His tongue teased along the seam of her lips, silently commanding her to open for him, and she did, helpless to do anything else. Her heart stuttered and then pounded like mad. A thousand butterflies took wing in her stomach. It was impossible not to get lost in the fiery paradise of his mouth. Flames raced down her throat, spread through her veins, straight to her sex.

For the very first time, his fist bunched in her hair, his first sign of aggression. For one brief second panic welled, but his kisses were possessive, and he poured himself into her. Taking her into him. Breathing for both of them. Sweeping her up into a world of color, of magic and perfect cleansing fire.

Everything around her receded until there was only Gorya. Only him. This man. Her arms were around his neck, fingers digging into his short hair. She found herself kissing him back, giving him everything she was. Wanting to give him so much more. For her, he managed to wipe out the past in these golden, glittering moments she got to spend with him. He gave her laughter. Fun. Ensured Wraith's survival. Appreciated the warrior in her and saw the woman even when she didn't. And he gave her this— making her feel like a sexual being when she'd been certain she never would or could be.

He kissed her over and over, breathing for them both when he stole the breath from her lungs. She found she liked hard and demanding kisses. Possessive kisses. She even liked his fist bunched in her hair. There was no hold-

ing back from him, not a single part of her. She didn't
want to and she didn't try. She surrendered everything she
was to him. Melting into him, giving up heart and soul,
needing him to know she was ready for step one hundred.

The most important step of all.

*The most important step was the first, Maya. Your
trust. When you gave me your trust. I hadn't earned it and
you still gave it to me.* He lifted his head and looked into
her eyes. *I'm a fucking Amurov.*

Maya framed his beloved face with her palms. *You're
my fucking Amurov. You always will be.*

His smile started in his mind. Right there first. She felt
joy in him. His eyes lit up, the frost disappearing, and then
his lips curved and his white teeth flashed at her. "Are you
ready for this, baby?"

Gorya asked the question, and everything in him
stilled, waiting for the answer, sending up prayers to whatever forces there were in the universe that she was ready.
He needed her desperately.

Her lips trembled, and just for a moment fear skittered
across her soft features, but she nodded. "I want to make
love to you, Gorya. With you. I just don't know what to do."

There was a tiny bit of frustration in her voice. He
didn't want to lose the moment, and she was skating close
to panic despite her determination. He lifted her back into
a sitting position. His cock was so damn hard it looked
like a spiked tower.

Fortunately, he had long arms. He pulled a bottle of
lube from the drawer of the end table and poured some
into his palm. "We want this to be as easy as possible on
you. You're going to be tight, baby."

He had anticipated that. She hadn't been with anyone
in a long time. He had girth to him. She could control how
much of him she took in. That should make it easier.
"You're going to straddle me just the way you are and sit
right over the top of me."

He wrapped his fist around the base of his cock and kept one hand on her hip. He didn't urge her to move. That was her decision. She had to make up her mind whether she really wanted to have sex with him or not.

This was Maya. His woman. He should have known she wouldn't be clinically detached. She had said she wanted to make love to him, and she obviously meant what she said. She ran her palms along his chest and then wrapped one fist around his cock.

"You do know I think you're beautiful, don't you? I've never thought a man's cock was beautiful until I saw yours."

The feel of her fingers sent fiery flames darting down his spine. The sight of her moved him the way nothing had ever moved him in his life. She lifted herself and slowly began to lower her sheath over the broad, weeping head. He wanted to watch her face, her expressions, but he couldn't take his eyes from the sight of her little body trying to stretch around his cock's head.

The burn was exquisite. Unbelievable. The first touch of her slick heat set his blood roaring and his pulse pounding. His cock throbbed and pulsed. He gritted his teeth, holding on to his control as she worked at giving him entry. He helped, pushing gently with his hips, a small nudge to open her enough to allow the first inch to pass her tight entrance.

At once her silky-smooth, scorching-hot muscles surrounded him, gripping him so hard he had to pause to catch his breath. It was like being in a vise of pure fire. Both hands went to her hips. He wanted to slam her down over him while he surged upward to bury himself balls deep. Nothing had ever felt this way. Nothing. No one.

"Relax, baby. Try to relax for me."

She hissed something, but he couldn't pull his gaze from the sight of the two of them coming together. She made some little movement with her body. A tiny swirl that allowed the folds to open enough to give him room to push another inch inside. The friction sent jagged streaks of white-hot lightning through him. The top of his head wanted to blow off and he wasn't even all the way in her. *Bog.* His woman. Once he was in her and moving, he wasn't certain he would have any control at all, when he'd always had the stamina of fifty men.

Her fingers stroked his belly, close to his cock. *Do you feel me? Hot like a volcano. That's how I am inside when I think about how much I love you.*

She pushed down, taking him deeper, swallowing more of his cock until she surrounded him with silk and fire and love. For the first time, he lifted his gaze to hers. There was no fear. A little discomfort, but he expected that. He would work through that and give her pleasure. Mostly he saw love shining back at him.

Do you want me to help you?

She nodded. *Yes, please.*

There it was, the absolute trust in him that he would make this good for her. For the two of them. No matter her past or his, this was their time together, binding them. She believed in him. He'd never had that, and it was sacred to him.

I love you, Maya. Never forget that.

He gripped her hips tighter and surged into her, burying himself completely. That exquisite scorching fire clamped around him like a silken fist, leaving him gasping, desperate to drag in enough air to breathe.

Baby. So fuckin' tight. He waited for her body to adjust when all he wanted to do was move. He needed to move.

Is that a good thing?

Trust me, it's more than good. Feel what I'm feeling.

I am. You feel much different than I do.

It will get better. Give yourself a minute to adjust. He took that same minute to absorb and savor the perfection of the moment. She was his. Entirely his.

Actually, I believe you're mine.

She moved first, lifting and undulating her hips in a riding move that shocked the hell out of him. Her muscles slid over his shaft, gripping and massaging, sending shock waves through his body. She was flushed, beautiful, her eyes wide and dazed, lids at half-mast. She looked sultry and sexy. His little siren.

She ground down again and again, her hips moving over him, and he gave her control, let her take the lead. The sight of her added to the increasing pleasure coursing through him. It also allowed him to breathe through the raging fire enough to get back more of his discipline.

He concentrated on the desire etched into her soft features. The passion in the green-blue of her eyes. Her ragged panting. The gasping moans that escaped. The way she threw her head back and ground down harder. She breathed his name in a kind of reverence.

I need more. I can't take us there.

He didn't want it to end. Not yet. He wasn't ready for their bodies to be apart. He could live right there, inside her, sharing her skin.

Are you certain you want me to take control?

She hadn't stopped moving, picking up the pace, grinding faster and harder, doing little swirls, her inner muscles suckling like a million greedy mouths. Each one sent more streaks of fire shooting through him, sent more flames rolling through his veins. His heartbeat pounded in his cock, and blood roared in his head, thundered in his ears. He was the one who might not survive. But he never wanted this to end.

Yes. You have to. She nearly wailed her answer. Demanded it of him at the same time.

Bossy little thing. He loved the demand in her voice. The way she looked. The fear was gone, replaced by pleasure—pleasure they were giving each other.

He caught her hips, lifting her as he drew back, and then surged deeper and harder with a stroke she'd never experienced before. He counted the pulsing heartbeats in his chest. In his cock. Would going from gentle to harder and his taking control be a trigger?

Gorya. She wailed his name. *Move.*

That was his answer. The best answer. He repeated the action, burying his body deep into her scorching-hot channel. Her silken muscles clamped around him, causing an amazing friction that made the firestorm rage hotter and wilder, burning out of control.

His woman was a wild little thing, moving with him, matching his rhythm, her body following every command of his hips and hands. She had a need to please him, to give him everything he'd given her, and was determined to be the best at loving him. And she was more than enjoying herself.

He kept his mind in hers to ensure she wasn't fearful. Every move he made sent pleasure racing through every cell in her body. She writhed and moaned, grinding down over him, throwing her head back, hair spilling around her.

It feels like an electrical storm. Building and building until I think I'm going to explode into a million fragments. It's terrifying and spectacular at the same time.

He loved that she felt that way. Gripping her hips, he stormed into her over and over, allowing the streaks of fire to engulf him with roaring flames. The intensity of each thrust sent that sizzling burn ripping through them, driving them both higher. He felt the tension in her coiling tighter, building higher.

Give yourself to me. He made it nothing less than a command. Even in her mind, his voice was hoarse. He could barely find a breath. *Give yourself to me. I'm giving myself to you. All of me. Everything I am.* He poured love and reassurance into her mind.

For a moment she hesitated, but his words gave her what she needed to have, the courage to let go, to surrender completely.

His fingers dug into her soft hips. *Look at me, baby.*

She lifted her long lashes and he found himself looking into her blue eyes. There was love there. Love for him. She took a deep breath and, with his next surge, let the fireball take them together.

The torrent ripping through her was massive, and Gorya felt every single wave centered around his cock. Her silken muscles clamped around his shaft like a vise, grasping and milking with scorching-hot fingers, sucking with molten mouths, taking him with her. Thunder roared in his ears so loud he couldn't hear his own hoarse shout as his cock pulsed and jerked inside that inferno.

The entire space of time they stared at each other, they kept their minds firmly merged. The torrent seemed endless, the waves rocking them while the fires leapt from one to the other. Gorya touched her tear-wet face.

"Did I hurt you?"

She slumped forward, arms sprawling across his chest, the action sending streaks of electricity arcing through his groin. He felt every aftershock in her body. Every ripple. She lay over him like a rag doll, too weak to move.

"Not hurt." She pressed a kiss over his heart. "I can't breathe."

He could see that. "You aren't trying. Slow your breathing down. I think you deliberately forget how."

"It's highly overrated," she murmured.

He lifted her off him and laid her gently on her back. "Give me a minute, and I'll get a washcloth and then run us a bath."

She waved a finger in the air and then dropped her hand back to the sheets as if her arm was too heavy to hold up. "It's okay. I'll just lie here and bask in the beauty of all things you."

Gorya found himself smiling up at the ceiling fan. "I'd be fine with that, but you'll be sore, and since I like step one hundred quite a bit and want to practice, I think soaking in a bathtub is necessary."

She gave a little frown to the ceiling. "And there it is. Your bossy is coming out. Although practicing step one hundred is a good idea." She turned her head to look at him. "I'm still not ready for leopard sex."

He swept his palm over her thigh. "The leopards can handle their sex, baby, just as they did before. They aren't worried, and neither should we be. We're all in this together."

Maya stretched her arms over her head languidly. "Who knew sex could be so good? I had no idea it would feel like that."

A dark, malevolent shadow slithered through Gorya. He rolled over, partially covering her body, still careful not to pin her down. Catching her chin between his thumb and finger, he tipped her face up so she was forced to look up at him.

"I'd kill any man who dared to touch you." He made that an absolute decree.

Her wide blue eyes searched his for a minute, and then her slow smile curved her lips, the one that always got him in the gut. "Are you acting like a jealous lover? Seriously? As if I'd ever let any man put his hands on me other than you. You aren't really jealous, are you?"

Shit. He was acting worse than a teenager with his first crush. What the hell was wrong with him?

Rogue. I'm blaming this on you.

She won't believe you. The cat sounded just as amused as his woman did.

Gorya knew she wouldn't. *No, but she'll let me off the hook. She's sweet that way.*

She's going to spoil you. Timur said you were going to be whipped. I think he's right.

"I'm not jealous, baby. I know you wouldn't take on another lover. It's that ridiculous cat of mine. He can't stand the thought of any man getting close to you. His mood riles me up, and I find myself blurting out outrageous things."

Maya leaned into him to brush a kiss across his mouth. "No worries, honey. Rogue will settle once Wraith is through her heat and emerges fully for him to claim."

Gorya sighed. He'd promised her he'd be honest with her, even if he had to sacrifice his pride and admit to being a jackass. "I'm lying my ass off."

She rewarded his confession with a girlish giggle. "I know. Fortunately for you, I love you even when you're being a jackass."

16

SAN Antonio, Texas, wasn't nearly as sultry as the swamp he now called home. Gorya tightened his hand around Maya's, pulling her closer and tucking her under his shoulder protectively. She didn't like crowds. There would be a crowd at his cousin's estate—a large crowd. He was looking forward to introducing her to his cousins. She wanted to hide in the house they were staying in. It wasn't just the fact that there were going to be so many people, it was that they were all Amurovs.

Fyodor's wife, Evangeline, owned a little jewel of a house in town hidden on a cul-de-sac. At one time Gorya knew Timur and Ashe had thought to purchase it from her and make it their home, but they lived on the same property as Fyodor and Evangeline. Timur was head of Fyodor's security, and the estate was immense. Timur and Ashe had decided to add to an existing house there they'd fallen in love with. Evangeline had offered the house in town to Gorya and Maya to stay for the night should they need a place. That gave Maya comfort, knowing they would have a place of their own, apart from others, to go to at the end of the day.

Time was short and they would only have one day for San Antonio. Jaoa Escabar Velentez wouldn't be happy with the lack of communication from his son. And Artur Krylov, the current *pakhan* of the lair that had belonged to the Amurov family, would be anxious to hear from his brother. This was only the first visit of several they had to carry out quickly in order to ferret out and eradicate traitors and spies.

A small tremor went through Maya's body as they walked into the enormous great room of his cousin's massive estate. The stone fireplace was gorgeous, and a curved staircase wound around the room up to the next level. The floors were gleaming hardwood, with a starburst pattern ingrained deep in the polished wood. The hardwood floor extended into the sitting room, a much smaller and cozier version of the great room.

They could hear the sound of children laughing and the soft murmur of adults speaking together. Then Fyodor's large frame was filling the doorway, his eyes lighting up when he caught sight of Gorya, a rare occurrence for him unless he was home with his family. Then his gaze found Maya and he stilled. He glanced behind him as Evangeline came to greet them.

"Gorya, we're so happy you've come home. And you've brought your mate with you." Evangeline sounded sweet and welcoming the way she always did. She stepped forward, immediately going straight to Maya and reaching to catch Maya's hands in hers. "We're so happy he found you, Maya. Ashe told me she's never seen him so happy."

Maya took her hands without a single sign of reluctance, but Gorya felt it. She'd never liked anyone to touch

her, male or female, although most people found Evangeline to be soothing.

"Thank you," Maya replied simply.

"I hope you're hungry. We have breakfast ready. Gorya
said you were arriving early and would only have a short
period of time before you had to leave. Everyone has come
to meet you. Gorya"—Evangeline leaned into him to kiss
both cheeks—"the children can't wait to see you. They've
gone a little wild on us. I told Fyodor not to tell them
ahead of time, but he couldn't resist."

Gorya was very aware of Fyodor's frown of disapproval as he stared at Maya in disbelief. Mitya and Sevastyan, his other cousins, didn't hide their shock at Maya's
appearance either.

Timur didn't warn them about you. He poured amusement into his voice and took her hand, pulling her protectively under his shoulder as if she would need it from his
big bad cousins. *They're buying right into your girl-next-
door act.*

*More likely they think you've robbed the cradle just
like everyone else.*

*That, and they really think you're an innocent lamb,
too innocent to be with the likes of this family. Although
Fyodor can't be saying much.*

"A word with you, Gorya," Mitya said. "Fyodor and I
have business to discuss before we go in."

Evangeline looked horrified. "This is a celebration,
Mitya. We agreed. A party. Fyodor, you promised me.
Mitya, you gave your word to Ania that all of you would
behave at least through breakfast so the family would have
the time to give Maya a proper welcome."

Gorya did his best not to laugh. That was Evangeline.
She might be sweet, but she could stand up to Fyodor
when no one else could or would dare to.

"Timur set them up to make fools of themselves," Gorya

said. "It's a brotherly cousin thing. They were just going to give me advice on how best to take care of my fiancée. She's young, and they worry she might have a problem with the life. I've explained the difficulties to her. She's gone into our relationship with her eyes open."

"She can actually talk for herself," Maya said.

That startled his cousins and made Evangeline laugh. "Good for you, Maya. Never let these men push you around."

They went into the dining room to find it filled with family. His family. To his astonishment, Gorya found himself inexplicably happy to see everyone there. His cousins were married with wives they loved. Fyodor and Evangeline had twin boys. Fyodor was so proud of them he could barely stand himself. He made a good father. He was firm but surprisingly gentle, not raising his voice to them when they were rough little things, tumbling all over the floor the way kittens often did.

The two boys made everyone laugh with their antics, even Maya, and she was tense throughout the breakfast. Mitya and Fyodor asked her several pointed questions. Before Gorya could direct the subject away from Maya, Ashe or Timur did. Sometimes Evangeline did, as if she could sense that Maya was uneasy with so many people around her. Sevastyan watched her closely, but he was quiet—mostly, Gorya was certain, because his wife, Flambe, would look up at him with a small shake of her head if he started to ask Maya anything. Gorya liked that the women were so protective.

It was a good morning spent with his family. Maya began to relax a little after breakfast and they moved into the great room, where the twins showed off their tumbling skills and used Sevastyan and Timur for a jungle gym. Gorya caught Maya giggling a few times as she watched the little ones scrambling over the intimidating men.

Finally, he caught her hand, kissed her knuckles and told the others, "I'm going to show Maya around the grounds. We'll take my security with me. Don't look disappointed, Evangeline, we'll be back inside shortly. I just need to stretch my legs. You can get to know her in a little while. I promise." He gave Gedeon a quick signal and nodded to Timur to alert Fyodor, Mitya and Sevastyan that they should be prepared to have their security personnel checked for traitors.

"The various security teams are outside on the grounds, Maya. We'll take a stroll around to familiarize you with the layout, but mostly so we can walk through the men and get a reading on anyone you think is betraying Fyodor, Mitya, or Sevastyan," he told her as they used a side door to go out into the large garden.

"Are you certain Wraith is going to behave herself surrounded by all those male leopards?" Gedeon asked. "Most of them are without mates."

"She's been very quiet lately," Maya answered. "I think she's getting close and gearing up for her big moment. Rogue would warn us."

He would, wouldn't he, Gorya?

Gorya tightened his hand around hers. *Yeah, baby. They're watching out for us too. They know we're in a dicey situation. All the Amurovs are right now. If we're going to protect Drake and shut down this ring, we have to play this thing just right. The timing must be fast and tight. Our leopards are on board. Both are.*

She only has so much control.

She'll warn you, he assured her.

Gedeon took her at her word because despite asking for Gorya's reassurance, she had sounded confident. Matvei, Rodion and Kyanite accompanied them as they wandered outside, seemingly just walking along various pathways. Gorya knew Meiling was close, somewhere high. She wasn't alone. There were other snipers on rooftops doing the same. With so many family members gathered, no one was taking chances.

The children were playing inside under close guard.
Evangeline and Fyodor protected them carefully. Each
time they had playdates with other children, even more
guards were put in place. Gorya understood the need, but
several times he'd seen Maya assessing the situation and
she didn't look happy.

You're worried about having children. He chose a path
that would take them through Timur's security team.

Why would you think that?

Amusement shimmered in his mind. *Nice way to avoid
answering.*

Her lashes lifted and she sent him a quick sideways
glance from under them. *I was giving myself time to think.
Unlike you, I like to consider what I'm going to say before
I commit to something.*

She put a little pressure on his side to move toward his
left. A couple of Timur's men were lounging beneath a
low-hanging branch drinking water. They looked as if
they'd just come back from a run. Without missing a beat,
Matvei engaged them in a friendly conversation. Gorya
knew them well, and he spoke to them too, accepting their
congratulations and introducing Maya.

She smiled demurely, looking as sweet and innocent as
she could possibly look. Beside her, Gorya thought he appeared to be the big bad wolf.

*They're completely loyal. They think you robbed the
cradle.*

*I did. I'm trying to feel remorse, but it's just not hap-
pening.* He waited, knowing she would circle back to his
question. It was important to him, and she didn't ignore
anything important to him.

He greeted the men he knew as they moved through
them. He'd been part of Fyodor's security team from the
beginning, working with Timur and then Sevastyan. He'd
protected Mitya, so he knew the men on both teams. Some

he knew from the old country, like Matvei, Rodion and Kyanite.

He pointed out various things of interest on the property to Maya and introduced her to different men he called friends. She often indicated they were all loyal.

I'm not ready yet. I'm getting used to us. I didn't think I could ever be with someone, Gorya. I never expected to have a relationship. You're extraordinary. I'm just getting adjusted to the fact that we can work.

That was Maya. Honest. Assessing. He understood. He was just as broken. Just as damaged. It wasn't like they were ever going to be a normal couple. But leopards couldn't prevent pregnancy. He was well aware of that fact. Preventive measures didn't work. That didn't mean the female always got pregnant, even in a heat. No one knew why. And they didn't always carry. Mitya's wife had trouble carrying a baby.

I understand.

Are you going to stay on as leader of the lair in the Atchafalaya River Basin territory? Leading a total criminal life as a crime lord doing nefarious things?

It was all he could do not to burst out laughing. *For God's sake, woman. You're going to blow our cover with your nonsense. Nefarious things? Like what? Gambling and arms deals? We're both fucking assassins.*

She gave a disdainful little sniff in his mind. *We only assassinate really bad men.*

Baby, I hate to point this out to you, but I'm a really bad man. You were going to shove one of your favorite knives into my heart before you decided you liked my pretty-boy face.

She moved into him, sliding beneath his shoulder. He slowed his steps to match hers. They turned toward a group of four men who seemed to be playing dice together. He didn't recognize any of the four.

"Gedeon? I've never met any of these men. Don't introduce us. We'll keep a distance and just assess them," Gorya instructed.

"Two of them joined Timur's team recently and two Sevastyan's security team," Gedeon briefed him.

Assassinating criminals isn't the same as running an entire organization, especially if you're very good at it, which, unfortunately, you are.

He had to work at keeping his expression blank, although he allowed her to see the amusement in his mind. *Why, thank you for noticing. I am very good at being the top boss. And to answer your question, I took the job and can't very well quit, not when I cleaned the lair up so nicely. I have to ensure it runs smoothly and everyone makes a decent living.*

She was silent a moment as they wound their way through several trees. *Do you think it's a great environment for children to grow up in? Look at the way Fyodor and Evangeline worry about their children's safety.*

He took his time answering. He couldn't very well leave who he was behind. There was no escaping being Gorya Amurov. They would eventually have children. They were leopard. He was a criminal. It didn't matter that he was doing his best to be as clean a criminal as possible; he was still a criminal. And he had more blood on his hands than most did.

We'll find ways to keep our children safe if we have them.

She slid her palm along his ribs. He knew that small gesture was a sign of needing to say more. She was intelligent. She knew there would be children.

We can handle anything together, Maya. We aren't alone. We'll have Wraith and Rogue. My family will help us. Some of them are already experienced, and we'll do our best to put off having children as long as possible.

She rubbed her palm along his ribs again. *I would*

*never get rid of our child, Gorya. No matter how afraid I
was. Never think that. It would be part of you, and I love
you. I would guard that child with everything in me.*

*I know you would, baby. I have absolute faith that you
would.*

Her breath hitched suddenly, and she abruptly came to
a stop, leaning down to fiddle with her shoe. She slipped
it off and shook it out as if she had a rock in it. Gorya
crouched beside her.

What is it?

*Those men. The things they're thinking. The things
their leopards remember. They're part of a trafficking
ring out of Panama, straight from Escabar Velentez's lair.*

All four of them? I can do this one.

*No. Give me a minute. There are four leopards. This
isn't easy. Just make it seem natural to give me the time I
need.*

Gorya signaled Gedeon and his crew and they surrounded him, bringing out a small pack and handing
around sandwiches and waters. They kept Maya in the
center, surrounded by the larger men so that as they talked
and laughed in low tones, it was impossible for the four
men to really do more than get glimpses of her through
the solid wall of shifter security.

Gedeon, like Maya, reached out to the leopards, to ensure she wasn't detected and to record any evidence
against them with his leopard.

The gathering of information from the four leopards
took longer than Gorya was comfortable with, and he realized both Gedeon and Maya were extremely uncomfortable with what the leopards were revealing. He couldn't
touch Maya's mind to alleviate her stress while she was
working, but it was clear the longer she stayed in the situation, the more anxious she felt.

When she pulled away, she was pale. She wrapped both
arms around her stomach and hunched forward, rocking

in a self-soothing motion. Gorya immediately swept his arm around her and drew close to hide her from the others. He didn't like the fact that she stiffened at first, but when he continued to hold her close, she relaxed against him.

"Tell me."

"Later. Inside. Away from them." Maya's voice was a mere thread of sound.

Gedeon nodded his head. "Let's get the hell away from here."

"I'd like to know what upset Maya," Gorya insisted, pinning the head of his security with a look that he rarely, if ever, had given him, reminding him he was the boss.

Gedeon refused to budge. "I've been around the Amurovs for years, working through private contracts with your family and now as head of your security. You don't forgive enemies. You don't abide human trafficking. And spies in your midst? Especially around your women and children?" Gedeon shook his head. "If we're playing this smart and we want to get any other information from them, it's best you don't question them or get your answers until we get inside, away from them. You'll need to be in complete control."

"I'm known for my complete control," Gorya countered, lifting his head to stare at the four men with glittering eyes.

"It's true," Kyanite agreed. "Rogue loses it, but Gorya stays calm."

Rodion nodded. "Known him since he was a kid. Always the voice of reason when his cousins were losing their damn minds."

Matvei rubbed his chin. "I don't want to add to his arrogant-ass ego, but he is the one always in control, Gedeon. Back in the day, when Fyodor and Timur would tear down the world, no matter what, Gorya stayed cool."

Gorya nudged Maya with his shoulder. *There you have*

*it, baby, eyewitness testimony. These things you accuse
me of can't possibly be true.*

She was too pale for his liking. Whatever the four leopards had revealed to her had made her sick, triggered too many memories. He wanted to change the subject. Make her laugh for a minute. Give her time to recover while they gathered up the leftover items from their impromptu picnic.

*You have an atrocious temper. I have no idea how you
managed to hide it from everyone.*

Despite the trauma, she was willing to let him lead her. How had he ever gone through life without her?

*Have you considered you've been wrong all along,
blaming me, when clearly the culprit for those foul moods
is Rogue?*

Rogue gave an inelegant snort. He thought Wraith may have sent a small curl of amusement as well, but if so, it was so fleeting, he couldn't be certain. Gorya tucked Maya under his shoulder without looking toward the four men. The temptation was there. They'd put that haunted tension back in her mind when the four of them had finally managed to push past it. He didn't, because when it came to his woman, his atrocious temper bordered on rage.

His comment earned him Maya's laugh. The sound was golden in the sunshine. It blended in with the way the birds sang to one another and the squirrels chattered. Nature moved all around them, adding to the beauty of the afternoon. They were walking through various groups of men, looking for traitors, something he would have done with Gedeon. It would have been a grim walk, although he would have looked easygoing and casual. Inside, he would have felt dead, the way he'd gone through most of his life feeling. Dead with enough of that rage Maya teased him about. He needed violence the way others needed air. Now, with her, everything was different.

Gorya glanced down at the top of her head. She appeared so small and delicate, but he knew she was every bit a warrior as the men surrounding her. She was pure steel. At the same time, she made his life fun. An adventure. He had a reason to live. And she'd saved Rogue. Hearing that laugh of hers was worth every bad moment he'd ever gone through.

She tilted her head back and looked up at him. *You're choosing not to see the broken and damaged parts of me.*

I love those parts. Those are the parts that allow you to live with me. You would never have looked at me twice, nor would I have been able to live with you.

Another smile broke out on her face and flashed through her mind. She knew what he said was the truth. The reason they worked was because they fit. They could make concessions for each other. With all four working together—Rogue, Wraith, Gorya and Maya—they had a real shot at living their life together.

They spent a good portion of the afternoon walking through the gardens and trees, making certain to check every single one of the security people brought on the property by his cousins. The only traitors they found were the four strangers. Gorya felt very satisfied that the plants hadn't had the time to set up any of the crew members he knew and liked so they could be blackmailed into helping them betray those they worked for.

It wasn't difficult to set up a festive room for the security teams to enjoy the baked goods from Evangeline's now famous bakery. Everyone loved the pastries from her shop, and setting up a long buffet table seemed normal to most of the security guards. Fyodor was generous with his teams, as was Mitya. Both had been in security themselves and took care to see that their men were paid well and lived in good conditions. They were treated with respect and, for the most part, as family.

Gorya gave the men in the room his easy, charming smile, keeping their full attention on him once he entered the room with Gedeon at his side. They'd left the women behind. He thought it best to handle this without any of them being close, especially Maya. He didn't want that trigger, not when he had the reports from both her and Gedeon of what these four strangers' leopards had revealed to them. He didn't want the men to see that each of the exits was blocked by his security force. His security did so casually, but if one really paid attention, they would see that it wouldn't be easy to get out of the room.

Evangeline's baked goods helped, no question about it. Her scones, cookies and pies were sought after, and with platefuls of them set out like a banquet for the men to feast on along with pots of coffee, they probably thought they'd hit the jackpot. There was no reason for their leopards to feel uneasy either. No one had threatened them in any way. Gorya had created a festive atmosphere.

His cousins had thrown a party in his honor, and he'd merely extended that festivity to the security of each of those who came to celebrate. He greeted those he knew by name, asking how they were, spending a little time with them so it would seem natural when he got to the four men who were strangers to him. Two of the men under suspicion were on Timur's crew and two on Sevastyan's crew.

Gorya had thought the Amurov family would have been off-limits to anyone in aggressive takeover bids. Krylov had shown no signs of respecting them. He wasn't afraid of taking them on. That meant he believed his allies in Houston and Panama were more than a match for them. That would have to come up in a discussion with his cousins and their allies. They would need as much information as possible.

The young man wolfing down the cinnamon-and-apple coffee cake wasn't much older than Jeremiah Wheating. He had dark hair with lighter streaks of blond running through it, as if he spent a lot of time in the sun. He didn't have the scars on his throat that Jeremiah had, but his eyes were harder, the lines cut deeper into his face. His eyes were green with an amber tint. As he approached, Gorya saw the man's leopard assessing him.

Gorya kept his energy low and friendly as he held out his hand. "I'm Gorya Amurov. I don't believe we've met yet, although Timur mentioned you were on his crew."

"Ian Razor." He had a firm handshake.

Gorya flashed another quick smile. "I see you appreciate Evangeline's coffee cake. I think that's how she ensnares all of us."

"You could be right. I don't think I've ever had anything that tastes quite so good. If I keep eating it, I'll have to double my training."

Gorya and the others laughed with him. Jeremiah reached out and took a handful of cookies. "You're lucky you weren't there when Ashe tried baking. She makes a mean latte though."

"Watch your mouth, kid," Timur said, but there was no bite in his voice.

"Just saying, boss," Jeremiah didn't sound in the least remorseful.

Gorya flashed a grin at the man standing next to Ian and held out his hand. "Gorya Amurov."

"Liam Kensie. Was just brought in with Ian a couple of weeks ago. Nice setup, and the food's especially good."

"You trained with Donovan?"

"We both did. Ian and I arrived around the same time in Borneo, and Drake took us on. When we wanted more training, he had us sent to Bannaconni's ranch and then here. He's moving us around to get more experience. We haven't had a chance to work with Timur yet, but my understanding is your cousin is one of the best security men in the business."

Gorya nodded. "And exacting. He doesn't take crap from anyone, nor will he let you shirk your duty. He isn't tolerant of mistakes. Ask Jeremiah."

"Mistakes cost lives," Jeremiah quoted, and stuffed another cookie into his mouth.

Gorya turned to the other two newcomers, greeting each with a handshake. These were the two on Sevastyan's crew.

"I'm Han Bastill," a sandy-haired man of about twenty-five introduced himself.

"And I'm Idris Malone." The second man was a bit older, perhaps twenty-eight, and heavier built, with very dark hair and eyes. "We also trained in Borneo and came to the United States with Drake. We recently signed on for more training under Sevastyan."

"It's interesting that all four of you trained with Drake," Gorya said. "Not surprising though. His expertise with shifters is renowned." He reached out to snag one of Evangeline's famous cinnamon cookies. "Where are each of you originally from?"

"We're all from Panama," Idris answered. "Grew up together, actually. When we were kids, we were orphaned. A family looked out for us, keeping us fed and clothed, and made sure we had schooling. We never went hungry. We were lucky. We weren't the only ones they took in."

"Jeremiah's from Panama as well." Gorya turned toward Jeremiah as if he could provide some explanation for them all coming from the same place.

"Panama is a big place, Gorya. I've never met them before," Jeremiah said. "Remember, I do have a mom and sisters. My mom is trying to marry me off to anyone who will have me just to get grandbabies."

The room roared with laughter.

"I guess there are advantages to being raised in an orphanage," Ian said, nudging Liam. "It was more a boarding school than an orphanage though. We were required to learn, but we were treated well."

"Who ran the boarding school?" Jeremiah asked. "I didn't know many people. I was a punk kid, but my mother knew a lot of people. She might know them."

"Jaoa and Carolina Escabar Velentez," Idris replied. "Jaoa's name carries a lot of weight with shifters in that country. With everyone. He's done a lot of good for the economy there. Turned things around."

Gorya thought it significant that Idris was the one the others allowed to speak for them. His voice rang with not only pride but almost a fanaticism. They may have been orphaned by Escabar Velentez and then brought to the boarding school to be programmed and shaped to be used as his agents. Escabar Velentez had seen the Cortez family fail when they'd tried to rule Panama with a bloodthirsty reign of terror. He was much more intelligent and made those around him fiercely loyal to him.

Gorya nodded thoughtfully. "We have a few friends in Panama. I believe they've mentioned Escabar Velentez many times and make him out to be a good man, although his opinion on a variety of subjects differs greatly from mine."

Ian's eyebrow rose. He caught up another piece of the coffee cake. "What opinion?"

"He believes in human trafficking. I draw the line there. Drugs. Guns. Gambling. Prostitution. There are plenty of ways to make money without selling human beings."

Liam frowned. "How would you know what Jaoa believes in or doesn't?"

Gorya sent him an easygoing smile and gave a casual shrug as if the conversation was of little consequence. "I took over the territory in the Atchafalaya River Basin and had to shut down the trafficking ring. There were several in the lair not happy about it."

"It's a lucrative business," Idris pointed out. "Very lucrative. And if done right, can turn an economy around quickly." Again, there was pride in his voice.

"Perhaps, but on the backs of children and young women and men. You make them sex slaves. They're subjected to rape, torture and often murder." Gorya kept his voice low, mild, not in the least challenging. "As orphans, all four of you could have easily been sold into that trade. You were lucky you weren't."

"And how many others are saved because of the sacrifices of a few?" Liam asked. "You should talk to Jaoa. If you listen to him, he can explain the pros and cons and lay it all out for you so it makes sense."

"I grew up in a lair that believed in human trafficking," Gorya said. "Nothing about it makes sense. My cousins grew up the same way. We witnessed how it tore apart our families and eventually destroyed everything we had from the inside out. It was killing our leopards. Killing our people. We've worked hard to rebuild. Trafficking is not something we would ever allow."

"Unfortunately for you, that's outdated thinking," Idris said. "It happens and it's here to stay. No one can stop it. It goes on all over the world. We may as well cash in on it and do good for our people. Many were starving. It can be done right."

"There's a right way to buy and sell human beings?" Gorya asked.

"Clearly, I'm not the one to discuss this with you. One of these days, you really should talk to Jaoa. I think you'd find him very interesting," Idris insisted.

The men didn't seem to notice that the room had gone eerily silent. Gorya sighed. "Sadly, I will be talking to him a lot sooner than I ever expected. I must personally deliver very bad news to him."

Instantly, the smiles were gone from all four men's faces. "What is it?" Idris asked.

Gorya shook his head. "It is very personal to his family. I plan on flying in our private jet to visit with him myself and tell him the news. I don't want him to hear any other way."

"It's possible we should fly home to be with him if this

will in any way impact the family," Ian said. "It isn't just curiosity. Jaoa has been a father to us."

Again, Gorya heaved a sigh and put on a somber expression.

"Raul, Jaoa's middle son, was visiting Derk Malcom, a college friend and the son of one of the more prominent leaders in our lair. Raul and Derk were caught red-handed in front of witnesses kidnapping, raping and torturing a fifteen-year-old girl. I'm certain Drake Donovan drilled into you the consequences of that kind of behavior."

All four men straightened simultaneously, clearly horrified. "There's a mistake." It was Idris who spoke for the others.

"There was no mistake. The two of them were brutal and caught in the act. They were executed."

"You don't understand. Family is everything to him. He'll go to war," Ian said.

"Evidence will be presented to the council. I will also give it to him." Gorya turned as if to walk away but then turned back. "A couple of other things you might find interesting. Those young women you kidnap and rape, quite a few are shifters. The mate to a leopard. You might not think it's important because you've spent a good part of your life enjoying raping young girls and think that's your right. You don't think about what that's doing to you or your leopard. You've been brainwashed by your mentor and believe whatever he tells you."

The four men glared at him. "You have no right to accuse us of such a thing," Idris snarled.

Gorya rolled his shoulders in a casual shrug. "I see no reason to get upset over things you know are facts. Haven't you ever heard of leopard whisperers? I'm sure you've heard the rumors. One leopard can talk to the other, and the other tells them every memory. Those memories are recorded. They can be entered into evidence. Just today I was walking on the grounds with my woman. We strolled right past the four of you. I found out quite a bit about you, none of it very nice, starting with the things you would like to do to the woman I love. I'll admit, it wasn't easy keeping Rogue from ripping the four of you into tiny pieces."

"I don't know what you're talking about," Hans snapped. "That can't possibly be true. No one can really do that."

Gorya leaned against the wall, crossing his arms against his chest. As always, he kept his voice very low and matter-of-fact. He could have been discussing the weather. "You wanted to repeat the time the four of you were together in Panama with a girl given to you by your mentor. You each raped her in every way possible, together and separately. You made her beg for her life. Crawl to you. You promised you would spare her if she pleased you. You caned her. You called it practicing your technique. Each of you practiced a different type of whip. Idris used a thin razor strap on her. That's what the four of you wanted to do to my mate."

The men looked at one another, unease on their faces, then around the room at the disgust plainly showing.

"You tortured Raul, and he made that up," Liam accused.

"Raul wasn't there. Jaoa was there, instructing you, mentoring you, ensuring you would learn the right way to be cruel to the women he trafficked."

Idris glanced toward the door.

Gorya shook his head. "You'd never make it. You came here to recruit for Escabar Velentez. That isn't going to happen. We don't like snakes in our midst. Usually, I deal with anyone who threatens my woman, but in this case, Timur and Sevastyan have the prior claim."

All four men had whipped out their phones.

"Your phones are useless," Gorya said. He turned and sauntered out the door as the security teams surrounded the four men.

17

THANK you for seeing us on such short notice, Mr. Caruso," Gorya said, holding out his hand. "The matter is extremely urgent, or I wouldn't have bothered you."

"No worries, and call me Marzio." The older man waved him into his office. "Your call intrigued me. Few things intrigue me at my age." He remained unruffled as Gorya escorted Maya in as well, one hand on her back. Gedeon entered with them.

"This is my fiancée, Maya. And you know Gedeon." Gorya said.

"Maya, very pleased to meet you. Please take a seat." He waved his hand toward the comfortable chairs across from his desk. It wasn't an opulent office by any means. One would never know the man was extremely wealthy. His desk was a beautiful carved cherrywood, the only truly expensive item in the room that Gorya could see. The walls were bare other than professional photographs of Marzio's wife, Ann, and their four sons. It was the office of a man who loved his family and didn't mind his business associates knowing he did. That was a rare thing in the world Gorya had grown up in.

Is he clean? If Rogue and Gorya had read the old man correctly, he knew nothing of what the Anwar family was doing on the docks of Houston. He had nothing at all to do with human trafficking, but Gorya needed it confirmed.

Maya inclined her head. Gedeon did as well.

"I've come across some very disturbing news that involves your family as well as mine. I thought it best to bring you the reports and have you read them. This isn't the kind of thing to tell you where it can be overheard or sent over a phone. If you don't mind, before I proceed, I'd like your permission for Gedeon to sweep your office for bugs."

Caruso leaned forward in his high-backed leather chair and regarded the trio, his dark eyes suddenly alive with interest. "By all means."

Gedeon took a few minutes because he was a very thorough man. "It's clean."

"Thank you," Gorya said, putting respect into his tone. There was something to admire about the man. He hadn't even insisted on having his security with him, and that said a lot about him seeing as how the Amurovs had quite a reputation. They were allies in business, but they were wary of each other.

Gorya took the report Maya had compiled under her alias Teona Kyva. It was extremely detailed. Gorya had included everything, so Caruso could judge for himself the extent and power of the ring. More, it was easy enough to see how the Anwar family set up the Caruso family from the very beginning to take the blame should they ever be caught.

The Anwar family had ruled Houston for generations, the docks a large part of that. It had been a shock to everyone when Bartolo had so generously offered the port to his closest friend, Marzio, and his family when things had gone badly for them in Florida. Marzio's wife, Ann, had become ill, and the doctors insisted they relocate. Bartolo had come to Marzio's rescue, giving him a lucrative portion of his territory. The Anwar family had their own freighters and one small section they used in the early morning one day a week, and they handled their own business. Little did Marzio know that the business was an extremely lucrative trafficking pipeline with Russia and Panama, shipping to New York and other places by land, air and sea. As Marzio read the report, it was easy enough to see when he reached the part where Giacenta, Anwar's daughter, was doing her best to seduce Cristo, one of Marzio's sons, using a drug procured from a black-market source.

"It is only by the grace of Cristo's leopard and his strange suspicions that he hasn't fallen for her wiles," he murmured. "This is bad. Very bad." He looked up. The old man had disappeared, and in his place was a shark with teeth. "You are Amurov. You must have come here with a plan. Tell me this report isn't going to the council before action is taken."

"That wasn't our first thought, no," Gorya conceded. "I know you and Anwar go way back."

"This is a betrayal of the worst kind." Caruso nearly spat the accusation. "By the time the evidence is verified by the council, Bartolo would have his family gone. No, we can't give him time or let him have an inkling anyone is onto him. If he has already found a way to lay blame on me and my boys, he must have a way to disappear."

Good for the old school. They aren't going to take this kind of shit lying down. Anwar betrayed him. They had an alliance, a friendship. Anwar had ruled a good portion of Houston for years, but in Florida, Marzio had had a big territory. He'd held an empire. He's a legend. Anwar should have remembered that.

"The first thing we must do is check every member of your security and crew to ensure there are no spies. As you have heard over the years, there are leopards that are able to do such things."

Marzio's eyes widened. "You have such a gift?" He looked from Gorya to Gedeon. "Such a gift would be incredible. Invaluable."

Gorya found it significant that it didn't occur to him that Maya also could have such a gift. She not only had it, but hers was far stronger. Marzio was old-fashioned. He might take care of his women, but he still regarded them as inferior to men when it came to business. They were not partners.

Gorya inclined his head. "It may be best to bring your sons in on this. Say nothing until we ensure that they haven't been compromised though. Albert Krylov was known to use drugs to influence people without their consent. Who is to say what the Anwars have done?"

"You checked me?" For the first time Caruso looked challenging.

Gorya gave him an easy smile. "Naturally."

Caruso glared for all of five seconds but then broke into a smile. "I would have done the same. I'll text my sons. They knew I had a private meeting this morning and will be close."

Gorya was certain their father would have told them to be alert. The fact that all four of Caruso's sons appeared in less than five minutes proved Gorya's theory correct.

The older man introduced his sons to Maya. Only the oldest had met Gedeon, so he was introduced to the others. Gorya knew them and engaged them in a brief, friendly conversation, simply stating he had recently been lucky enough to find Maya after he'd been challenged for leadership in the Atchafalaya River Basin. He'd taken over the territory there, was the new *pakhan*. He was Russian, not Italian, but they had joined the American council, mostly made up of Italian families, and were subject to the approval of that council. He was certain they weren't too happy with having the Amurovs taking over so many territories.

All the brothers are clean. Cristo has a strong leopard, which is a good thing. The spray Giacenta uses is meant to simulate a leopard in heat and confuse his leopard. He has not claimed her because something about her repels him even as he is attracted.

How does Cristo feel about Giacenta?

He doesn't care for her, but if her leopard is his leopard's choice, he will accept her.

Gorya didn't care for the speculation in her mind. *You are my choice, Maya.*

I wasn't at first. We would not be together had our leopards not insisted, she reminded him.

Rogue interrupted. *Which only goes to show that human shifters need guidance. Cristo is lucky his leopard has been able to guide him.* As usual, the male cat sounded smug.

Gorya hid his smile and met Marzio's inquiring gaze. "I believe we're ready to proceed."

"Before we go any further," Marzio said, once again sitting back in his chair and regarding Gorya over the tips of his joined fingers. His gaze was diamond hard. Gorya was looking at the man who had held an immense territory for years and ruled with an iron hand. "There's a price for everything, Gorya. I'll want to know what that price is before I involve my sons."

Gorya respected him all the more for asking the question. "An alliance between our families. Before there is any agreement, know this—on both sides, when an Amurov gives his word, he binds all family members, and the penalty for breaking that word is death. We would carry out that sentence on our own. If an ally betrayed us, it would be war and a death sentence. It would be annihilation. We don't expect aid with anything unless we go before the council, or you do, and we speak and agree beforehand. And human trafficking is off the table. That is an absolute."

Alessandro made as if to speak, turning toward his father with a small shake of his head, but Marzio held up an imperative hand. "I am still the head of this family and I make the decisions for all of us. We don't believe in selling other human beings. We've spoken of this often. My sons believe as I do and feel just as strongly. That is not a barrier to the alliance between our families."

Gorya thought it tribute to Marzio's authority that his sons didn't interrupt or act impatient. They waited quietly, arms folded across their chests, listening to their father and Gorya carefully.

"Your family will not be asking for territory in Houston? Or a tribute of any kind?"

Gorya shook his head. "We don't want or need such things. This is your territory, Marzio, not ours. When the Anwars are gone, every ally we have will aid you in taking over all of Anwar's assets and will back you with the council. We want nothing here. I've laid out our terms. We don't enter into alliances lightly. It's as much for your protection as for ours."

"There are advantages on both sides," Marzio conceded. "And helping our family to acquire what the Anwars leave behind is very generous."

Gorya didn't respond. Often silence was the best response. Marzio knew that to wipe out the Anwar family without the consent of the council, he would need the Amurovs. If he informed the council, there was no doubt word would get to the Anwars before they could be taken down. Marzio wouldn't want that. He wanted to take the Anwars down, to destroy them. He thought the way the Amurov family did.

Gorya's family had spent a great deal of time gathering

information on the other *dons* and *pakhans* who had territories in both the United States and overseas. It was a case of knowing your enemies. They'd studied strengths and weaknesses. It was engrained in them. Marzio was close enough and ruled by the same council. They did business with him on a regular basis. He and his sons were men they'd spent a great deal of time studying.

Marzio nodded. "You speak for Fyodor and Mitya? This agreement stands with all three of you?"

"Yes, as well as Sevastyan and Timur. They don't hold territories, but they are included in all decisions. It was Timur's decision to remain as Fyodor's head of security. Sevastyan chose to remain with Mitya."

Marzio handed the report to his eldest son. Beside him, Bendetto leaned closer to read it as well. Cristo and Donato waited patiently.

Alessandro's handsome face darkened as he read through the report, and then he glanced at his brother before looking at his father. Silently he handed the papers to his younger brothers.

"You don't look as shocked as I thought you would be," Marzio observed. "Did you know about this?" His tone was mild, but there was an ominous glint in his eyes.

Alessandro shook his head. "I suspected something was going on. Remember when one of our crew, Ciro, was killed in an accident near the docks? I never bought that story. Something didn't ring true. We even discussed it."

Marzio frowned. "Yeah, I remember. You were insistent, but I told you to tread carefully. Bartolo had been my friend for years."

Alessandro sighed. "Nothing added up. The accident report didn't make sense. And when I talked to our cop, he said he got stonewalled. That convinced me someone higher up had been bought off. None of the dockworkers would talk. Not a single one. Didn't matter how much money they were offered. The only time one came close was in a bar. Bendetto bought him a few drinks and he was beginning to get friendly, went to the men's room and never came out. Cops said it was a drug overdose, that he'd shot up in there, but he didn't have a history of taking drugs. He drank, but drugs were not his poison."

"You didn't bring this to me," Marzio said.

"I didn't have anything to give you," Alessandro admitted. "No evidence. Nothing concrete. Only a bad feeling about Ciro and that the Anwar family was up to something. I had no idea what. When Giacenta began coming on to Cristo, we talked it over and thought maybe he could get information out of her. She may have overheard her brothers and father talking, but then Cristo and his leopard were confused. We feared she was drugging him, but we didn't know how."

Marzio turned to Gorya. "What's the plan?"

"We're taking down the entire ring. All of it, from here to Panama. Shutting it down. To do that, we're on a very close timeline. We've started already, and word can't get out before we're ready. That means we hit the Anwar family tonight. We free their cargo, take back your territory and kill their people. If you're not prepared for that, we ask that you step aside and allow us to handle it."

Marzio's features darkened. "Bartolo betrayed our friendship and our agreement. He lied. He did share a very lucrative business with me when he knew my family was in a vulnerable position, but it was to set us up and at the same time make me always indebted to him. All along he was playing me. His family has tried to trap my son." He stood up slowly, his fists on his desk. "No, we will be part of this. And part of the rest. I ask that you allow me to attend to Bartolo and his daughter."

"If that is at all possible, just as long as both are dead in the end and it is impossible for them to communicate with anyone."

"That will be guaranteed. You have my word. Tell me what you need to get this done on such short notice."

"You and your sons know the docks and the surrounding area better than anyone else. We need detailed maps. One will do. We can memorize the map between all of us. If you have anywhere you suspect they would take prisoners to be held before being shipped out to other locations, those places should be raided. If you find prisoners, they need to be taken back, cared for and kept under wraps until we get this entire thing done."

"You believe you can take them down tonight?" Marzio asked. "All of the Anwar family and their crew?"

"We've got them under surveillance. We've been trained for this, Marzio. This is our field of expertise, as much as it pains me to say it. We were raised on it. We can get in and out of their homes without raising an alarm. That isn't all we want. We want everything they have as well as the key men in their crew. If anyone is left alive to report to someone higher up, we're blown. We still have two stops to make in New Orleans tomorrow, then Russia and finally Panama. That's a tight schedule and anything can go wrong."

"I trust you're already setting things up ahead of you."

"This isn't our first war. When we decide to act, we have all the pieces in place. That doesn't mean something can't go wrong."

Marzio indicated for his sons to begin preparing the information needed for Gorya and his family to raid the docks. "We'll handle all the possible places they might be keeping prisoners. We have the capability to take out the cameras and phones."

Gorya didn't tell him that was already being handled. His family wasn't about to take any chances. There wasn't going to be any blackmail. His family was too careful and saw to every detail. If Marzio hadn't agreed to the deal, they had been prepared for that as well—in a couple of different ways.

Marzio indicated for his sons to begin mapping out the docks for Gorya and his family before he turned back to Gorya.

"You speak in front of your woman."

Gorya didn't change expression, but instantly Rogue went as still as he did. Coiled. Ready to strike. He chose his targets carefully. No doubt all the Carusos were armed. The old man had a panic button in his desk to call his security people. That wouldn't matter. They had Gedeon. Maya could fight as well. Between the three of them, they would make it out of the building.

He didn't answer, but he did turn his gaze on the old man, let him see the killer in him for the first time. The easygoing negotiator of the Amurov family was gone, leaving the deadly predator facing the old man. He had to see what was in that room with him. If he made a wrong move or said the wrong thing, that predator would be unleashed, and nothing could call it back.

"I was raised in a different time," Marzio said, addressing Maya, not Gorya. "In my day, we didn't believe women should ever know our business. Female shifters weren't acknowledged to have any talent when it came to defending themselves. I've kept an eye on the Amurovs since they've taken over the territories of my fallen allies. All of them appear to treasure their women, but they also seem to include them in their business." He quirked an eyebrow. "Am I behind the times? Is that why my sons have not found their rightful mates?"

The four men stirred as if they might protest, but Marzio held up an imperious hand. "I wish to hear what she has to say. I have no grandchildren. I was lucky to find my Ann. I want nothing more than for each of you to find a woman you can love and respect, not someone you can tolerate for your leopard's sake." He turned back to Maya. "Am I wrong in my thinking?"

I'm the last person he should ask such a question of, Maya protested in dismay. *He means it. He's very sincere.*

Wraith stirred sleepily. *You are very wise, Maya. Tell him honestly what you think. That's all he's asking.*

Maya gave the older man a tentative smile. "I believe we're all different, sir. We're products of our environments. You were raised in a different time. But it isn't wise to underestimate women. We have our strengths too. Those strengths can help our men. Some of us need to be partners to our men in ways others do not. Some women prefer not to know what is going on in their man's world. I'm not one of those women. I think with shifters, because we have leopards, it's important to communicate. If you do know, there's no mistaking what each person needs in the relationship."

"You do feel you contribute to your man's business."

She shrugged. "I'd like to think I do. Only he can say whether I do. The fact that he wants me with him says something."

"In any case, it's something to think about," Marzio mused.

"If your sons are serious about finding the right mates, Marzio," Gedeon said, speaking for the first time, "you might consider that they look outside this area. Send them one at a time to Borneo. Have Drake Donovan take them for extra training."

Donato bristled at the idea, looking up from where they were marking a map laid out on the desk. "Training in what? What could Donovan possibly teach us that we don't know?"

Gorya and Gedeon exchanged a quick look. If there was amusement, it didn't show on their faces. Gedeon shrugged. "It was merely a suggestion."

Marzio indicated the map with a scowl. "I'd like to hear what you had to say, Gedeon. What does Donovan teach these shifters? Why are his bodyguards considered so superior? I hear that from everyone."

"He requires them to learn to shift with incredible speed. The training starts there and continues in every form of combat. Humans are required to be physically fit in the forest, working every day, and the leopards are as well. They are in combat situations daily. Hours of shifting increases speed. Your sons may be challenged for leadership. They're shifters. It could happen. Training just seemed a good idea to me. I didn't mean any disrespect," Gedeon answered.

Marzio tapped his fingers on the desk. "I've thought quite a bit about something that was said once. A young lady I cautioned against choosing one of your cousins was quite adamant when she thought one of my sons might challenge her intended. She was alarmed. She tried to backtrack, obviously worried she had pricked his sense of pride and possibly mine, but it was the alarm in her eyes and the honesty in her voice I couldn't forget. She didn't think my son had a chance in a fight against him."

His gaze met Gedeon's and then Gorya's. "After seeing the real you, Gorya, I don't believe he would have had a chance. None of my sons would be able to defeat your leopard. Even with the weapons we have on us, you intended to kill all of us if we had threatened your woman, didn't you?"

"Yes, sir," Gorya answered without hesitation.

Alessandro very carefully put the pencil he'd been using down on the top of the map and turned fully to face Gorya, partially blocking his father's frame. "You targeted my father."

"Naturally. I protect my woman above all else. He's sitting in front of a window. A perfect target. You're standing in front of that same window. Do you think the head of my security works alone? Your family has worked on the docks and in the city. From the time I was an infant, I grew up fighting for my life. We've had to fight for everything we've ever gotten. You've grown complacent, Alessandro. Your father and every one of you has been in danger since the Anwars brought you to Houston. Just one challenge from a shifter could swing the balance of power here."

Gorya reached between Alessandro and Bendetto and took the map. "I came here with a great deal of respect for your father, enough that I considered he could be a threat to us, and I took him as such. I'd be a fool not to be prepared to fight our way out of here." He folded the map and thrust it into his jacket. "Marzio, we'll have to check all your men, starting with your personal security and then those assigned to your sons. After them, call in your soldiers, any you trust to keep this night under wraps. Keep your strike teams small. Your sons will be leading them, and you'll be directing them. My cousins and I will penetrate the Anwar homes. We aren't going to leave anyone behind alive other than to try to keep my promise to you to bring you Bartolo and Giacenta."

"I'll start ordering the men to assemble in my conference room."

"It will have to be a room with a bank of windows," Gedeon said. "My backup must be able to take out a traitor in a roomful of shifters. If there's more than one, things can get dicey. It takes concentration to go through the memory of a leopard."

Marzio's sons just stared at Gedeon. They were learning at an alarming rate. Gorya had to give them respect that they didn't waste time arguing or protesting. They'd read the report and had already had their suspicions about the Anwar family and trouble on the docks. Their father had agreed to an alliance, and that bound them. They were willing to get on board, and all four seemed capable of absorbing information quickly. Gorya found himself respecting the family even more, and he respected few others.

"One more thing before we do this," Marzio said. "Gorya, after it is all over and we have taken down the entire ring, I would very much like you and Maya to come to dinner and meet my Ann. My leopard thinks her leopard is very soothing. He thinks Ann would find her quite enjoyable and Ann has precious little to look forward to these days. I would consider it an honor."

My understanding is that no one sees his wife anymore, Maya. He is being very sincere. You've made quite an impression on him.

It's Wraith, not me.

It's both, Gorya corrected.

"It would be our pleasure, sir."

Marzio gave an old-fashioned bow toward Maya and then began texting his private security to meet them in the designated room. His sons did the same. The real work of the night was about to begin.

THE Anwar family had become wealthy enough that they had built their own private gated community, where they could invite people to move into the homes they provided on the prestigious grounds. It didn't appear much different from other exclusive gated communities, with golf clubs and swimming pools and lavish estates dotting the landscape. But if one looked closely, they would see that the number of security guards was tripled, if not quadrupled, and the weapons they carried had serious firepower. The family was free to throw their extravagant parties, providing their sex slaves to their friends and entrapping officials and other members of the various lairs they invited. Compromising anyone who came wouldn't be a problem given what Maya had told them went on during the parties.

It was safe to say that anyone residing in that community was a member of the Anwar's inner circle and aided in their trafficking ring. They were the higher echelon, profiting the most from it and drawing others into it. Most of them pretended to be Marzio's friends. Some were shifters, some weren't. All were guilty, humans and shifters alike.

The roving patrols had to be removed first. Those on the grounds and those in cars. The phones had been dealt with, the towers taken down, affecting not only Anwar's area but a large grid, so it wouldn't seem as if he was specifically targeted. Next, they jammed all radio and internet access as the Amurov soldiers proceeded through the large community, silently killing the guards and removing the bodies from sight.

Enrico Anwar lived in a long, sprawling U-shaped house with an inner courtyard. Gorya had the interior of the house mapped out in his head, the long hallways and various rooms. Which room was Enrico's bedroom. His playroom. He had every luxury a man could want and then some. He believed in indulging himself. Gorya found it strange that there was very little to accommodate the man's leopard. No high perches. No plants to lounge under. Didn't Enrico allow his leopard freedom?

Gorya reached out to the leopard first, allowing his mind to travel through the house, energy low and non-threatening. There could be no prior warning, not that it would matter. He had no doubt that he would kill Enrico, but he wanted this night over with as quickly as possible. This was a large group of men and women involved in the trafficking, a big cog in Jaoa Escabar Velentez's wheel. It was imperative that they take it down swiftly and silently.

The leopard was lazy. Indolent. Enrico indulged in drugs, by turns sedating his leopard or hyping him up. His memories were of indulgence, but also work. Bartolo expected his sons to run the docks on the days and times they had to bring in their cargo, and they did. They were hard workers and didn't shirk, running the crews and keeping track of shipments, but when they played with the merchandise, they played just as hard. Enrico preferred to keep his leopard tuned to his moods and needs by enhancing him with drugs.

Gorya moved through the house unerringly, following the directions in his mind. It wasn't difficult with the wide hallways. The archways were open, leading from one entry to the next. The rooms were spacious, with comfortable furniture. Abruptly, Rogue snarled, warning him Enrico wasn't alone.

Gorya dropped to a crouch, annoyed that he hadn't been given that information. They had eyes on the houses. It should have been relayed to him that Enrico had company. He was lucky that Rogue alerted, warning him before one of the other leopards sensed their presence. He kept his energy low and nonthreatening as he moved toward his target, which served him well in this instance.

It took a few more minutes to tap into the four leopards. One of the shifters present was Enrico's younger brother, Samuele. The other three seemed to be close friends of the oldest Anwar son, now serving as his personal security. Only one of the three friends was tainted by drugs. Like Enrico's, the male's cat was disoriented and confused. The other two leopards were on edge. Samuele definitely hadn't taken drugs, and his leopard was alert and, like the other two, restless and stressed.

It took some time for Gorya and Gedeon to calm the leopards and keep them from alerting their human shifter counterparts to their presence before they proceeded toward the playroom. Gorya could hear the sound of a cue stick hitting pool balls and then a voice.

"I don't understand why Braum can't take care of Amurov. His rep isn't all that great," Enrico's distinct voice said. He had a slight accent, reminiscent of his father's. "I've met him. Believe me, he isn't very impressive. On a bad day, Giacenta could take him."

The three others in the room laughed. "Your sister could take Braum. He's a chickenshit, sitting back and getting everyone else to do his dirty work for him," one commented.

IT might be a good idea if you opened your eyes about now," Maya told Giacenta. "We've found all the evidence we need in your little secret safe behind the wall. Not a very clever hiding place when you consider how the perfume and pills that were smuggled from New Orleans are in such short supply."

Giacenta sat up with a curse, reaching for the gun she always kept next to her. It wasn't there. She glared at Maya. "Who do you think you are, sneaking into my home and robbing me? Do you have any idea who I am?"

Maya ignored her and indicated to Meiling, who was in the shadows. "She's ready for pickup. She's a bit of a mess, but no one's going to care what she looks like. I'd say she drank a little too much last night."

"My security people are going to tear you to pieces. You have no idea what you've let yourself in for, you scrawny little nobody. Get the hell out of my house." Giacenta's voice rose to a high pitch. She leaned over and pressed a button over and over again.

"They're all dead," Maya informed her. "Every last one of them. Your brothers as well. Your father, like you, will be taken prisoner, but it would have been far kinder to just kill you."

Giacenta hissed her displeasure and swung her legs over the side of the bed. Her hair fell in tangles around her face. "Who are you?" She tried to pour reason into her voice, but it still came out haughty.

"It doesn't matter. Get up. You're coming with us. If you give us trouble, one of the men will be happy to drag you out by your hair."

"You wouldn't dare touch me." She folded her arms across her chest. "I'm not going anywhere."

"Suit yourself," Maya said. "Meiling, tell Fyodor we need a garbage collector."

BARTOLO paced restlessly across the floor of his private den, glass of whiskey in hand. He didn't like when things went wrong. Not even small things. This night had seemed to have some kind of weird domino effect, starting with phone towers going out and then the internet. Radios failing. He couldn't raise his sons, either one of them. He'd tried his security people. He employed a shit ton of them just outside his house as well as roving walking patrols and patrols in vehicles. Two-man teams and four-man teams. Where the hell was everyone?

He kept his family and community safe. Their secrets were safe. They had places underground where they could interrogate prisoners. Anyone looking would expect it on the docks, not in their upscale neighborhood. Beneath the sprawling golf clubhouse were a gambling club to rival the best casinos and a party room where they brought the whores to entertain their guests any way their guests saw fit. If things went too far, there were always the ovens made just for the purpose of getting rid of shifter bodies or those they tortured and killed. He carried it all out under the nose of Marzio Caruso, the hot kingpin of Florida and the docks of Houston.

Marzio. His nemesis. He'd grown up with his father always pointing out how Marzio was such a success, ruling a huge territory in Florida. How everything Marzio touched seemed to turn to gold. No matter what he'd done, he'd always come up short in his father's eyes.

"Bartolo." The low voice came out of nowhere, seemingly disembodied, as if the shadows in the room had leapt to life. He whirled around, nearly dropping his crystal whiskey glass, only keeping his composure at the last moment. In the dim lighting, even with his superior vision, he had to blink several times before he made out Gorya Amurov sitting so still in his favorite leather chair.

"How did you get in here?" Bartolo demanded. "My guards . . ."

"Are dead. I killed them. It wasn't that difficult. They really haven't had any opposition, so they haven't trained hard in years. Your sons are dead as well, in case you think they may come rushing to your rescue."

Bartolo tried not to believe that quiet matter-of-fact voice. The features were expressionless, but those eyes gleamed like a predator's and didn't blink once. His mouth went dry. "What do you want?"

"I would prefer to kill you outright. Everyone else in your little empire is dead. We don't tolerate human trafficking, but then you knew that. Marzio isn't happy with you, and he'd like a word with you and your daughter before you die."

Bartolo's heart accelerated to the point it could be heard throughout the room. He reached for his leopard, but the leopard seemed to be sleeping. Totally unaware. Instead, he hurled the whiskey glass at Gorya's head and turned to rush out of the room. He ran right into Gedeon Volkov. There was no escape, no matter how hard he fought. He would be facing Marzio, and he knew from past experience, Marzio had no pity for his enemies.

18

JOSHUA Tregre had made it easy for Gorya and the crew he brought with him to examine his men. He had taken over the lair in New Orleans when his corrupt and extremely brutal predecessor had been killed, leaving a vacancy. Unfortunately, the majority of the men in his lair had been just as depraved and corrupt as the man leading them, and Joshua had been forced to weed them out.

Gorya knew him to be steady, dependable and extremely intelligent. He had formed alliances with the *bratva* in Florida and was an asset to Donovan's overall plan in his effort to stop the worst of the atrocities the crime families committed, especially human trafficking.

Joshua seemed to have a tight crew, one he trusted. Most of the men had flourished under his leadership. To the outside world they looked as if they worked for Donovan's security company. They were good to their neighbors and well liked—a big difference from his predecessor.

If there was any dispute, Joshua stepped in immediately and settled it amicably. His wife, Sonia, was best friends with the wife of the head sheriff.

Sonia had made a name for herself restoring old homes to their original glory even as she modernized them. She was a wonderful artist, but her first love was home restoration, and she ran a crew of carpenters. It was impossible not to respect the pair of shifters as they quickly and efficiently assembled their men in the large backyard leading to the swamp. Gorya knew Joshua had deliberately chosen that particular spot because if a traitor was found, he would be disposed of immediately.

Gedeon, Gorya, Maya and Meiling drifted through the crowd of men as they talked quietly, waiting for Joshua to address the reason he had ordered them to come together. It was time-consuming to check each man, but thankfully the lair wasn't large and they were able to process them quickly. They had divided the groups of men into four quadrants, with each of them taking a section. As they cleared a man, they would indicate to Joshua to move him to a different area.

Timur, Joshua and Fyodor stood quietly on the steps above the area where the men who had been cleared waited to hear what they had to say. To Joshua's relief, there were no traitors found among his crew.

Gorya allowed Joshua to explain to his men that he would be going to the rainforests of Panama, slipping in under the radar as part of an army to defeat the kingpin, who had set up the largest known trafficking ring. He was leaving that night and none of his men were required to go, but any volunteers had to understand they would be going up against shifters familiar with the territory where they would be fighting. It was a stealth mission. Get in and get out. Take out every member and dispose of the bodies. It wouldn't be easy work and the chances of losing one's life were moderately high.

Every member of Joshua's crew volunteered, which didn't surprise Gorya. These men were loyal to their new leader. Joshua wasn't Russian. He wasn't a member of the *bratva*. He had been trained in Borneo with Donovan but was originally from right there in New Orleans, and Gorya knew he was a man who would choose to bring his best with him. He indicated that they were on a tight timeline and needed to reiterate to his men to keep silent about what would be taking place in Panama. Gorya left with his cousins and their crews to make his way to Drake Donovan's territory.

Drake Donovan was responsible for a large lair, seven families of shifters. This was not a territory claimed by a crime lord—and God help them if someone tried it. Remy Boudreaux was a member of the lair along with his entire family. Saria Boudreaux was Drake's wife and mother of his son, Elijah. Remy was a detective and a darned good one. Nearly every male member of the Boudreaux family was in law enforcement.

To expedite things, Drake did exactly what Joshua had done—called a mandatory meeting requiring every single member of the lair to be present. Saria and Drake owned the La Font Inn, a bed-and-breakfast that backed up to the canals and marsh. Because the lair was so large and the notice was short, there was quite a bit of grumbling. He held the meeting behind the inn. Chairs and tables had been set up, and as always, Saria had provided food for her guests.

She was nowhere in sight, and neither was Drake's son. Gorya asked that Drake seat the family members together so they could examine each quickly and efficiently.

"This is bullshit, Drake," someone called out. "We all have work to do."

"I don't see Remy Boudreaux here," Armande Mercier added. "That's favoritism."

"You might call it that, but he was called away for work

and asked to be excused. He received irrefutable evidence on a huge drug ring he'd been quietly investigating for some time. His people are in the process of taking it down now. Your sister, in case you're worried about repercussions for her, called in asking to be excused. She's on her retreat. Naturally, I didn't ask her to return."

"Well, let's get this over with. What the hell is going on?" Mercier demanded. "I'm a busy man. I have commitments."

"I have a charter today," Gaston Mouton said. He sounded the way he always did. Cooperative and pleasant, but firm. "Jules is taking a second boat out into the gulf."

"We should be done in an hour or so," Drake said. "The names of your families are on the tables. I'd like you to go to those designated areas with your crews. We have guests. Some you know, some you don't. The faster you cooperate, the faster you can leave."

There were seven families making up the lair. Generations had lived in the swamp. The children would grow up and leave, but they always returned to make the swamp their home. Drake regarded most of them with affection now. He'd come to know them over the years, and it was going to be wrenching, especially for his wife, if there were others involved in the drug and trafficking ring. He could barely make himself look at Tonio Escabar Alba, who sat beside Armande, acting as his bodyguard. Drake had taken the kid under his wing and trained him. Tonio was the biggest traitor of all.

Maya and Gorya moved around the Pinet table, where the parents and their four grown children were seated. They had three sons, Leon, Charles, Philippe, and a daughter, Sabine. As they did so, Gedeon and Meiling circled the Jeanmard table, where the old leader, Amos Jeanmard, sat with his daughter, Danae, and his son, Elie.

"There's been an unfortunate development that will affect our lair and many of our people in it as well as their livelihood," Drake said. "We live by extremely strict rules for a reason. We aren't human. We can't be arrested and thrown in jail. All of us know the consequences when we choose to break the laws of the lair."

A hush fell over the expansive lawn. For the first time, the men and women sitting at the tables seemed to notice not only that grim-faced shifters had been brought in from Donovan's security company but also that many of the *bratva* security crews were openly armed and blocking access to the swamp and marsh.

Even Armande Mercier remained silent. Gorya and Maya moved away from the Pinet family table and circled the one labeled *Tregre*. This was not only Joshua's immediate family; Evangeline, Fyodor's beloved wife, was related to them as well. Two younger men, Ambroise and Christophe Tregre, sat together there. They couldn't be any different if they tried, but the brothers were intensely loyal to each other. Drake liked them both and would detest it if Gorya gave an indication that either of them was in any way part of the trafficking ring.

"This lair will never at any time allow the selling of drugs. We don't make arms deals. We don't take any part in the enslaving or selling of men, women or children in any way. That is not our way. I thought that was made perfectly clear to everyone when it was found out that the Tregre brothers were using the Mercier business for their own purposes."

Drake looked around the lawn at his people. The afternoon breeze had come up, alleviating some of the heat. Gedeon and Meiling had moved from the Jeanmard family table and were now circling the Lanoux family. They'd lost Robert to addiction and weakness.

Drake had no way to prove it, but he was suspicious that Fyodor may have killed Robert. There had been a rumor that Robert had accosted Evangeline at her bakery in San Antonio. If that rumor was true, then it would certainly explain his disappearance. Fyodor would never allow anyone to put their hands on Evangeline and live.

At the Lanoux table was Robert's long-suffering mother, Jenna; her husband, Bruno; and their two youngest boys, Duc and Loic. The boys were just entering their early teens and already were a handful. Jenna had four boys to raise and her husband worked from sunup to sundown. The oldest son was in the rainforest, hopefully learning to become a decent shifter.

Gorya and Maya gave Drake a slight nod as they moved away from the Tregre table toward the Boudreaux family table. Technically, Saria, Drake's wife, could have been seated there. Only two of her brothers were there, because most were with Remy raiding the Mercier properties. Drake's remaining brothers-in-law were there more for backup than for any other reason. His security crew was here to back him up. He didn't need Saria's family to put themselves on the line, but at least Mercier couldn't complain that none of them had to show up for a mandatory meeting.

Gorya and Maya barely slowed down as they moved past the Boudreaux family table and strolled in a circle around the Mercier table. Gedeon and Meiling had moved to circle the Mouton family table. Drake had known those two families would be left for last. He still held out a faint hope that Maya had been wrong and the information she'd acquired on the Mouton brothers was incorrect.

So far, five of the seven families had been cleared. Drake knew he should be grateful for that much. He didn't want any member of his lair to be guilty of the heinous crimes that Mercier had been committing right under his nose. Not just Armande, but Tonio.

Drake sighed and shook his head, wishing for the comfort of his wife. Maybe he was getting too old for leadership. He looked across the lawn at Amos, the man who'd held the position before him for so many years. The old man met his eyes. He knew something huge was up, and those faded eyes held sympathy. The moment he saw the Amurov family entering La Font Inn he had been worried.

Drake knew Gorya, Maya, Gedeon and Meiling were gifted in a way most others weren't. They could connect with other leopards, read their memories and record them. They were able to get evidence from a shifter's leopard if the shifter was involved in any criminal activity. Drake was well versed in the lore of shifters. He was from Borneo and had grown up with the elders, hearing all the stories. He'd heard of such things, but never met any shifter who had such a gift until he came to the States.

For the first time, Armande Mercier, always arrogant and sure of himself, acted a little nervous. His gaze swept the ring of security surrounding them and jumped to Gorya and Maya as they wove in and out of the tables close to Mercier and Tonio Escabar Alba. Drake could actually see the tension gathering on his face. Armande leaned close to Tonio and whispered. Tonio nodded and slid his mirrored sunglasses onto his nose with a flick of his fingers, making Drake want to shake his head at the practiced move.

Gorya and Maya returned as Gedeon and Meiling came toward him from the other side of the lawn. Drake had no recourse but to finish this.

"There are certain leopards with the ability to read and record other leopards' memories. Very few have this ability, but when the leader of a lair wants irrefutable proof before he passes the death sentence on any member of his lair, those leopards, if they are known to him, may be asked to come. We've worked hard to overcome the problems in this lair. We've been turning things around for our younger people, sending our men to train and giving them opportunities to find mates. We've been finding ways to bring more money legally into each of your family homes. What we have never condoned is turning our lair into a criminal operation."

He moved two steps up the porch to better look at Armande and Tonio. "Tonio, I personally mentored you. I sent you to the places I thought you would get the best training. I gave you every opportunity, and yet you came here under false pretenses, at the bidding of your father, on a mission to draw others into your trafficking ring. There isn't any denying it. Your family has been investigated thoroughly and your leopard has all the images in his memory bank. Your brother, Raul, was caught torturing and raping a fifteen-year-old girl. Even though he was caught outright, his leopard's memory and that of the child's were examined and proof taken. Those have been transferred to show evidence that there was reason to end both his life and yours." Drake knew he sounded weary because he felt that way.

Tonio stood up slowly, looking as cocky and arrogant as a young man raised to believe he was above all rules could look. "I guess I'm supposed to challenge you for leadership or something equally as silly as that."

"No. You haven't been listening. Your brother is dead. He was executed for his crimes. Just as you are to be." Drake nodded his head.

One of Drake's men, Kian, stepped in front of Tonio and in one swift movement brought up a gun and shot him between the eyes. He did so with the blurring speed Drake's security team was infamous for. He didn't wait for the body to drop, just turned away in contempt and moved back to the line with the others.

Armande stood up slowly, his impeccable suit and shoes stained with drops of blood. His face had gone gray. "Drake."

Drake shook his head. "Every excuse you made for your behavior in the past we wanted to believe, Armande.

For your sister. For your aunt. For all of us. I didn't want to think you were capable of selling human beings. Running drugs was bad enough, but selling children? You didn't need the money."

"It wasn't like that. I was protecting Charisse. They threatened to kill her. I had no choice."

Drake shook his head. "Your leopard doesn't lie. The images in his head are always the truth."

"This lair—hell, the entire parish will fall without the Mercier business. We're too important for you to threaten me this way," Armande blustered.

"I don't make threats, Armande. You should know that by now."

Kian moved fast, a blurring speed in human form. He came in from behind Armande soundlessly, then suddenly was in front of him. Before Armande had a chance to react, Kian shot him with a single bullet between the eyes. Again, he walked away before the body had time to fall to the ground.

There was a stunned silence. No one spoke. No one moved in their chairs.

"I would very much like to say those were the only two depraved individuals we have living among us, betraying us, but unfortunately, there are two more. Gaston and Jules Mouton, you've been condemned to death for your crimes of drug running and human trafficking. For betraying every single person in his lair."

Drake felt sick. He'd sent his men out on terrible missions, ones he knew they had little chance to come back from. He'd seen friends die. He'd had close calls himself. He liked Gaston and Jules Mouton. Granted, he hadn't spent a great deal of time with them; he'd been too busy seeing to the numerous problems of the lair. He ran a huge business. And Saria had been pregnant with their first child. Still, the little time he'd spent around the brothers, they'd seemed like good, solid, steady men.

He wasn't an executioner. He glanced at Gorya. At Fyodor. Mitya. Joshua. These were men he'd asked to place their lives in untenable positions to help fight human trafficking. In doing so, he'd forced them to make these very kinds of decisions, to become executioners.

"Drake," Jules began.

He shook his head and flicked his gaze toward Kian. The head of his security had quietly worked his way around to the other side of the tables so he could come up behind the brothers. With him was Riggs, another one of his personal security guards. They didn't make a sound, pure stealth. Moving into position swiftly, they simply stepped in front of the two men and executed them simultaneously.

Drake sighed. "The rules of the lair are absolute as always. No one speaks of this to anyone for any reason. The bodies will be cremated."

He wanted to go to his wife, but he knew that wasn't possible, not yet. Amos Jeanmard was coming toward him, and he had to see to the bodies. The Amurov family would leave quickly. They were on a precise timetable and had to get on a plane to Russia.

Russia, Primorye Region

Fyodor, Timur, Mitya, Gorya and Sevastyan led their small army of shifters through the pass in the mountains toward the lair they'd called home while growing up. They knew the entire area intimately, having explored it as children. With them were the others who had grown up in the lair, Matvei, Rodion, Kyanite and so many others who had followed them to the United States and eventually found their way to work for them as trusted members of their new territories.

Gorya had done his best to try to convince Maya to stay home with Evangeline, where Fyodor had some of his very skilled security men protecting her. He thought bringing her back to the place where she had been so abused as a child was a terrible idea, but she refused to be separated from him. She used the excuse that Wraith was too close to fully rising, but he knew her decision had nothing to do with Wraith and everything to do with her needing to be with him. He felt the same way about her. He didn't want a separation and Rogue hadn't either.

They knew approximately where Krylov would position his outer guards. Gorya was fairly certain those guards would be bored. How often would neighboring *pakhans* send their soldiers against Krylov? So far, there had been no reports of that happening. What had been discovered with careful research was that small incidents were disrupting the lair from the inside out. Much like when Gorya had disrupted Patva's brutish rule. Arms deals fell apart at the last minute because the shipment disappeared and couldn't be traced. Children who were in the whorehouse for training went missing. There was no sign of them, and they couldn't be tracked even when Krylov put his best leopards on it. Fires broke out in warehouses. Krylov's men were becoming paranoid because a leopard seemed to be entering homes without raising an alarm, leaving everyone inside dead and no tracks to follow outside. It didn't happen that often, but often enough that the men were trying to stay awake at night to guard their homes.

Gorya found it interesting that whoever was wreaking havoc in Krylov's territory was doing so in a way that was almost a complete duplicate of what he had done when he was a teenage boy. Someone had a plan to undermine Krylov and was methodically carrying it out. His crew had to be careful that they didn't harm any innocents.

Meiling, Maya, Gedeon and Gorya moved ahead of the

others, spreading out toward the areas they considered most likely to be guarded by sentries. They reached out looking for leopards.

Something's out here watching us, Maya reported. *I can feel it.*

Three sentries, Gedeon said. *I can take the one straight ahead, Gorya. You're probably feeling them, Maya.*

No, that's not it. Something else. Meiling? It's faint. Above us. To the right.

Gorya didn't make the mistake of looking in that direction, nor did he dismiss Maya's instincts. She'd never been wrong, even when Rogue hadn't alerted.

I'm getting a faint reading, but it comes and goes, Meiling agreed.

Gorya could feel a stillness in Maya, as if whatever was watching them bothered her on a level she had never experienced before. He tried to connect, but it was too elusive.

Is it a direct threat to us? A sniper?

Maya frowned. *I don't feel that. It's a female. She's puzzled, trying to understand who we are and what we're doing here. She doesn't understand why she can't . . .*

The thought trailed off in her mind before Gorya could catch it, or maybe it wasn't fully formed. Now wasn't the time for any of them to be distracted. He was bringing in an army to annihilate Krylov's lair and free any prisoners. He would have to do it fast while shutting down all communications.

Marzio had handled the fallout beautifully at the harbor. The shifter bodies had been burned. No shifter could be autopsied. The women taken from warehouses had told tales of gunfire and dockworkers turning on one another. It appeared to the investigators as if the workers had become angry and had broken into two factions. Most had been killed outright, and those who weren't died before the paramedics could save them.

The Carusos had heard the screams of the women and

children as fires broke out in crates and containers, and they had organized a rescue quickly. His family had become heroes. No one knew where the Anwars had slunk off to, but it was clear they had been the ones involved in trafficking. It was assumed they had used one of their vessels to escape overseas. Marzio was a brilliant man to have orchestrated such a believable scenario in such a short time.

Everyone in New Orleans had bought the story. Gorya considered that by now Krylov would be anxious to hear from his brother. In Panama, Jaoa Escabar Velentez had to be very nervous, most likely demanding that his contacts find his sons and give him an update on their whereabouts. If this venture took more than a night, they could lose the element of surprise.

They had allies in Panama. Connor Vega and his crew were already there, setting things in motion, assembling their army, bringing them in through the rainforest a few at a time. A local tribe Vega was close with was aiding him, bringing in the shifters and keeping them hidden from any others who were friendly with Escabar Velentez. The man seemed to have eyes and ears everywhere in the rainforest, so they would have to be especially careful.

Gorya had a sudden desire to grab his woman and get out of Russia. He didn't like that she seemed distracted when she was always so focused.

"We can't have someone potentially warning Krylov," he mused aloud.

Maya shook her head. *I don't feel that at all from her. Confusion. But she isn't in league with Krylov. When I attempt to get closer to her leopard, I feel more of a deep-seated rage against him. A determination to end him. She feels about the Krylovs the way I do about the Amurovs.*

He remained silent, waiting for her to realize what she'd just said to him. When she didn't clarify, he was gentle. Guiding her back when she seemed as if she was drifting too far from him. He never should have allowed her to come back to this place.

Baby. I'm an Amurov. Timur and Ashe are. Fyodor. Evangeline. You are going to be my wife as soon as we can make that happen. Not every Amurov is a monster. He paused. Allowed humor to creep into his mind and hers.

Perhaps I should rephrase that.

Her laughter felt good. He could always count on those little golden notes of joy to turn him inside out and brighten his world.

She wouldn't report us to Krylov. That was decisive.

Let's deal with the sentries and then we'll find who is watching us and why, Gorya suggested. *Maya, you're the one who has the best chance of spotting where she is. The three of us will go after Krylov's guards, and you watch our backs.*

Kyanite suddenly broke through the brush. He stood for a moment out in the open, taking a long, slow look around, uncaring that he'd disobeyed orders.

Gorya hissed his displeasure at the bodyguard for breaking all protocol. "Have I lost control of everyone?"

"Not sure what's happening, Gorya, but Bahadur, my leopard, is losing his mind. I mean *losing* it. He's always calm. Steady as a rock. Not now, and he's determined to drag me up this mountain toward those rocks up there. I know something's up there and so does he. He says it's his female. The one he claims belongs to him."

Gorya knew Kyanite was stressed if he was using the Russian version of his leopard's name. Normally he would call him Warrior.

"If that's a female in heat watching us," Gedeon said, "why is it we can't scent her? Does everyone have this scent-blocking shit from the Mercier family? Is it sold on the internet?"

"I wouldn't be surprised," Gorya agreed. "Flea markets. Garage sales. Who the hell knows these days? Stay put, Kyanite, and get under cover. We need to take out the sentries. Keep your leopard quiet so the sentries aren't alerted." That was a strict order.

"I'll do my best. He's never been like this." There was a grimness to Kyanite's voice that had never been there before, and Gorya looked him over carefully. He sounded so unlike the man Gorya had always known. Was something amiss in these mountains? Rumor had it that a certain hybrid flower Charisse Mercier had cultivated had gotten loose from her greenhouse into Fenton's Marsh and affected the male leopards adversely. The flowers had to be eradicated.

Maya, keep your eye on Kyanite. He's acting strange.

It's his leopard. I'm doing my best to soothe him. If he keeps it up, I'll take him over, but it won't be easy. I'm not even certain I can. He's that excited and a bit on the ferocious side. Kyanite isn't wrong. He's difficult to control. He's certain his female is close. He never thought to find her.

We need Meiling to take out one of the sentries or I'd leave her to back you up. "Kyanite, I trust that you'll guard Maya while we're dispensing with the sentries. Get your leopard to understand she's too important to leave without a guard."

"Of course, Gorya." Kyanite looked resolved.

Gorya once more tuned to Maya. *Is he good?*

Yes. His leopard understands duty. He won't act up while you're gone.

Keep me apprised of what is going on here, Gorya instructed. *And stay in my mind.*

If a female leopard was in heat, why couldn't he scent her? Why couldn't any of the other males? Normally if a leopard went into heat, she gave off enough pheromones to call every male leopard for miles. The only female he'd ever known who could suppress her scent when in heat was Maya.

He signaled the others to move toward their intended targets. *Be safe, Maya. Stay focused.* She wasn't though. A part of her was paying attention to him, but at the same time another part was puzzling out what was so familiar about the feel of the watcher. She wasn't looking after her own safety, and that worried him.

Gorya moved quickly through the rough terrain in the direction in which he knew the sleepy sentry had a little shelter built for himself. The sun had set and there wasn't much to do to keep the man awake and alert when he was alone. He did have a regular route he patrolled. Gorya saw evidence of a path trodden in the grass by shoes rather than lighter paws. He found that astonishing. Why wouldn't the sentry use his leopard and the cat's superior senses to guard the city below?

Keeping his energy low, he reached out slowly to find the leopard's brain pattern to enter. They'd already made certain to keep the animals from alerting the sentries to their presence, but approaching closely when the guard had been on duty for days, possibly weeks, might have made the leopard even more wary than usual and resistant to direction.

The cat was strangely compliant, as if it was too sleepy to bother being part of the sentry's warning system. Gorya didn't have time to find out why. He only took enough time to ensure that this guard was part of Krylov's trafficking ring, sifting through the memories of the leopard until he reached the distasteful scenes of violence, rape and imprisonment of women and children. He slammed a knife into the base of the sentry's skull, severing the spinal cord, and then cut his throat to ensure both leopard and shifter died immediately.

As Gorya dragged the body out of the open and into the makeshift shelter, he felt a soft, steady pressure moving against his mind. Rogue reacted instantly, snarling and clawing.

Maya reacted as well, deftly blocking the female while Wraith hissed her displeasure that another female so close to heat would dare to get near her male.

Definitely a young female, Gorya reported. *I took down the sentry. She's trying to get into my mind and take over Rogue.*

Wraith is giving me some trouble. Give me a minute and I'll go after her, Gorya. Maya locked on to her furious female. *Let me handle this, Wraith. We must be careful. This is Kyanite's mate, and she has no idea if we're friends or enemies.*

She knows. She's being a bitch, trying to show her superiority and trap all the males for herself. She can't have mine. I would fight to the death for him.

Gorya hid his smile as he made his way back to the others. Wraith was a fierce little thing, just like her human counterpart. Meiling and Gedeon were already waiting.

"I feel like I know her. Or met her somewhere," Maya said aloud. "You'll have to give me a minute to do this. She has skills."

Maya reached out tentatively, keeping her energy lower than she ever had. Gorya stayed in her mind, as invisible as possible but ready to help get her out of trouble if there was any problem. Taking over a leopard and looking into memories was always a risk. Gorya was astonished at Maya's patience. She took her time, the flow so even and slow, so nonthreatening and even noninvasive, that it would be nearly impossible to detect. Gorya wasn't certain he would have been able to feel her entrance into Rogue.

Once Maya had found a pathway into that female leopard, she didn't just take over. She was slow, keeping her energy low as she joined the patterns in the leopard's mind. Amur for certain. Maya was correct in feeling a strange familiarity with this creature and her human counterpart. He did as well, which was odd when he had no idea who she was.

Maya began to examine her memories without trying a takeover. The little leopard was indeed in her first true heat, close to her emergence, but like Wraith, she had, for her human's safety, managed to find her way out. She could shift. And she could fight. She had excellent fighting skills. Her human seemed reliant on her in more ways than usual, but it was clear the woman was getting restless. If Maya didn't act soon and take over the leopard, the shifter was going to do something unpredictable.

Maya made her decision and, as usual, acted on it without hesitation. She was in, surrounding the cat with her superior strength, forcing her will on the animal, wrenching her away from the watching shifter. The reaction was unexpected. The sensation of being watched was immediately gone.

There was shock and silence at first. Horror. Fear. *Give her back. You don't know what you've done. The danger you've put all of you in. Or me. I can't see or move without her. I'm stuck here on this cliff and could fall without her vision. Release her or you'll force me to sound the alarm, and others will come, believing all of you are enemies. I don't think you are, but you're leaving me no choice.*

The woman, using the leopard's path, spoke directly to Maya. It was her voice. The pattern of her mind. The brilliance and signs Gorya caught of elite gifts. This woman was somehow related to Maya. She had to be. At the same time as he was absorbing that information, he knew the truth had hit Maya even harder. She had known she had siblings but believed them dead. She had been the youngest, barely two when her family had been murdered. She was paralyzed, unable to think or breathe, and then she crumbled to the ground, her legs going out from under her.

19

GORYA realized that the woman above them on the rocks must have also recognized that an invader was related to her. She, too, had gone perfectly still. He feared if she fell, she might really go over the cliff. He signaled to Kyanite. His leopard had the best chance of finding her quickly. He certainly had felt her presence when others hadn't.

"Go, she's in trouble. Be gentle with her, she's just had a shock. Have your leopard hold off his claim for a few minutes while we sort things out."

Kyanite didn't have to be told twice. He was gone in an instant, shifting on the run, his clothing tucked into the pack at his neck the way he'd been taught by Donovan in the rainforests of Borneo. He was incredibly fast and very skilled. One of the best the Amurovs had. They worked on their fighting skills every day. All of them worked with Donovan to improve shifting times as well.

Meiling trailed after Kyanite to protect him. He wouldn't see her, that slight shadow in the darkness. Bahadur might sense her eventually, but Gorya doubted it. She was elite and working with Gedeon; her skills had become even better than they had been when he'd first met her.

Gorya dragged Maya into his arms, sitting on the ground with her in his lap. She was trembling. The moment he had her close, she burrowed into his chest, taking in deep breaths of air. One hand caught at his so she could rub the backs of his fingers where the tattoo of his Amur leopard was spread across his hand. He had thought she would hate that tattoo, but it gave her comfort in a crisis.

I'm Maya. What is your name? Maya paused, waited a moment, and then pulled into him even more, as if seeking shelter. *Do you remember me?*

Maya? There were tears in the voice. In the mind. *I don't think I can stand up much longer. This is too much of a shock. You were the baby. Our little baby. I was four when they came for us. Mama let me hold you sometimes when you were first born. You were so beautiful. I tried to protect you, but they dragged me away by my hair. Do you remember me at all? I am called Tanja.*

At once Gorya saw the childhood memories surfacing between the two women. The laughter as Tanja, her long golden curls falling all over Maya's head, planted kisses over Maya's upturned face. The two girls had looked remarkably alike as toddlers. It was easy to see why the older sister had been named for a fairy princess. She looked like one as she danced and twirled for the little girl watching her so adoringly. They both had the same large blue eyes and strangely pale skin. Already one could see the cat features in the eyes.

There is a man coming to aid you. He will ensure you don't fall, Tanja. Kyanite is one of our sweetest and best. He is part of our security force. His leopard is Bahadur, or Warrior, as we often call him. He'll protect you.

Release my leopard. I cannot function properly without her. I'll make my way down to you and we can meet properly and talk.

You tried to take my fiancé's leopard from him. Wraith, my leopard, is in the midst of her first heat. She went a little crazy, and I've had to calm her. She's extremely close to emerging. She'll fight to the death, Tanja, and she's very skilled in combat. Now, knowing you're my sister, more than ever I don't want that to happen.

I call my leopard Savior. She saved me when I had no chance. None. I still wouldn't without her. We function well together. There was a small gasp. *He's here. He's speaking to me. His leopard is close, I can feel him as well.*

Gorya and Maya could feel Savior responding to Bahadur's nearness. The leopardess wanted to rise to inspect him, to see if he was worthy of her. She didn't like Tanja being unable to protect herself.

If I return your leopard, can you control her? We are on a very close timetable this night and I want to speak with you, but we can't have our leopards fighting.

Yes. Savior will do as I order her.

Maya didn't pull completely away, monitoring the events taking place on the cliffs using the leopard's vison, since she didn't have access to her sister's.

The leopard stared at Kyanite through Tanja's eyes, assessing the man. Kyanite had managed to pull on a pair of soft trousers, the kind they used for fast shifting. He was barefoot and shirtless, his powerful chest and arms betraying the fact that he was a man housing a leopard of equal strength.

"I'm Kyanite Boston. I've come to escort you down the mountain."

"Tanja Averina. I'm Maya's older sister. I recognize the name Boston. Are you related to Damir Boston? Or Melor Boston?"

Kyanite didn't change expression. "They're related to

me. Cousins. Younger. I've never really met them other than briefly. I was raised in this territory when it was run by Patva Amurov. It was worse than you can possibly imagine. Worse than Krylov has managed to make it, and the truth is, we're here to take his ass down." He studied her and the leopard as he gave her complete honesty. "The two you just mentioned were just babies."

Maya let out her breath. "He just confirmed what Tanja already knows. She's relaxing a little bit."

"I'm ready to go down to meet with Maya and the others."

"We have something to do before we go meet with the others." Kyanite was firm. Resolved. Utterly implacable.

She backed up a step. "I don't think you really looked at me. You don't just get the leopard if your leopard claims mine, you take on the human. You aren't getting a bargain."

"I looked at you and I see more than you think I do. I also had Bahadur speak to Savior. She tells him you are the one responsible for fucking up Krylov's lair, keeping him off balance. He also tells me you've risked your life over and over, freeing his trafficking victims and secreting them away, training them to fight back when the time comes. You've been acquiring supplies, medical equipment, weapons and food. I think that says more about who you are than anything else. On top of that, you're one of the most beautiful women I've ever seen. Tiny, like that little spitfire Maya, but stunning."

"My sister is a spitfire?"

"She's a little hellion. In a fight, I've never seen anything like her. Lightning fast. She can take down a man three times her size, leopard or not. If you're anything like her, I'll tell you up front, I don't have the special gifts Gedeon and Gorya have, but I'm loyal and I've looked all over the world for you. For me, not just for Bahadur. Let her choose, Tanja. See if she's interested. If she's not, you don't have to worry, I won't force the issue no matter how attracted I am to you. I'm not that kind of man."

Gorya was proud of Kyanite. He'd stated his case as well as a man could have in the limited time that he had.

"I have issues. Terrible issues." She took another step back. "You don't understand. I can't see at all. Without Savior, I'm totally blind. Not just that, I have trouble walking. She keeps me walking steady. I have to work at it all the time in order to . . ." She broke off, shaking her head. "I refuse to be a burden to anyone."

"Are you a burden to these people you house and feed? You rescue. You're a leader. You're the brains behind the rebellion going on here. You're taking back this lair a piece at a time. You're recovering victims."

"Not enough."

"Without you, the ones you saved would have been sold or dead. And you have recruits. Allies in the lair. That's why you mentioned my cousins. They're part of that network."

"They risk their lives every day."

For the first time, Kyanite smiled. "Good genes. Take a chance, Tanja. Just let her decide. Let her have a look at him. Talk to her."

Gorya wanted Maya to tell them to get on with it. He knew Kyanite was resolved, utterly resolved. He wasn't going to back down. The Bostons had immigrated to the lair. They had Persian leopards, although they were Russian or Patva would never have allowed them entry. They were the second generation of the Primorye lair, and Gorya didn't know the history of the family other than the fact that once Kyanite had left the lair, he'd traveled extensively, ended up with Donovan and stayed with his company a long while before traveling to the United States and coming full circle to work for the Amurovs.

Maya. I'm so afraid. Tanja reached out to her sister. *I*

never thought I would have a man of my own. Savior is eager for his leopard. She says this man is good and kind and that he genuinely wants me. I have physical problems beyond the normal. I can't see without Savior. I can't walk very well without her. This man is built like he could run for miles and never stop. What should I do?

I can only tell you he is one of the best men I know, and I am fond of few men. I don't let them close to me. My past experiences were rather terrible. When Gorya's leopard claimed mine, I nearly suicided. I wanted to. He was as broken as I was, but he convinced me to give the relationship a try. We made it work on our terms. We communicated our fears and what each would need to go forward. So far, I've never been happier in my life. He makes me feel safe for the first time in my life. I know I can trust him fully. He listens. I believe Kyanite will listen to you and put your needs first, but you have to be willing to give the relationship a real try if you decide to give your leopard her chance at happiness.

Gorya thought that last part was very clever of Maya. By including Savior, she was reminding Tanja of everything the leopard did for her. The cat did deserve to have her mate.

"Okay, then. What do I have to do?" Tanja's voice trembled, but there was determination in her tone.

Kyanite gave her another smile. "Unquestionably a warrior woman. Never say you're not. Turn around and place your palms on the rock behind you. I'm going to raise your top to your neck and allow Bahadur to come to the surface. He'll do his best not to hurt or frighten you, but he'll inject his hormones into your bloodstream. If Savior is willing to be his mate she'll rise and touch him, injecting him with her hormones in return. It's an exchange of acceptance between them. A promise. From that time on, he'll be there to protect both of you. We both will."

Again, Tanja hesitated, and then she took a breath. Maya took another breath with her, and her sister turned and placed her hands on the rock. Kyanite bunched her shirt in his fist, tracing her spine with one finger as he drew the material to the nape of her neck. The feel of fur against Tanja's back was soft, almost alluring. Hot breath exploded against her shoulder. A rough tongue lapped there and then the leopard bit down in a holding bite while he injected the male hormones into her bloodstream to call to the female. Tanja cried out. Kyanite soothed her with one paw.

There was the briefest hesitation as the female leopard studied the male. He was patient. Steady. Calm. The way he always was. Just the way Kyanite was. Gorya waited, wanting this for a man he considered more than deserving. He respected any man who could manage to win Maya over even a little bit. Sometimes with Kyanite, her laughter was genuine.

The female suddenly rose and touched her nose to Bahadur's in complete acceptance. Tanja caught her breath as the male leopard carefully withdrew his teeth and used his saliva to lap at the wound to close it. For one brief moment, the large animal nuzzled Tanja's neck with his head before Kyanite shifted fully back to his form. He pulled the small first aid kit from the pack he carried.

"Do you need to sit down for a minute while I do this?"

"No, I think I'm fine. This is just unexpected. I had planned to take her away until her heat passed. I've been masking her from any males when they've been close. How did you know?"

Kyanite used antibiotic cream over the punctures and covered them before dropping her shirt. "Bahadur knew. We were a distance away, but he went wild. He just kept telling me he'd found her. I've never felt his joy like that. Thank you, Tanja, for taking a chance on us. Let's get down to the others. We have an army waiting to take down

Krylov and we're on a limited time schedule. The main players are in Panama. After we remove Krylov and establish new leadership here, we'll go there and destroy the main power. If we manage to take them down, this ring is permanently broken."

As he gave her the information, he slipped on his shoes and began the walk down the mountain to Gorya, Maya, Gedeon and Meiling. He should have been surprised when he caught a glimpse of a small shadow moving just ahead of them toward the same destination. Meiling, watching his back. That made him smile.

"You plan to hit them tonight?"

"That's right. We don't have much time before Panama will be warned. We've hit several of their major ports and there's no way the mastermind isn't going to figure out what's happening, that he's under attack."

She's a brilliant strategist, Gorya said. *Do you feel her mind working with just the small bit of information he's giving her?*

Maya nodded. She indicated that she wanted to stand. He knew she wanted to appear strong so her sister would respect her. It was the first time he could remember Maya caring about anyone's opinion of her.

She's going to love you, baby. How could she not?

I'm so broken, Gorya. I don't want her to see those pieces of me. She's so strong. Look at what she's done here.

Look at what you've done. She'll be proud of you. He wrapped his arm around her and drew her beneath his shoulder.

Tanja came into view, Kyanite looking every bit as protective of her as Gorya felt of Maya or Gedeon did of Meiling. Tanja had the same diminutive build as Maya, although she was much curvier. Her hair was just a little more like spun gold, but she had the same curls. Her eyes were a darker blue, with deep green and golden flecks revealing Savior studying them through her eyes. Mostly, she was taking in Maya, just the way Maya was taking in her.

Tanja clutched at Kyanite's wrist. "I had no idea you were alive. I would have searched to the ends of the earth to find you had I known. I'm so sorry, Maya." It came out a whisper.

"I didn't know you were alive either. I thought everyone was dead."

"What happened to you? After they took you? How did you survive? Where did they take you?"

Maya hesitated. Gorya knew she was very conflicted. She glanced at Kyanite and then up at Gorya's expressionless features.

You don't have to give details.

She's my sister. She deserves the truth.

His woman. So brave. He held her tighter, trying to give her courage.

"They brought me here, to this terrible place, where I was with several women. I was just a toddler, but it didn't matter to Patva or his men. He delighted in brutally raping and torturing women and children."

Maya turned her face into Gorya's ribs. *I can't tell her.*

She hadn't given specifics. She made it sound like the trauma had happened to other children, not her.

Tanja was intelligent. She blinked back tears. Kyanite casually put his arm around her waist and pulled her into him, beneath his shoulder. Tanja allowed the familiarity, needing the comfort.

"I've seen what they do to women and children. Krylov must have learned from Patva. He's attempting to spread that teaching by sending his brother out to other lairs and recruiting as many as they can to join their ring."

"He's dead," Maya said abruptly, her chin going up. She met her sister's leopard's eyes steadily. "Albert Krylov is dead."

Tanja frowned and shook her head. "We would have heard. Artur, his older brother, would lose his mind. He'd go on a killing spree."

"He doesn't know yet. But I assure you, Albert is dead. He was silly enough to challenge Gorya for leadership of the lair. Not that he would have lived if he hadn't, but his leopard had no chance against Rogue. Albert tried to cheat and attempted to get to me. Rogue got a little angry."

"That's putting it mildly," Kyanite confirmed.

"It's also one of the reasons we have to move on this lair tonight. He wasn't the only one to die that night," Gorya explained.

"Let's go where we can be more comfortable talking. Your people can relax for a few minutes while I tell you my story and let you know how many fighters I have available to aid you. We can get word to the others inside the lair. I can show you our supplies and give you any information you might need," Tanja said. "There's an entrance not very far from here." She gestured toward their right. "It's just a little farther down the slope."

Gorya had spent his entire youth exploring the region, including the mountains above the city. Even as a boy he had never found the opening concealed by rocks. Tanja deftly squeezed through a thin crack. It was much harder for the men to find a way to pass through. Timur really had to do some maneuvering and Mitya cursed repeatedly as he got stuck. His chest was thick with muscle, making it difficult for him to get through. Maya's little giggle was shared by her sister as their army of men struggled to make their way into and through that narrow crack.

Once inside, the going wasn't all that much better. The floor of the cavern was dry, formed of compact dirt, but the walls were narrow, so their wide shoulders brushed against rock and dirt on either side. They had to bend to keep from hitting their heads on the low ceiling. Fortunately, the winding trail led to a much wider set of chambers, one after another, until they were greeted by four women with very businesslike automatic weapons.

Tanja smiled at them. "Help has finally arrived. These men will be taking the lair from Krylov and shutting down the trafficking ring for good," she announced. "Have the others prepare food and drink. They don't have a lot of time. Jessica, contact Damir. Tell him to get ready, if possible, and to meet us here as soon as he is able to get free. Tell him his cousin has arrived and is anxious to give him news."

One of the guards nodded, turned and went down another corridor of the cave. Looking around, despite the low ceilings, the caves were an extensive labyrinth.

"What a great find, Tanja," Gorya said. "How long have you been here?"

"I escaped when I was a little girl." Tanja continued to lead them past the guards, through another chamber to a larger one where there were tables and benches made from planks of wood. "This is as good as it gets, gentlemen. You can rest in here, and my friends will bring food. It's simple but, I can guarantee, good for you."

Timur groaned. "My wife, Ashe, has used that very line on me on more than one occasion and it was not a good sign of things to come."

Ashe bumped his shoulder. "Unfortunately, that's the truth. I'm the worst cook in the world, but he loves me anyway, don't you, babe?"

Timur wrapped his arm around her neck. "I couldn't live without you."

His men made kissy noises.

Are they always like that? Tanja asked Maya.

Gorya was pleased to note that Tanja sounded as if the teasing gave her hope that she could have a relationship with Kyanite after all.

They get worse. They're crazy about each other, Maya confirmed.

Once their army was settled, Gorya and Maya followed Tanja and Kyanite into a smaller chamber where they could have privacy.

Tanja shrugged out of the small pack she had and gestured toward the crude seats made of planks of wood. "I'm sorry we don't have anything more comfortable."

"This is just fine," Gorya said. "You're the unexpected treasure we never hoped to find. Please tell us how you managed to survive."

"Savior. She did it. I was only four. I was given to this huge man and because I was fighting him and managed to kick him in the balls, he was furious. I wanted to get to Maya, but that sealed my fate. I was dragged outside. Maya and my mother were still inside. My father and brothers had been killed. I saw their bodies. The man's friends followed us outside and they were laughing at him. That only made him madder, and he grabbed me by my hair and slashed at my legs when I tried to kick him again. He cut the backs of my legs."

Involuntarily, Tanja reached down and rubbed her calves. She didn't seem to notice she was doing it. Kyanite immediately lifted her left leg into his lap and began to massage it.

"It hurts, doesn't it?" he asked, his voice gentle.

"Sometimes."

"All the time," he corrected. "You don't have to pretend with me."

"Quite a few of the girls I bring here have worse things to contend with," Tanja explained, her voice soft. "I try to tell them it's important not to give in to self-pity."

Kyanite didn't stop the slow massage, and Gorya noticed Tanja didn't pull her leg away from him.

"Please continue, Tanja," Maya pleaded. "How did you manage to escape? It seems so impossible. You were so tiny."

And surrounded by those men, she added to Gorya, a little sob in her mind. *I wasn't with her. I couldn't help her.*

You were a baby. He put his arm around her. Maya and Tanja hadn't embraced. Neither had touched the other. He knew Maya was afraid that if she did put her arms around her sister, she might shatter into a million pieces.

"He told me he cut my legs so I could never run from him again. And then he slashed the knife across my eyes. When he did, he laughed and laughed. My world went bloodred and then dark. The pain was so bad I nearly passed out. He thought I had. He dropped me on the ground and kicked me out of his way while he and the others dragged a couple of women who worked on our farm over to the stairs. They had bottles of something they were drinking. I couldn't see, but I could hear them beating and raping the women. That's when I heard Savior talking."

Her leopard, like yours, came to her rescue, Gorya said. He couldn't help but be a little shocked. Savior had been a toddler too. Technically, she shouldn't have even been aware. Somehow, she had managed to become Tanja's eyes and legs.

"There was so much blood from all the people killed around the houses, Savior told me not to worry about binding the wounds yet, just to run toward the hills, away from the farm. The pain was very bad, but I just did it. I did everything Savior told me to do, such as collect water bottles and then rags to bind my legs. She was the one who found the opening to the cave, and she also showed me how to erase tracks. I was so small I didn't really make many impressions on the ground anyway."

"I can't imagine the agony you must have gone through to make your way here from where the farms were located, dragging water bottles and rags with you when you were wounded so severely like that," Kyanite said. "You have courage, woman."

Tanja flashed him a smile. "I think it's called being stubborn. It took a long time to heal and to learn to work with Savior. I would steal food, but mostly I learned what plants I could eat and where to find fresh water to drink. I was here alone for several years."

Gorya exchanged a long look with Kyanite. As far as he was concerned, the two men had hit the jackpot. They'd somehow managed to find the two strongest women on the planet.

"And then you decided to start taking back trafficking victims," Gorya guessed.

Tanja's gaze met her sister's as she nodded. "I did. I hated those men so much. I was certain Maya was dead. I knew they would kill my mother. By that time, I'd snuck down to the port enough times to see what happened to the victims. But I just couldn't bear thinking of my Maya gone from the world." Tears filled her eyes. "You were the brightest light in my world when I was a child."

"I understand how you feel, Tanja," Gorya said. "She's my brightest light. I sometimes feel as if I can't breathe without her."

We can't stay any longer, baby. I'm sorry. I know you want to stay and just look at her.

Maya leaned into him. "When this is over, Tanja, please say we can spend time getting to know each other again."

"I would love that," Tanja said. "I guess you have a plan."

"Our specialty is going into their homes and cutting their throats," Gorya said. "We don't intend to leave any of them alive. Your jobs will be to get the prisoners to safety, burn down warehouses, destroy Krylov's drug supplies, steal his weapons and take his money. Every man and woman dealing in trafficking needs to die tonight. We've got the manpower to accomplish this."

Tanja gave him a small smile. "Don't leave out the power of the women."

Gorya returned her smile. "I don't think that's going to happen. We're counting on it."

ARTUR Krylov had never been more furious in his life. He'd been awakened from a sound sleep by his guards and given the report that several of his key people had been found dead in their homes. *Dead. Murdered.* Fires had broken out at every warehouse where the shipments of drugs and arms were held before being crated for the freighters. Millions of dollars going up in smoke. And the women and children they'd had ready for market? Gone. Vanished into thin air.

He'd been steadily losing prisoners over the last few years. The number had started small, just one or two gone with each shipment, but then a steady drain. He knew he had a few rats, and this time he was going to get answers.

"Bring me the Boston brothers. I know they're behind this," he snapped. "And find out how many of my men we lost tonight." He'd texted just about everyone he trusted in his crew and no one, not a single man, had texted him back.

A chill slid down his spine. First his brother went silent on him and now this. He paced outside, back and forth, his leopard every bit as restless and as edgy as he was. He knew something was very wrong. His five personal guards stayed close, as if they felt that same unease as he did.

It seemed as if it took forever before his enforcer returned, dragging Melor Boston with him, hands tied behind his back. The prisoner was thrust onto the ground a distance from Artur. Melor struggled to his knees and regarded Artur calmly, which only infuriated him more. That was one of the reasons he despised the Boston brothers. They gave him no respect. He was the lair leader, for fuck's sake, and they looked at him with contempt.

"Where's his brother?" he demanded.

"He wasn't home. Just this one," his enforcer told him.

Artur drew his knife—the one he loved, the one with the long, gleaming blade that scared the hell out of everyone—and took two steps toward Melor. "I know you're part of this. Where's your brother?"

A leopard's roar filled the night, stilling all other sounds. It was one of rage. Of challenge. The menacing sound stopped Krylov in his tracks. He looked carefully around and then at the five guards and his enforcer, the ones always shadowing him. They gripped their weapons as they peered out into the night, trying to pierce the veil of eerie fog that had crept in off the sea.

"I challenge you for leadership." The voice was very clear. Unfamiliar. Unafraid. Extremely confident.

"Shoot the bastard dead," Artur ordered his men. "I don't have time for this crap. I need to know what's happening to my crew and every one of my warehouses." He had taken two steps toward Melor when another voice came out of the darkness.

"I don't think it's a good idea to ignore a legitimate challenge for leadership of a lair. No true leader can afford to do such a thing and keep the respect of his men. If you try to avoid a valid challenge or cheat by having one of your men use a weapon to prevent your leopard from having to fight, that brands you a coward in the eyes of all shifters."

A shadowy figure emerged from the darkness. Gorya Amurov. Artur gripped the hilt of the knife so tight his knuckles turned white. More shadows emerged. Too many. A virtual army. Amurov hadn't come alone. Artur recognized Fyodor, Mitya, Sevastyan and Timur. There were others he knew from his childhood. And so many more. He was surrounded. His pitiful five security guards and lonely enforcer weren't going to cut it. It would be suicide for them to go up against that army of grim-faced shifters. His only recourse was to meet the challenge.

He shrugged his shoulders. His leopard was in shape. Fast. A killer. The cat enjoyed killing. He'd never been defeated. He wasn't being challenged by one of the Amurov leopards. He tossed the knife on the ground and signaled to his crew to put down their weapons. The idiots had already done so. That made him look weak, but he refused to acknowledge it to the audience. He was too aware of the rest of his people moving forward, looking on. They'd heard that roaring challenge.

Artur pulled his shirt over his head and tossed it aside as he toed off his shoes. Flexing his muscles so the audience could see the ripples of power on him, he dropped his hands to his trousers and unfastened the band and zipper as his challenger came striding out of the darkness.

He was still fully dressed. A big man coming out of the fog and darkness with shaggy hair and blazing eyes. Kyanite Boston. He might be older, but Artur recognized him. He looked powerful, but he'd made one huge mistake. Amateur. He wouldn't have a chance against Czar, his leopard. Artur would end this before it got started. Artur had his trousers gone in seconds and shifted, his golden Amur leopard leaping across the thirty feet in one bound, claws extended, teeth exposed, fully expecting to rip the human shifter's head right off.

Kyanite shifted in midair, clothes gone, his Persian leopard fully emerged. Bahadur's powerful gray body with his thick fur, black rosettes and dense muscles met Czar in the air. Claws like stiletto hooks tore at Czar's belly and genitals, ripping great lacerations as they slammed together and tumbled to the ground snarling.

Artur felt as if he'd been hit with a battering ram. Czar rolled over and over in an effort to get away from the tearing claws and ripping teeth to regain his feet. The Persian leopard was lightning fast. Almost a blur as it ripped and tore at Czar's golden fur in a fury. Artur's leopard had been in hundreds of fights over the years, but nothing like this. He'd hunted prey mainly, been set loose on humans by his shifter counterpart for sport. The other leopards he'd fought were pathetic in comparison.

Bahadur fought viciously, breaking away and returning with a roar of contempt, sinking wicked teeth into his spine and leaping away, ripping great gashes in his sides to leave him bleeding great globs of blood. Czar's fur should have protected him from those punishing claws, but there seemed to be no defense.

No matter what he did, twisting and turning, trying every trick he knew, he couldn't get a retaliatory strike on the challenger. The Persian leopard was slowly ripping him to pieces. It was a savage, brutal, ferocious killing. Artur realized when he was able to push past the panic and rage in Czar that it was also deliberate. Kyanite wanted him to suffer. To be humiliated. There would be no submission. No mercy. This was a fight to the death.

Czar lifted his bloody muzzle and stared malevolently at Melor. Was this because Artur had threatened the betrayer? He charged at the helpless prisoner everyone seemed to have forgotten. As fast as he was, Bahadur was faster. The cat seemed to be a whirlwind of terror. In a blur of speed, the leopard streaked between Melor and Czar so that the Amur leopard found himself facing a mouthful of teeth and those savage, relentless claws.

With no hesitation, Bahadur struck, the claws ripping open Czar's muzzle and sweeping across his eyes, taking one out completely and scratching the other one severely. Czar howled in pain and tried to turn tail and run. Bahadur was on him, dragging him down by his back hips, vicious teeth meeting, snapping the bones of his right hind leg.

"Kye, stop playing around," Gorya called. "We have

planes to catch. Finish him off so we can send everyone out. We can't be late."

Tanja leaned close to Maya. "He's playing around?"

Maya nodded. "He could have killed him within the first thirty seconds. He's angry because his cousin was threatened, not to mention what Krylov did to all those women and children. Kyanite might be sweet, but he's got a protective streak."

Gorya watched Bahadur deliver the kill bite to Krylov. Kyanite allowed the leopard a few roars of triumph and a couple of swipes of contempt-filled dirt and leaves flung over the carcass before he took back the form. Catching his trousers and jerking them on, he nodded toward Melor. Rodion freed Melor's hands and helped him to his feet.

Kyanite indicated the six remaining Krylov men—his five personal security guards and the enforcer. "Execute them." There was pure steel in his voice.

20

EVERY rainforest looked, sounded and felt different to Gorya. Each had its own beauty. The sounds of birds, hundreds of varieties, harmonized with the hum of insects and the shrieks of the howler monkeys. The flowers winding their way up tree trunks to the tall canopies above gave off a distinctive perfume.

The wildness called to Rogue. The leopard was eager for a run. Eager for his mate. He had been patient. He had put the concerns of humans first. So had Wraith, making a tremendous effort to suppress her heat so their shifters could work out their relationship and carry out the war against those committing trafficking.

"Wraith is in distress," Maya reported, slipping her hand in his as she moved with her usual grace along the narrow trail winding through the trees. "She can't be expected to hold out much longer, Gorya. What she's been doing is nearly an impossible feat for any female leopard."

He glanced down at her bent head. "This isn't your fault, Maya. We all agreed to putting off the heat as long as possible. We're nearly finished. Everything is in place. The moment we've taken down Jaoa Escabar Velentez and his organization, we'll give Rogue and Wraith all the freedom they'll ever want or need. That's a promise to the three of you." Gorya was sincere.

I admire and respect you, Wraith. I doubt any other leopard could do what you've done.

It is getting very difficult.

Gorya could see the very real distress in the leopard. She was squirming continually. Hot. Burning up in reality. He had to give Maya credit for the fact that she was stoic, not letting on that her leopard clawed and raked to emerge. That burning had to affect Maya as much as it did Wraith, yet she had closed her eyes on the plane and was still, curled up in her chair beside him.

I should have checked in on you. Gorya meant both. Woman and leopard.

The lush vegetation thickened around them. Light streaked in ribbons through the canopy to highlight the ferns, seedlings and saplings on the mushroom-and-debris-covered floor. Millions of insects kept the leaves moving so the ground beneath their feet resembled a living carpet.

What good would it have done for you to know? Wraith asked. *You cannot change a leopard's heat.*

You did, he pointed out, exorbitantly pleased that Maya Averina had been chosen by the universe to belong to him. She had given Wraith to Rogue.

We gave Maya to you, Rogue corrected. Everything about him felt smug.

Wraith felt amused. That same almost-little-girlish feeling of feminine laughter that Maya gave to Gorya mind to mind, her leopard did as well. Maya tipped her face up and smiled at him. He leaned down and brushed her lips with his.

"Connor, my woman's leopard is extremely close to emergence. I'm hoping we can get this done quickly. It could be a matter of urgency. And perhaps a cabin somewhere for the two of us for after? We'll need privacy."

Connor Vega had been born and bred in the rainforest of Panama. He had known Drake Donovan for years and reestablished his connections with the tribes that had held his mother in high regard. Vega had met them at the boat that brought the small group of shifters who would go directly to Jaoa Escabar Velentez's personal estate.

Connor looked civilized in his casual jungle garb, but he didn't feel that way to Gorya. He felt as wild and feral as the surroundings they were in. He was from a long line of fast, dangerous shifters, and it showed in every line and movement of his body.

"We can provide the cabin for you, no problem. I've got your army in place and identified the targets. My men are in place. We just need the signal for a go." His gaze slid over Maya. "Your woman is going to be a trigger for Jaoa and his wife, Carolina. She has the exact look that sets them off."

He turned back to the narrow path and continued to walk. While he'd been speaking and looking at them, he hadn't broken stride or stepped off that tiny trail.

I've done quite a lot of research on Jaoa and his wife. I don't know what he means.

"What do you mean she'll be a trigger for them?" Gorya asked.

"Her looks," Connor said without turning around or slowing down. "She looks innocent and pretty, very young. Carolina will hate her on sight. Jaoa will be attracted."

Connor was silent a moment. Gorya could almost hear the ebb and flow of the sap in the trees and the call of the wildlife to Rogue and Wraith—it was that strong. This was a primitive place and it called to the very nature of every shifter.

"Carolina isn't Jaoa's true mate, at least no one thinks she could possibly be."

"How can that be?" Timur asked. "He keeps her as if she is. He married her. She's the mother of his children."

"They've been together for years," Fyodor added.

Connor shrugged casually, rolling his shoulders without turning around even as he led the way through the maze of flower-covered trees. "He likes to have his fun. Carolina is a very jealous woman. She also has a cruel streak. It's possible Jaoa indulges her cruelty because he feels guilty about cheating on her, but more likely, the steady supply of women he's able to play with is his reason for trafficking. That and the money. He might spout to others that he does it for the good of the economy, but he's got more money than he knows what to do with."

"You're glad to see us," Gorya said.

"Very glad and grateful," Connor said. "When we clear this lair of the depraved shifters, Drake has convinced me to step up and fill the vacancy so no one else does. It isn't something I aspire to. I'm no leader. I like my freedom, and as far as I can tell, anyone ruling a lair has a yoke around their neck."

Fyodor and Mitya laughed. "You've got that right," Fyodor agreed. "Worst damn thing Drake could have asked. I should have shot the bastard instead of agreeing."

THE Jaoa home was a sprawling two-story mansion built inside what could only have been designed to be a fortress. There were high walls surrounding the estate. Roped vines covered the walls. There were two sets of patrolling guards around the outside and two more inside. Gorya noted cameras in various locations.

The moment the heavy iron gates swung closed, trapping them inside, he knew his people would dispose of the patrolling guards outside the estate. Their army was already on the move, quietly going through the rainforest, taking down targets and disposing of the bodies. Jaoa was soon to be without his personal army.

The private airstrip where prisoners were brought in and out had already been destroyed, and at that very moment their fighters were engaged with Jaoa's shifters at the mouth of the river. They'd already recovered every victim locked in the various holding areas Jaoa had near the airstrip and river. They also had attacked the school and rescued the children there. Jaoa was unaware, but he had few resources left who could come to his aid.

A pretty but downtrodden woman opened the door for them and beckoned them into the cool interior of the house. The foyer was large with a high ceiling. Fans with wide paddles turned above their heads. The woman led the way into a very large rectangular room filled with plants and low rattan furniture. Windows allowed light to stream into the room during the day, but thin lacy curtains filtered out the brightness.

The sun had set, streaking the night sky in deep purple across the growing darkness. The colors against the vivid greens of trees and plants outside the windows cast an eerie effect onto the walls of the room through the lace. Carolina was seated in one of the few high-backed chairs, facing away from the ferns, looking as if she were sitting on a throne. Jaoa came forward to greet Connor and then each of the Amurov cousins. Gorya couldn't help noting that his gaze continually slid to Maya, just as Connor had predicted.

With Gorya and his cousins had come their security force. It would have been suspicious for men of their stature not to bring them. Gedeon, Rodion and Matvei were with Gorya. Timur and Sevastyan accompanied Mitya and Fyodor along with three of their top people, including Jeremiah. They moved soundlessly across the room, facing Jaoa's bodyguards.

"Gentlemen, it's such a pleasure to meet you. When Connor reached out and said you would be traveling this way, I had hoped you might come to see Carolina and me." Jaoa waved them toward the low-slung couches.

Gorya deliberately took the one directly in front of Jaoa's chair and in Carolina's line of vision. The tension in the room increased dramatically.

She despises Maya, Wraith reported. *Her leopard is going wild.*

Is it worth controlling the animal? Gorya asked.

No, Maya replied sharply. *She is guilty of so many deaths. Women and young girls dying in hideous ways. Her leopard contributed.*

Gorya had heard and felt Maya in many moods. This one was new. This was full assassin.

"We came to Panama specifically to speak with you," Gorya conceded. "We asked Connor to arrange the meeting."

Jaoa looked pleased. He glanced at Carolina. She hadn't taken her malevolent gaze from Maya. Jaoa cleared his throat as if that might get her attention. When it didn't, he scowled. "Carolina." His voice was extremely harsh, making his wife jump.

Carolina paled and turned her attention to him immediately. He gave her a benevolent smile. "Send for refreshments for our guests."

"Yes, of course. Merida, that should have been taken care of already." Carolina glared at the young woman who had allowed them entry into the house. Merida disappeared into another section of the house.

Jaoa turned his attention back to Gorya and his cousins. "This is a visit to discuss business, then. I had hoped for such an alliance between us."

"I'm afraid not," Gorya said. "I've come in person to bring you news. I'm the new *pakhan* of the Atchafalaya River Basin. I don't deal in human trafficking, and the first order I gave was to clean it up. When I give an order, I enforce it. I also uphold every law of the shifters. All of them. I hold them sacred."

Gorya maintained eye contact with Jaoa. A small part of his attention, as always, remained lodged in Maya's mind. She was locked on to Carolina. Gorya trusted his cousins and the security force to handle everyone else in the room.

Jaoa's mind worked, trying to puzzle out where Gorya was going with his line of thought. Gorya didn't make him wait.

"Your son Raul was visiting with Derk Malcom, a friend from college. The two men were caught kidnapping, torturing and raping a fifteen-year-old child. We have the proof recorded straight from their leopards as well as eyewitness accounts. We have the photographic evidence of what was done to the child, all to present to the elders."

Jaoa sat up very straight. "What are you saying?" His voice was low.

Gorya could see knowledge working behind his eyes. "Shifter law is very clear. Rape is not tolerated in our society."

Carolina shrieked. She leapt to her feet, her face twisted into a mask of hatred. She was built in the way many female shifters were, with curves and muscles and gleaming hair. She looked like she was extremely strong. "My son was born with a legacy. He has the *right* to any woman he desires. He can do whatever he wishes with her. No one can touch him. *No one.*"

Maya stood slowly. She looked as if she were a tiny doll in comparison to Carolina. She met the other woman's yellow gaze with her cool frost-blue eyes. "I was born with a legacy as well. I am the executioner of the depraved, disgusting monsters who have no business being alive. I caught Derk and Raul with that child between them, and I killed them both."

Carolina screamed again, tearing at her dark hair, her eyes going completely cat as she hurled her body at Maya, hands contorting into hooked claws. No one moved or made a sound. It seemed as if time stood still. Maya waited until the last possible moment. With blurring speed, she stepped to one side, avoiding the charge, one hand moving fast— up, down—she spun, and the other hand did the same on Carolina's other side. Blood spurted like a fountain from Carolina's neck and under her arms. She staggered. Teetered. Coughed. Maya slammed her knife into the base of Carolina's skull and then shoved her foot into the small of her back. Carolina crumpled to the floor.

Jaoa stared at his dead wife with a kind of macabre fascination. He looked up at his security force. They lay on the ground in a pool of blood. Every one of them. He hadn't even seen or heard them go down.

Jaoa swallowed his pride and forced himself to sit back in his chair. "She was out of her mind. She went insane a long time ago."

"I understand now," Connor said. "You took her when she was just a child and shaped her the way you wanted her. You were the one to convince her she was your mate."

Jaoa smiled at him, a false, shark's smile. "She was easy enough to manipulate. I wanted sons."

"And you fed her the bullshit of cruelty and hatred until she was so twisted, she did exactly what you wanted," Connor continued.

"She was an asset at first, although she began to grow so crazy. I knew that sooner or later I was going to have to dispose of her. I was discussing it with Roque just the other day. I wanted him to get used to the idea that she had to go." He sounded matter-of-fact. As if he were still in control of the situation. "Where is Tonio?"

"Tonio? The one you sent to New Orleans to be with Mercier?" Gorya asked. "I'm afraid Tonio and Mercier met the same fate as Raul and Derk. They had more company. The Mouton brothers and a few others. In Houston, the Anwars are gone. In Russia, the Krylovs."

Jaoa shook his head. "You don't know what you've done. I built this empire from the ground up. What are these whores? They'd be nothing anyway. We're organized. We pour money into the neighborhoods that need it. These women serve men the way they should."

Gorya was sick to death of the same rhetoric. He stood up, walked across the room, pulled out his gun and shot the man three times. Once was enough, but he couldn't stop pulling the trigger.

"We'll find Roque, his oldest," Connor said. "And finish the mop-up. Let's get you and Maya to the cabin."

Gorya was more than happy to take his woman away from the smell of depravity, blood and death.

THE "cabin" was actually a small structure built high in the branches of a tree. A porch with an overhang and low railing gave added space. They had no time to inspect. The shower was on the ground, below the tree, and Wraith didn't wait. The moment the cleansing water poured over Maya, her body began to burn.

"Gorya," she called. This time, rather than being terrified, she felt triumphant. Joyful. "She's ready. I'm burning up."

The fire came on fast, flames rolling through her, consuming every part of her, waking every cell, bringing her alive. Heat banded in front of her eyes, and she stepped naked out of the small half stall that had been constructed for the crude shower.

Come out, Wraith. This is your time. You've waited. Rogue is close. Can you feel him? He thinks you're the

most beautiful leopard in the world because you are.
Maya was so proud of her, and she wanted Wraith to
know. *You saved us all. Gorya thought I was going to be
the miracle, and all along it was you.*

We did it together, Maya. All of us. The cat was writhing, burning up in a fever of need.

Maya took one last look around her at the beauty of the
rainforest using her human eyes. Then she stared into the
eyes of the man she loved. Gorya Amurov. An Amurov.
His eyes were going from silvery blue to a ghostly blue.
His strong body went to the ground, on all fours, fur
emerging as Rogue waited for his mate.

Maya stepped back and Wraith burst through with her
smooth, practiced ease. She pushed her nose against
Rogue's and then whirled around and sprinted away.
Rogue easily kept pace with her. She lifted her voice to the
canopy with sawing calls declaring her need for her mate.
Over and over, setting the night on fire with her desire.

Rogue answered, roaring a challenge to any male daring to cross into his territory. Wraith was his and he would
fight to the death for her. Shifter or feral leopard, it mattered little, he would take on the challenge. He proclaimed
his intention loudly, in no uncertain terms, the roar like
thunder, echoing through the trees and rolling down the
slopes and rivers.

They spent the rest of the night playing in the rainforest, exploring hollow logs and shallow creeks. They found
great piles of leaves they could roll in together. They tumbled down slopes of grass and righted themselves, shaking
off the debris and nudging each other affectionately with
their muzzles.

Every few minutes Wraith crouched submissively, and
Rogue covered her. They rested. Played. He blanketed her
often throughout the night, assuaging the terrible burning
heat until they were both completely sated.

At dawn, Rogue led the tired female back to the shower. Maya emerged there, in Gorya's arms. They made their way up to the cabin. He carried her to the bed and followed her down, kissing her over and over, the heat blazing between them.

Gorya lifted his mouth from hers only to nip her earlobe. "How brave are you feeling?"

She tilted her chin at him, eyes sparkling. "Are you challenging me?"

He grinned at her. "Hands and knees, baby. Let's try this and see how you do."

"Let's see how *you* do."

"Now you're challenging me."

"You are quite a bit older than me, and it is dawn. You didn't get any sleep. Rogue kept you out late."

As she gave that little giggle that caught at his heart every time, he flipped her over and yanked her up onto her knees. She was so beautiful to him. He ran his palms along her sides, feeling the indentation of her waist and the flair of her hips. He nuzzled the length of her spine and then took his time kissing his way to her silky bottom.

She was ready for him. He bent his head to taste her. Just get one taste of that elusive marigold-and-snow combination. As he did, a whisper of sound alerted him. Alerted Maya. Wraith. Rogue. Something stalked them, stealthily climbing up the branches of the neighboring tree toward their snug little cabin.

Roque heard me calling out to the males that I was in heat, Wraith said.

He heard my challenge, Rogue said.

Good, Gorya answered. *He came straight to us. We don't have to search an entire rainforest for him.*

A shot rang out. A second one. Nearly simultaneously. Both reverberated loudly through the dawn, setting the birds fleeing into the air and the howler monkeys shrieking. The sound of a heavy body crashing against branch after branch was loud as it fell through to the ground below. There was a thud, and then silence settled once more over the rainforest. The insects began their steady drone as if nothing had happened. The birds landed back in the trees. The chatter of the monkeys resumed.

Roque is down. You two carry on, Gedeon reported.

Maya giggled. *Thanks, Gedeon, Meiling.*

So glad we have your permission, Gorya said dryly. He bent his head once more to the temptation of the love of his life.

CHECK OUT THESE UPCOMING TITLES FROM
#1 *NEW YORK TIMES* BESTSELLING AUTHOR

CHRISTINE FEEHAN

SCAN ME
or visit
prh.com/christinefeehan